Thousand Islands:
Inspired by True Events

An "on-going" law enforcement investigation.

by **Tom Reilly**

D1518197

Brooklawn Production Press

www.tomreillybooks.com

Cover Design by Jon Van Gorder

Back cover aerial photography
©Ian Coristine/1000IslandsPhotoArt.com

Illustrations by Kitty Mitchell

In Loving Memory of
Irene Juliana Izak
Scranton, Pennsylvania
AGE 25
Died Here 6/10/1968

Murder never solved

PREFACE

Thousand Islands is the second in the *Inspired* series, following in the footsteps of *Bridgeport: Inspired by True Events.*

Like *Bridgeport*, this fictional tale is woven around historical facts. In this case the historical facts concern the brutal murder of Irene Izak.

I first learned of Irene Izak's murder when I picked up a copy of Dave Shampine's *The North County Murder of Irene Izak*. Shampine was a *Watertown Daily Times* reporter who methodically investigated the murder. Unfortunately, Shampine's impressive investigatory efforts didn't lead to an arrest since he began unearthing the evidence 30 years after the murder; critical evidence had gone missing and witnesses had died.

Curious, in late 2022, approximately 55 years after Izak's murder, I sought records from the New York State Police regarding the investigation of Izak's murder pursuant to the New York's Freedom of Information Law, known as FOIL in legal parlance.

The NYSP informed me in 2023 that its investigation of Ms. Izak's 1968 murder was still both "active " and "on-going" and disclosure of the records would interfere with the troopers' investigation. I appealed the initial decision and was once again told that the investigation was "active and on-going."

The state police's mind boggling response forced me to take legal action (details of the legal action may be found at the end of this book). Right before my court date, the NYSP relented and provided me with most of the documents I sought. The documents I had to pry away from the NYSP revealed that in 1968 considerable evidence incriminated a New York State Trooper. In fact, that after the murder investigation was reopened in 1998, Trooper David Hennigan became the state police's main target.

Despite the strong evidence implicating Hennigan in the murder, the New York State Police did not zero in on him for the first three decades after the murder. Common sense indicates that, in fact, some troopers likely did just the opposite: they turned a blind eye to the truth.

Jefferson County District Attorney

The records which the NYSP did not want to disclose also revealed that the-then Jefferson County District Attorney was actively involved in Irene Izak's murder investigation and issued strong declarations of support for Trooper Hennigan, as Hennigan came under suspicion.

Intrigued by the District Attorney's role in the murder investigation, I sought the D.A.'s records regarding the 55 year old murder.

My request, like my initial request to the troopers, was denied on the basis there was an "open" investigation in the 1968 murder. My appeal was granted but my FOIL request was "deemed moot in light of the lack of possession of any responsive records." I was informed that, pursuant to a court order, District Attorney Kristyna Mills destroyed all the records regarding Irene Izak's murder in 2018. I was provided with a "copy of the order and proof of destruction of the records." However, upon inspection, the "proof of destruction" did not identify the files related to Ms. Izak's murder investigation. I requested clarification and all digital files related to my FOIL request.

I have not received a single document from the Jefferson County's District Attorney.

Instead, like clockwork, every month the Jefferson County's Record's Access Officer notifies me that more time is needed to determine whether the District Attorney destroyed the documents or possesses any records regarding Ms. Izak's infamous murder investigation. It seems the Jefferson County

District Attorney, like the NYSP, will comply with the Freedom of Information Law only if I bring legal action.

Ms. Izak's murder investigation is still shrouded in mystery and the historical stink of injustice still hangs over it. It was a horrific crime that screamed for justice. A young woman, in the prime of her life, was murdered in cold blood.

Justice was never served.

And shockingly, the agencies responsible for bringing justice to Irene Izak's family, are still keeping details of the injustice shrouded in mystery.

Legal Cases

Lastly, the numerous legal cases referenced in this novel are actual cases. For narrative purposes, however, I have taken liberties with the dates of several.

Thus, this fictional tale, set in modern times, was weaved around a few historical facts and lingering mysteries concerning a horrendous and officially unsolved murder.

Thanks

I'm grateful for the considerable assistance and insights from the many people who have shed light on the history and workings of the New York State Police and other law enforcement agencies in northern New York. Additionally, the input from forensic scientists made the complex world of DNA analysis a bit less daunting. As noted earlier, the records which I've incorporated into this largely fictional story had to be pried from the NYSP. New York's Committee on Open Government which issued an advisory opinion supporting my effort proved very helpful in my successful battle to obtain the documents.

While I am solely responsible for the book's shortcomings, I cannot take full credit for any patches of smooth prose. Such credit must also go to my sister, Patti Reilly, a talented writer, who went through boxes and boxes of pencils running her diligent and creative eye over every line of the manuscript. Additionally, the hunt for typos and grammatical gremlins was a family affair. My wife, Ellen and my daughter, Charlotte, zealously hunted for imperfections while also offering valuable suggestions.

Lastly, my multi-talented friend, Jon Van Gorder, has provided the graphic artistry and technological horsepower needed to get this book published. Without him, this book would still be marooned on my computer.

Dedication

This book is dedicated to the memory of my dad,
Frank R. Reilly, a role model for the ages.

THREE MONTHS AFTER STATE'S ATTORNEY FRANCIS X. DURKIN RETURNED FROM THE THOUSAND ISLANDS

```
Connecticut Criminal Justice Commission
Hearing, Hartford, Connecticut

Questioner: Honorable Wayne Batise.
Witness: State's Attorney Francis X. Durkin

1 Q  State's Attorney Durkin. Were you a

2     suspect in a murder investigation?

3 A  That's a question best left to the

4     New York State Police.

4 Q  Okay. Then let me try a question best

5     left for you. Did the New York State

6     Police ask you to submit a DNA sample?

7 A  Yes.

8 Q  And did you voluntarily provide your DNA
9     sample to the New York State Police?

10 A No.
```

CHAPTER ONE

Francis X. Durkin couldn't sleep.

For the past two hours the 56 year old State's Attorney tossed and turned in bed. His legs twitched as troublesome thoughts swirled in his head. He tried sleeping on his side, on his stomach, then on the other side. His legs still twitched.

Durkin then laid perfectly still and regulated his breathing. He pursed his lips and drew a long stream of air through his nostrils. He filled his lungs and steadied himself before visualizing the spent air as billowing clouds slowly escaped through his nose. Then he repeated. After five minutes he laid wide awake, looking at a ceiling full of imaginary clouds.

With a gush of exasperation, Francis Durkin reluctantly accepted the fact that sleep was not coming anytime soon. With his head resting on his pillow, his brain sent an instruction to his body to sit up. There was a delay as if his body parts were separately debating whether or not to comply. Then, as if different parts decided to obey at different times, his legs, arms and torso rolled to the side of the bed in an out-of-sync jumble.

Hunched over the side of the bed, Durkin's muscles felt withered; like a gnarly leather baseball glove found in the back of a garage. He clicked on his bedside lamp and squinted as his eyes adjusted to the light bulb's glare. As the shock to his optical nerves subsided, his thoughts returned to the source of his insomnia: Roslyn Jones, Connecticut's Chief State's Attorney.

Hell, Durkin groaned, he deserved better. By any benchmark, he was far and away the best state's attorney in Connecticut. In a burst of immodesty, Francis Durkin was sure no state's attorney or federal prosecutor anywhere could hold a candle to his courtroom accomplishments.

Most prosecutors would agree with him. Other prosecutors could only dream about his conviction rates. In law-and-order circles a halo hovered over his name when colleagues or judges discussed his work, his strategy, his cunning, his brilliance. His tenacious legal assaults on the wolves; the violent bastards who inflicted wanton violence against society, were legendary.

But his track record didn't cut him any slack with Roslyn Jones. A week ago, Jones forced him to take a two month sabbatical.

Officially, Jones claimed that her star prosecutor was recharging his batteries. There was more than a grain of truth to Jones's story. Decades of working around the clock to avenge the wrongs of murderers, rapists and gang members would take a toll on anybody; even Francis X. Durkin. His batteries needed recharging.

But unofficially, his sabbatical was due to Jamaal Shavers.

Sixteen year-old Jamaal Shavers sprayed a rival gang's drug den with 47 bullets from an AR-15. He didn't hit any low-life gang members but Shavers did kill a father of six working on his car a half block away.

Durkin charged the 16 year old with capital murder, a class A felony and manslaughter, a class B felony. Fifteen year olds charged with Class A and B felonies are automatically tried as adults. But Connecticut law allows a state's attorney to file a motion to move cases back to juvenile court if he thinks it's in society's and the offender's best interests.

Durkin didn't. He thought the reckless and wanton act of spraying a neighborhood with over 47 bullets that left six children fatherless warranted that Shavers be tried as an adult.

Roslyn Jones was besieged with calls from liberal politicians and civil rights groups lobbying for Jamaal Shavers to be tried as a juvenile. He was too young to know what he was doing. His brain wasn't fully formed. He was the product of the mean streets and never caught a break. He could be rehabilitated. Try him as a juvenile.

Jones felt the heat and began softly lobbying Durkin to take a hard look at trying Shavers as a juvenile. But she knew by her star state's attorney's body language his mind was made up. It was. Only 16 years old, Shavers already had a rap sheet that including four arrests for car theft, two armed robberies, possession of illegal guns and 7 arrests for shoplifting.

Francis Durkin never considered sending Shaver's case back to juvenile court. Not for a moment. As far as he was concerned, rehabilitation for Shavers was a pipe dream and his job was to protect society from him. When Shavers was sentenced to 25 years with a minimum of 15 years in state prison, a political tempest tore through the state capitol. Jones was torched by the newspapers for locking up a young black man and throwing away the key. State legislators called for hearings and proposed legislation to try all juveniles, even for murder, in juvenile courts.

A state senator called for Francis X. Durkin to appear before the General Assembly's Judiciary Committee.

Jones knew the hearing would be combustible. She shuddered at the thought of Durkin speaking his mind. She shuddered at the thought of the headlines. She shuddered at the heat Durkin would take at the hearing. She needed time to lower the political temperatures. Her solution was to get Francis Durkin out of town. So Jones forced Durkin to take a sabbatical.

Durkin protested. He pleaded. He tried a charm offensive.

Nothing worked. Her decision was final.

"Bullshit," Durkin groaned as he rolled out of bed and noticed the digital clock read 3:30 a.m. He slipped on cut-off shorts and an old pair of sneakers and lumbered down the rickety wooden stairs. He walked onto the screen porch and eyed the moon beams skipping over the St. Lawrence River.

He suddenly shivered as if an electric current ran down his spine. It was a raw, primordial foreboding. He stilled himself and stared at the river for a long second to see if the sensation would return. When it didn't, he turned his attention back to the river and suddenly got the urge to kayak on the dark and still water.

Durkin turned on the kitchen lights and ambled towards the basement stairs. He stopped at the top of the staircase and peered down into the basement as if searching for any signs of danger.

He flicked on the lights and slowly descended into the basement. His mind's eye saw a small kayak perched in the corner. He saw it clearly. It was five feet long, red, and a plastic oar leaned against it. Durkin figured it was decades ago when he last stood in the basement but his mental image was crystal clear.

Durkin cleared a path through dusty vacuum cleaners and stacks of dented paint cans on his way to the corner. When he reached the edge of the basement, the kayak was gone. Only a broom with curled up straw bristles stood where the kayak once rested.

He searched for the kayak amongst the rusted saws, porch spindles stacked in bundles, and jam jars filled with copper colored bolts. He stopped and peered into a line of rusted Chock-Full-of-Nuts coffee cans holding crooked nails; relics of the cottage that was pieced together by men who worked on the river in the summer and swung hammers in the winter.

Durkin slowly pivoted and his eyes fixed on a grimy, green Schwinn bicycle leaning against the wall. It had to be 40 or 50 years old he thought as he eyed its fat rubber tires, wide handlebars and winged chain guard.

Durkin navigated his way around cardboard boxes and gripped its handlebars which squeaked in protest for waking it from its decades-old rest. He stepped back and admired the Schwinn with its rusted link-chain drooping off the crankset. In an odd way, he felt kinship with the dilapidated bike.

A grin crept over Durkin's face as if the mental vision of him riding the bike amused him. He dusted off the bike's spongy seat and fitted the link chain over the crankset's teeth. He scanned the room and grabbed a small tin of WD-40 resting on the workbench. To his surprise, he heard sloshing when he shook it. He tipped the rusted can over and squirted oil on the chain. He then grabbed a thin screwdriver off the workbench and poked out the dirt and grime that clogged the links before coaxing each one over the crankset's teeth. He sniffed his finger tips which smelled of degraded petroleum and rubbed his greasy hands against the side of his shorts. It was a lifetime ago when his hands last smelled of grease, he thought.

With the chain on, he lifted the back tire off the ground and pushed the pedals with his hands. The wheel whirred back to life.

He then found a foot pump in the corner of the basement and injected air into its flat tires, one heel stomp at a time. After two minutes of stomping on the plastic pump, he pressed his weight on the bike. The wide rubber wheels bulged but didn't blow. It might just work he chuckled as he rolled the bike out of the basement into the early morning quiet.

As he struggled with the pedals, the prosecutor with a photographic memory couldn't remember the last time he rode a bike. It had to be decades. Shit, he corrected himself. It had to be more than three decades he thought as the Schwinn creaked as he strained to keep from falling over.

He wobbled as the tires rolled over the gravel road that passed a line of Victorian summer cottages built a 150 years ago to house those who flocked to a Methodist summer retreat. The wonderland of gingerbread cottages, built during the long-forgotten era of lazy summers, were all still.

As he reached the entrance to the Thousand Island Park, Durkin made a resolution to get in shape. He admitted to himself that he had let his body go to pot. Decades of 18 hour work days and a bachelor's diet left him with a soft gut and sagging muscles. On the spot, in mid pedal, Durkin resolved to drop 20 pounds. At least 20 pounds, he huffed out loud. He'd start immediately and make the early morning's ride a long one.

The road was deserted as he pedaled towards the first of a span of bridges that connected the United States and Canada. As he reached the foot of the Thousand Islands Bridge he considered taking its footpath to watch the freighters pass on their way either to or from the Great Lakes. No, he decided, he'd keep true to his minute-old resolution and keep pedaling.

Durkin steered the creaking bike down a country road and didn't take any notice of the sign that pointed to the Dewolf Point State Park, one of three state parks on Wellesley Island. He just concentrated on pedaling.

Durkin cycled less than a mile when he began to experience pangs of fatigue. He wheezed, slid off the seat and came to a full stop with the bike frame resting on his crotch. Peering down the dark road, the tingling premonition resurfaced. Again, Durkin brushed the sensation aside. It was a primitive fear of the dark he told himself with a rush of embarrassment. He pushed himself back onto the bike's seat and pressed with all his might on the pedals. Slowly, he propelled himself towards a turn in the road.

As he rounded the dark corner, he suddenly saw the glow of flickering lights against the sea of trees. As he rolled closer, Durkin immediately recognized the short, authoritative bursts of colored light. He had visited hundreds of crime scenes surrounded by a sea of flashing cop cars. But this was different.

As he rolled nearer, he saw two muscular cop cars with tinted windows. One was adorned with the markings of a New York State trooper car. Durkin was sure the other was an undercover cop car.

Both engines were idling and radio chatter filled the darkness of the early morning air. He pedaled up to the trooper's car. Its interior lights were on but was empty. He dismounted and propped the bike up on its rusty kick-stand and walked to the undercover car.

The undercover car was also abandoned. That's when he saw the vintage VW Beetle parked next to the trooper's car. It was the same era as his Schwinn, he thought. The Beetle's driver side door was flung wide open and the scene pulsed with signs of distress: a single shoe on the road. A pair of eye glasses on the asphalt.

"Hello?" Durkin yelled out. He stilled and listened for a response. The only sounds he heard were the rumble of the car engines and the cackle of the police radios.

"Hello?" he shouted louder.

Durkin shivered again as his internal alarms sounded. Something was wrong, terribly wrong. He patted his short's pocket and was relieved to feel the outline of his cell phone. He pulled it out and dialed 911.

"911. What's your emergency?"

"This is Francis Durkin, I'm a state's attorney from Connecticut. I just came across two empty troopers' cars." He paused and looked up and saw the sign for the entrance of a state park, "at the entrance to DeWolf Point State Park."

With his cell phone pressed to his ear, Durkin walked over to the guardrail running alongside the edge of the road. He set his left hand on the rail and peered into the dark woods. He thought he heard twigs snapping, leaves compressing against earth, the unmistakeable sound of a man walking in a forest. He stepped over the guardrail. "I hear something in the woods."

"Sir, stay where you are," the dispatcher commanded, as if she was watching him on a security camera inching towards danger. "Troopers will be arriving momentarily."

On cue, Durkin stepped back from the guardrail and heard police sirens off in the distance, piercing the early morning's peacefulness. Then from behind him he heard an angry voice. "Hold it! Don't move!"

Before Durkin could respond, he felt a crushing blow on his head. For a second, the world swirled before him as he fought to maintain consciousness. He then lost the battle, spilling onto the asphalt like a ripped bag of groceries. His shoulder hit the pavement and then the side of his face dragged over the coarse, asphalt surface, tearing a gash across his cheek.

As he lay helplessly on the pavement his brain's connection flickered on and off as he felt his body being manhandled. Someone wrenched his arms behind his back. An unseen club struck his kidney and a knee pressed painfully into his back. For a second, Durkin thought he was going to die as he laid hogtied, face down on the pavement. His body screamed from being unmercifully contorted.

"You got someone?" another voice cried out from the woods. From the sound of their voices, Durkin was sure the men were troopers.

"Sure do," his captive yelled as if celebrating hooking a prized fish.

Durkin's skull throbbed. He winced as the pain in his ribs and kidney spiked. He wanted to shout that he was a state's attorney but speaking was too painful. He just moaned.

Durkin heard the men speaking in hushed tones. The talking stopped and he heard one of them speak into a cell phone. He couldn't make out what he was saying but he knew by the pauses the guy was listening intently to a senior officer.

A second later Durkin heard a car with a powerful engine shriek to a stop. He heard the crack of a car door opening and shoes running over asphalt. Then he felt a pair of strong hands roll him over. His eyelids flittered open and he saw the hands were connected to a baby-faced trooper. He couldn't be more than 22 years old Durkin thought as a groan slipped involuntarily from his lips.

"Sir, did you call 911?"

Durkin nodded as he spit out bits of gravel from his mouth and crooked his neck to lessen the growing pain in his neck. "Yeah," he gasped.

The baby-faced trooper was Trooper Andrew Loughlin, a rookie, on the job for less than 6 months. Loughlin shot a confused look at the other troopers as if to ask how they could've messed up so badly. They were going to catch hell.

The other trooper was a 23 year veteran, David Hennigan. Broad shouldered and plain faced, Hennigan vigorously defended himself. "There's a body in the woods," Hennigan yelled pointing to the woods next to the entrance to the state park. "I heard someone moving around." He paused as if wondering if he persuaded Loughlin on the necessity of striking Durkin. "It makes sense that the killer would circle back and try to escape," he added.

Loughlin wore the face of the unconvinced.

"I saw him heading for Haskin's car so I apprehended him. Ask Haskins."

The other trooper was Don Haskins. Five foot, 9 inch with a slight build and weighing less than a 150 pounds. Haskins came with 6 years on the job and a grating, cocky attitude.

"What's the guy doing out here at night?" Haskins shouted in defense of Hennigan. "We couldn't take any chances."

"He called 911," Loughlin said, shaking his head disapprovingly. Trooper Loughlin was a rookie but smart enough to know not to argue in front of a civilian. He sighed and gently ushered Durkin into a sitting position.

Loughlin focused on Durkin's bloody face which resembled a patch of highway under repair. He gently brushed the gravel clinging to Durkin's shirt and motioned for Hennigan to unlock the handcuffs tightly binding Durkin's wrists. Hennigan shot an annoyed look at Loughlin but followed the rookie's instructions like an adult reluctantly following the directions of a smart child.

As Durkin rubbed his wrists, Loughlin guided Durkin to the passenger seat of his trooper's car. He pulled out a towelette and handed it to Durkin.

"Thanks," Durkin groaned as he matted his face with the thin, wet gauze. He then removed it and his eyes bulged with disbelief as he looked at the bloody patches on the towelette.

"Are you okay?" The voice was deep, official sounding, devoid of any sympathy. It was a factual question, meant to elicit a plain, yes or no.

Durkin gathered strength and swiveled his head. Without yet seeing the trooper's face, Durkin knew he was looking the chest of a senior trooper. He dabbed the cuts on his face and slowly looked up at the trooper.

For a second, Durkin froze as if startled by the trooper's impenetrable mirror glasses. Durkin felt like he was speaking to a surveillance camera that periodically adjusted its angle. He sighed at his bad luck: a trooper on an authority-kick was in charge.

"I've been better," Durkin wheezed as a patrol car's flashing lights bounced off the trooper's glasses. When the trooper stepped closer, Durkin could see his bloody face reflecting off of the trooper's mirror glasses.

"I'm Commander Rasmutin. Are you a District Attorney?" Rasmutin asked sounding as if his interest in Durkin's welfare was conditioned upon Durkin's profession.

Durkin's eyes slowly drifted up to Rasmutin. He emitted a coldness under the one-way glass that covered his eyes and his jaw seemed in perpetual motion as if he was chewing a wad of tobacco.

"Well?" Rasmutin followed up with an irritatingly impatient tone.

Durkin shrugged. Kind of. State prosecutors went by a host of names. District Attorneys, County Attorneys, State's Attorneys, Prosecuting Attorneys, Circuit Solicitors and more. In New York the state prosecutors were called district attorneys and were elected.

"I'm a state's attorney," Durkin finally replied in a tone that suggested he didn't suffer fools and he considered Rasmutin one.

Rasmutin surveyed the area crawling with law enforcement agents. His eye stopped on the old Schwinn that had been knocked to the ground.

"You usually ride a bicycle this early in the morning?" Rasmutin's question was wrapped in an accusation.

Durkin stiffened as if pricked by Rasmutin's implication. "Your troopers usually assault civilians?"

Rasmutin stopped chewing as his clenched jaw vibrated with anger. In Connecticut, Rasmutin and Durkin would have been allies, working cooperatively to put the criminals away. Not in the Thousand Islands.

Rasmutin ran his thumbnail over the edge of his front teeth and glanced down at the leafy ravine where the other troopers had gone. With his head pointed towards the ravine, he said, "I'm not making excuses for Troopers Hennigan or Haskins, but Hennigan just found a dead body in the woods." Pause. "Everybody reacts differently when they encounter death."

Durkin nodded lightly. That's true.

Rasmutin modulated his tone to try to sound as if he was extending Durkin an olive branch. "I'm sure you know cops who've made good-faith mistakes."

"Oh, cops make good-faith mistakes all the time," Durkin said with a wince.

"Then you can understand how a trooper would think you had something to do with the murder."

14

Durkin shook his head. No. That was a leap of logic that he wasn't going to make. "This wasn't a good faith fuck-up. This was…." Durkin's voice fell off as if he hadn't concluded what it really had been. He just knew he was in far too much pain to forgive and forget.

Rasmutin shrugged. Have it your way, asshole. "I would appreciate it if you would stick around until our investigators arrive." Rasmutin pointed to his car. Then, sounding as if he rectifying an oversight, he asked,"Do you need medical attention?"

"I'll be going soon," Durkin replied in an authoritative tone.

Rasmutin stepped back and glared at Durkin through his mirror glasses. His glasses then darted to Durkin's hands. "Do you mind showing me your hands?"

"My hands?" Durkin's eyes shot daggers at Rasmutin. He shook his head as if he was silently chastising the commander before stretching his fingers and extending his hands, palm down.

"Would you turn them over?"

Durkin flipped his hands over. Oily bicycle-chain tracks ran over his fingers and both palms.

"How'd you get those marks on your hands?"

"Marks?" Durkin pushed his hands towards Rasmutin to show he had nothing to hide. He motioned to the bicycle and then back to his hands which had the outline of thin bicycle chain. "That's grease from the bicycle chain. Why don't you grab the chain and see for yourself?"

Rasmutin eyed Durkin like he was eyeing a petulant child. He motioned to Loughlin and spoke loudly for Loughlin's benefit. "Trooper Loughlin will get you anything you need."

"I don't need anything."

Rasmutin shrugged. Again, have it your way, asshole. As Rasmutin walked away Durkin noticed the circle of cop cars arranged to block traffic in either direction. No one was coming in or out of the area without Rasmutin's authorization. Durkin suddenly felt like a captive. A bruised and battered captive.

Durkin sat back in the passenger's seat and took stock of the situation. What the hell just happened? His head and body pulsed with intense pain. He winced as his finger tips dabbed the large bump on his head. Hell, maybe he did need medical attention, he thought as Trooper Loughlin handed him a cup of coffee.

He then watched the stream of troopers, deputy sheriffs and medical personnel trampling over the crime scene. Durkin shook his head. Any

15

defense attorney worth his salt would have a field day with a contaminated crime scene. Everything should have been cordoned off and only a few investigators allowed down into the crime scene.

Suddenly, Durkin felt drowsy as if a tidal wave of exhaustion washed over him. He leaned back and closed his eyes. After a few false starts, he fell asleep.

*****

Durkin's eyelids fluttered as his eyes adjusted to the morning sunlight. For a second he sat catatonic like, unsure of the time or his surroundings. As he got his bearings, he figured he had slept for at least an hour.

He breathed heavily and then realized he had been awakened by the vibration of his cell phone's buzzing. It buzzed again.

He pulled the phone from his pocket and saw the caller: Dem.

Dem was Sergeant Angelo DeMartin.

In the whirl of the early morning events, Durkin had forgotten his guests were scheduled to arrive midday. As his kidney screamed in pain, the vision of his guests driving up to his cousin's cottage flashed in Durkin's head. A 68 year old retired Bridgeport cop and a 20 something year old Bridgeport cop known world-wide for his bravery. The fact that the retired cop was bald, misshapen and white and the young cop was black and had movie-star looks busted the adage that birds of a feather flock together. All three of them were very different men from very different generations. But their special bond bridged the age gaps and differences bestowed at birth. Now they were all eagerly awaiting the chance to drain a few bottles of Irish whiskey together on the banks of the St. Lawrence River. They'd clink their glasses but they wouldn't share any war stories about their greatest battle. No, the details of their greatest battle would remain unspoken and be forever buried when the last one of them passed to the other side.

"Hey," Durkin answered unsteadily.

"Francis! Are you ready for us!" DeMartin's voice was hyper-charged like a college kid setting off for spring break. "PJ dragged my butt out of bed in the middle of the night. We're crossing the bridge right now. This place is beautiful."

"You're where?"

"Don't sound so happy to see us," DeMartin joked.

"There's been a…" Durkin stopped and searched for the right word. "There's been an incident this morning."

Silence.

"Francis, is everything okay?"

"Yeah, sorry," Durkin replied, sounding like he was catching his breath. "I stumbled across a murder scene and…" His voice trailed off.

"You what?"

"It's a long story."

"Are you pulling my chain?"

"No. Take the first exit over the bridge. Take a left. I'm two miles down the road in front of the DeWolf Point State Park."

DeMartin reacted to Durkin's somber tone. "Francis, are you really okay?"

Durkin ignored him. "About a mile and a half down the road you'll see trooper cars. Tell them that you're coming to meet me and Commander Rasmutin."

"Who?"

"Just say Commander Rasmutin. I'll tell you everything when I see you."

Before DeMartin could ask any more questions, Durkin killed the call.

Durkin sat in the trooper's car and sipped the rest of his cold coffee. He pushed himself out of the car and crushed the coffee cup in his hand as if hoping to release some of his stress. As he felt the styrofoam crumble in his hands the sounds of a disturbance on the perimeter drew his attention. Then he heard raised voices. No one was shouting but he heard forceful, authoritative verbal jousting. It was clear no one was backing down. The jousting continued and the volume increased.

Three troopers circled a man as if they were readying to subdue him. Durkin recognized PJ McLevy's bald, egg shaped head. PJ used his forefinger to forcefully emphasize whatever he was saying. When PJ finished, a thick-chested trooper broke away from the other troopers and hustled to find Commander Rasmutin who was huddled with three plainclothes troopers and a medical examiner by the side of the road. The trooper waited deferentially until Rasmutin acknowledged him. The trooper then pointed to PJ McLevy and then towards Durkin.

From under his mirror glasses, Rasmutin followed the trooper's fingers and stared at Durkin. Rasmutin shook his head, broke off eye contact and issued an order to the trooper. His gestures and body language were designed to send a message to Durkin that he was in charge.

The trooper hustled back to the perimeter and escorted Angelo DeMartin and PJ McLevy to Durkin. The first thing Durkin noticed was that Angelo

DeMartin's arm was in a sling but he had jettisoned his crutches and now walked, stiff-legged, in a moon boot. He still looked like a wounded warrior. The second thing was that every trooper stared at Angelo DeMartin, the famous cop. Could anyone blame them? Even a New York State trooper working on the border of Canada was familiar with the youngest Public Service Medal of Valor winner. Every trooper and deputy sheriff had seen the famous video of the black cop firing his gun through his patrol car's front window as he barreled towards bank robbers toting automatic weapons. The video was in the top ten videos for two straight years. At least 100 million people had viewed it, including everyone now hovering around the entrance to Dewolf Point State Park. Several troopers battled the urge to ask for his autograph as DeMartin walked gimpily past them.

Angelo DeMartin was the fist to reach Durkin. He stopped and ran his eyes over the deep cuts and streaks of blood on Durkin's face. "Francis, what the hell happened to you?"

Durkin waited for PJ to arrive and then ran through the morning's events. He was out for a pre-sunrise bicycle ride. Everything was serene and peaceful until he came around a bend and saw two trooper cars with their engines running. He called 911 and then a trooper hit him from behind. He rubbed the bump on his head. Based on what he overheard, the troopers saying, he thought he stumbled upon a murder scene. He pointed to the guardrail. He was pretty sure a trooper found a woman's body in the ravine.

When Durkin finished, their cops' brains considered every angle.

First, they considered the unfathomable. Could the state's attorney have killed the woman? Could a state's attorney have met the woman for an early morning sexual rendezvous and it all went terribly wrong? Their cop's brains were wired to consider every possibility. It was possible for a legal genius to snap during a sexual encounter. Both cops knew countless men who grew horns when they sprouted hard-ons. For those twisted guys just the prospect of an orgasm triggered a primordial frothing like bluefish in mating season, slashing at everything in its reach. Maybe the state's attorney went through an evil transformation when his testosterone raged. Maybe Durkin couldn't sexually perform and lost it. Maybe Durkin was just riding by and tried to take advantage of a damsel in distress? Did he offer to help her in return for sexual favors and go bat shit when she refused his advances? Both cops encountered hundreds of cases of twisted men who beat women who wouldn't submit to their sexual demands.

But PJ and DeMartin's cops brains quickly cleared Durkin. They saw immediately that the murder occurred 20 feet from the guardrail. An earlier rain left the ground muddy. Anyone who walked down to the murder scene returned with mud up to their ankles. DeMartin's canvas sneakers were dirty but dry. No, almost instantly the cops' brains had cleared Durkin. He never stepped anywhere near the body.

PJ pointed to Durkin's face. "How'd it turn physical?"

Durkin shook his head. "I yelled out a couple of times. I went over to the guardrail. A trooper yelled 'freeze'. I froze and before I knew it, I was hit from behind. It felt like I got hit with a shovel."

"I'm sure it was his flashlight," PJ said a matter a factly.

Durkin nodded. Could be. "When I was lying on the ground he flung me around like a rag doll and cuffed me."

"This place is a real vacation wonderland," PJ joked as he scanned the perimeter of the crime scene. He then turned to Trooper Loughlin who had drifted within earshot. "What's going on down there?" he said, pointing to the woods.

"It's a murder," Loughlin answered. His face tightened. "It's awful. A woman's head was bashed in."

Before he could say anything more, Commander Rasmutin summoned the young trooper in an angry voice.

PJ lowered his voice as Loughlin hustled off. "Francis, you said you were riding a bicycle?"

The men all turned and eyed the Schwinn that someone had tossed to the side of the road.

Durkin winced with embarrassment. "It's my cousin's."

"So you weren't kidding about riding a bike?" PJ asked.

"I know how to ride a bike," Durkin said more defensively than he intended.

PJ gestured towards Commander Rasmutin who huddled with troopers by the guardrail. "Why's there so much tension?"

"Because that asshole in the mirror glasses hasn't cleared me as a suspect."

DeMartin and PJ exchanged quizzical looks. It took them less than a minute to rule out Durkin as a suspect. There was no mud on his sneakers.

"They just have to be thorough," DeMartin said with a shrug. No big deal. It's just normal. "They'll clear you in less than an hour."

PJ shook his head in disagreement. "No, I'm with Francis. Something doesn't sit right with me." Before Durkin or DeMartin had a chance to say anything, PJ added, "Don't ask me why. It just doesn't."

That was enough for Durkin. "Hey," he yelled to Trooper Loughlin who had drifted back to keep an eye on him. "Tell the commander I'm leaving."

Loughlin winced, knowing Durkin's decision would trigger fireworks. Durkin shook his head at the rookie trooper. It was non-negotiable. He was leaving.

"Give me a second so I can inform the commander," Loughlin said almost pleading.

"Sure, but only a minute."

Trooper Loughlin hustled off to the huddle of troopers surrounding Rasmutin. He whispered to Rasmutin who immediately spun out of the pack of troopers and marched back to Durkin. His body language screamed that he was readying for a fight.

"I'm leaving," Durkin announced when Rasmutin was five feet away.

Rasmutin stopped and slowly observed DeMartin and PJ through his mirrored glasses. He then turned back to Durkin. "We need to speak with you."

"You can get in touch with me through the Connecticut State's Attorney office."

Rasmutin stood back and gestured to a guy in a plaid suit jacket who Durkin hadn't noticed before. He reminded Durkin of a stamp collector.

"This is District Attorney McClusky," Rasmutin said as if it was distasteful for him to introduce the two prosecutors.

The man pivoted slowly and held out his hand. "Bill McClusky," he said. "Jefferson County District Attorney."

Durkin shook McClusky's hand. "Francis Durkin. I'm a state's attorney in Connecticut."

McClusky nodded as if Durkin's reputation proceeded him. McClusky then stepped back and examined Durkin's ripped shirt and the cuts on his face. "I'm sorry to hear about the misunderstanding."

Durkin pointed to his face. "You call this a misunderstanding?"

McClusky's eyes blinked and his lips made an awkward circular motion. Rasmutin then fixed a cold stare on Durkin. "Would you submit to a DNA swab?"

Durkin drew a deep breath as he felt rumbles of rage stirring inside him. For a long second he eyed the ground before raising his head and fixing his eyes on McClusky. "I understand it's standard practice to take DNA samples from anyone found in the vicinity of a crime scene," Durkin said with the tone of man straining to sound like he hadn't a care in the world. "Because it's best to eliminate suspects early on."

McClusky nodded with a faint look of appreciation for Durkin's pending cooperation. Durkin pointed to the woods. "But I never crossed over the guardrail or stepped into the woods. I wasn't in the vicinity of the crime." He patted his cheek with a towelette. There wasn't any chance he'd be giving a DNA sample.

Durkin paused as Rasmutin and McClusky's faces tensed. "In fact, when I arrived, I called 911, identified myself and was rewarded with a beat-down by one of your troopers."

Durkin dabbed the cuts on his face as if to emphasize the severity of the beating.

Rasmutin cleared his throat louder than necessary. "If you don't have anything to worry about, why not just submit a DNA swab?"

Durkin vibrated as if Rasmutin struck a raw nerve. "I think you should focus on finding the murderer," Durkin said, hitting a purposefully superior tone.

Rasmutin pointed to Durkin's ripped shirt. "You'll need to leave your shirt."

Durkin glared at Rasmutin. Then, as if he reached his boiling point, jabbed his finger at the commander. "That's not going to happen."

Rasmutin rubbed his temple, conscious that everyone's eyes were on him. He then stepped back and slowly removed his mirrored glasses and leaned towards Durkin.

That's when Durkin saw it. Rasmutin's right eye was totally black: there was no white around his eye. There was no iris. It looked like a black, impenetrable marble. But it moved as if Rasmutin could see through the dead, evil eye.

In the split-second it took Durkin's brain to process the trooper's facial image, he began to shiver as if overcome by revulsion. The white hot intensity of his revulsion sped up his heart rate. His face twisted in disgust. It was as if a dog suddenly snarled as it detected an evil aura around a stranger.

"I can arrest you," Rasmutin said, staring him down through his dead eye.

Durkin recovered from the shock of looking at Rasmutin's dead eye and gathered himself. He turned to McClusky. "You might want to remind this trooper that the Fourth Amendment requires a thing called probable cause for an arrest."

Rasmutin smirked and slipped his mirror glasses back on. "Probable cause is not a high bar."

Durkin tensed, wondering if Rasmutin knowingly quoted a U.S. Supreme Court opinion. Time and again the Supreme Court has emphasized that

21

probable cause is not a high bar to clear. Hell, Durkin had used the same quote himself a hundred times in court.

"No, it's not a high bar but it's still a bar," Durkin replied as he activated his encyclopedic knowledge regarding probable cause standards. He pointed to McClusky. "Since your trooper likes to quote the Supreme Court he should know that *U.S. v. Sokolow* states that probable cause means a 'fair probability'. It doesn't mean a hunch, a gut feeling or something he feels just ain't right."

"I know the law," McClusky replied with a trace of a singed ego.

Durkin reverted to his courtroom swagger. "Well, then you know that the touchstone of the Fourth Amendment is reasonableness, not individualized suspicion. Try *Samson v. California* or *Maryland v. King* or the *U.S. v. Knights*. Probable cause is an evidentiary threshold that isn't close to being met here."

Durkin straightened as if spitting out legal cases temporarily numbed the pain of his injuries. "And you should also know that a false arrest will trigger a 1983 action against state and local officials for deprivation of my Constitutional rights."

1983.

42 United States Code, Section 1983.

Section 1983 empowered people to sue state and local government officials who violate their federal constitutional rights. The law, known as the Ku Klux Klan Act, was aimed at protecting black Americans during Reconstruction. Now a state's attorney from Connecticut was waving it at New York State troopers like a torch to keep a pack of wolves at bay.

Rasmutin stared icily at Durkin. "Don't you think it's reasonable to have suspicions when someone rides a bike around a murder scene in the middle of the night? We have the authority to stop someone in the middle of the night."

Durkin's face exploded in disbelief. He turned to McClusky. "Did he really say that?" Durkin asked mockingly. "Does he believe that the Nightwalker statutes are still in effect?"

Nightwalker statutes? McClusky's confused face sought an explanation.

Durkin assumed the air of a law professor. "Yeah, in medieval England, watchmen could arrest any nightwalker and hold him until the morning when he could be brought before a magistrate. But those laws went away with the advent of electricity."

"This bullshit isn't going to get you anywhere," Rasmutin blurted as his head seemed to bulge under the confines of his Stetson.

Durkin leveled his forefinger at the troopers circling them like he was pointing a gun. "Every trooper and state official who observes or assists in an arrest not based on probable cause is liable for not interceding to prevent an arrest not based on probable cause. That's O'Neill v. Krzeminski."

Durkin jabbed his finger at McClusky. "You should make sure that the troopers know they have an affirmative duty to intercede on the behalf of a citizen whose constitutional rights are being violated in their presence."

There was a long, awkward silence. Durkin dabbed his face and glared at Rasmutin. "I'll be seeing you in court."

Rasmutin and McClusky bristled at being threatened by the chubby, patronizing, legal-case spewing, state's attorney from Connecticut.

"What about the DNA swab?" Rasmutin huffed impatiently. He touched his mirror glasses as if threatening to expose his dead eye again.

"It's not going to happen."

Rasmutin played another card. "We can always get a warrant."

Durkin's eyes turned dark. He pivoted away from Rasmutin with a look that he wouldn't dignify his comment with a reply. He instead stared directly at McClusky. "Mr. D.A., I think you should advise the commander not to waste his time. He'll need probable cause to get a court to issue a warrant to compel a DNA swab."

McClusky stood awkwardly with his lower lip protruding over his top lip.

"All you have is a man on a bicycle who called 911," Durkin said, talking in the third person. "And then he was attacked by troopers. You can't draw probable cause from those facts."

McClusky blinked as if he was experiencing a flutter of nerves. He stared at Durkin, unsure of how to reply.

"I'm leaving," Durkin said as he hobbled over and picked up the rusty Schwinn which seemed more battered in the daylight. Then he, PJ and DeMartin shuffled like three wounded soldiers through the line of troopers surrounding the entrance to DeWolf Point State Park.

"Did you see that guy's eye?" PJ asked, shaking his head.

"That's one weird looking dude," DeMartin replied.

When they reached PJ's car, it suddenly struck the men that there was no room for the Schwinn. PJ reached into his back seat and pulled out two straps. He fastened the ends to hooks inside the trunk and then pulled a carabiner from his belt buckle and used it to pull the two straps securely around the bicycle.

DeMartin and Durkin exchanged a bemused look.

"What?" PJ asked. "You guys should learn to carry carabiners with you. You never know when you'll need them."

The three men squeezed into PJ's car and waited until a trooper moved his car that blocked access to and from the crime scene. As they drove by the long line of troopers' cars, an uncontrollable shiver rippled down Francis Durkin's spine.

CHAPTER TWO

James Alexander Breen wore a yellow raincoat over his jean shorts, his favorite ripped flannel shirt and yellow rubber boots. With his boyish looks, the 38 year old looked like an oversized kindergartner frolicking near the water in the steady, morning rain.

Known as JB to everyone, he perched himself on the edge of his fishing boat and picked up a glass mayonnaise jar full of spare nuts, washers, bolts and screws.

"For want of a nail the shoe was lost," JB said to himself in a sing-song voice. "For want of a shoe the horse was lost, and for want of a horse the rider was lost." JB chuckled as he squeezed his hand into the glass jar in search of a nut that would attach to a post that supported his outboard engine.

His cell phone interrupted his search.

JB instinctively knew the call was not bringing good news. Maybe it was the timing of the call. Who calls at daybreak? Maybe it was how the snappy ringtone clashed with the sound of water gently lapping up against the dock and the drops of rain falling softly on the water. Maybe it was his reporter's instincts kicking in.

JB frowned as he struggled to free his hand from the mayonnaise jar. With a pop, he pulled his hand out of the jar and dug out his cell phone from his breast pocket. With one glance, he knew his instincts were right.

Larry Costello, the editor of the *Watertown Daily Register*, was calling. His boss. At least one of his bosses, JB corrected himself as he deployed his cheeriest voice with one of the men who controlled his livelihood.

"Good morning, Larry."

"JB, I know you're taking a personal day," Costello began in a rushed voice, "but a young woman's body was just found at the entrance to Dewolf Point State Park."

The glass mayonnaise jar sounded as if it was going to shatter as Breen dropped a large bolt into it. A death? JB's first thought was that a young woman had drowned and her body washed up on Wellesley Island. His mind instantly recalled interviewing a Coast Guard officer a few months back when they discovered a middle-aged man's body floating in the St. Lawrence River.

"A drowning?"

"No. She's been murdered." Costello's shocked breath streamed through the phone as if he was still coming to grips with the gruesome information. "I hear someone bashed her head in with rocks."

"Holy shit," Breen exhaled.

"Can you get over there right away?"

JB eyed his clothes. He considered racing to his house to change but time was of the essence. He'd sacrifice his dignity for his trade.

"I'm in A-bay," JB said, referring to Alexandria Bay, the small town 10 miles downriver from Dewolf Point State Park. "I'll be there in 15 minutes."

"Great," Costello replied. "Oh," he hesitated, sounding reluctant to bring up an awkward subject, "McClusky and Rasmutin are both on-site. I just wanted you to know."

"No worries," JB said breezily as he hung up. But he was worried.

JB was the Watertown Daily Register's crime reporter. His success depended on prying information from clerks, coroners, dispatchers, sheriffs and district attorneys. He couldn't afford to burn bridges but a reporter had to report the facts. If he couldn't report the facts for fear of making enemies, he should find another job. But JB never wanted another job. After he graduated from Potsdam State, he started as a gopher at the Register and worked his way up as a general beat reporter. He was good and after five years he worked his way up the ladder to become the Watertown Daily Register's crime reporter.

The power of his pen brought a small-town prominence. Mayors, sheriffs and troopers went out of their way to curry favor with him since his pen could shape their reputation.

With two exceptions.

The first was William McClusky, Jefferson County's District Attorney. McClusky was outraged by Breen's account of how he botched the murder trial of the Egans. The Egan murders were as high-profile as it got in Watertown. Three Egans were killed in cold blood on New Year's eve at a rest stop on I-81. Everyone; the man in the street, cops, troopers and district attorneys were sure they arrested the right man.

Everyone except the jury.

In Breen's estimation, McClusky committed one gaff after another in the courtroom. As far as JB was concerned, the killer walked because of McClusky's incompetence. And he didn't hide his opinions from his readers.

But it was JB's coverage of McClusky's plea bargain in the Shawcross murders that caused the irretrievable breach between the crime reporter and the District Attorney. Shawcross was a twisted deviant who fished in the small rivers that ran through the small, aging town of Watertown. He was also a sadistic, demented, pedophile who sodomized and raped a boy before suffocating him by stuffing his throat with rocks. While the Watertown police searched for the boy, Shawcross raped and brutally murdered a little girl.

Shawcross was finally arrested. The public called for him to be strung up to the electric chair and fried. The people expected McClusky to throw the book at Shawcross. But when it came to filing the charges McClusky folded, only charging Shawcross with manslaughter for the two cold-blooded killings.

Families ruined. Citizens traumatized. The twisted rapist spent only 10 years in prison and was then released. Free to kill and maim.

The Police chief shrugged. They caught him. That's all they could do. The parole board shrugged. The charge was manslaughter; they had no choice but to release him. McClusky shrugged. The people just didn't understand how the legal system works. What could he do?

When the parole board released him, Shawcross immediately did what sadistic rapists do; he went on a sadistic raping spree in Rochester, mutilating eleven prostitutes. The psychotic child killer, cut out vaginas and ate them in his car. What could the D.A., the cops, the parole board do? They shrugged.

Breen did what he could do. He kept to the facts. A travesty had occurred. The travesty could and should have been avoided. How could Shawcross not have been tried for first degree murder of the two young children? Thousands of men have been convicted of murder on far less evidence. There was no excuse for not securing a first degree murder charge. There was no excuse for releasing Shawcross to maim and kill.

James Alexander Breen, the lead crime reporter for the *Watertown Daily Register,* called for accountability. It was a code word to throw McClusky out of office and investigate the state parole board. Accountability was a code word for heads-rolling.

Now with only five months left in his term, McClusky saw the writing on the wall. McClusky hoped for an appointment as a judge since there'd be little chance of securing another term as District Attorney. And McClusky blamed his need for new employment on James Breen who turned the people against him.

As JB crossed over the Thousand Islands Bridge, he shrugged off the thoughts of his impending confrontation with McClusky. It came with the territory for a crime reporter, he told himself.

27

But Commander Rasmutin was another matter. Rasmutin resented any penetrating questions. He expected the reporters to toss him soft balls and JB threw fast balls. Rasmutin would stare icily at him and his dark, sinister eyes gave JB the spooks. He wouldn't admit it but Rasmutin intimidated him.

As he neared the Dewolf Point State Park, JB spotted a scrum of sheriffs' and trooper cars cordoning off the area in both directions. The deputy sheriffs from the Jefferson County Sheriff Department covered 1,272 square miles and 585 square miles of water. Now the deputy sheriffs lined the area looking like bored security guards at a mall.

JB parked on the side of the road and fished out a small notepad he kept in his glove compartment. He zipped up his raincoat and exited his car, searching for a familiar face.

He quickly found one. He recognized Deputy Sheriff Phil Potter's meaty face as he stood next to his patrol car and looked off into the distance. JB had interviewed Potter countless times, the last being two weeks ago when a car filled with drunk kids side-swiped an Amish horse and buggy.

JB walked briskly towards Potter, hoping to leverage their friendship. "Morning Phil."

Potter nodded tiredly. He was the fourth person on the scene and hadn't left his post in four hours. He needed to pee and desperately wanted a cup of coffee.

JB flipped open his pad and assumed his casual, disarming North Country air. He was one of them, their neighbor.

"Can you tell me anything about the murder?"

"I hear it's pretty gruesome." Potter shivered as if he was thinking that the dead woman with the disfigured face could have been his 14 year old daughter. "What kind of sick fuck does this sort of thing?"

JB's head bobbed in agreement. "Who found the body?"

"I hear it was Hennigan." Potter's face scrunched up as if he disliked saying Hennigan's name.

"What are you saying?"

Potter shook his head. "He's a funny guy."

"Funny, ha-ha?"

"No, funny weird. Somethings not right about him. He's the type who won't look you in the eye. I never trust those types. You know what I mean?"

JB shrugged. He knew that Hennigan grew up in Watertown, joined the Army and then the state police. But that's all he really knew. He made a mental note to dig up some background information on Hennigan.

"About an hour ago, they rushed him out of here," Potter continued.

"Hennigan?"

"Yep."

"Why?"

"I don't know. It just was odd. The troopers are acting secretive. When I asked them what was going on, they all got tight-lipped." Potter's nose pulled up as if he detected a foul odor. "My guess is that Rasmutin issued a gag order. They're all scared of shit of him."

JB nodded. He was too. He absorbed Potter's information as a battered car chugged up to the road block, sounding like an asthmatic on his last breath. Potter pointed to the line of cop cars. No one was permitted through. The driver pointed at the cars and gestured like it was his god-given right to pass. This was the only road that led to his camp. What the hell was he going to do?

Potter shrugged. He had his orders: no one was passing through. JB didn't recognize the driver. He was in his late-seventies and his face reddened as he realized that Potter was not going to bend. How long was it going to take?

Potter shrugged again. He had no idea. Maybe you should find something to do for a while and then come back. The man gritted his teeth and pulled a jerky, three-point turn and sped away leaving a gust of charcoal colored exhaust behind.

"Anything else going on?" JB asked Potter as they both watched the tailpipe's smoke dissipate.

"A prosecutor from Connecticut was here."

JB pointed to the ground. "Here?"

"Yup." Potter pointed to where the troopers were congregating. "I couldn't hear everything but there was a lot of high testosterone, chest-bumping going on."

"With who?"

Potter chuckled. "Who else? Rasmutin."

"About what?"

"Not sure. I walked over and heard bits and pieces. The prosecutor was spewing a lot of legal shit like he was in court."

"No kidding."

"Yeah, he walked by me. He had cuts all over his face. And get this. Remember the video of the black cop shooting the bank robbers through his front windshield?"

Potter shook his head. It didn't ring a bell.

"Well, he's really famous. The cop is a hero and received a medal from the President."

29

"The President of the United States?"

"Yeah. That President. The hero cop was with him. He was all banged up. His arm was in a sling and he was wearing one of those moon boots. You just missed them."

JB stared disbelievingly at the remote area in front of the Point State Park. What the hell was a Connecticut prosecutor and a medal winning cop doing on Wellesley Island?

"A little later, McClusky arrived," Potter continued. "There was a big pow-wow. I couldn't hear what was being said but I could see a lot of long faces."

What the hell is going on? JB asked himself as he tried to make sense of what Potter told him. He turned back to Potter. "Have you ever heard of a murder on Wellesley Island?"

Potter scoffed. Murder? There were less than a 1000 year-round residents on the island. Everyone knew everyone. People didn't lock their doors. "Nope. I've never heard about a murder on the island."

"Me neither," JB replied. He'd do some fact checking but was confident that this was the first recorded murder on Wellesley Island. He made a mental note to find a way to weave the fact into the story.

"Take care," JB said, hustling over to the crowd of law enforcement officials huddled outside of the guard rail.

No one seemed to notice the man in a rain coat and yellow rubber boots approaching the crime scene. JB pulled out his notepad and held it up as if it was a pass to enter beyond the guardrail. He stepped over the guardrail, expecting to hear a voice calling out for him to stop.

No one called out.

He pressed on and his boot immediately sunk into the deep mud. He began sliding down the slippery ravine and grabbed onto a thin limb to save himself from going ass-over-tea-kettle down the ravine. Still, no one called out to stop him.

When he reached level ground, he saw a search light on a stand was set up, beaming light on a lifeless body under a brown tarp. Troopers searched the area and an older man in a rumpled suit stood silently with his eyes transfixed on the tarp.

JB recognized the man; Richard Spanks, the Jefferson County Coroner. Spanks moved like a bag of old bones and his skin had a yellow tinge like a newspaper left in the sun.

JB stepped carefully as if he was navigating through a minefield and made it to Spank's side without detection. JB's presence finally broke Spanks out of his trance.

"Breen! What are you doing here?" Spanks blared like a startled man roused from a deep sleep.

"Just doing my job."

Spanks paused as if grading JB's reply. He then slowly nodded. Yes, they were both just doing their jobs. "You know you're in a restricted area."

JB ignored him and looked at a foot that stuck out of the tarp. As if reading JB's mind, Spanks said, "You don't want to look under the tarp."

"Is it that bad?"

Spanks nodded, wearing a melancholy look. He then gritted his teeth and shook his head as if shaking it at the murderer. "Her left cheekbone was punctured by a sharp object right below her left eye. The bridge of the poor woman's nose was split open. That's just what I can see from here. The back of her head was also beaten in." He pointed to large, sharp stones beside the body. "My guess is that whoever killed her, used the stones."

"And when did this happen?"

Spanks looked around to see if anyone was within earshot. Seeing they were alone, he then stepped closer to JB. "You didn't hear this from me."

JB nodded.

"You're not going to use my name, will you?"

"No, not if you don't want me to."

"Good. Don't. I overheard them speaking. Trooper Hennigan stopped the woman at around 3:34 a.m. Hennigan crossed over the Thousand Islands Bridge at 4:09. She came through the tollbooth at 4:10 and Hennigan then found the woman's body at 4:28 a.m." Spanks cocked his eyebrows skeptically.

"What the hell?"

"Yup. Remember, you didn't hear this from me."

JB stepped closer to the body. The bulge under the tarp looked smaller than he imagined.

"Breen! Get the hell out of here!"

JB knew his luck had run out when he heard the booming, angry voice he knew belonged to Commander Rasmutin.

JB turned and in a low, calm voice said, "Commander, can I get a quote from you?"

Rasmutin rumbled like a volcano. His face was beet-red and a thick vein on his neck pulsed ominously. "Who let you down here?"

31

JB ignored his question. "Can you tell me anything about the murdered woman?"

"Get out of the crime scene!" Rasmutin screamed like a lit fuse.

JB flipped his pad closed and traced his muddy tracks back to the road. When he reached the guardrail he was glad to see Paul Sterling from the North County Radio and Sarah Billings with WWNY News. He quickly gravitated to them as if there was safety in numbers.

An hour later, the state police said they wouldn't be making any statements until the victim's family was contacted. JB eyed his notepad. The body of an unidentified woman was found near the entrance to the Dewolf Point State Park. She was brutally murdered. Her face and head had been crushed by rocks. He could cite the chief coroner as an anonymous source that stated that her nose had been smashed open. He'd quote Deputy Sheriff Potter as a long time law enforcement officer who said it was the first murder he could recall reported on Wellesley Island. He shook his head despairingly. He needed to corroborate the exact times Hennigan stopped the woman on the highway. He spotted the late model VW Beatle wrapped in police tape and jotted down the Pennsylvania license plate number. He'd figure out a way to get a friendly cop to run a check on the car.

But why was a Connecticut prosecutor with a bloody face at the scene? And who was the famous cop with him? JB gnawed on his knuckle as he tried to piece together the bits of information.

CHAPTER THREE

Francis Durkin sat on the wooden dock still dappled by the early morning's rain. Holding an icepack on his head, he studied the quickly moving clouds. It looked as if a film was sped up; dark clouds were quickly displacing gray ones and white clouds appeared on the horizon. A few sun rays began peeking through the white clouds. The prospects for a sunny day were damn good, Durkin thought.

Durkin's gaze shifted to a freighter off in the distance. He couldn't determine if it was headed towards the Great Lakes or the Atlantic Ocean. His eyes darted over the river as his thoughts turned back to the morning's events.

What the hell were the odds of stumbling upon a murder scene in a remote area of a remote island? The odds were the same as being struck by lightning. No, he corrected himself. The odds were higher. Much higher. He looked up at the clouds again. The odds were the same as a plane suddenly blasting through the clouds and landing on his head. A billion to one, he mumbled as he scanned the sky in search of a plane.

Durkin's eyes dropped to his chest and seemed surprised he still was wearing the ripped and bloody polo shirt. When they arrived back at his cousin's cottage, PJ and DeMartin hit the phones to dig up information on what happened at Dewolf Point State Park. They had sources everywhere and were owed countless favors. Durkin was still buzzing from the morning's events so he sought a few minutes of solace by the river. He hadn't moved for an hour.

Durkin peeled off his torn and bloodied polo shirt and was about to toss it on the dock when he suddenly reconsidered. The sight of a ripped and bloody shirt lying in a pile would dampen the mood. He picked it up and walked unevenly, as if one leg was shorter than the other, into his cousin's boat house and draped the shirt on a rusty nail.

Bare chested, he headed for the ladder on the dock. He felt the warm breeze on his skin and realized he hadn't experienced the sensation of being half-naked in the open air for years. How long? He could remember walking bare chested on a beach while he was in law school. That was a long time ago, he chuckled.

His body ached as he trudged towards the ladder. He stopped and glanced down at his stomach. It drooped like it was a sock carrying a lump of cottage cheese. He shrugged. A soft, round body was an occupational hazard for a prosecutor.

He kicked off his sneakers and seemed captivated by the river as the morning sun stirred it from its sleep. He eyed a lone motor boat slicing through the glistening water leaving a line of white foam dissolving in its wake. He watched as the last trace of the foam disappeared and scanned the horizon not taking any notice of the paddle boarder and fishermen across the bay.

He turned his attention to the water slapping gently against the dock. It was crystal clear. He could see the river's floor. His brain calculated that it was about 10 feet deep and the landing area was free of rocks. He watched two small fish swim by as he summoned the nerve to jump. He was far too sore to dive. If he entered the water it was going to be feet first and cautioned himself to avoid a belly flop.

Durkin positioned his feet to the edge of the dock and paused as he assessed the dangers once more. He was over-thinking it, he admonished himself. Just do it.

Durkin took a baby step towards the water and then, as if half his body wanted nothing to do with the water, he half-fell, half-jumped into the river.

Like the wind on his bare chest, the sensation of his body submerging in the river, broke free the good memories of visiting the river when he was a kid. The cold, clean water enlivened his mind and body even though the water seemed to loosen the newly formed scabs on his face and awaken his sore muscles.

He doggy paddled back to the ladder and held on to the bottom rung as he caught his breath. A sharp pain shot through his ribs as he raised his arm. It was like with every new movement, he was discovering a new injury.

"Fuck," he hissed, unable to get his leg onto the last rung. He cursed whoever built the ladder. There should be at least one more rung for older, fat guys. Durkin was sure he looked like a beached whale as he stepped on a rock and pushed his knee on top of the lowest rung.

The pain in his back was excruciating. He dropped back into the river, thinking it would be far too painful to climb up the ladder.

But there was no other way out. He forced his knee up and onto the lowest rung and was sure, to anyone walking by, it would look as if he was humping the ladder. He slowly fought through the pain and forced his right foot up onto the ladder. Each step up the ladder felt like someone was stabbing him in his ribs. He reached the top rung and plopped his butt on the dock and gently rubbed his ribcage. Damn it hurt, he hissed.

Durkin's phone buzzed. He found his cell phone atop a towel. He slid the towel towards him and picked up the phone. His face tightened the second he eyed the caller's name. Jones.

Chief State's Attorney Roslyn Jones.

Durkin was not surprised that the morning's news would filter back to Roslyn Jones. He was just shocked at the speed.

"Good morning, Roslyn," Durkin said, straining to sound as casual as possible.

"Is it?" Jones began in high gear. There'd be no ice-breaking, small talk. "I just got a call that leads me to believe you had a shitty morning."

"Who called you?"

"Don't play games with me," Jones snapped with an angry burst of authority. "I was told you were at a murder scene this morning."

Roslyn paused for his response.

"A-hum. I was."

"I was also told that you locked horns with the troop commander and the Jefferson County D.A."

Durkin scrunched his face as he envisioned two rams head butting. It was actually an apt visual, he thought. He then shivered thinking of the trooper's menacing dead eye. "We had a disagreement."

Jones held her tongue, hoping her silence would pry the details from him. Her hopes were dashed as Durkin remained silent. Jones expelled a breath of frustration. "Francis, I sent you——". Jones stopped mid-sentence and chose other words. "You're on a sabbatical. It's madness to knock heads with New York State troopers and the local D.A. while you're on a sabbatical."

"What exactly is the purpose of my sabbatical?" Durkin pushed back.

Jones instantly regretted giving Durkin an opening to air his grievances. She slammed it shut. "We're not going there," she said sharply. "I'm calling to discuss what happened this morning."

"What did you hear?"

"Francis," Jones sighed, "without hearing your side, I have to admit what I was told sounds troubling, to say the least."

"Did they tell you that I came across abandoned trooper cars?"

"They say that's your story."

Irritation spurted out of Durkin. "My story?" Durkin moaned audibly as he sat up. He took a moment before continuing. "Well, my story is that I called 911 when I came across the troopers' cars. My story is verifiable. "

"Yes, they said that."

Durkin felt an uncontrollable swell of anger take command of his emotions. His voice tightened as he struggled to regain his composure. "Right now my face feels like a smashed pumpkin."

"I'm sorry to hear you were injured. It does seem like the troopers overreacted."

"Overreacted?" Durkin spit the word out as if he was offended by the euphemism. "Roslyn, would you like me to text you a photo of what my face looks like because the trooper overacted?"

"That's not necessary." For a fraction of a second she considered lightening the mood with a joke that if he texted her the photo they'd risk being accused of sexting. She reconsidered. No, it wasn't the time for levity. "I'm sorry to hear that you're injured."

"May I ask who the hell you have been talking to?"

Jones considered her response. She knew her star prosecutor was close to his boiling point. And once Francis Durkin boiled over there was no reasoning with him. Maybe the truth would lower his temperature.

"Superintendent Joseph C. Crowley. He's the head of the New York State Police. Does that tell you how seriously people are taking this?"

"It is serious," Durkin shot back. "There's been a murder and the troopers beat the shit out of me."

"Francis! Crowley said you implied you're going to sue the troopers. Is that true?"

Durkin exhaled and thought back to what he said. "I'd be totally justified if I did."

"Francis? You of all people," Jones said with a tinge of exhaustion. Her point was crystal clear. Francis X. Durkin was the staunchest law-and-order prosecutor in the country. How'd it look if he sued the troopers?

"Roslyn, the trooper struck me from behind and beat the shit out of me. You sure you don't want me to send you a picture of my face?"

Jones reconsidered her joke. His mood had softened a bit. The timing was now right. "No, we don't want to be accused of sexting," she joked.

It worked. Durkin laughed so hard he audibly winced as a knifing pain shot through his ribs.

"Listen, Francis. You may want to consider submitting a DNA swab and putting this all behind you."

Durkin stiffened and let out a moan as another knifing pain tore through his ribs. No way. No fucking way was he going to suffer the indignity of submitting a DNA swab, he seethed as he battled to hold his tongue.

Jones sensed the tension in Durkin's breathing and changed the subject. "By the way, is it true you were riding a bicycle before the sun came up?"

Durkin bubbled with anger. "I wouldn't have been riding a bike if you hadn't forced the sabbatical on me." He instantly regretted sounding like a whiny kid.

"Wow, now *I'm* responsible for this? That's a bit of a stretch, Francis, isn't it?"

No, it wasn't a stretch. It was all Roslyn Jones's damn fault, he fumed. He wouldn't have been in the Thousand Islands if it wasn't for her. He wouldn't be in agonizing pain and his face wouldn't be torn up but for her. But he knew how childish he'd sound if he gave voice to his feelings.

"Since you're asking, yes, I went for a ride this morning," he said indignantly.

"Francis, don't take this the wrong way," Jones said and then paused, "as long as I've known you, you've never exercised. You've never ridden a bicycle and you've never taken walks in the middle of the night. What gives?"

"Roslyn, what are you saying?"

"I'm just—-"

"You think I'm mixed up with a murder for God's sakes?"

"No! Of course not. I'm just telling you as a friend and a colleague the optics are crap."

Durkin held his breath as he considered the optics. Roslyn Jones had a point. Anyone would ask themselves why he was in the middle of nowhere in the middle of the night. He drew a long breath through his nose and held the air in his lungs. He didn't have an answer; at least not a plausible answer.

"Francis, you should consider cooperating with the police."

"I'm not being un-cooperative."

"They tell me that you won't provide a DNA swab."

Durkin extended his left hand and stared at the grease smudges smeared across it. "They have no right to ask me for my DNA."

"You sound like a silly defense attorney, for God's sake."

"That's a low blow, Roslyn."

Jones breathed heavily. She knew accusing Francis Durkin of acting like a defense attorney was the ultimate put down to him.

"The bottom line is that you don't want to be considered a person of interest."

"A person of interest?" Durkin said, testing how the phrase sounded to his own ears. "A fucking person of interest?"

"Roslyn, make sure you tell the Superintendent that I'll sue his ass if anyone attaches that label to me."

"Francis—-"

"I'm not kidding," Durkin said, interrupting her stiffly.

"Listen, I understand you're pissed off. You have good reason to be. But I'm also sure that when you cool off you'll see it's best just to cooperate."

"Roslyn, I told you. I'm not refusing to cooperate. I was beaten pretty badly and that kind of soured me on cooperating with the troopers."

Jones hesitated. "Listen, I get it. But if things aren't managed properly they could get out of control."

"Roslyn, stop speaking in code. What are you trying to say?"

Jones carefully chose her words. "Okay, I also spoke to District Attorney McClusky." She paused for effect. "And he says the troopers are gathering facts and are expediting the DNA analyses."

"So?"

"Francis, for the record, I don't think you had anything to do with the woman's murder and I think it's preposterous for anyone to suggest there's any connection between you and the murder." Jones paused. "But I know you. And I know you can spout off like an Old Testament prophet when you think you were wronged. And that doesn't solve anything."

"What are you saying?"

"I'm saying you need to reconsider your decision not to give them a DNA swab."

Durkin moved the phone away from his ear as if her request irritated his ears. He sat in stunned silence and gazed up at the clearing sky as if the clouds held answers.

Jones sat in silence. Her star state's attorney was too hot to think reasonably and if he didn't think and act reasonably there'd be a shitshow. She envisioned the headlines. She grimaced. She sent Durkin on a sabbatical to get him off the grid. Now he'd be a headline.

"I'm going to call back Superintendent Crowley and the district attorney. I'm going to lie through my teeth for you and say that you cooled down and will smoke the peace pipe with the troopers."

"I have cooled down."

"Francis, you haven't. You sound like a defiant adolescent who wants to poke the troopers in their eyes." Jones let a long breath of frustration escape from her lips. "You need to pull back, go see the troopers and put this behind you."

"If I do, will you let me handle the appeal *State v. Terrance Police*?"

Jones could feel his smile through the phone. "Francis, are you bargaining with me?"

"I guess I am. Roslyn, I can win. What are you hesitating for? Are you afraid of pissing off—" Durkin stopped himself in mid-sentence. It was far too sensitive. He was essentially accusing the Chief's State Attorney of putting a greater premium on not rocking the boat than fighting for the right legal principles. He firmly believed the Connecticut Supreme Court ruling should be appealed to the U.S. Supreme Court and he was the man who could shepherd the case to victory.

He tacked. "I would win. You know that."

Roslyn sighed. "Francis, they don't pay me enough for this."

"I'll catch up with you at the law school in a few days." Durkin was referring to his upcoming speech. He was slated to speak at the Benjamin Cardozo Distinguished Lecture Series before he was sent away on his sabbatical. A half year ago, Roslyn Jones signed off on Durkin giving his address with no strings attached. Now, as the chief state's attorney held her cell phone to her ear, she regretted her decision.

Durkin waited for a long second and just as he was about to disconnect the call, Jones interjected. "Oh, I hear that Sergeant DeMartin is convalescing with you."

Durkin inhaled loudly. "Roslyn, are you asking me if Sergeant DeMartin is my guest?"

"No," she answered with a dash of defensiveness. "I was just relaying the information from the troopers. Their description of the black man with his arm in a sling and limping in a moon boot fit Sergeant DeMartin."

"Roslyn, what are you saying?"

Jones huffed. "Francis, do I have to spell everything out for you? Only a few months ago there were riots in Bridgeport and Sergeant DeMartin killed a grad student in the Remington Shot Tower. Have you forgotten?"

Durkin held his cell phone close to his mouth as if he didn't want anyone to overhear him. "Officer McGuinness was also murdered. The FBI gave DeMartin a proctology exam and found there was no evidence of any wrong doing on his part."

"Yes, I heard the same thing. And right now I think it's best if no one draws attention to the fact that a state's attorney and a cop who was in the

FBI's crosshairs," Roslyn paused as she searched for the best phrasing, "are vacationing together on some island near Canada."

"It's called the Thousand Islands."

"No matter," Jones snapped, making it clear she didn't give a shit about the name of the area. "I hope you're smart enough to just play ball."

"I always do."

Jones laughed at the absurdity of his statement. "Just remember what Thomas Jefferson said."

Durkin winced, knowing what was coming.

"When angry, count to ten before you speak. If very angry, count to one hundred."

"Thank you Roslyn for sharing a bit of Jefferson's wisdom with me."

"Count to one hundred. Now goodbye," Jones finished the call sounding exhausted by their conversation.

Durkin placed his cell phone back on his towel and dug a can of Miller High Life from the cooler at his feet. He popped it open and stared at the glistening St. Lawrence River. He then took a long swig and swirled the beer in his mouth like it was a fine wine, appreciating the watery mixture of barley and hops. For some unknown reason, the beer tasted particularly good in the late morning.

He suddenly noticed PJ McLevy sitting next to him, holding a beer. His eyes drew wide. Where the hell did PJ come from? Had he been listening to his call with Jones?

PJ smiled and raised his beer as if toasting to their mutual health. A thin smile appeared on Durkin's face as he clinked beers and both men swigged the Miller High Life as if in a drinking contest. Damn, it tasted good, Durkin thought again. Maybe it was because he hadn't had a beer before noon in his entire adult life. He felt a tinge of relaxation and began leaning towards taking Jones's advice.

The distinct sound of rubber boots atop a wooden dock drew the men's attention. Durkin lowered his beer can and turned towards the direction of the footsteps. Ten feet away a man in shorts, a flannel short and yellow rubber boots approached. Durkin didn't recognize the man but he'd bet his paycheck he wasn't a cop. He just knew by the casual way the man carried himself. Probably a neighbor just saying hello.

"Hi," Durkin said, sliding his beer can under his chair as if he was self-conscious about day drinking bare-chested. He instinctively pulled his towel over his body. "Excuse me for not getting up. I had a fall," Durkin said with a soft smile, suddenly becoming acutely aware of the open wounds on his face.

"No, sit, please," the man said, extending his hand. "I'm Jim Breen." Durkin shook his hand and pointed to PJ. "PJ McLevy."

PJ waved. "You want a beer?"

JB smiled. "Normally yes, but I'm working."

Durkin surveyed his clothes. "What are you working on?"

"On a story. I'm a reporter with the *Watertown Daily Register.* Everyone calls me JB."

Disappointment flashed across Durkin's. He wanted to put the morning's event behind him. Was this the first of many reporters to come knocking?

"I heard I just missed you this morning at the Dewolf Point State Park."

Durkin eyed the water and seemed fixed on a power boat off in the distance. "Yep, I was there," he said quietly, telling himself that the friendly sounding guy was not his friend.

"I also hear that you're a state's attorney in Connecticut."

"Guilty."

"Mind if I ask you a few questions?"

"I can't stop you from asking questions but I probably won't be able to provide you with much information."

JB nodded as his eyes absorbed the beauty of the river. "This murder may be the first recorded murder on Wellesley Island."

"Recorded?"

"Ah, I just figure an Indian must've killed another Indian sometime or other when this was all Indian country. I read somewhere that the Iroquois and Onondaga supposedly fought a lot in these parts."

JB pointed to a island off in the distance. "There's a story that a man was murdered on Maple Island during the Civil War. The story goes that the victim was a Confederate soldier who stole gold and was tracked down and killed all the way up here."

"You don't say?" Durkin replied. "You sure you don't want a beer?"

JB shook his head. "No, I have to file a story today."

"Well, we're on vacation so we're going to have one," PJ said, fishing two more Miller High Lifes out of the cooler. He handed one to Durkin and they popped the tops at the same time.

"What time did you reach Dewolf Point State Park yesterday?"

"It's all in the police report."

"I'm sure it is but the troopers aren't releasing the report for another few days."

"Don't you find that a little odd?" PJ McLevy asked.

JB shrugged. "They delay it sometimes."

"They'll delay it more if the press doesn't make a stink about it," McLevy replied with a swig of his beer.

JB grinned. The old guy was probably right. The press is a check on the government and JB knew he could do a better job in that department.

"How'd you find us?" Durkin asked.

JB's grin widened to a full smile. The cagey prosecutor turned the table; he was now the questioner.

"I guessed you would be staying in Thousand Island Park. I have a few friends who have cottages here." JB grinned and let out a light chuckle. He didn't share that a black guy in a sling and walking boot stood out. "She calls it Thousand Eyes Park. She says everyone knows everything about everyone in the park."

Durkin snorted, looking around at the cottages which lined the river. "She's probably right. It's beautiful, though. Ain't it?"

"It sure is," JB replied. "Now, if you don't mind me asking, what time were you at Dewolf Point State Park?"

"I don't mind," Durkin responded with a friendly ring. "It was approximately 4:15-ish. The timing can be verified by my call to 911."

"That's my next question. What made you call 911?"

Durkin recounted how he was on a bicycle and rode up to the empty troopers' cars.

"Were the engines on?"

"Yeah."

"Were their lights flashing?"

Durkin closed his eyes and thought back to when he came upon the troopers' cars. "Yeah, their lights were flashing and engines running."

"How'd you get the——," JB stopped and pointed to the bandages on Durkin's face. "Injuries?"

JB was good at his job, Durkin thought. Good at disarming a person with stories of Indians and Confederate soldiers hiding out in the islands before asking his questions. Durkin composed his words carefully in case the words made it to a courtroom. "I was attacked. I didn't see it coming. I was told to freeze and I complied. I put my hands up in the air and remained rigid." Durkin paused for effect. "Then I was knocked unconscious." Durkin pointed to a bump on his head. "You want to feel this?"

JB hesitated and then shrugged. Why not? He was an investigative crime reporter. He raised his hand and Durkin guided his fingers down on top of his skull so JB's fingertips could run over the bump.

"Feels like an egg."

"Yep."

JB scribbled in his notepad. "Are you going to take legal action against the troopers?"

Durkin sighed, unhappy about being put on the spot. "It's too early to make any decisions. I'd appreciate it if you didn't write anything about a potential lawsuit."

JB studied his notepad for a bit. "Sure. I don't think that adds anything to the story at this point. Did you pass anyone on your way to the park?"

Damn, Durkin thought. The troopers hadn't even asked him the basic question. "Nope."

"Well," JB hesitated, looking like he was about to apologize. "Do you mind if I ask you what you were doing out there at that time?"

Durkin's shoulders sagged as he wondered how many times he was going to have to repeat the story. "I couldn't sleep so I went for a bike ride."

"Do you normally do that?"

"I normally can't sleep so it's not unusual for me to get up and do things in the middle of the night."

"No, I mean is it *normal* for you to ride a bike in the middle of the night?"

It was a fair question but it triggered Durkin's irritation. "I found an old bike in the basement and I decided to give it a shot. There really isn't much to do around here at 4 a.m."

JB nodded. He circled the word "bike" in his pad but decided not to press the subject. He had a good ear and sensed Durkin's defensiveness.

JB pointed with his notepad towards the cottage. "I was told that Sergeant Angelo DeMartin is visiting the Thousand Islands with you."

Durkin and PJ exchanged smiles. Word gets around fast.

"Frankly, I think I was the last guy in the world to see the video of him saving his fellow officer," Breen said.

Durkin and PJ laughed knowing the reporter had no idea that the old cop DeMartin saved was sitting on the dock with him.

Durkin winked at PJ. "Yeah, the video is pretty amazing."

"You think I can have a word with him?"

"Unfortunately, he's sleeping," Durkin said just as the cottage door opened and DeMartin began maneuvering in his moon boot down the front steps . "I guess he's up," Durkin quipped.

JB stared at the celebrity cop laboring in the walking boot and sling. For the first time in the morning, he thought he'd have enough to cobble together a story.

JB pulled out a business card and handed it to Durkin. "Would you mind if I called you to follow up on a few questions?"

What could Durkin say? Besides the beer was loosening him up. "Sure, no problem."

"Thanks." JB positioned the tip of his pen against his notepad. "What's your cell number?"

"Damn," Durkin said, hoping that JB would've been too starstruck to remember to ask for his number. Durkin grinned and gave him his number. "I appreciate it if you don't circulate it."

"Of course not. Nice speaking with you," JB said as he pushed off towards DeMartin.

CHAPTER FOUR

New York State Police
Troop D
Alexandria Bay Station

The interrogation room wreaked of a musty, rancid mix that troopers described as a cross between cat pee and smelly sneakers: a smell which no amount of air freshener could cover. The heating and ventilation system had never worked properly because the room had been originally designed as a storage room. The natural light consisted of a four-foot-wide slit of opaque glass and the two ceiling lights cast a yellow-green hue over everyone who sat in the eggshell white room.

The conference table was designed for 8 people. On one side sat detectives Ray LeFleur and Charlie Parker. LeFleur and Parker looked like brothers. Both had thinning black hair, oval cheeks and square jaws. Dark sweat rings sagged from under their armpits and their faces were covered with a greasy sheen. Tired, zig-zag lines cut across the whites of their eyes. The look-alike detectives also wore the same stress-filled expressions as they gazed at Trooper David Hennigan who sat across from them.

Ray LeFleur breathed loudly and began tapping his right forefinger on the table as if he was sending Hennigan a message in morse code. As if responding to LeFleur's message, Hennigan tilted back in his chair. "I've already told you everything that happened. Nothing is going to change." Hennigan's voice was growing hoarser by the minute. "I want to go home."

LeFleur flashed a frustrated look at Parker and then closed his eyes as if seeking to calm his mind. He blew a stream of air through a small opening in his lips as if he was trying to whistle and opened his eyelids. He began to talk and then stopped as he coached himself to strike a sympathetic note. "Listen, we all want to go home but first we need to clear some things up."

Hennigan pushed his weight forward so his chair's front legs banged against the linoleum floor. "What's not clear?"

LeFleur's eyes bulged. Was this a guy a total moron? Nothing was clear! And the facts were becoming murkier by the minute. Take Hennigan's body camera. Every trooper was required to wear a BWC —a body worn camera— and activate it when he exited his patrol car. Hennigan didn't activate his BWC until after he had subdued the state's attorney at the entrance of Dewolf Point State Park.

LeFleur sighed and then lowered his head, thinking how the press was going to twist the facts about the GPS system and dash cam. The GPS system in Hennigan's unmarked patrol car wasn't working. The detectives discovered a work-order to repair it had been submitted two days ago. The dash cam on Hennigan's car was also not working. LeFleur confirmed that Hennigan reported the dash cam problem to his supervisor about a week ago. But the technical malfunctions were going to smell rotten to the outside world.

LeFleur eyed his notes, searching for a way to keep the interview streamlined without provoking Hennigan.

DH stated he stopped a young female for speeding south of the Thousand Islands Bridge. 3:34 a.m.

LeFleur asked around. Every trooper in the Alexandria Bay barracks told him that Hennigan was known for pulling over young female drivers for kicks.

DH states he drove ahead on I-81 to the bridge and was "pretty sure" he crossed it just prior to the victim.

DH crossed the 1000 Islands Bridge at 4:09 a.m. (Verified)

Approximately 19-23 minutes later DH discovers body at entrance to Dewolf Pt. St. Park???

LeFleur struck the question marks he had instinctively written next to Hennigan's statement.

DH says he saw bloody rocks next to body——presumably murder weapons.

LeFleur pushed a stream of air through his nostrils. "What you say now is important for the record."

Hennigan rolled his eyes like a wise guy. No shit. Tell me something I don't know.

"Okay, then tell me again how you got the blood on your uniform."

Hennigan began to gently karate chop his left thigh as if LeFleur's question triggered an impulse to hurt himself. "I told you. When I saw the body I ran down to her. I had to touch her to see if she was alive."

"Show us how you touched her."

Hennigan's cheeks puffed and he released a gust of frustration. He then demonstrated how he cradled the woman's head in his hands using an imaginary mannequin. "I reached my left arm under her head." He dropped his hands in frustration. "I don't know exactly how I touched her. It happened so fast."

Parker cleared his throat loudly as if announcing he had something to say. "It was wet and muddy. You probably slipped when you approached the body, didn't you?"

LeFleur shot a hot glare at Parker. Are you coaching him?

"Yeah, it was wet and I probably slipped," Hennigan replied, sounding relieved at the softness of the question.

LeFleur's eyes looked as if they'd pop out of his sockets. Probably? "Show me where your leg touched the ground when you slipped."

Hennigan glanced down at his legs as if trying to recall if the uniform pants that now hung in the next room together with the rest of his uniform, were lined with mud. "My shoe slipped. I'm not sure if my leg or knee touched the ground. As I said, everything happened so fast. Parts are blurry."

Yeah, and Hennigan's recall was getting blurrier by the minute, LeFleur thought, as he rubbed his tired eyes. But he couldn't write that Hennigan's recall was blurry. Troopers find dead bodies all the time. They're trained to operate in high stress crime scenes. In the last 60 minutes Hennigan said he turned her head and saw bloody vapors. Then he said he slipped and fell on the victim's body. His latest statement was that he turned her head quickly and her bloody hair flicked blood on his uniform.

LeFleur pushed back from the table. "Let's take a five minute nature break, okay? Get a cup of coffee or something to drink."

LeFleur's tone made it clear he wasn't asking for anyone's concurrence. LeFleur pushed himself to his feet and opened the door. His eyes instructed Hennigan that the clock was ticking on the mandatory five minute nature break. "Stretch your legs."

Hennigan didn't argue. He got up and walked briskly out of the room. When he was half-way down the hall, LeFleur closed the door and turned to Parker. "What the hell are you doing?"

Parker expected the rebuke. He gave Hennigan a leading question; a cardinal sin of a law enforcement interrogation. "I'm just trying to help a brother out."

"Why's he need your help?"

Parker screwed his eyes on LeFleur. "You and I know damn well he didn't do it."

"We do?"

Parker craned his neck and looked stunned. His look then morphed to disappointment. "Hennigan was just doing his job. He needs our help. Any one of us could've been patrolling around Dewolf Point State Park last night and found the body."

LeFleur's face scrunched up. "Really? Hennigan's job was to patrol I-81 for speeders. There was no reason for him to be on Wellesley Island."

"That's bullshit."

"Is it? His job was to give speeding tickets. No one is speeding on a sleepy island at 4 a.m."

Parker waved his hand dismissively at LeFleur. "You know that the guy on the bicycle did it."

Hints of doubt surfaced on LeFleur's face.

"At the very least he was part of a group that killed her," Parker added.

Parker and LeFleur arrived at the crime scene about the same time. They both stared at the three men who pushed the dilapidated bicycle to a car and hooked it up with a carabiner. They both took careful notice of the men. The detectives both agreed that the group was odd. Suspicious.

LeFleur's facial expression changed as he reminded himself to focus on the task at hand: obtaining Trooper Hennigan's contemporaneous statement.

"Okay, say I agree," LeFleur began. "We still need a clear statement from Hennigan or Rasmutin will drill us another asshole."

Parker nodded and drifted off in silence. The detectives sat in an awkward silence for five minutes. The men pulled air through their noses and cleared imaginary obstacles from their throat. LeFleur's eyes fell on his notes but he was too wired to concentrate on the written words. All he saw were ink squiggles on paper. He then eyed his watch. "Where is he?" he asked with a rush of impatience. Parker checked his watch. The five minute nature break was going on ten minutes.

"Shit," Parker said, popping up. "I'll get him."

48

A minute later Parker stuck his head back in the doorway wearing a troubled look. "I can't find him."

LeFleur looked stricken. "Holy shit," he said, springing to his feet. The two detectives hustled into the small area behind the security shield.

"Conroy, have you seen Hennigan?" LeFleur shouted at Sergeant Thomas Conroy, a five year veteran who manned the barrack's front desk. Conroy thought for a second and then pointed to the rear door that led to the parking lot.

A muffled curse slipped past his lips as LeFleur speed-walked to the rear door. He pushed the door open with the sinking feeling that Hennigan had gone AWOL and he and Parker were going to catch hell for letting him wander off in the middle of their interview.

The sound of a compressed stream of water battering steel drew their attention. In the corner of the parking lot Hennigan stood spraying his unmarked patrol car with a thin, powerful blast of water that sounded as if it could remove the car's paint. In his left hand he held a soapy sponge.

"Hennigan!" LeFleur screamed. "What the hell are you doing?"

Hennigan looked irritated by the interruption. What the hell does it look like I'm doing? He continued to spray the car as the detectives half ran, half walked, to him.

"I just needed some air," Hennigan said in anticipation of their questions. LeFleur stared disbelievingly as water bounced off the unmarked trooper car. It had been scrubbed clean. Its bumpers gleamed.

"Stop," LeFleur said with a forced calmness that threatened to shatter if Hennigan did not instantly comply.

Hennigan shook his head and turned the spray nozzle that capped the flow of water. For a long second neither LeFleur or Parker knew what to say. Finally, LeFleur broke the silence.

"We need to finish your statement or Rasmutin will have our heads."

Everyone nodded in agreement, envisioning Rasmutin's terrifying dead eye. Parker gestured towards the door and made it clear that he and LeFleur would escort Hennigan back into the barracks. Hennigan dropped the spray nozzle in a clump of rubber hose and trudged back into the barracks with a sigh of protest.

When the troopers were back in the interrogation room, LeFleur scanned his notes, searching for where they had left off before the break.

"I know this is hard," he said, trying to hit a supportive note, "but while everything is still fresh in your mind we need to get everything straight."

Hennigan waved to the detectives. "Tell me what you want."

"We want you to tell us in your own words what happened once you saw the VW parked in front of Dewolf Point State Park."

"I drove up next to it and flashed on my spotlight. I didn't see anyone around."

LeFleur and Parker nodded in sync. Go on.

"Then I got out and looked around."

"Did you activate your body camera?"

"I don't remember."

"Were you carrying your flashlight?"

Hennigan shook his head as if afflicted by a small tremor. It was at 4:30 in the morning. Of course he would be carrying his flashlight. "Yes. I flashed it around. I saw a pair of eye glasses on the ground. I took a few steps towards the woods and then beamed my light into the woods. That's when I saw her."

LeFleur's head bobbed. Okay, now we're getting somewhere. "What did you do next?"

"I went into the woods. It was muddy and I had trouble with my footing."

LeFleur nodded and jotted something down. Yep, go on.

"I didn't know if she was dead or not so I turned her over. I kind of cradled her head in my arms." Hennigan demonstrated how he held the small woman's head in the crux of his arm.

LeFleur scrunched his lips and tried to recall the blood stains on Hennigan's uniform. He envisioned a bloody palm print on the back right side of his uniform. Nothing Hennigan said so far accounted for the hand print.

"When I realized she was dead I thought I heard movement in the woods. I proceeded to exit the woods and then I called the report in."

LeFleur played the recording of Hennigan's call to the dispatcher over in his head. Hennigan was excited, almost fearful. He said he discovered a possible homicide. Possible? Why did he say that? Did he think there was any chance the woman tripped and her face and the back of her skull was shattered by her fall?

LeFleur and Parker exchanged a skeptical look: they both detected an inconsistency. The look was not lost on Hennigan. He sprang to his feet. "Mind if I stand?"

LeFleur and Parker both shook their heads. Knock yourself out.

Hennigan began to regulate his breathing as if warding off a heart attack.

"At that time, did you see anyone else around the crime scene?" Parker asked.

Hennigan began to wiggle his legs as if warming up for a road race. "After I called it in, I went back into the woods. I heard what sounded like someone walking around in the woods. I went back to the road and that's when I saw him."

"Describe what you saw."

"His back was to me. He was about 5 foot 10 inches or so. He was chubby and was wearing a green polo shirt. I ordered him to freeze and raise his hands. He refused to comply and I was forced to apprehend him."

"How did you apprehend him?"

"I tackled him."

"Before you tackled him, did you hit him with your flashlight?"

Hennigan breathed deeply and began to walk in place.

"Oh, yeah. I think I hit him with my flashlight as I tackled him."

"Why did you crack him with your flashlight?"

"I was worried he was reaching for a gun." Hennigan sped up and began to jog in place. Parker and LeFleur shot each other looks. Is the guy cracking? The detectives watched Hennigan jog in place for five seconds.

"What are you doing?" LeFleur asked.

"I'm burning up nervous energy," Hennigan answered, sounding out of breath as he kept his legs pumping.

LeFleur shook his head. Screw it. It was strange as hell but he and Parker had a job to do.

"What was a guy doing out there in the middle of nowhere at 4:30 in the morning?" Hennigan panted.

The detectives didn't reply. Hennigan was beginning to open up. The room was silent except for the sound of Hennigan's shoes slapping against the linoleum tile as he continued jogging in place. "I can't believe the guy's not locked up."

The detectives nodded. It didn't make sense to them either.

"I think he intimidated McClusky," Hennigan huffed.

LeFleur and Parker again nodded. They both held the D.A. in low regard. He always wanted to play cop during investigations.

There were two loud raps on the door before it swung open and Commander Rasmutin stuck his head in the room. They could sense the heat of his eyes emanating through his mirror glasses. Hennigan instantly stopped jogging-in-place.

Rasmutin's face contorted with confusion and disgust. "What the hell is going on?"

"Sir, Hennigan said he needed to burn up nervous energy," Parker replied nervously.

Rasmutin brushed away his confusion so only the disgust remained. "Why hasn't this man been allowed to go home?" The panning movement of his mirror glasses made it clear that he was directing his question equally to LeFleur and Parker.

LeFleur pointed to his notes. "We are just finishing up with Trooper Hennigan's statement."

"That's not what I asked," Rasmutin snapped. "Trooper Hennigan has not slept for," he turned to Hennigan for confirmation, "for what, 20 hours? How's he supposed to keep anything straight if he's sleep deprived?"

Rasmutin motioned with his thumb for Hennigan to leave. "Get some sleep and report back here at 0900."

Hennigan exited the room rapidly like a kid relieved to be dismissed from the principal's office. Rasmutin waited for Hennigan to move out of sight before he closed the door and set his scorching scowl on LeFleur and Parker.

"What's wrong with you guys?"

LeFleur face drooped, looking speechless. Rasmutin had directed them to take Hennigan's statement. Hennigan was all over the place and they needed to go over his glaring inconsistencies before they put pen to paper. What else could they do?

"The man is going to fall apart if he doesn't get any sleep."

"Sir, we gave him a break," Parker said meekly.

"Sir, um," LeFleur interjected, I need to inform you that during the break Trooper Hennigan left the barracks and cleaned his patrol car."

Rasmutin fingers softly gripped the edges of his glasses as he considered LeFleur's words. "A trooper is responsible for leaving his car in a clean and orderly condition. Sounds like he was just doing his job."

"He cleaned the exterior of his car with a power washer."

The troopers all thought the same thing: if the press ever learned that Hennigan was permitted to clean the car that he was driving soon after he found a brutally murdered woman, there'd be a shitshow.

Rasmutin correctly read LeFleur's face. He couldn't afford to be accused of white washing the investigation. "That reporter is going to be all over this case like flies on shit." Rasmutin's sneer revealed his life-long disdain for meddlesome reporters, especially James Alexander Breen, whom he considered a righteous prick. "We need to ensure every trooper is on the same page. Everyone needs to be a team player."

LeFleur and Parker parsed Rasmutin's words. Team player.

"We need to apprehend the suspect as soon as possible before rumors run wild."

The detectives' eyes widened.

"What I'm saying is that the irresponsible rumors have to be cut off at their knees. You know what I'm saying."

LeFleur and Parker nodded. Kind of.

"Every stone needs to be turned over," Rasmutin added, sensing the detectives' unease. Rasmutin stared at the detectives who stared back with blank faces. "You're both up for the task, right? You can meet the demands of the moment, right?"

LeFleur and Parker deciphered Rasmutin's questions. The detectives sucked in a mouthful of air and nodded in unison. Of course, Commander Rasmutin could count on them.

"This guy, the prosecutor from Connecticut," Rasmutin's voice trailed off. "It just doesn't sit well with me." Rasmutin jabbed his fingers at LeFleur and Parker. "Mark my words. That guy's DNA will link him to the murder. I just know it in my bones."

LeFleur and Parker nodded. They were all in agreement. There was something suspicious about the prosecutor.

"Good. We need to stick together," Rasmutin said as he stepped towards the door. "I'll see you after you get through with Hennigan tomorrow."

Rasmutin exited the interrogation room with a gust of renewed determination.

New York State Police Crime Laboratory
Albany, New York

Danielle Keegan peeled the blue lab glove off her fingers and dug her knuckle into her blood-shot eyes to soothe the burning. She inhaled until her lungs were full and then, after holding the breath, let the spent air rush out of her mouth. Was she ever going to make a dent in the back log of unprocessed DNA tests?

She turned her focus to the rows of miniature plastic test tubes lined up in front of her. An hour ago she inserted the DNA she had scraped off a black hoodie into the tubes. Danielle had meticulously segregated the DNA from each area of the hoodie. The hoodie's cuff had traces of saliva and snot; more than enough to determine the owner of the DNA code. She then deposited particles from a dried white spot on the hoodie's hem. Danielle's experience told her that it was a fleck of semen. She was sure the DNA codes in the semen would lead the police to the man who left the stain.

She glanced back at the data sheet. All that was listed was the date, the name of the technician who collected the evidence, and the location; Utica, New York. There was one other handwritten notation that was circled: homicide.

The data sheet was bare-bones by design. After scandals rocked the trooper's forensic lab, new procedures were put in place to eliminate "mental contamination." The evidence was to be stripped of context, anything that could influence the forensic scientist was supposed to be omitted. The lab director for the Biological Sciences Division harped about the need for the forensic scientists to divorce themselves from the stories behind the evidence. Focus on the science and block out the human element.

For Keegan, it was easier said than done. She was curious by nature.

She reviewed her check-list once more. She had precisely extracted the DNA from the physical evidence. She deployed chemicals, heat and centrifuges to break the cells down and extract the DNA from the flecks that held the human code. She used high-tech machines to create graphs that located genetic markers at different locations of the DNA strands for each sample of saliva, speck of snot and fleck of semen. Then she ran the same tests on the suspect's DNA to determine the probability of a match.

Years of using the cutting edge machines didn't diminish the magic of DNA fingerprinting for Keegan. Hell, Keegan marveled, 10 thousand cells can fit on the head of a pin and she could produce a DNA code from only 16 cells. As far as Keegan was concerned, that was magical.

Keegan paused once more to make sure she had not overlooked any step. She rechecked a plastic card that listed every step. When she was sure she hadn't missed anything, she pressed the start button on the square machine. There was a whir that always reminded her of the sound of a miniature electric subway pulling away from an underground station.

Danielle Keegan felt a surge of satisfaction flow through her as the cutting edge laboratory equipment started processing the results. A light flashed and Keegan envisioned her Betty Crocker Easy Bake oven she had as a kid. She never told anyone she always thought of her Easy Bake oven when the results came in. It was too goofy a secret to share. But the inner nerd in her enjoyed it.

Seventeen minutes later, the whirring ended and Keegan eyed the computer. The snot and saliva samples were a mixture of three people; one woman and two men. The genetic markers from the semen on the hoodie and the DNA swab taken from a suspect's mouth lined up at all 20 locations on the DNA strands.

"Bingo," she whispered to herself. She then used a computer to run a highly complex algorithm to determine the probability that the swab from the suspect did not come from the suspect. Keegan made herself a bet: it'd be one in a quadrillion.

Danielle Keegan was also a math nerd. She was comfortable around statistics, algorithms and large numbers. She named her tiny kitten Cajillion, the largest possible number in the entire universe. A cajillion was so big no one could even fathom its size. She loved the humor in it every time she said her tiny kitten's name out loud.

"Quadrillion," she mumbled to herself as she repeated her bet on the odds that the DNA belonged to someone other than the suspect.

A quadrillion.

A quadrillion was also beyond human comprehension, she thought. It's a thousand trillion. Hell, a trillion is a thousand billion. The numbers invigorated Keegan. She marveled at the fact that one million seconds equaled

12 days. A billion seconds totaled 33 years. How big was a trillion? One trillion seconds was more than 32,000 years! And a quadrillion? One quadrillion seconds totals over 32 million years. Mind blowing. How did anyone not find the concept of a cajillion mind blowing?

Keegan then chuckled, thinking of her little Cajillion curled up on her bed.

The computer completed the process quicker than Keegan expected. One in six billion. She shook her head in disagreement with the computer's random match probability. No way. It was far higher, she silently argued with the multi-million dollar computer.

Keegan knew the random match probability was the numerical estimate that a DNA match would occur by chance. The lower the probability, the higher the chance of guilt.

"At least a trillion," she said under her breath as if she was arguing with the designer of the computer program. Keegan knew the manufacturer skewed the figures on the conservative side. Since there were only six billion humans on the planet, a one in six billion yield would mean that there was a one in six billion chance that a random person's DNA would match the semen sample. For Keegan, her tests just proved with a scientific certainty that the semen found on the victim's hoodie belonged to the suspect.

Keegan saved the computer results and made sure all the information was compiled in one digital file. She then meticulously cleaned up the lab area and headed to the clean room to shed her lab jacket, hair net, goggles and boot covers. She worked quickly and moved with an excited purpose.

Two minutes later, Keegan sat behind her desk and used her personal cell phone to search the internet. She punched in the date the sample was taken, 'Utica' and 'crime'.

Besides the magic of DNA and the excitement of incomprehensibly large numbers, Danielle Keegan was also attracted to forensic science because of its connection to real life crime. From a safe distance, she experienced a thrill knowing she was an important cog in the criminal justice system. Her test results proved the guilt of violent criminals and occasionally exonerated the innocent. Now, after the tests were performed, when there was no chance of injecting her bias into the results, she searched for the human story behind the hoodie and spot of saliva, snot and semen.

Instantly, the story from the Utica Times appeared. Body found behind Dredger's bar. Shakeema Stores, a single mother of two boys, was found next to Dredger's garbage dumpsters. Police reported that Shakeema Stores was beaten and sexually assaulted.

Shakeema Shores died of exposure. After she was knocked unconscious, her attacker left her in the snow like a bag of garbage. In the morning, two inches of snow covered her frozen body.

Keegan then turned her thoughts to the swabs from the suspect's cheek. The article said the swab was taken from the mouth of Wayne Brooks, a drifter, well known to the Utica police. He was found stumbling drunk through the snow the night after Shakeema Stores' body was found behind Dredger's. On a hunch, the Utica cops arrested him on a drunken and disorderly charge. Brooks agreed to let the cops run a cotton swab over the inside of his cheek. He had nothing to hide.

Keegan thought of the computer's results. The odds were one in six billion that a random person would match the DNA found on Shakeema Store's hoodie. There was no doubt the semen belonged to Wayne Brooks.

But Keegan wondered whether Wayne Brooks killed Shakeema Stores. There was no doubt his semen was on her hoodie. But who knows? Maybe Brooks paid Shakeema for a hand job and left his genetic calling card on her hoodie long before she was murdered. Who knows? All she knew was that Wayne Brooks better get a damn good defense lawyer.

Keegan's office phone buzzed as a small light bulb flashed. Keegan shot a displeased look at the phone. It buzzed again but Keegan hesitated, hoping the buzzing would stop, hoping that whomever was calling would go away. It buzzed again and Keegan reluctantly answered.

"Keegan," she said into the old fashioned hand phone. Identifying herself by her last name sounded strange to her ear. But that's what she was told to say. That was part of the New York State Troopers' military culture and the Forensic Sciences Laboratory was run by the New York State Troopers so that's how Danielle Keegan identified herself.

"Keegan. This is Ben down in the lobby."

Ben was Ben Stewart, a prematurely balding employee of the security firm the troopers hired to watch over the sprawling trooper complex in Albany, New York. He was nice enough. He always greeted her with the excitement of a Labrador Retriever. But he wasn't Keegan's type and she knew her natural tendency to stop and chat with him probably fueled his hopes. But his hopes weren't going to be realized, she said to herself. There was less than one in a quadrillion chance. Maybe a less than one in a cajillion, she'd date Ben Stewart.

"Is Russo in his office?" Stewart asked.

Russo? Dante Russo? Danielle reflexively wrinkled her nose. Russo annoyed her. It wasn't just his bad hygiene. It wasn't because she thought he was just plain stupid. His error rate was the highest in the state and brought down their lab's ranking. And he was also dog-lazy which meant more work for her.

"Why would Russo be here? It's after three p.m."

Stewart got the joke. He chuckled and then lowered his voice to a whisper. "There's a Trooper Maloney in the lobby. He's carrying a box and says he's waiting for Russo. He won't give it to anyone else."

Keegan checked her watch. It was 7:20 pm.

"That's weird."

"Can you do me a favor?" Ben asked sheepishly.

Keegan muffled her tired sigh. "Sure, what is it?"

"This guy is making me antsy. He keeps staring at me and tapping his foot loudly. Something's not right about him."

"What do you want me to do?"

"Russo isn't answering his phone, but I just want to make sure he's not in his office."

"You want me to see if I can find him?"

"Just take a quick look if you don't mind."

Keegan minded. After working long hours in the lab wearing a hair net she had hat-head and hated to be seen in public with her hair matted to her skull. But what could she do? A trooper was tapping his foot in front of a guy who had a crush on her.

"Hold on." Keegan put down the receiver and quickly ran her fingers through her hair. She glimpsed at her reflection in her office window. She thought her hair was shaped like one of those flat berets intellectuals parade around in. "Jesus," she huffed as she walked through a line of empty cubicles. At the end of the hallway was Russo's office. Keegan walked to the entrance of his office. She looked through the skinny door window. The lights were off.

For some reason, Keegan reached down and turned the doorknob. The door was open and the motion detector switched on the ceiling lights as she opened the door. Russo's desk was a mess but a white, NYSP Forensic Lab notepad caught her eye. She stepped closer and studied Russo's scratchy handwriting.

-clothes: panties, bra, shoes
-pocket book, wallet
-trace swabs-7-10- car
-Wellesley Island-homicide
-RUSH - Comm. Rasmutin- Col. Kordas

-POI- Francis Durkin-

'Rush' was circled three times.

Danielle Keegan shook her head as her face pinched with confusion. Forensic scientists never were supposed to know the names of the Person of Interest before they analyzed the DNA samples. Everyone knew that biases crept in if the scientists knew who the troopers were targeting before running the tests. They were scientists, Keegan huffed. Not troopers in lab coats.

Keegan heard the ping of the elevator. Her heart skipped at the thought of her being caught trespassing in Russo's office. She raced out of his office and quietly closed Russo's door. She then ran back to her laboratory station. Out of breath, she picked up the receiver as Russo and a trooper turned the corner.

"Ben, he wasn't in his office."

Ben was still on the line. "No. He arrived right after you went to check on him."

Out of the corner of Keegan's eye, she could see Russo approaching her. "Okay," she said, quickly hanging up.

"Keegan, were you in my office?" Russo's hands were on his hips, demanding an answer.

Danielle Keegan's face flushed. She hated confrontation. Any form of confrontation. She was also a horrible liar. "Ben in security called me and asked if I would see if you were in your office so I walked down there a minute ago."

Russo eyed her suspiciously. "Did you go into my office?"

"Listen, Russo, I've got too much work to do to care about what you're doing."

Russo shook his head as suspicion leaked into his face. His ceiling light indicated his privacy had been violated. He started inching backwards and was about to say something when Keegan beat him to the punch. "How are the SAKs coming along?"

Sexual Assault Kits. Clearing out the bulk of the tedious and time consuming SAKs had been assigned to Russo.

"I don't report to you" Russo snapped, before turning around and striding back to his office.

Keegan sagged with relief as Russo retreated but then confusion splashed over her face. What the hell was going on? Who is Trooper Maloney? The forensic lab wasn't like a walk-in clinic. Troopers didn't arrive with evidence and stick around as the scientists performed the DNA analyses.

The lab had over 1900 unprocessed DNA samples to process. There were strict protocols. A forensic scientist had no say which cases she tested. Murder cases received the highest priority. But the lab even put a 10 sample limit on murder cases. Russo's list must have contained twice that many, Keegan huffed. Everything about this smelled rogue. And Russo's face? Why was he so agitated? What was he hiding?

Keegan sat in her office and considered her next steps. She copied down what she could remember seeing on Russo's notepad. Panties. Trace swabs. Col. Kordas. Wellesley Island. And POI. She forgot the name written next to 'POI' but she was sure that Russo's notes specified a POI. Rush. Yes, 'Rush' was emphasized. The word was circled three times.

Keegan concluded she needed to speak with Stephanie Cotton, the Assistant Director of the Biological Sciences Division and her boss. But Cotton was more than that. She was Keegan's unofficial mentor and Cotton was the only supervisor whose talent and expertise Keegan respected. So many managers in the lab were oily, sycophants with limited forensic science expertise. But Cotton was different. She was smart and professional.

Cotton routinely worked late but Keegan knew she was out of the office recruiting future forensic scientists at a local college job fair. She'd talk to Cotton first thing in the morning, she whispered to herself as a dark frown spread across her face.

New York State Police
Troop D
Alexandria Bay Station

A clammy sheen covered Commander Rasmutin's face. He removed his mirror glasses, revealing dark, tired rings sagging like spent tea bags below his eyes. He squeezed his eyes shut and then opened them as wide as his eyelids would stretch, revealing his black eye that looked like a malevolent orb.

He picked up the coffee mug that sat on the conference table and blew air over its surface before taking a swig. As he set the mug down, he blinked twice, steeled himself with a deep breath of air and put his mirrored glasses back on, signaling to anyone watching he was in full battle mode.

Ray LeFleur and Charlie Parker were watching. The NYSP detectives sat across the conference table, wearing the nervous expressions of men readying themselves for a blow. For the past minute, the men sat in silence. Neither dared moving lest they ignite Rasmutin's wrath.

The only sound in the room was the sound of Rasmutin's starched uniform shirt crinkling as his chest rose and fell with each breath. To the two detectives, Rasmutin was a rumbling volcano on the verge of erupting.

LeFleur and Parker exchanged nervous glances as Rasmutin shattered the silence with a guttural cough. "I brought Trooper Hennigan in this morning for a lie detector."

The detectives' faces telegraphed their concerns.

"It was all very straight forward," Rasmutin added. Rasmutin delayed a beat. "Hennigan passed with flying colors."

Flying colors? Lie detection exams weren't graded in colors. An examiner had three grading options. Deception detected, Non-detect or Inconclusive. Both LeFleur and Parker's faces twitched as each detective fought to mask his thoughts.

"Who administered the test?" LeFleur finally asked in a tone designed to suggest it didn't matter. But it did. A polygraph's results are highly dependent upon its examiner. It was virtually impossible not to allow biases to leak into the interpretations.

Rasmutin's nostrils flared as if he did not like the question. "Senior Investigator Cordon."

LeFleur and Parker both took a breath and nodded in unison as they both concluded the polygraph was worthless. A polygraph administrator had to be neutral, fully objective and administer the test without any emotion. He alone determined if the person was truthful, deceit was not detected or lying, deceit detected.

It was well known in the state police that Senior Investigator Larry Cordon and Rasmutin shared the same academy class and had remained fast friends and watched each other's backs as they rose up the ranks. LeFleur and Parker were sure that Rasmutin had shared the gossip about Francis Durkin and how he thought it was unfair to focus on Hennigan. Hennigan was just doing his job.

"How long was the polygraph?"

"How long?" Rasmutin repeated LeFleur's question as if it was a stupid-ass question, undeserving of a reply.

"The duration. How long did the test take?" LeFleur clarified in a steady, placating voice.

Rasmutin shrugged with an annoyed look. "I don't know exactly. It was short and to the point. Hennigan was asked if he killed a girl on Wellesley Island. Hennigan answered 'no'. He was also asked if he hit a girl with a rock on Wellesley Island. He answered no."

LeFleur and Parker nodded in silence. They both knew a professional polygraph took an hour or more.

"Cordon noted that Hennigan consented to the polygraph and was fully cooperative."

Fully cooperative. The detectives nodded. I'm sure he was.

"He was absolutely honest in his responses," Rasmutin continued.

LeFleur suppressed the urge to correct Rasmutin and say that a lie detector couldn't detect honesty. A polygraph measured the reaction of a person's nervous system to questions. That's it.

Rasmutin rearranged himself in his chair as he reaffirmed his decision not to tell the detectives that Cordon actually administered two polygraph examinations. Cordon was troubled by some spikes in the graphs during the first. He declared the test "Inconclusive" and rebooted the polygraph and sent

Hennigan out of the room to relax. Twenty-five minutes later he administered the second test.

"I just wanted you both to know about the polygraph. But you still need to go wherever the facts take you." Rasmutin's tone was flat like spent seltzer bubbles.

"You need to go wherever the facts take you," Rasmutin repeated in the same monotone as if he was regurgitating mandatory safety instructions at the beginning of an airplane flight. The detectives remained stone-faced, unsure of what to say.

"Do you understand?" Rasmutin asked with rising emotion.

They both replied crisply. "Yes sir."

"What else do you got?" Rasmutin asked sharply.

Parker drew a deep breath and said, "Two waitresses said they thought they saw a man speaking to a woman shortly before Hennigan found the woman's body."

"Where?"

"Near where the victim's car was found."

Rasmutin's face exploded with displeasure.

Parker looked like he regretted sharing the information. "One seemed real confused and the other one says she was sure she saw two cars and the woman's Volkswagen."

"She doesn't know what she's talking about," Rasmutin blurted as he waved his hands as if swatting the waitress' credibility away. "They were probably drunk. Where do they work?"

"At a bar in A-bay called Swingers," Parker replied.

Rasmutin shook his head with disproval at the degenerates who frequented Swingers. "A hundred bucks says they were drunk," Rasmutin scoffed.

"I agree," Parker said with a nod. Definitely drunk.

"What else?"

"The tollbooth collector reported that the murder victim was pretty shaken up when she came to the bridge."

Rasmutin shot a death stare at Parker. Parker swallowed hard. "We pulled the video. There's no audio but they looked like they were just talking. She didn't look flustered. If anything, she looked tired."

Rasmutin nodded. "Go on."

"The toll collector is an ex-Watertown cop. He says Hennigan seemed to be in a rush when he crossed the bridge a few minutes before the victim."

Rasmutin pressed his thumbs against his temple. Once a cop, always a cop, eh? "So?"

Parker shifted in his chair as if signaling his discomfort at what he was about to say. "Sir, um," he said, still shifting in his chair, "Hennigan stopped the victim on I-81 about 50 minutes before he found her body."

Rasmutin performed a half roll of his eyes. "That's Hennigan's job. What else you got?"

Parker nodded. Okay, you asked. "Trooper Pilgrim reports seeing blood on Hennigan's jacket."

"Hennigan found her body, right?"

"Yes, sir."

"So, would it be unusual for her blood to be found on Hennigan's uniform?"

"Of course not." Parker dropped his eyes to the ground and seemed to study the floor tiles before finding the courage to look directly at Rasmutin's mirror glasses. "Pilgrim thought he also saw blood splattered on the bumper of Trooper Hennigan's unmarked patrol car."

The wooden floor creaked as Rasmutin pressed his feet into it.

"Have you checked the bumper?"

The detectives exchanged nervous looks as Rasmutin's hot eyes demanded an explanation.

"We told you. Hennigan washed the unmarked car yesterday. Right in our parking lot."

"So you didn't find any trace of blood on the bumper?"

"No, sir. As I said, Hennigan power sprayed the bumpers."

Rasmutin sneered. "If Pilgrim was so sure he saw blood on Trooper Hennigan's bumper why didn't he say something to me when I was at the crime scene?"

Parker looked to LeFleur for support. None was coming. "I'm not sure."

Rasmutin broke off eye contact with a dismissive shake of his head. "No, Pilgrim didn't say anything because he wasn't sure. It was five in the morning, for Christ's sake." Rasmutin shook his head. Case closed. For a second, Parker considered advising Rasmutin that he was troubled by Hennigan's inconsistent statements. They just didn't sit right with him. Then he reconsidered as Rasmutin glared at him through his mirrored glasses.

Rasmutin tapped the conference table impatiently. "What do you have on the state's attorney?" Rasmutin steered his question to Detective LeFleur.

LeFleur straightened and looked relieved that Rasmutin changed the subject. "Um, I don't buy his story."

Rasmutin nodded. "Good. You shouldn't. It doesn't pass the smell test."

The three troopers nodded in unison. The state's attorney's story that he was just riding his bicycle because he couldn't sleep failed all of their smell tests.

"Nobody just goes for a ride in the middle of the night," Parker offered. "The bicycle has got to be 50 years old. I was told that the chain was rusted and the tires were crumbling. My bet is it was driven over there to give the guy an alibi."

Rasmutin vibrated with the energy of a hunting dog about to be released. The detectives were following the right scent. "He had to communicate with the woman. There's got to be a way to find a call or a text between them."

Parker had done his homework. "I contacted her family. Fortunately they knew her cell phone password and gave permission for us to access it."

Rasmutin's head bobbed. Hurry up and tell me what you found.

"So far, we haven't found anything on her phone."

Rasmutin glared at Parker. "Look harder. Was there a call to her from an unknown number?"

Parker broke off eye contact as he recalled every call to and from the victim during the last week of her life. There was only one call from an unknown source. He tracked it down and it was a marketing call from Pennsylvania. "I'll check again," he said softly, careful not to displease Rasmutin.

"What about encrypted chat sites?"

The detectives stared blankly at Rasmutin. What about them?

"Could they have used one of them to communicate? There's no way they arranged the rendezvous by mail," Rasmutin said sarcastically. He rubbed his neck as if trying to knead a crick.

"They'd most likely have to connect from their phones. So far, there's no trace of her connecting to an encrypted site from her phone."

Rasmutin pushed back from the conference table. "There's going to be pressures to cut the prosecutor slack because of his position." He pointed threateningly at Parker and LeFleur. "Don't succumb to the pressure. No one is above the law. No one."

There was a squeak of chair legs scraping the floor as Parker and LeFleur both pushed their chairs away from Rasmutin and nodded.

"Anything else?"

"We secured the prosecutor's shirt with the assistance of the CBP," Parker replied.

65

Rasmutin pulsed with nervous energy. Yes, he knew that. He was the one who called in the favor with the Customs and Border Protection to get it done. Tell me something I don't know.

Rasmutin zeroed in on Parker. "Get the D.A. tee'd up for an arrest warrant."

Parker flashed a confused look. Wasn't an arrest warrant premature? Parker pursed his lips, making sure his thoughts didn't leak out his mouth.

Rasmutin slapped the table. "Everything points to this fella Durkin! I'll bet my pension that his DNA will be found on her body. I don't want us to get bogged down in bullshit bureaucracy."

Parker and LeFleur stared back at Rasmutin with an identical confused glow as he exited the room.

CHAPTER SEVEN

"Well, now the world knows we're vacationing together," Durkin said, sounding mildly irked at the invasion of his privacy. Both PJ McLevy and Angelo DeMartin shrugged. It was no big deal. The reporter who left 15 minutes ago was just doing his job.

Durkin's nose twitched. He wasn't so sure it wasn't a big deal. He hadn't thought that there were any downsides to inviting the men to the Thousand Islands. After a Bridgeport cop had been murdered, DeMartin's Achilles's heel was savagely cut, riots tore through Bridgeport, everyone was dazed and depleted. It was simple: everyone needed to get out of the city and get some R & R. So when Roslyn Jones force-fed him the sabbatical, he invited the men. It was a simple and seemingly uncomplicated decision.

Now it wasn't so simple.

"Roslyn says I should give the troopers a DNA sample and move on."

Durkin drew a long breath and savored the feeling of his lungs expanding. He held his breath for a few seconds and then enjoyed the sensation of his lungs collapsing as the air rushed out of him. "I'm not sure what I'm going to do."

Durkin didn't have to explain. He was a man of principle. His entire life had been devoted to putting the scum who preyed on society behind bars. He never took short cuts or compromised for politics. He was criticized for being pigheaded but he never shied away from toeing tightly to his ethical line.

Durkin pulled another Miller High Life from the cooler. "If I don't take Roslyn's advice it could cause complications for both of you. Especially," Durkin hesitated, choosing his next words carefully. "Especially since Dem was recently under the FBI's microscope."

Before DeMartin could respond, PJ interrupted. "Hey," he said standing up on his creaky legs which threatened to buckle like a cheap aluminum folding chair, "we need to speak but first I need to piss and get another beer."

PJ wobbled off to the boathouse and when the retired cop's bladder was drained he plopped himself back in his chair and fished out another beer from the cooler. He popped the lid and took a long, satisfying guzzle. "If we tell you something, would it be protected under the attorney-client privilege?"

"If I was your attorney, it would." Durkin left unsaid that he wasn't their attorney so, no, it wouldn't apply. Anything they said to him could end up biting them in their asses.

"What I'm getting at," PJ continued, "is since you're on sabbatical, would you be free to represent us? Legally speaking, I mean."

A crystal clear image of the two-page document he signed three days ago appeared in Durkin's mind. The sabbatical was officially voluntary. Roslyn Jones was far too clever to allow Durkin to later claim she compelled him to step away from his state attorney's duties. He'd be paid for a 12 week sabbatical. He could do anything or nothing. He could engage in either for-profit or pro bono activities as long as such activities did not bring his office into disrepute.

Hell, there was nothing disreputable about having cops as clients.

The pleasant sensation of cold beer and warm sun relaxed Durkin and brushed the ethical complications of being a state's attorney and a private counselor aside. "While I'm on my sabbatical I can represent you and everything you tell me would be forever protected by the attorney-client privilege."

PJ raised his beer can in a toast to his new lawyer. "Okay, then you're hired."

"But only while I'm on sabbatical."

"I gotcha." With a casual shake of his beer can, PJ signaled for DeMartin to fire away. The state's attorney is now your attorney as least as long as he's on sabbatical.

DeMartin began but then stopped as if he was uncomfortable sharing his deepest secrets. Secrets could be twisted and land him in prison if the wrong people were privy to them.

Durkin read DeMartin's unease. "Only share what you're comfortable with."

"No, I'm fine with you Francis. I'm just," DeMartin bubbled with emotion. "It just brings back tough memories." Angelo DeMartin wiped tears from his cheeks as PJ patted him on his back. Everyone knew DeMartin was thinking about McGuinness. Officer Kelton McGuinness who was brutally killed patrolling the streets of Bridgeport. Officer Kelton McGuinness who was killed in the prime of his life.

"Here's to Kelton," Durkin said as he raised his beer in solemn reverence. The men all raised their beers and instead of clinking them they pushed them together as if they all sought solace in the cans' connection.

For the next half hour, DeMartin and PJ methodically detailed what transpired in Bridgeport only months ago. As each secret was revealed, Durkin squirmed, shifting his rear-end in his seat as if his butt was itchy. So much of what Dem said conflicted with the official police reports. The state's attorney was growing visibly more uncomfortable with his decision to take on new clients. What was he thinking?

When DeMartin finished, Durkin sat quietly, sorting the facts and applying the law. Sure PJ McLevy was justified using lethal force to save DeMartin's life. That was cut and dry. But his new clients faced serious exposure if all the facts surfaced. Durkin sighed. He could think of at least 10 other criminal charges that could be levied against his clients.

Worst of all, the investigation wasn't closed and buried. The feds could revive the matter. And if they did dig up new facts, they'd twist them and go for DeMartin's jugular.

And now PJ McLevy's.

Before today, PJ McLevy was not on anyone's radar. But that would all change once the *Watertown Daily Register's* article was published. The FBI would learn that a legendary ex-Marine sniper and knife throwing expert was Angelo DeMartin's close friend. It wouldn't be long before they theorized it was PJ who stuck the knife in the killer's neck and PJ McLevy would be in the FBI's crosshairs.

"I just thought you should know everything," PJ shared, "especially given what went down this morning."

This morning. Yes, for the first time in Durkin's life he found himself in law enforcement's cross-hairs. For the first time in his life, cops eyed Durkin suspiciously. It was unnerving how the three men were members in the same fraternity; good guys under suspicion.

A state's attorney's life is complicated, Durkin thought as he took another sip of beer and gazed up into the sky as if looking for answers. Far too fucking complicated for what the state pays him.

"Francis," DeMartin asked, as if he was apologizing for changing the subject.

"Yeah?"

"You remember the woman I met when I was investigating Kelton's murder?"

Durkin shook his head. No, but he heard rumors that DeMartin was dating a sexy professor.

"Well, anyway," DeMartin continued sheepishly. "We've become friends."

Durkin's eyebrows raised. "Friends? Are you asking me if she can visit?"

"Yeah," DeMartin replied in a hushed voice.

Durkin sipped his beer and used the can to mask his feelings. He was under siege and the last thing he wanted to do was be around outsiders. They wouldn't be able to speak freely around DeMartin's girlfriend. He took another quick sip to shield his thoughts. But on the other hand, DeMartin was an injured hero-cop who put his life on the line to bring a cop-killer to justice. The least he could do is let him use his the cottage as a love nest. He lowered the beer can and forced a smile.

"Of course, but…." Durkin wavered.

"But what?"

"The cottage is like a wooden tent. Noise carries easily so move the headboard from the wall."

The three men laughed as only good friends could. The laughter lowered and then spiked two or three times before it petered out.

PJ cleared his throat, announcing he had something to say. "I also asked a friend to come up here."

Durkin and DeMartin looked to him for an explanation.

"A girl—friend?" Durkin asked, sounding pissed off he'd be the only guy without a date.

"No, this is an ex-cop."

Durkin placed his beer can on the dock. "What gives?"

"There's a few things that just don't sit right with me."

"Like what?" Durkin asked.

PJ's shoulders raised up and down as if communicating through his body language. "I didn't like how that trooper and D.A. were looking at you."

"I didn't either," Durkin replied earnestly. "But why are you asking an ex-cop to come up here?"

"He's going to look into a few things for me and," he pointed to DeMartin in his sling and moon boot, "this guy ain't going to be able to help me with shit."

DeMartin ran his eye over his sling and boot. The doctors told DeMartin that his shoulder would take two months to heal. His Achilles heel would take at least twice that long before he was able to rejoin the force.

"He's an ex-cop and he owes me." PJ McLevy, the 68 year old oddity, smiled as he recalled what he did to earn the favor. "He won't be shacking up with us, though."

Durkin searched for clues in PJ's face. What was really bothering him?

"It's just in case," PJ answered.

"Hey!" a skinny man with a withered face yelled out as he walked towards them with a youthful bounce in his bare feet. As he neared, Durkin gauged his age: early seventies but he was in good shape. A glint in his eyes and a slight smirk gave the impression he was perpetually concocting practical jokes.

It was still too painful for Durkin to push himself out of his chair. "Hi," Durkin said. "Forgive me for remaining sitting. I hurt my leg."

The skinny man ran his eyes over Durkin and was about to remark about the cuts on Durkin's face when a mischievous smile washed over his face. "I'm Kyle Johnston."

"Francis Durkin."

"I know who you are," Johnston said as if he knew all of Durkin's secrets.

"You do?"

"Your cousin Bill told me you'd be here."

Kyle pointed to Durkin's bandages. "Did you get those up here?"

Durkin ignored the question. "It's a long story. What can I do for you?"

Kyle swiveled around to PJ and DeMartin. First things, first. He stuck his hand out to shake. "Hi, Kyle Johnston," he said, shaking DeMartin's hand and then PJ's. He then turned back to Durkin. "Bill asked me to give you and your guests a tour of the river. Since the sun is out, I thought now may be as good as any time."

Durkin looked unsure.

"It's no trouble and there's no cost," Kyle said, raring to go. "Bill's a longtime friend of mine. What do you say?"

The three men eyed the cooler and then the river and thought the same thing: the beer probably tasted even better on the river. PJ and DeMartin nodded. "Sounds good."

"Okay," Durkin said. A tour of the river would be a good distraction. Durkin made a mental note to follow up with PJ on why he felt it was necessary to drag one of his cop buddies up to the Thousand Islands.

"I'll bring my boat around," Kyle said, already halfway down the dock. "It won't take but a moment."

As Kyle hustled off, none of the men noticed the construction worker parked in a pick-up truck in front of the cottage. None suspected he was an undercover trooper. Dressed in worn Carhart jeans and a shredded baseball cap, the undercover trooper unpacked his tools and lowered a ladder from the roof, blending seamlessly into the Thousand Island Park.

Ten minutes later, Kyle captained his 25 foot Grady White up to their dock. As they hoisted their cooler onto the boat the sun seemed to shine even brighter. The sky was a brilliant blue and cloudless. The aqua-colored water rolled lightly as Kyle pulled away from the dock and burst out in rhyme.

"Hail! River of the Thousand Isles,
Which so enchants and so beguiles,
With Countless charms and countless wiles,

Kyle beamed and looked for applause like a street performer seeking tips. PJ and DeMartin clapped while Durkin's head tilted, wondering about his guide's mental stability.

"That's impressive," PJ said to placate Kyle whose broad smile begged for more enthusiasm.

"Learned that poem as a kid," Kyle said proudly as he pointed up river. "I grew up on Grindstone Island. It's not far from here," he added, inviting conversation. It was clear that Kyle was a man who dreaded silence.

"Year round?" PJ asked to save Kyle from a patch of silence.

"Yep." Kyle grinned as if he anticipating PJ's next question. "Went to school there. We had two schools. Mind you, neither was very big."

"Must've been great," PJ said, sounding genuinely interested.

"It was. If you ever want to see Grindstone, just let me know. My cousin spends the summer on Jolly Island which is right off Grindstone. She gives a good as tour as anyone. My expertise is the river tour."

As the men sipped beers, Kyle talked. He listed the tycoons who flocked to the Thousand Islands; the Astors, Pullmans, Vanderbilts. He talked about when Ulysses S. Grant ventured to the river. He talked about the famous hotels and castles that once lined the St. Lawrence River.

For a brief moment, Kyle stopped talking as they came beside a giant tanker motoring up river. The men marveled at its steel nose slicing through the St. Lawrence River and the two large H-shaped cranes protruding from its deck.

Kyle pointed to the Thousand Islands Bridge that lay five hundred yards down river. "That bridge was the first bridge between the U.S. and Canada. FDR kicked off three days of celebration commemorating its opening in 1937. Bands played God Save the King and ended with the Star Spangled Banner. There were parades, boat parties and fireworks."

Kyle grew nostalgic as they drew nearer to sounds of the car and truck wheels whirring over the steel and concrete bridge. "There's five spans to the bridge. It hops over the islands to Canada."

Kyle spun the steering wheel to the right and pointed up river from the base of the bridge on Wellesley Island. "That's where my great, great grandfather sunk the Sir Robert Peel on May 30, 1838."

The men looked in the general direction where he pointed. Only medium sized river houses lined the river. Kyle's face sagged when no one asked him about his lineage. "Haven't you heard of Bill Johnston?"

The men shook their heads, no. With a disappointed shake of his head, Kyle pushed on. "Bill Johnston was born on the Canadian side of the river and made a fortune smuggling between Canada and the States." Kyle's eyes widened to emphasize that he meant a real fortune. "He built an estate near Kingston, which is over on the other side of the river in Canada. But the powers-that-be then made the fatal mistake of messing with my great, great grandfather."

"What did they do?"

Kyle was ready. "They meddled in his business," he said with a glint   in his eye. "When the War of 1812 broke out, the British tried to arrest him for spying for the Americans. When they couldn't put their hands on him, they confiscated his estate." Kyle paused for a long beat. "That was a mistake."

The men nodded. Sorry to hear. Shit happens during wartime.

"My great, great grandfather then declared war on the British. He made the British's lives hell on the river," Kyle said with mounting pride. "He plundered their supply boats and burned their ships. He wreaked havoc on the St. Lawrence River for the British. They couldn't catch him. He stayed a step ahead of him for years. He hated the British and led an expedition and captured and sank a British boat called the Sir Robert Peel." He pointed to the water in front of them. "It was anchored right there."

Right there.

Kyle pointed to the shoreline that consisted of a few docks and a boat house. A kid chased a dog across a lawn. "There's a marker up on the road commemorating the sinking of the Sir Robert Peel. He snuck up to the steamer when it was collecting firewood. He got all the passengers off and then scuttled the steamer." Kyle pointed to the bottom of the American channel as if they were floating above the Sir Robert Peel.

Off on the horizon, a power boat grew in size as it neared them. Durkin could see the boat's nose slice through the water sending water spraying in its wake. The boat seemed to be on a beeline, straight for them.

"Is that boat headed towards us?" DeMartin asked, tipping his chin in the direction of the boat. It had a steel hull, large console and powerful engines. It was either a fast workboat or a police boat.

"No, it'd be just passing by," Kyle said as a hint of uncertainty crept into his voice. "I've only been boarded once in all my years. He'll veer off in a few seconds."

Durkin eyed the vessel intently; he wasn't so sure. A light pulse of jitters rippled through him; jitters of a paranoid person of interest. As it came closer into view, Durkin recognized it was a law enforcement vessel. Twenty yards away, the boat slowed and motored up to the starboard side of Kyle's boat.

New York State Troopers was emblazoned on its side. Two troopers were on board with gray shirts emblazoned with large square letters on their back: STATE POLICE. One trooper was a meaty guy who looked like a high school fullback and the other was a wiry guy who could have been mistaken for an intern if he didn't have a gun strapped to his belt.

"Good afternoon, gentlemen," the beefy trooper said, looking through his dark sunglasses. The trooper then stopped and eyed the bandaids on Durkin's face. He then peered at PJ and held his stare on DeMartin's sling. In a barroom his prolonged stare would've triggered a fist fight.

PJ, DeMartin and Durkin exchanged irritated looks. There was nothing random about the troopers' boat sidling up to them.

Durkin's instincts kicked in. He made a mental note of their name tags. The thick bodied trooper was Carlson and the other was Piper. Piper typed Kyle's boat's registration number into a portable tablet and his head bobbed as if he possessed important secrets.

With his good arm, Angelo DeMartin dug his wallet out and flashed his badge. "Bridgeport police," DeMartin said, hoping to leverage the good will of the law enforcement fraternity.

"Bridgeport?" Trooper Carlson asked as if he had never heard of the largest city in Connecticut.

"Bridgeport, Connecticut. We're up here on vacation."

The troopers both nodded, looking unimpressed.

"Do you have alcohol on board?" Trooper Carlson asked, sounding as if the question was a test and he possessed the answer.

Durkin felt his forehead tighten as anger welled up inside of him. He urged himself to keep calm. He reminded himself he was on sabbatical. He drew a deep breath. For a few seconds, he held his anger in check. Then it bubbled over. "Is it illegal to have beer on a boat?"

"It is if the operator is over the legal limit," Carlson replied testily as if Durkin was challenging his authority.

"Then you should've asked our captain whether he had consumed alcohol. Not whether we have any on board."

"I can ask any question I want," Carlson replied defiantly.

"You can but it'd be better if you asked relevant ones," Durkin replied with the air of a pissed-off, smarter man. "So, is it illegal to have beer on the river?"

The troopers looked to one another for advice. They knew it wasn't and if it was they'd have to arrest every boat on the river. Trooper Piper pointed to the large white cooler. "Would you open the cooler?" he asked, sounding like he was issuing an order more than making a request.

All eyes turned to the cooler sitting in the well of Kyle's boat.

"Trooper, you'll need a search warrant for that. You should know that," Durkin said.

Carlson and Piper looked at each other, hoping the other would suggest their next move.

"But before you consider a search warrant," Durkin continued, "I think you should consult an attorney. When I file a harassment suit against Troopers Carlson and Piper I'm going to subpoena your phone records and texts. I'm going to outline how you received a call or a text from Commander Rasmutin or one of his lackeys that will show that you didn't stop us randomly. You came looking for us. I can assure you that a federal jury won't take harassment lightly."

Trooper Carlson's face broke into spasm of concern as he envisioned himself in a poorly fitting suit on the witness stand in federal court. He broke off eye contact with Durkin. "I don't have a clue what you're talking about."

"No? Let me refresh you then," Durkin said with a beer-fed swagger. "A trooper informed you that we were on the water. They provided our location and a description of our boat. They probably told you to bust our balls."

Durkin paused and used his lifetime of experience grilling men on the witness stand to read the troopers' faces. He knew instantly he was dead right.

"Before you say another word," Durkin continued with the confidence of a law professor who knew far more than his class, "remember I can subpoena your cell phone and text records. Don't try to be clever."

"Sir, upon arriving at your boat I observed that individuals were consuming alcohol in state waters. It's reasonable to ask how much alcohol you have on board."

"Oh, this has nothing to do with what you observed."

"I'm not sure what you mean," Carlson said with the ring of a bad liar.

Durkin eyed the shining water as if composing his parting words. "Trooper, tell Commander Rasmutin that I will contact him tomorrow. Right now, my guests and I are going to continue enjoying ourselves on the river."

Carlson's face drooped as if he dreaded communicating with Commander Rasmutin.

"Tell him nine-o'clock," Durkin added.

Carlson pressed his lips together as if suppressing what he really wanted to say. He eyed Durkin for a long moment. "Just some friendly advice." He paused for effect. "I'd put some sun screen on."

Without another word, Trooper Piper shoved off Kyle's boat as the engines roared, leaving foamy trail in their wake.

Kyle Johnston shook his head as he watched the troopers boat gain distance between them. "What the hell was that all about?"

Durkin, McLevy and DeMartin exchanged concerned looks as they all pondered the question. Finally, PJ said, "That was a "fuck-you" from the troopers."

CHAPTER EIGHT

New York State Police
Troop D
Alexandria Bay Station

Francis Durkin drove over the Thousand Islands Bridge on his way towards the police barracks. He cast his eye over the horizon at the miles of forests springing from the countless islands below. A freighter approached the bridge as a handful of pleasure craft sliced through the river. The view reminded Durkin of a photograph from a hot air balloon.

Durkin's thoughts then drifted to his conversation with Roslyn Jones. Just go and smoke a peace-pipe and enjoy your sabbatical. Don't screw up the only vacation you've had in 25 years. Swallow your pride and move on. Don't take it personally.

Durkin parked his car in the Troop D's barrack's parking lot. He got out and eyed the barracks which had the feel of a pre-fabricated, plastic toolshed lining Home Depot's parking lots. He then glanced into his side-view mirror, taking one last look at his puffy face and cuts covered by four different shaped bandaids. He straightened and ran his fingers over the bump on his head. It was still sore to the touch. He smiled tiredly. If he was going to smoke a peace pipe, he was only going to take one puff.

Inside the barracks a middle-aged trooper sat behind a desk protected by a thick security window, looking bored from shuffling the same papers, day-in and day-out.

Durkin paused at the sight of the protective shield as if its symbolism suddenly struck him. The fact that the trooper had to sit behind a security shield was a sad commentary on the world. Cops were targeted by crazies and terrorists. Machine gun fire riddled police headquarters in Dallas, New York, San Francisco and countless other cities. Molotov cocktails had been tossed at police headquarters. Cops had been shot and killed sitting just where the trooper sat.

Durkin recognized a flicker of recognition in the trooper's eye. He was positive that the trooper had been told to expect a prickly state's attorney plastered with facial bandaids.

"Can I help you?"

Durkin paused and shot an amused look at the trooper. You know who the hell I am. No matter. With a sigh, he introduced himself, "State's Attorney Durkin to see Commander Rasmutin."

The trooper nodded nonchalantly. He wasn't impressed. He pointed to a bench in the foyer. "Take a seat. The commander is on a call. I'll tell him you're here." The trooper's delivery was scripted, almost robotic. The trooper then rose and disappeared into a room behind him.

Durkin surveyed the antiseptic surroundings decorated with the obligatory photos of the Governor, the Superintendent of the New York State Police and the Troop Commander. All were in standard, black plastic picture frames designed to easily swap out photos to keep up with the constant changing of the guard. Durkin zeroed in on Rasmutin's photo. Without his mirror glasses, he was almost unrecognizable. It looked as if someone blackened his right eye with a magic marker and he sneered at the world through his dead, left eye.

A minute later, the trooper reappeared, carrying a glass of water wrapped carefully in a paper napkin. He handed Durkin the glass of water while making sure not to touch anything but the napkin. "Commander Rasmutin has to deal with an emergency. He says he'll be with you in a few minutes."

Durkin nodded understandingly. Emergencies pop up for cops every day. "No worries."

Durkin sipped the water and began warming to the idea of cooperating with the troopers. For the second time in the morning, he thought of Jones's counsel to smoke the peace-pipe.

Suddenly, his thoughts were interrupted by the ping of his phone. He pulled his cell phone from his front pocket and his eyes screwed up in confusion. It was a text from a number he didn't recognize.

CALL IMMEDIATELY! HONDO.

Hondo. Otherwise known to Durkin as Assistant State's Attorney Alex Phillips. A long time ago, Phillips once shared with Durkin that his hero was the once famous basketball player John Havlicek. Havlicek spent his entire career with the Boston Celtics and went 8-0 in NBA finals. That's the type of guy Phillips wanted to be: strong, reliable and always a winner. From that night on, Durkin always called Phillips by his nickname: Hondo.

But why was Phillips calling from the different phone number? Phillips eyed the message again.

CALL IMMEDIATELY! HONDO. The text's capital letters and exclamation point signaled Hondo was screaming at him to call asap.

Durkin caught the trooper's eye and pointed to his cell phone. He was going to step out and take a quick call in the parking lot. The trooper scrunched his lips and nodded.

As he pushed through the barrack's front door, Durkin thought about Phillips. Phillips had a sharp mind and possessed a Herculean work ethic. He was 12 years younger than Durkin and since he graduated Fordham Law School, his only job has been in the state's attorneys office. For the past 6 years, Phillips and Durkin worked side-by-side. Phillips was his loyal wing man and when Jones sent Durkin away on the sabbatical, Durkin appointed Phillips as Acting State's Attorney. There was no one that Durkin trusted more in the office.

He hit the return call speed dial. Phillips answered immediately. "Can you speak?"

Durkin scanned the area. The parking lot was almost empty. "Yeah. What's up?"

A beleaguered sigh slipped out of Phillips. He felt sleazy using an untraceable burner phone. He felt even sleazier sending his sister to a hookah lounge to buy it with cash but he knew cops could get a copy of the store's surveillance footage and he could never risk being seen buying a burner phone.

"I just got a call from a friend in the troopers' office."

"Our troopers?"

"Yep, the Connecticut troopers." Phillips took a breath. "This morning a New York State trooper named Rasmutin requested that our troopers pick up your trash."

Pressing his phone closer to his ear, Durkin looked like he was having difficulty processing Phillips's words. A request was made from the New York State troopers to the Connecticut State troopers to pull his trash? He glanced back at the barracks imagining Rasmutin talking on the phone with Connecticut State troopers as he stood in the parking lot.

"That son of a bitch," he hissed like an air hose.

For the second time in two days, Francis Durkin raged at being treated as if he was on the wrong side of the law. His entire career he had been on the side of the wolf hunters. Now he was being treated as a wolf. He felt his body tense as cortisol, the fight or flight hormone, pulsed through his veins.

And there was no chance Durkin would take flight. His brain accessed his limitless repository of legal support for his battle. The Fourth Amendment provided the people the right to be secure in their persons, houses, papers, and effects against unreasonable searches and seizures.

But damn, he didn't feel secure. He felt violated, he growled to himself. But Durkin knew the law supported Rasmutin. Digging through a state's attorney's trash was legal if Durkin left it on the curb for collection. And he had.

"Francis, are you there?" Phillips asked as if he sensed Durkin's mind was adrift.

"Yeah, I'm just thinking," Durkin answered in hushed voice as his mind dredged up *California v. Greenwood.*

In *Greenwood,* a cop rifled through a garbage left on a curbside and tested the garbage for traces of drugs. Bingo. Traces of cocaine and hashish were found on plastic cups and papers. The cops then used the test results to obtain a search warrant of the house. Bingo. They found illegal drugs everywhere in Greenwood's house.

Greenwood moved to suppress the evidence claiming the cops searched his garbage without a warrant. He lost. The Supreme Court ruled that Greenwood had no reasonable expectation of privacy when he set the garbage out to be collected. It is common knowledge that plastic garbage bags left along a public street are readily accessible to animals, children, scavengers, snoops, and other members of the public.

Hell, he had no more protection than Greenwood, Durkin fumed. Durkin's brain then instantly scoured every leading case on the legality of cops rummaging through suspect's garbage.

Every case on the history of search and seizures flashed through his head as if his brain's survival mode was stuck in high gear.

Abel v. U.S.

Berger v. New York

Katz v. U.S.

None offered him any relief.

Durkin felt like he was suffocating as his thoughts flashed to the glass of water the trooper gave him.

"Hold on!" he yelled to Phillips. He didn't wait for a reply as he ran back to the barracks. He swung the door open and his eyes darted to the small coffee table in the foyer. His heart pounded as he spied the glass—his glass—with his DNA on it —sitting undisturbed. It suddenly was crystal clear why the trooper wrapped the glass in a napkin: he didn't want to have his fingerprints smudged next to Durkin's.

Durkin rushed into the foyer and snatched the half-full glass and turned to the trooper who looked up with surprise in his eyes. "I'll be right back," he yelled as he hustled out of the barracks holding the glass. He cursed to himself. The sick bastard with the evil eye arranged for the trooper to give him a glass of water. It was all a ruse to snare his DNA fingerprint.

As Durkin strode to his car, his thoughts returned to his garbage. His garbage, laden with his DNA. Before he left his house in Fairfield he put a bag of trash in his garbage can. It was Tuesday and his trash was picked up every Friday morning.

"I need you to put my garbage can in my kitchen," he blurted to Phillips.

Phillips quieted as if he was unsure of what Durkin had said. But he had. The legal implications of his boss's request gave him pause. The state's attorney was asking Phillips to thwart a law enforcement investigation. How could Phillips rush to Durkin's house and put the trash into his boss's house without jeopardizing his career?

Durkin's emotions spilled out as he read Phillips' mind. "I assure you my request is kosher. This son of a bitch trooper is going to war with me and I'm not going to take it lying down."

Silence.

Durkin sensed Phillips was weighing both the legalities and ethics of complying with his request.

"The bastard had a trooper's boat pull us over on the river yesterday," Durkin fumed.

Phillips cleared his throat, unsure of how to respond. "Roslyn directed me to not speak with you while you're on sabbatical."

Durkin had expected as much. Jones agreed that Phillips could assume the role of acting state's attorney on one condition: Durkin could not have any contact with him during the sabbatical. She was not going to allow Durkin to rule from afar like a mafia boss issuing orders from prison. She said it with a smile, but it still rubbed Durkin the wrong way. To make it clear she meant business, she suspended Durkin's official email account and half-jokingly said she'd inspect Phillips's work phone.

Durkin lowered his voice. "Hey, if you don't feel comfortable, don't do it."

Silence. Of course, he didn't feel comfortable. He was already putting his career at risk by calling Durkin. Phillips answered with a heavy breath.

"Hondo, forget I asked you the favor," Durkin replied. "It's not right to drag you into my fight. Just forget it."

"I'm good. I know you wouldn't ask me to do anything illegal."

Illegal. There was nothing illegal about putting a friend's trash can inside his house. But moving a trash can full of garbage that an assistant state's attorney knew was going to be picked up by a state trooper? That had career-killer written all over it. Roslyn Jones would crucify them both if she got wind her prosecutors thwarted a police investigation.

"Forget I ever asked you to move the garbage," Durkin said plainly, without a bite. "I wasn't thinking. I'm pissed. I know how to handle this. I really appreciate you passing on the info." Durkin's rage surged as he looked back at the barracks, thinking Rasmutin was likely on the phone with the Connecticut troopers.

"Hey, I know you took a risk calling me. Don't do it again. I'll be coming back for the Benjamin Cardozo Lecture in a few days. If you want to meet me, come by my house. We can catch up without leaving a digital footprint."

Before Phillips had a chance to reply, Durkin hung up and dialed Michael Cornelius, his long-time neighbor. Cornelius was known to everyone as Corny. Durkin and Corny looked after each other's houses and both had a copy of one another's house keys. Corny was retired and his wife passed away two years ago. Durkin pictured Corny reading the papers and sipping coffee in his boxers as his cell phone rang.

Corny answered on the second ring.

"Francis! How's Canada?"

Durkin had no time for small talk. He needed a favor. Right away. Would Corny hustle, yes hustle, over to his house and drag his garbage cans into his kitchen? Yes, his kitchen. Put the two outside plastic garbage cans right in the middle of the kitchen floor. It is a long story but he didn't want Corny to go through the garbage. Just leave the garbage cans in his kitchen and he'd go through them when he got back.

Don't worry about the garbage smelling up his kitchen. Corny! He had to go. It was a rush. Corny began to ask about the fishing in the Thousand Islands.

"Corny I can't talk now. Please do this right away. I know it sounds weird but time is of the essence. Thank you. Look forward to drinking the beer with you."

Durkin hung up and immediately dialed DeMartin. DeMartin answered on the second ring and Durkin told him about Rasmutin's request to the

Connecticut State troopers. Durkin could hear DeMartin suck in a long breath as he processed the information. "You're shitting me."

"I know I'm sounding paranoid but just be sure not to put any garbage out."

Nerves spilled from DeMartin. "You're not being paranoid."

"What are you saying?"

"PJ's buddy just got a call from his friend inside the troopers. Do you remember seeing a construction guy working in front of the cottage?"

A faint image of a worker outside his cottage flashed onto Durkin's mental screen. "Yeah, faintly."

"Well, he's an undercover trooper. They've had the cottage under surveillance since yesterday morning."

Durkin's heart raced. "Damn, that's how they knew we were on the boat yesterday. I'll speak with you soon."

Durkin hung up and walked to his car. He casually opened the door and shoved the water glass under his front seat as he considered his options. He could just drive away. He came to the barracks as a cooperative witness and Rasmutin had the balls to make him wait. Sure he should have been more patient but he was on his sabbatical and waited for 20 minutes. Jones would give him shit but his story was plausible. He was pissed off and hard-headed enough to walk off in a huff.

Before he considered his other options, the barrack's front door swung open and Rasmutin stepped out. His chest heaved as if he had been running. Rasmutin's biceps bulged through his tight fitting uniform, looking like a military officer itching for a fight. He was wearing his mirror glasses and with a flick of his head summoned Durkin.

Durkin splashed a phony smile to shield his anger. You bastard, Durkin hissed under his breath. As he walked towards the barracks he had the sinking feeling the meeting wasn't going to go well. No, it was going to be exceedingly bad, he concluded.

Inside the barracks, Rasmutin signaled to the trooper behind the protective glass to buzz them through. He motioned for Durkin to enter the door. Durkin took a step and then stopped abruptly. He dug his hands into his pockets and motioned for Rasmutin to take the lead and open the door. He wasn't going to touch anything, especially the doorknob.

Rasmutin eyed Durkin through his mirror glasses and then, after twisting his lips together, pushed the door open and walked purposefully to a conference room.

The small room was hot and smelled dank. Durkin noted that it was also out-fitted with surveillance and recording devices. Everything he said and did would be recorded. Everything he said and did would be used against him in a court of law if Rasmutin had his way.

Rasmutin pointed to two middle-aged men in plain clothes. "Detectives LeFleur and Parker."

Durkin nodded and dug his hands deeper into his pockets. He wasn't going to shake their hands. Rasmutin closed the door and quickly took a seat.

As Durkin's eyes fell on Rasmutin, his dislike for him congealed into a brew of hatred. Durkin knew there was no rationale explanation for what triggered his powerful revulsion. Maybe it was Rasmutin's distrusting eyes. Maybe it was his aggressive body language. Maybe it was just combustible human chemistry. Who knows? Whatever it was, Francis Durkin was filled with an unalterable hatred for the trooper seated across from him.

Rasmutin began. "Would you take us through how you came to be at the entrance of Dewolf Point State Park yesterday at approximately 4:05 a.m."

"I couldn't sleep so I decided to go for a bike ride. I rode from Thousand Island Park to the entrance of the state park."

Rasmutin interrupted, "Do you mind if I ask you what was keeping you from sleeping?"

Durkin instinctively wanted to tell Rasmutin that it was none of his goddammed business but he reminded himself he was being recorded. "Insomnia."

"What type of bike do you own in Connecticut?" Detective Parker cut in. Cute, Durkin thought. Really cute. Parker had likely been asking around about him and learned that Francis Durkin was allergic to exercise.

"I don't know. It's an old one."

"How often do you ride a bike in Connecticut?" Parker quickly followed up as if he didn't want to give Durkin time to formulate a lie.

Irritation bubbled up inside of Durkin. There was no doubt Parker's questions were wrapped in the knowledge that no one had ever seen Francis Durkin on a bicycle before.

The conference door opened and the trooper on desk duty entered like he was walking on egg shells. "Commander. There's a call for you."

Rasmutin looked like he was going to rip the trooper's head off for the interruption.

"I think you need to take it."

Rasmutin snorted and used the conference table to push himself up. "I'll be right back. This will be quick."

The detectives stared at Durkin, hoping the awkward silence would dislodge a few words from him. It didn't. Francis Durkin stared back at the detectives with a plastic smile.

Thirty-seconds later, Rasmutin burst into the conference room. He glared at Durkin with red-hot anger. Durkin smirked, sure that Rasmutin had just learned that his garbage had been moved inside his house. Way to go, Corny, Durkin cheered to himself as he envisioned Corny dragging his garbage cans into his kitchen dressed in pajamas and slippers.

"I was asking you about how often you ride a bike when the Commander left to take a call," Parker said, jump-starting the questioning. "When you can't sleep, do you usually go for a bike ride?"

Confrontation crackled in the air. Durkin pinched his lips and again reminded himself he was being recorded. "Nope."

Rasmutin clicked the top of his pen furiously. "Is there any reason why we would find your fingerprints on the guardrail next to the state park's entrance?"

Durkin raised his right forefinger. "If it's there, it's because I touched it."

The room quieted as tension swirled in the small room. Durkin broke the silence. "You are aware that I called 911, right?"

Rasmutin cleared his throat. "As a prosecutor, you know that criminals have been known to call the police."

Durkin's eyes widened as if he wanted to signal the importance of his next words. "Were any grease stains found on the woman?"

The troopers' faces hardened as if they resented Durkin turning the tables on them. They asked the questions. He was supposed to provide the answers.

"The investigation is on-going," Rasmutin spat out as if each word pained him.

Durkin's head bobbed and Rasmutin tapped the conference table as if one wrong word from Durkin would spark an outburst.

Durkin held out his hands. "I fixed a bike chain yesterday morning and had grease all over my hands. I showed you them yesterday." Durkin paused but held his stare on Rasmutin. "Now, did you find any grease on the woman?"

Rasmutin stared at him, stone-faced. He wasn't going to be answering any questions. "I was led to believe that you would consent to a DNA swab," Rasmutin said as he cracked his knuckles.

Durkin looked unsure how to respond. He was sure Jones told the Superintendent of the New York State Police that Durkin would provide a DNA swab and put the matter behind them. But that was before Rasmutin

85

tried to obtain his DNA from his garbage like he was some sleaze-ball criminal. No, Rasmutin crossed the line. He wasn't going to cooperate with the bastard. In fact, he was going to press charges for excessive force and he'd do his damndest to prove that Rasmutin was the architect behind a culture that turned a blind eye to civil rights violations. He was going to swing and swing hard.

"Sounds like someone led you astray," Durkin replied coldly.

Rasmutin's face reddened. The other troopers' eyes widened. They had never heard anyone speak to the commander like that.

"Are you refusing to voluntarily submit a DNA sample?"

Before Durkin had a chance to respond, the door opened and District Attorney William McClusky entered the room. His tie was loosened and he was out of breath. In his tweed blazer and khakis, he reminded Durkin of an associate professor at a community college.

"Sorry gentlemen. I had another matter to attend to." He quickly found a seat. "Now please carry on."

"Is it customary for the District Attorney to attend a fact-finding meeting?" Durkin's tone had more of a bite than he intended.

"We're less formal in Jefferson County," McClusky answered. "I was in the area and given that we're both prosecutors, I felt like sitting in with the troopers was the right thing to do."

The right thing to do? Durkin fumed. The right thing was to get cracking on the investigation and stop wasting time speaking with a guy who happened upon a murder scene.

The room quieted as if no one knew what to say to break through the tension. Rasmutin broke the silence. He turned to McClusky. "I was just asking the state's attorney, if he would consent to a voluntary DNA swab."

Everyone looked to Durkin for his answer.

"I was in the process of telling Commander Rasmutin that under the circumstances I wasn't going to supply one."

McClusky's lips moved as if he was chewing on Durkin's words. "That's unfortunate. We can always get a search warrant to force you to submit a DNA sample."

Durkin looked as if he was going to smash McClusky in his nose. "I told you yesterday that you need probable cause to get a search warrant." Durkin coated his words with condescension.

"Several sets of fingerprints were found on the guardrail outside of the park. If one of those are yours, we'd have probable cause for a warrant."

Durkin shook his head, appalled by McClusky's lack of intellectual horsepower. "I made the call from the guardrail. A fingerprint from the guardrail would never be sufficient probable cause." Then for emphasis, he spit the word out again. "Never."

"I'm not so sure about that," McClusky said cockily as if he had already consulted with a local judge. "You have numerous cuts and abrasions on your body. Those injuries are consistent with a physical struggle. Your hands were covered in grime."

"The wounds were inflicted by troopers." He showed his palms to McClusky. "And I had grease on my hands from the bicycle chain."

"We are investigating that," Rasmutin chimed in.

"You can test my bicycle chain if you want." Durkin sniffed like he was telling Rasmutin to kiss his ass.

"I'd like to get to back to the DNA swab," McClusky interrupted.

Durkin's patience snapped. "What don't you understand? Courts won't issue warrants for fishing expeditions." Durkin stared McClusky down. "Even if you got a kangaroo court to issue one, I'd have it quashed in a heartbeat."

McClusky glared at Durkin. "I have to say it's mighty unusual for a state's attorney not to cooperate with an investigation."

The room crackled with tension, waiting for Durkin's response. McClusky was right, Durkin thought. He couldn't recall a state's attorney ever refusing to submit a DNA swab. He also knew the optics of refusing to provide a DNA swab were horrendous.

Durkin stood, dabbing his bandaids. "You'll be hearing from me."

"Oh, you'll be hearing from us too," Rasmutin said in a tone that matched Durkin's threat and raised the stakes.

Durkin took one step towards the door, spun around and fixed his eyes on Rasmutin's mirrored glasses. "Hey, if your undercover trooper outside my cottage wants a cup of coffee, tell him to just knock on my door."

Durkin pulled a handkerchief from his pocket and covered the doorknob before he turned it. He exited and left the door open. See you later assholes.

CHAPTER NINE

Durkin followed Rt. 12 past the entrance to the Thousand Islands Bridge without a clue to where he was going. He just needed time to think. Think and sort out what the hell just happened at the barracks.

A few hundred yards down the road, he saw the 1000 Island Bait store, a large white building with gas pumps outside. He headed towards its parking lot as he recalled the store carried newspapers. He parked and found the newspaper stand wedged in between an ATM machine and a rack of hand-made key chains that resembled fishing lures.

He grabbed a copy of the *Watertown Daily Register*, dropped a dollar on the counter, drove across the street and entered the North Country Welcome Center parking lot, studiously avoiding the front page until he parked his car far from the others. When he reached the far corner of the lot, he lowered his windows, killed the engine and sat looking up at the base of the Thousand Islands Bridge.

He unfolded the paper and ran his eyes over the photos. There was a photo of the woman's VW Beetle. The passenger car door was flung open, like a ransacked dresser draw. Trooper Loughlin, the baby-faced trooper, was in another photo. Loughlin struck Durkin as level-headed and honest but his youthfulness in the trooper uniform gave the appearance of a boy wearing a trooper's outfit for Halloween.

Durkin's eye caught the byline. J.B. Alexander. He pictured the reporter standing in his yellow rubber boots trying his best to draw a comment from him. Durkin blew a stream of frustration. How was he caught up in this? It was a train wreck. A f'ing train wreck, he repeated to himself as he creased the paper and started reading the article.

WOMAN MURDERED ON WELLESLEY ISLAND
Victim Discovered by Trooper Shortly After Speed Warning
Badly Beaten Body Near Car

It was a young woman's worst nightmare. An unidentified woman, driving alone in the early morning hours, was found brutally savaged at the entrance to one of New York's renowned state parks. A deputy sheriff believed it was the first reported murder on sleepy Wellesley Island, nestled amongst the Thousand Islands.

At approximately 4:30 am, the young woman's brutalized body was found by a New York State Trooper. A Jefferson County official who requested anonymity stated that the victim suffered "gruesome and disfiguring injuries which only a psychotic could inflict."

There are countless questions that require answering. Who was the woman? Did she pull off the road for a smoke? To rest? Was she forced off the road? Did a late-night rendezvous go terribly awry?

Adding to the mystery, a highly regarded state's attorney who is a recognized Constitutional and Criminal law scholar, stated that he cycled upon the murder scene minutes after Trooper David Hennigan found the victim's body. "The patrol cars were running and their lights were flashing," said Francis X. Durkin, the Connecticut state's attorney who was vacationing on Wellesley Island and decided to take an early morning bicycle ride. "There was no one in the cars so I called 911. I was almost immediately assaulted by a New York State trooper."

Durkin reported that he was struck in the head and manhandled by a trooper. Durkin claims to have suffered multiple facial abrasions and a large, egg-shaped bump on his skull at the hands of the troopers. He declined to comment on whether he will pursue legal action against the NYSP.

A spokesman for the NYSP, Major Terrance Wallace, stated that for the past 48 hours both the dash cam in Trooper Hennigan's car and the GPS locator had been malfunctioning. Wallace commented that "Trooper Hennigan reported the faulty body camera to his superiors three days ago but a backlog of repair work led to delays in the repairs."

District Attorney William McClusky reiterated that he was confident there were no irregularities in the technical malfunctions in Hennigan's cruiser. McClusky additionally praised the state police for their tireless investigation over the past 24 hours and singled out Trooper Hennigan "for his professional actions that has sped up the investigation so far."

Major Wallace indicated that many garments and other items had been sent to the state police laboratory in Albany and all evidence will be tested on an expedited basis.

The motto in the crest of the County of Jefferson seal is Fiat Justia which means "Let justice be done." The people of Jefferson County will likely call out, Fiat Justia.

Durkin's head lifted from the paper when he finished the rest of the article. He stared blankly at the Thousand Islands Bridge. He needed time to clear his head before he returned to the cottage. He needed to sort his thoughts he told himself as he sat alone in his car.

To anyone walking by he looked like a man with the weight of the world on his shoulders. But there wasn't anyone around. He sat alone, looking at the river from the base of the bridge, cooling off like an overheated engine.

His cell phone's ring was jarring. With a ticked-off expression, he pulled his phone from his pocket and eyed his phone. "For Christ's sake," he muttered, seeing Roslyn Jones's name. It couldn't have been more than 15 minutes since he left the barracks.

"Durkin," he answered in a husky voice as if he was recovering from an all-nighter at a bar.

"I thought you were going to play ball with the troopers," Jones snapped.

"Change of plans," he replied cavalierly.

"Cut the shit, Francis."

Roslyn Jones' sharp tone felt like a whip cracking on his back.

"When I entered the meeting, I planned to be a good soldier. I really did."

"Then what the hell happened?"

"They tried to pull a DNA swab from my garbage."

"They came to your," Jones's voice fell off. "Wherever you're staying."

"No, Roslyn," Durkin said, almost in a whisper, "the New York State troopers called our troopers and asked our guys to collect my garbage from my house in Fairfield."

"How do you know?"

"After 30 years, I have friends in the state police."

"But," Jones began, "You know—legally speaking— a cop can pull your DNA from your garbage if you leave it out for collection."

Of course he knew. *California v. Greenwood.* But that wasn't the point. The point was that it was his goddamned garbage and he was a goddamned state's attorney.

"I get why you're pissed." Her voice was plain, unemotional. "But," she paused, "it's going to be hard to explain why my law-and-order prosecutor refuses to provide a DNA swab."

"The pricks tried to go through my garbage, so I told them to shove the swab up their asses," Durkin replied with a tad more emotion than he intended.

"Francis. You need to contain this. This sounds like it's turned personal."

It had. Rasmutin turned his stomach the second Durkin set his eyes on him. And it went downhill from there. When Rasmutin requested the Connecticut State troopers pick through his garbage, Durkin's hatred for Rasmutin boiled over.

"It became personal when Rasmutin directed our guys to my home," Durkin said in a steely tone with a delivery as tight as piano wire. To Roslyn's ear, Durkin could snap at any second.

"Francis, you can't let it become personal."

He knew Jones was right. No one makes the smart decisions when a confrontation turns personal. Durkin dabbed the bandaids on his face. It felt like they were the only thing holding his face together. "Of course it's personal. I got the shit kicked out of me and they asked our troopers to snoop in my garbage. What the hell are the Connecticut troopers thinking now?"

"Francis, listen to me! You have to take the emotion out of this!"

Emotion. That's what separated Francis Durkin from the pack. Emotion. To Durkin, prosecuting crime should be emotional. He approached every criminal trial with the ferocity of avenging a wrong as if the defendant injured his family. If the defendant didn't plead guilty and accept a reasonable prison sentence, he would crush him in court and seek the maximum sentence. It was about retribution and, of course, it was emotional. It should be emotional. Now this was personal and emotional.

"Francis," Roslyn said in a tone pitched to appeal to his intellect. "You are smart. Damn smart. Your one weakness is you sometimes let your emotions get the best of you. This is one of those times. You need to start acting in your best interest. If you let this get out of hand, ruining your sabbatical will be the least of your worries."

"I didn't ask to go on a sabbatical."

Jones sighed. Durkin needed time to cool off but she needed to raise a question that had been nagging her. "Is there any reason why you're not sharing your DNA with the New York State troopers?"

Durkin shook like an old furnace about to explode. "No," he growled testily. It was inconceivable that he could be involved in any crime, let alone a heinous murder. "Roslyn, I can assure you that I had nothing to do with the young woman's murder."

Jones regretted asking the question but she had no choice. Nothing was making sense to her. She sighed sympathetically. "Francis, get some rest. You just came off weeks of non-stop chaos in Bridgeport. You probably got less than four hours of sleep a night for the last couple of months."

He was lucky if he got two hours of sleep most nights, Durkin thought. "I'm going to sue their asses for excessive force."

"Listen to yourself. You sound like a whiny, ACLU attorney."

"Roslyn, they're messing with the wrong guy."

Jones blew a stream of frustration into her phone. "Francis, for goodness' sake," she began, adopting the tone of an older sister. "Have you thought about what's going to happen once the Commission gets wind of this?"

The Commission. She loved to remind him that the Criminal Justice Commission wanted his scalp.

"You've also got to remember that you're out of your jurisdiction and your reputation doesn't carry any weight near the Canadian border. There's only so much I can do for you up there. You need to be careful."

"I will."

"You haven't been so far."

Durkin gripped his forehead. It was personal and getting more so by the minute. He was so angry he couldn't see straight. And when he couldn't see straight, he knew he'd crash into something or someone.

"Let's speak tomorrow," Jones said, sounding as if she was running out of gas.

"Okay. Talk tomorrow," Durkin replied as he ended the call. He sat back in the driver's seat and drifted into a semi-catatonic state as his eyes fixed on the sunlight dancing on the top of the river. What the hell is going on?

CHAPTER TEN

Durkin looked up from his chair on the dock and enjoyed the sunset; a glowing orb slowly descending, second by second, over the island's tree line. Minutes later, it was gone and darkness blanketed the river.

Where the hell did the day go? Durkin asked himself as he watched PJ and DeMartin work their phones from the boathouse. The two men spoke nonstop as if they were manning a phone bank. PJ would nod, say something in a low voice and occasionally make a note as he sipped his beer. Now a pile of empty cans rested next to his chair and his large, bald head and craggy face radiated with sun burn. DeMartin sat comfortably and used the fingers on his free hand to peck away on his cell phone.

Durkin pulled out his cell phone and saw his battery had only a ten percent charge left. He felt his own batteries were even lower. He picked up his glass of scotch and swirled the amber colored drink, savoring the tinkling of the ice cubes. He then noticed that for the first time in hours, PJ and DeMartin were off their phones. Durkin slowly rose and carried his drink over to them. For a minute all three of the men sat in silence as if decompressing to the sight of the dusky river.

"Where are we?" Durkin finally asked no one in particular.

PJ sucked in a long, loud breath. Where should he start? "A friend inside the New York State troopers says the trooper who roughed you up is named Hennigan. The other guy is named Haskins. He says both are odd ducks but Hennigan's odder."

Durkin instinctively touched the bump on his head at the mention of Hennigan's name.

"Hennigan grew up in Watertown, spent a few years in the military and then became a trooper. He's got 21 years on the force and is known for his stronger-than-average interest in pornography."

"Go figure," Durkin said sarcastically.

"What about the girl?" Durkin asked in a tone that suggested he'd return to Hennigan in a bit.

"She was from Pennsylvania. She came from a Ukrainian family. First generation American. Her father is a priest. By all accounts, she was a straight-laced, nice, average girl. She was a hard working French teacher. No one thinks she was running drugs or involved in other crap. She was just at the wrong place————"

"When the wrong fucking guy came around," DeMartin cut in sharply, finishing PJ's sentence.

"Was she sexually assaulted?" Durkin asked.

PJ shook his head. "Doesn't appear it got that far."

"Why the fuck would someone kill an innocent young woman?" DeMartin asked out loud, his face contorted with disgust.

"Can you get me background on Rasmutin?" Durkin asked PJ, wanting to know who he was up against.

PJ nodded as he crushed his beer can with one hand. He was way ahead of Durkin. "Rasmutin is a political animal. He's got his eye on becoming the Superintendent of the Troopers. He's connected and will do anything to get what he wants."

"Political cops are the worst," Durkin said as he sipped his scotch. He shook his head. "I didn't like the guy the second I laid my eyes on him."

"Unfortunately, I hear he's not stupid," PJ said. "And a political snake with brains can be dangerous."

PJ's phone rang. "Yeah," he said gruffly as if he thought the caller should've called him sooner. He listened intently and then hung up without a word. "That was my buddy Sam, the ex-cop I told you about. He wants to meet us tomorrow but he doesn't think he should be seen with us."

Durkin smiled to himself as everyone scanned the horizon as if searching for undercover troopers in the trees or floating in the river. No one saw anything but they all felt the heat of surveillance. They nodded in agreement, it made sense not to meet PJ's buddy here.

"Sam was made for this. He gets into the weeds and isn't afraid to stir things up." PJ laughed. "In fact, he prefers to stir things up."

Durkin turned back to PJ. "Are you sure you want to get mixed up in this?"

"Yep."

"Why?"

"Because my old cop's nose smells what you smell."

Durkin solicited DeMartin's input. "What's your read on this?"

94

DeMartin quieted as if he was drifting into deep concentration. For a few seconds, his brain pored over every detail about the murder and the jumbled investigation. "I agree. Something stinks."

Durkin looked satisfied with their answers. "All right. Tell me about Sam."

For the next half hour, PJ briefed Durkin and DeMartin on Sam Rome, the brash ex-cop who hop-scotched his way through Massachusetts law enforcement agencies. He made a career of transferring from one agency to another after clashing with his bosses. And he always clashed with his bosses. It was just a matter of time. He had stints in the Massachusetts Port Authority Police, Massachusetts Bay Transportation Authority Police and Suffolk County Sherriff's department. As long as Rome was able to transfer to a senior position in another agency, his career trajectory continued upwards. Rome knew a time would come when he ran out of agencies and he'd have to search for his next gig.

And that time was now.

CHAPTER ELEVEN

New York State Police Crime Laboratory
Biological Sciences Division
Albany, New York

Danielle Keegan paced back and forth in front of the corner office with a burning desire to speak with Stephanie Cotton, the associate director of the crime lab's biological sciences division. She looked up and caught her reflection in the office glass. She looked like a madwoman, she told herself. She had to relax. Besides, if Cotton appeared right now she'd just spew raw emotions; exactly the sort of drama that Cotton detested.

Keegan decided to return to her office and collect herself. She mechanically opened and closed the stack of manilla folders lying on her desk. She then began straightening her desk but stopped almost immediately; it was pointless. Every thing on her desk was already perfectly straight. Perfectly aligned. Perfectly organized. To give herself something to do she picked up a notepad and then laid it crookedly on the desk. Then she straightened it out. She wheezed. It was a horribly boring game.

She turned her attention to the award plaque on her desk. Forensic Scientist of the Year. Her chest puffed with pride when she first received it but now it had no effect on her as she slouched in her chair. She ran her eye over the Forensic Lab System seal that adorned her plaque. A scale that represented the scales of justice overlaid the outline of a silhouette of New York State. The scale's post was a twisted DNA helix. One side of the scale held a microscope and the other a beaker and test tubes. At the base of the scale, there was a handgun and a magnifying glass. Then there were eight rows of numbers signifying genetic codes. The crime lab's logo was so geeky only a true nerd could like it, Keegan chuckled.

As she sorted the reports, her eye caught the draft report that would be sent to the Utica Police. Her eyes traveled down the codes that identified the locations in the human genome where the unique codes were kept. The locations were called loci. She shook her head thinking of how many times she heard people mispronounce loci. It was low-shee. When she started in the lab, forensic scientists focused on thirteen low-shee.

CSF1PO, FGA, TH01, TPOX, vWA, D3S1358, D5S818, D7S820, D8S1179, D13S317, D16S359, D18S51, and D21S11.

Keegan loved the magic of some of the loci's names. The loci that fell within a gene were named after the gene. TPOX was named after the thyroid peroxidase gene. THO1 was named for the tyrosine hydroxylase 1 gene. vWA is located in the von Willebrand Factor gene.

At each genetic address, there are two genes called alleles. Uh-lelles. Every gene comes in pairs. Like the animals on Noah's Ark, Keegan would say. One of the genes is inherited from the father and one from the mother. Each member of the pair was called an allele. If the alleles matched the alleles at the same location at many DNA addresses, there was a DNA match. Keegan also knew that when the biological mother and the father passed on the same allele there'd only be one number at that address.

Her eyes traveled to the lab report. The suspect's DNA matched exactly with the DNA found on the hoodie. THO-1, the allele was 7. vWa, the allele was 16 and so on and so on.

Item #	THO-1	vWA	TPOX	D21S11	D2S1338	D7S820	D5S818
2-1 (hoodie)	7	15,16	NR	30,31	17,19,20,21	8,9,10,11,12	11,13
2-2 (pants)							
3 (Suspect)	7	16	11	30,31	20,21	9,10	11

Danielle Keegan hopped up from her chair. She was going to drive herself mad if she sat in her office any longer.

As she rounded the corner, Keegan sighed with relief at seeing the lights on in Cotton's office. When she reached Cotton's doorway, the assistant director was just settling down at her desk.

"Stephanie, I need to speak with you," Keegan gushed, sounding as if she had just held her breath for a minute. She wished she had slowed down and said,'good morning' first.

The sound of Keegan almost asphyxiating grabbed Cotton's attention. She motioned for Keegan to close the door and take a seat.

Stephanie Cotton was a decade older than Keegan and could be mistaken for Keegan's sister. They shared the same interests, same lack of fashion, same high intelligence. From the day Keegan joined the State Police's

Forensic Lab, Cotton guided her through the suffocating bureaucracy that constantly drove away talent from the crime lab.

As Keegan plopped herself in a chair, Cotton's mind raced ahead, searching for a clue to what had excited Keegan's mind. Was it a personal crisis? A man problem? Was it professional issue? Had she made a mortifying error in the lab? Worse, did Danielle Keegan finally succumb to a recruiter's pitch to leave for a much higher salary?

Cotton forced a smile as she steeled herself for bad news.

"It's Russo," Keegan said, still sounding as if she was out of breath.

Cotton's face exploded with confusion. Russo? Cotton knew how Keegan felt about Russo. Had Russo harassed her? Had she discovered a massive scandal? Like everyone else, Cotton had heard rumors that Russo was guilty of dry-labbing; documenting test results he never performed. If anyone was going to take short cuts, Cotton would guess it would be Russo.

"Last night, at about 7:30 a trooper delivered a package to Russo. He said he wouldn't give it to anyone but Russo."

Cotton stared blankly at Keegan. Troopers walked through the lab all the time. Did Keegan forget that the crime lab was run by the New York State Police? Cotton's eyes urged Keegan to continue.

"I saw his handwritten notes," Keegan said, handing Cotton a folded piece of notepad paper. He circled 'rush' and it had Commander Rasmutin's name on it and then a line with Colonel Kordas's name.

Cotton took the paper and unfolded it.

"But this is in your handwriting."

"Yes, I know. I copied what I remembered."

Cotton's eyes ran over the note. DNA. POI- person of interest. Rasmutin.

Kordas? Colonel Carl Kordas, the deputy superintendent in charge of all the mundane stuff that kept the New York State Police running: budget, facilities, records and the forensic crime lab. In Cotton's world, Kordas was on top of the food chain.

Cotton mentally reviewed Russo's workload. Russo was supposed to be chipping away on the backlog of Sexual Assault Kits. If he worked around the clock, Russo would finish in a year. He didn't have time for anything else. It didn't make sense.

"Are you sure?"

Before Keegan could respond, Cotton's eye returned to the note. 'Wellesley Island.' She felt her pulse quickening. Cotton had just read a report that a trooper had discovered a woman's body on Wellesley Island. She expected to be contacted for a pre-submission case review. Normally the victim's body and evidence would be at the Jefferson County morgue for at least a week. Cotton expected to get pulled into the case in a few days.

Cotton tensed. Why was she being left out of the loop? Was the top brass going around her because she felt that scientists, not troopers, should be running the crime lab?

Cotton wiggled the note between her thumb and forefinger. "I'll look into this."

Keegan sighed with relief. "Thank you."

"In the meantime, treat this information as strictly confidential. My main concern is that we don't have all the facts and we could be mistaken."

Keegan's and Cotton's eyes connected. They both knew there was no mistake. Russo's note indicated something dodgy was going on.

"Of course," Keegan offered as she stood. "Just let me know if I can do anything."

Both women exchanged pained expressions as Keegan exited the office.

*****

Stephanie Cotton instructed her secretary to hold all calls. She then sat down behind her desk and began jotting down notes. Russo. Lab protocols. NYSP resources. Wellesley Island. Why would a senior trooper circumvent the official chain of command and contact her least-skilled forensic scientist to handle a high-profile crime analysis? She didn't like her preliminary conclusions.

Cotton pinched the bridge of her nose and exhaled as she stared at her notes. She had worked her way up to Assistant Director of the Biological Sciences division and was 14 years younger than the current Director so she was well positioned to keep moving up the crime lab's ladder. But she knew that her continuing ascent required her to avoid career-derailing friction. Don't give offense. Don't speak ill of the other scientists. And don't be drawn into contentious issues.

And this had contentious written all over it.

It was going to be a long day, she sighed, pushing herself up from her seat.

Cotton headed to the laboratory. She peered through the glass windows and saw technicians and forensic scientists in lab coats, hair nets and protective eye gear in the climate controlled room. The lab seemed to be just waking up as the technicians examined reports and organized evidence to be analyzed.

Stephanie Cotton entered the small room the technicians used to change into their lab clothes. She donned a white lab coat, slipped on a hair net, pulled a pair of disposable covers over her shoes and slid her fingers into blue latex gloves.

Most of the forensic scientists were too engrossed in their work to notice their boss strolling through the lab. The ones who did, smiled broadly and greeted her warmly. Stephanie Cotton was the most-liked senior executive in the crime lab. To anyone watching her, she appeared to be just observing the lab at work.

"Russo," she said as she walked up behind Dante Russo. Russo didn't move. Cotton raised her voice. "Russo."

Dante Russo turned as if she had startled him. He straightened and came to attention as he saw Cotton standing in front of him.

"Ah, Assistant Director," Russo stammered like a high school kid caught red-handed, holding a case of beer.

Cotton nodded without revealing her concerns. She was a master of her emotions. "How's everything going?"

"Going? Ah, fine," Russo replied.

Cotton eyed the evidence laid out before him. "How's the backlog of SAK's coming along?" she asked, referring to Sexual Assault Kits.

Russo swallowed hard. "There's a slight delay."

"Really?"

"I've been asked to work on a high-priority matter."

"Really?" Cotton said, sounding only faintly interested. "And what is the high-priority matter?"

A pained expression flooded Russo's face. "I'm not at liberty to say," he stammered.

"Oh, is that so?" Cotton said with the expression of a cat toying with a mouse. "Who assigned you this high-priority matter?"

"Director Chilletti is aware of this," Russo replied defensively.

Russo looked relieved that Cotton showed little emotion. "So Director Chilletti assigned you this high-priority matter?"

Russo looked stricken. "I think it's best if you speak with her."

"Yes, I'll do that. Have a good day."

Stephanie Cotton strolled through the laboratory, greeting her staff by their first names. On the outside she looked as if she didn't have a care in the world. Inside, she boiled. She needed all her powers of self-discipline not to walk back and tear into Russo. He wasn't at liberty to say? Hell, she's in

100

charge of the damn laboratory! Cotton walked slower and counseled herself to breath deeper.

Five minutes later, Cotton slipped out of her lab clothes and marched directly to Darlene Chilletti's office.

Chilletti graduated from Oswego State University and worked for the NYSP her entire career. She spent little on clothes and less on make-up. Her voice sounded as if it sprang from her nose, causing people to focus on her nostrils when she spoke.

"Good morning," Cotton said to Chilletti's secretary. The secretary looked up and smiled as if to say she wished she worked for Cotton instead of Chilletti.

"Is the Director in?" I just need to speak to her for a minute."

"I think she's free. Let me see."

The secretary buzzed and whispered into the phone. Almost immediately, Darlene Chilletti swung her office door open. "Good morning, Stephanie." Chilletti's forced smile slid off her face like a fast melting ice cube.

"Darlene." Cotton greeted her boss with a tip of her head. "May I have a word?"

Chilletti stepped aside and gestured for Stephanie to enter. "Please."

Chilletti closed the door behind her and stood standing. "Yes?"

"Has Russo called you?"

Chilletti's eyes widened as if she was contemplating taking the Fifth. She sidestepped the question. "What can I do for you?"

"Well, I just saw Russo at the lab and he informed me he was working on something other than the SAKs. He said it was a high-priority assignment. "

Chilletti nodded and pressed her lips together. Yes? Go on.

"I was not aware of it and he led me to believe that you assigned him the case."

"That's incorrect," Chilletti said in her high pitched nasal twang.

"Oh. Then who assigned the case to Russo?"

"I'm not at liberty to say," Chilletti replied curtly.

Cotton summoned all her powers to remain calm. No one was at liberty to tell the director of the Biosciences division what the hell was going on in her lab?

"That's fine, Darlene," Cotton said in a controlled voice, "I just wanted to confirm that you were aware of what Russo is up to."

"Thank you."

Cotton took a step towards the door and then turned quickly around. She hesitated and then delivered her words as if she was a fisherman, expertly setting her fly on the surface of the water. "Oh, I just hope that you don't receive any blowback for this."

Chilletti took the bait. "What sort of blowback?"

"You know," Cotton answered.

Chilletti knew.

Screw ups were every directors' worst nightmare. Screw ups led to loss of accreditation and that led to terminations. Misidentification of hair fibers, destroyed blood samples, DNA contamination, false credentials, evidence integrity issues, theft of drugs. The list of career-ending screw ups in a crime lab was infinite. But the searing, white-flamed blowback was reserved for rogue scientists who tinkered with test results. And Chilletti knew that was what Cotton meant.

"I just hope you don't get criticized by the *Times Union* or the Inspector General."

Cotton got Chilletti's full attention. "Why would they criticize me?"

"It wouldn't be fair but someone could twist the facts and make it look like you allow troopers to cherry pick forensic scientists."

"That's not what happened," Chilletti shot back defensively.

"I'm sure," Cotton said, sounding doubtful. "I just hope it's not going to be misconstrued."

"Russo can be trusted."

"Of course. But what if the high-priority matter winds up in a high-profile trial?"

"What are you getting at?"

"*Melendez-Diaz v. Massachusetts.*"

Darlene Chilletti understood. The Confrontation Clause. The Sixth Amendment provides that in criminal prosecutions the "accused shall enjoy the right...to be confronted with the witnesses against him." In *Melendez-Diaz,* the Supreme Court ruled that the accused had a right to cross-examine the forensic scientist who prepared a lab report used as evidence because the report essentially acted as testimony against him.

"I shudder to think of Russo under withering cross-examination in a high-profile trial. Think of the press. How would that reflect on our lab?"

Chilletti stepped back, weighing Cotton's words. "Hasn't Russo gotten high ratings from his clients?"

Cotton remained poker-faced but inside she was celebrating how she was maneuvering the conversation in the right direction. "Yes, I'm troubled by that, too. It could be misunderstood."

"Misunderstood?"

"Well, Russo has the highest error rate in our lab but at the same time he received the highest ratings from law enforcement."

Cotton let the implications sink in. "I wonder if a crafty defense lawyer would question why Russo, who is so error prone, is held in such high regard by law enforcement?"

"What are you saying?"

"I don't think it would be fair," Cotton continued, "but I'm afraid a crafty lawyer could paint a picture that law enforcement likes him because he's pliable?"

"Pliable?"

"I'm concerned a lawyer could smear our lab with a claim that Russo bends to the will of law enforcement."

Chilletti shuddered at the prospect of Russo being cross-examined by a sharp defense attorney.

"And of course, there's the audit," Cotton said just above a whisper. The audit. The dry-labbing charge. An audit concluded that it was 'plausible' that Russo engaged in dry-labbing. Writing down lab results for tests that never were conducted was a mortal sin for a forensic scientist. A messy investigation followed and the state police issued a report that the dry-labbing claim could not be substantiated but noted many facts were "troubling." The report recommended Russo receive counseling on how to prepare detailed reports.

"There's no other forensic scientist that is held in such high regard by law enforcement and so low regard by his fellow scientists," Cotton added artfully as seeds of concern sprouted on Chilletti's face. "I also wonder what a defense lawyer would do if he learned how this case by-passed the lab's protocols and was rushed to the top of the line?"

Worry bled through Chilletti's cheeks as she envisioned herself being grilled by the New York State Forensic Science Commission. She still bore the emotional scars from defending her lab from charges that her forensic scientists disregarded DNA markers that did not match the suspect's. The scandal rocked the crime lab and Chilletti had to fend off charges that the lab was suspect-centric and failed to heed obvious warning flags.

Now, Chilletti could hear the flapping of the flags. She knew she'd be roasted if she ignored the concerns Cotton raised. She looked to Cotton for suggestions.

"I think we should have one of our best forensic scientists work hand-in-hand with Russo. She can review his notes and help prepare the reports. If the forensic scientist has to testify, we can send one of our best."

Chilletti chewed on Cotton's suggestion. "Who do you suggest?"

Cotton feigned a stumped look, knowing she couldn't recommend Keegan first. With a cagey absentmindedness, she floated names she knew would be out of the office this week. "Katie Morrissey would be perfect."

Chilletti nodded. "Yes."

"But I have to confirm her schedule. She may be in court. If she is, Wayne would be a good choice. He works well with everyone."

"Wayne would be ideal. He's a team player."

Yes, thought Cotton. He's a team player when he's in the office. But Cotton knew Wayne was out on a two-week vacation. She smiled inside, envisioning Wayne Rustoski on the beach in Hilton Head.

"Okay, either is a good choice. The tests need to be completed in the next 24 hours."

24 hours? What the hell is going on? In her entire career Cotton was aware of only a few cases that caused everything in the lab to come to a screeching halt. But she had never seen a case cloaked in secrecy and rushed to the head of the line like this. Chilletti was still not sharing who was pulling the levers but she had an idea. Colonel Kordas and Commander Rasmutin.

"Okay, I'll check with Katie and Wayne." Cotton headed towards the door. "If, for whatever reason, Katie and Wayne can't help out, I'll just put another high performer with Russo."

Chilletti nodded, too wrapped up in her own thoughts to respond.

"Will you advise Russo that he'll be working with another forensic scientist?"

Chilletti nodded. "Will do."

Cotton repressed a smile but she was glowing inside. "I'll have one of our top people on this shortly."

As Cotton stepped through the office doorway, Chilletti called out. "Stephanie."

Cotton turned and met Chilletti's eyes.

"Thank you," Chilletti said.

Cotton let a smile blossom. "It's not a problem. We'll get through this."

CHAPTER TWELVE

PJ McLevy's beefy hands clasped the large, ceramic coffee mug like he was trying desperately to warm his hands. Slightly hunched over, with his eyes glued on the mug, he seemed to be lost in faraway thoughts.

His thoughts were interrupted by the sounds of a man with aching muscles descending the staircase. A grunt followed the sound of bare feet balancing unsteadily on the wooden floor. He then saw a bulky shadow lumbering towards him. A second later, Francis Durkin's sleep-deprived face slipped into the cone of light shining above the kitchen counter. Durkin's puffy and stubble-filled face reminded PJ of a ball of lint that escaped from the dryer.

Durkin steadied himself against the kitchen counter as he counted three spent coffee pods piled next to the coffee maker. "How long have you been up?" he croaked.

PJ shrugged as if sleep was of little importance. "I'm an early riser."

Durkin's face curled up. It was a source of pride for Durkin that he always was first to arrive at the state's attorney's office. In some odd way, he felt like he had lost an early riser competition by arriving after PJ.

Durkin shuffled to the coffee maker, dropped a pod in and pushed a flashing button. The machine growled and hissed as it forced the heated water through the pod and coffee dripped into his mug.

"Sam Rome wants to meet us at eight o'clock," PJ said in a hoarse morning voice. "He recommended we meet at the Boldt Castle Yacht House."

Boldt Castle.

Durkin retrieved his Boldt Castle mental files. He remembered visiting the castle as a kid. The famous castle was built on Heart Island, located off the eastern tip of Wellesley Island. It was designed as a magnificent, sprawling castle, grand even by the standards of the robber baron era. The exquisite stone castle was decorated with Gothic towers and exotic gargoyles crafted by the then-leading masons in the world.

George Boldt built the stupendous castle for his wife, Louise. But she never saw it. When it was 90 percent completed, Louise died and with her death, her husband's passion for the castle died. Boldt Castle laid dormant for the next 80 years and became a home to bats and vagrants until it was restored and became the leading tourist destination in the Thousand Islands.

Across the river on the tip of Wellesley Island, Boldt also constructed a five story-high yacht house. Its gabled roofs were high enough to house tall ocean-going, sail boats and wide enough to house a massive collection of wooden boats. It was also open to tourists.

Durkin removed his coffee from under the coffee maker's spout and blew a soft stream of air to cool it. It was a good idea to meet in private, he thought as he sniffed the coffee. He looked out the kitchen window as if searching for a troopers's surveillance team.

Durkin checked his watch. 6:18. He had plenty of time to shake off the sleepy cobwebs that wrapped him like a tight cocoon.

*****

Durkin, PJ and Angelo DeMartin limped their way to PJ's car like a pack of wounded misfits. Each man felt the heat of unseen troopers' eyes. But who was the trooper? Was it the guy in the bathing suit reading the paper on the hotel porch? Was it the guy in the blue t-shirt on the bicycle? Was it the woman with the long pony tail on the golf cart behind them?

The trio drove slowly out of the Thousand Island Park and kept on the same two lane road that cut through Wellesley Island, past the Thousand Islands Country Club and a boat marina before they reached a small wooden sign for the Boldt Yacht House. PJ turned down the dirt road that winded down to the yacht house's gravel parking lot.

The parking lot had the feel of a shopping center with no tenants. Only two cars were parked in the lot and one had the dusty look of a car that hadn't been moved for months. A racing bicycle leaned next to the weathered front door.

The men exited the car and walked jerkily to the entrance. When they opened the door they were met with screeching seagulls, objecting to sharing the yacht house with the intruders.

There was only one other person in the yacht house; a man dressed in tight fitting spandex. The cyclist clomped in his metal cycling cleats to the edge of the yacht house and stood admiring a wooden sailboat.

PJ was the first to reach the cyclist. He shook the cyclist's hand warmly before turning towards Durkin and Angelo DeMartin who shuffled up behind

106

him.

"Francis, Dem, this is Sam Rome."

The glow in Rome's face brightened as Durkin and DeMartin studied the man in the tight-fitting cycling pants. He had a rubbery, boyish face and thin, sandy-colored hair. He also exuded a youthful air with a contagious, mischievous grin. Neither knew how PJ and Rome knew each other and if PJ didn't offer the information, they weren't going to ask.

From afar, Rome had admired Durkin. He knew Durkin's reputation as the ultimate cops' prosecutor with the impeccable record. "Nice to finally meet you," he said to Durkin, extending his hand. Francis shook his hand firmly.

Rome's attention shifted to DeMartin. He made eye contact and then his eyes drifted to DeMartin's sling before landing on his walking boot. Rome was at least 15 years older but his faced betrayed his excitement at meeting a celebrity. He had watched the video of DeMartin's heroism at least 10 times and each time was more impressed by DeMartin's fearlessness. He repeated his greeting and shook DeMartin's hand like he didn't want to let go.

"Nice to meet you guys," Rome said confidently and pausing as if giving their ears time to adjust to his thick Boston accent. His smile then disappeared and he turned all business. "Let's not make this long. Tell me what happened two nights ago."

Durkin ran through the facts of how he rode upon the murder scene, his confrontation with Rasmutin and his meeting at Troop D's barracks. Rome's lips curled up and nodded as if to confirm he understood every fact.

"So the troopers found a middle-aged guy on a rusty bike at a murder scene at four in the morning," Rome said as if playing back a condensed version of Durkin's account.

Durkin shrugged. "I get your point. It looks like shit."

Rome's head tilted and he rolled his eyes. It also smells and tastes like shit. If he was Francis Durkin, he'd be concerned with a lot more than the optics.

"I hear you banged heads with Rasmutin."

A slight grin escaped on Durkin's face. "You can say that."

Rome turned serious and set his eyes on Durkin. "Rasmutin is not someone you want to fuck with."

Durkin sloughed-off the warning. He had banged heads with men a lot tougher than Rasmutin.

"His full name is Karl Igor Rasmutin. His nicknames are Igor the Terrible and Rasputin because he's ruthless and just plain nasty. A trooper claims that when Rasmutin was a kid he buried cats in the ground up to their necks and ran over their heads with lawn mowers for fun."

Every face filled with disgust. "He's not married. His life is the troopers and he'll do anything to get to the top. My gut tells me he'd like to roast you alive."

"I don't see myself getting roasted alive," Durkin said as if he believed Rome was being overly dramatic.

Rome wasn't having it. "Maybe not, but you've got injuries they can claim are consistent with killing a woman with a rock."

"Rasmutin can say anything but that bullshit would never hold up in court."

Durkin pointed to his face. "My injuries were inflicted by the troopers. That's on the record."

"They could dispute that."

Durkin looked unconvinced.

"They're likely to point out that your injuries were sustained at the same time as the murder. You know, the case *In the Matter of Abe A.*"

Abe A.

Durkin shook his head. *Abe A* was not remotely on-point.

Abe A was bludgeoned to death in his apartment. Everything indicated he died a violent death. His face and body were brutalized. His windpipe was crushed. Blood was splattered on the walls and pooled on the floor. When the police arrived, a detective noticed a man standing nearby had cuts on his hands and face and his face swelled from recent injuries. It was obvious to the detective that the man's injuries were consistent with the injuries from a violent struggle. Based on his injuries alone, the detective arrested the man at the scene.

New York's highest court ruled that it was reasonable for a cop to arrest the suspect based on the cuts on his body in the proximity of the victim.

"This isn't close to be an *Abe A* case," Durkin groused impatiently like a law professor who had no time for a student who didn't do his homework. "The troopers inflicted my injuries."

Rome sighed. Tell it to the court. "Listen, there's a rumor they're working overtime to find your DNA on the victim's body."

"That makes no sense," Durkin barked.

Rome waved his fingers. Have it your way. "Let's hope you're right. But most people have a hard time believing that someone's DNA could be where they weren't. You know what I mean?"

"These are the facts," Durkin continued, sounding as if he was arguing to a skeptical jury. "After the trooper manhandled me, he went back down to the body. He had his arms and hands all over me. My DNA could have been on him."

"What are you saying?" PJ asked. "There was secondary transfer of your DNA?"

Durkin fixed his eyes on PJ. "That's the only way my DNA could be found on her."

The four men sank into subdued thought. They all knew that at the time DNA identification was discovered by an English scientist in 1988, the labs needed blood, semen or dried saliva to conduct a DNA test.

A decade later, Roland van Oorschot, an Australian forensic scientist, proved that DNA codes could be detected from as little as a microscopic touch; from as little as 16 cells of a human. An invisible fingerprint left on a doorknob, a table, a staircase left a sufficient amount of a genetic code to identify a person.

Now investigators only needed a fingerprint to run a DNA test.

But Oorschot also discovered that touch DNA could be easily swept up and transferred. Some people's DNA appeared on things that they had never touched; a phenomenon known as secondary transfer. Trace DNA.

"There's that case in California," Rome added.

Durkin nodded. That case in California. He gestured for Rome to share the facts with PJ and DeMartin.

"A house was invaded in Southern California. The attackers bound a husband and wife with duck tape and tortured them. The husband died of suffocation. The cops got a lucky break when they found DNA on the husband's body. The killers were identified by the DNA found at the crime scene and charged with murder."

"There was only one problem," Durkin chimed in. "One of the suspects identified by their DNA was in the hospital at the time of the murder. There was no explanation how his DNA was found in a house he never visited."

Rome took over. "It was the paramedic. You see, the paramedic attended to the suspect's wounds earlier in the night. Three hours later he rushed to the scene of the murder. He checked the victim's vital signs. He tried administering CPR. He touched him everywhere."

"You're saying the paramedic had another guy's DNA on him when he tried to save the victim?"

"Exactly," Durkin said. "The paramedic was the DNA mule, spreading DNA like a road crew spreads sand over an icy road. When he touched the victim's body, he spread the suspect's DNA onto him. It's a classic secondary DNA transfer."

"There was an experiment," Rome continued. "Six men sat around a table with a pitcher of beer. One guy poured the beer and shared the glasses. After 20 minutes, the chairs, the glasses, the pitcher were swabbed for DNA. Four of the men had another guy's DNA on their hands. Two of the glasses had traces of DNA of a person who never even touched the glasses. All secondary DNA transfers."

All the men wore uneasy looks. Okay, secondary transfer happens but it's hard to prove. And even harder to get a jury to believe.

Rome rolled his lips inward and turned serious. "Sorry to be a buzzkill but no one is going to believe your DNA was transported to the murder scene."

Rome squared his shoulders to Durkin as if positioning himself to deliver an important message. "In a couple of hours, the troopers are going to serve a search warrant to compel you to give a buccal swab."

A buccal swab, pronounced, 'buckle', was a swab of the inside of a person's cheek.

"Bullshit," Durkin blurted, thinking of his stand-off with Rasmutin and McClusky. "The cops need to establish probable cause that I committed the crime in order to get a swab."

Rome shook his head as if chastising Durkin for being naive. "They have a body. They have you at the scene. They may have your DNA on the body. Up here, that's more than enough for probable cause."

Durkin gritted his teeth. "I'll quash the warrant."

Rome ignored Durkin's outburst. "If the troopers show up with the search warrant, you're still going to have to give them the swab. If you're going to quash the warrant, you need to do it before they knock on your door."

DeMartin sighed loudly as if something was troubling him. He turned to Durkin. "Can I ask a stupid question?" He didn't wait for Durkin's answer. "Why do you care if the troopers have your DNA?"

Durkin stared disbelievingly at DeMartin as if DeMartin failed to grasp a simple concept.

"I mean you can't run from the troopers forever," DeMartin continued. "And DNA can exonerate you."

Durkin's eyes slowly rose and fixed on DeMartin's. Their eyes conveyed they shared the same unsettling memory.

Michael Brown.

Michael Brown was the eighteen year old killed in Ferguson, Missouri by a police officer. A white police officer. The killing set off protests, riots and mayhem. Ferguson burned. The National Guard was sent in. The St. Louis airport was closed due to gun fire lighting up the sky.

Durkin squirmed with embarrassment. He had never spoken about Michael Brown with DeMartin but he knew a year ago DeMartin had overheard him and Assistant State's Attorney Alex Phillips discussing the grand jury's report on the shooting. Durkin didn't mince words. He had cast his prosecutor's eye over every page of the grand jury transcript and as far as he was concerned the jury's finding was cut and dry.

Brown's DNA was found on Wilson's gun. Brown's DNA was found on the interior of Wilson's car, Wilson's shirt collar and pants. The DNA analysis backed up the officer's account that Michael Brown attempted to take his gun in a violent attack.

But the Michael Brown case was still a third rail for law enforcement. In the confines of their offices, white cops and prosecutors could freely discuss the case and how the DOJ's vilification of Darren Wilson and the Ferguson police department led to cops to stand back and not pursue the criminals. They'd discuss how the "Ferguson Effect" led to rise in violent crimes and murders. But the topic never came up among mixed races. No, it was too hot. Too emotional. Too charged.

And Durkin and DeMartin weren't going to touch the third rail in the Boldt Castle Yacht House.

"This guy is a bastard," Durkin answered DeMartin, sweeping away his lingering embarrassment of being overheard as he shared his views on the Michael Brown case. "He's poking me and I'm poking him back."

The men quieted as Durkin's words settled in. The legendary prosecutor was sounding slightly unhinged. The battle had become intensely personal and he wasn't acting rational.

"But I'll need some time to get the court papers drafted," Durkin said as he thought of the logistical hurdles involved in drafting them.

"Then let's buy ourselves some time," Rome said, sounding like the kid who always enjoyed a good fight.

"And how do we do that?" PJ asked.

Durkin's eyes danced around the yacht house. His eyes brightened as the answer came to him. He dug his hand into his pocket and pulled out a business card. Kyle Johnston, Fishing Guide.

"Hold on." Durkin stepped away and made a call. Johnston answered on the first ring.

"Kyle, this is Francis Durkin." He rolled his eyes as he listened to Kyle tell a story. "Hey, I don't have much time. Can you take me to that island you mentioned yesterday."

Pause. "Yes, Grindstone." Pause. "No. Can you pick me up at the Boldt Castle Yacht House."

Long pause. Everyone could hear Kyle's mental gears moving, oiled by suspicion. "It's just more convenient," Durkin lied. "I'm here now. Thanks. I'll be waiting on the dock."

Durkin stuck his cell phone in his pocket. "You guys go back to the cottage. I'll hang in here until Kyle picks me up. Let me know if we have any visitors."

*****

Less than a half an hour later, Kyle tied up his Grady White to the yacht house dock wearing a green t-shirt with 'Little Galloo Island Shoot-out' on its front.

"Francis" he yelled out like he was greeting a lifelong friend.

As Durkin boarded the boat, Kyle handed him a tube of sunscreen and immediately began backing the boat away from the dock. "You need to put on sunscreen," Kyle said as he planted a pair of sunglasses on his face. "That trooper yesterday was a prick but he was right. Your pasty skin will get burned up on the river."

Kyle quickly left the yacht house behind as Durkin dabbed on sunscreen.

"Why are you running from those troopers?" Kyle asked as he fed the engines fuel.

Durkin adjusted his sunglasses, trying to mask his surprise as he formulated his reply. "I'm not running from anyone. I just have some time on my hands."

Kyle's face curled up. He wasn't buying it. Durkin scanned the horizon and looked desperate to change the subject. He pointed to Kyle's tee-shirt. "What's Little Galloo Island Shootout?"

Kyle's face perked up. "Let me show you something," he said, turning the boat's steering wheel sharply and increasing their speed. "This will only take a minute."

Kyle navigated through a maze of islands and then Kyle abruptly slowed the engine, causing the Grady White to sink into the river and float to a stop.

"Is this Little Galloo Island?"

112

"Nope. We call that Alfred Hitchcock Island," Kyle said, pointing a barren rock island teeming with large black birds. The trees protruding from the rocks looked like skeletons serving as resting posts for hundreds of the black birds.

"What type of birds are they?"

Kyle's face turned dark. "Those damn birds are called cormorants," he said, looking as if he used a dirty word. "I call them the Devil's birds," he added. Kyle shook his head in disgust. "Look at those trees."

Durkin spied the bare, petrified trees holding hundreds of cormorants.

"Their droppings are highly acidic. They shit like hell and it kills everything."

Kyle motioned to the island like he wished he could blow it up. He spun the steering wheel and fed gas to the engine. He had seen enough.

"So I take it that the Little Galloo Shoot-Out had to do with shooting cormorants."

Kyle shook his head as if he was trying to dislodge a fly on his head. "I'd prefer to say it was about fishermen taking action to protect their livelihoods."

Durkin turned and eyed Alfred Hitchcock Island that was rapidly growing smaller and smaller as Kyle sped away from it.

"How many cormorants were killed?"

Kyle shrugged. "I don't think anyone knows. The feds claimed over 700."

Durkin's eyebrows pulled up as he envisioned 700 mangled cormorant carcasses littering the island.

"How were you involved?"

"I didn't shoot one damn bird but I was dragged into court."

Durkin looked for an explanation.

"Friends of mine shot some birds to protect the fish. They asked me to hold their rifles and I did what any friend would do. I hid them in my barn."

Kyle shook his head from side to side as if commenting on the injustices heaped on him.

"Let me guess," Durkin said, "You were tried for conspiracy after the fact for hiding the weapons."

"Yup, but everyone knew I didn't do anything. At my sentencing the judge even said it was difficult for him to determine who was guilty." Kyle smiled brightly as if remembering a pleasant moment. "My attorney was quick on his feet. He told the judge in that case it's better to let a guilty man go free than to convict an innocent man."

Durkin laughed. "That's what Blackstone said."

"That's exactly what the judge said though I never knew what he meant."

"Blackstone was a British legal theorist. Since American law is based on British law, he had a big impact on American law. He's credited with saying that it's better that ten guilty men escape than one innocent suffer."

Kyle flashed Durkin a look that he wanted to hear more.

Durkin paused as he thought about the moral mathematics of the innocent-guilty tradeoff. He wasn't sure he could stomach watching ten guilty men walk to save one man. "An ancient wise man named Maimonides argued that a 1000 guilty men should be freed rather than execute a single innocent man."

"That seems extreme. You agree with that?"

"Nope."

"What's your position?"

Durkin hadn't formed a satisfactory position but he felt his position shifting over the past few days. "I don't think you can put a firm number on it. I just think it's far worse to convict an innocent man than to let a guilty man go free."

Kyle looked disappointed they were nearing their destination before they finished their discussion. "That's the tip of Grindstone," Kyle said, pointing to a long dock lined with cabin cruisers and yachts as if giving Durkin a point to orient himself. "And that's Jolly Island over there," he said pointing to a small island off Grindstone.

Kyle motored up to the dock. Kyle fastened the ropes to the dock and gestured for Durkin to head up the path. "Walk down the dirt road. There's only one road from the dock. Cassie will meet you in about five minutes."

"Cassie?"

"She's my cousin. Salt of the earth. She'll take care of you."

"I thought you were giving me the tour."

"I'm a river guy. If you want to go fishing or anything on the river, I'm your man. Cassie knows Grindstone. She'll take good care of you."

"Okay," Durkin said with a shrug as he pushed himself off the boat and onto the dock. He watched Kyle gun the engine and speed-off without looking back.

Durkin set off down the road with the sensation of a fugitive on the run. Maybe it was the remoteness of the island that immediately engulfed him. Maybe it was the feeling that he had just stepped into another world, far from the craziness of the past few days. Maybe it was because he couldn't shake the thought of Rasmutin's dead eye.

The single lane, dirt road was cut through twisted pine trees, surrounded by high grass that was only tamped down by the occasional ATV's that rolled over the road. As he began to wonder if Kyle played a joke on him and just dropped him off on the island, he heard the rumble of an engine and the distinct sound of large, rubber tires churning over a dirt road and tall grass. The sounds grew louder and a few seconds later, a plume of dust revealed a four wheel, all terrain vehicle heading towards him.

The ATV slowed and rolled towards him before it skidded to a full stop, shooting up a cloud of dust. When the cloud dissipated, he saw it was driven by a woman who bore a faint resemblance to Kyle. She was makeup free, wore ripped jeans, work boots and a cut-off tee shirt. She had an organic sort of look Durkin found unusually attractive. Her hair was a natural salt and pepper mix with enough pepper to avoid the washed out look of gray hair. At closer inspection, Durkin guessed she was in her mid-to-late 40's.

"Can I hitch a ride?" Durkin asked with a smile as the driver straightened up and released the throttle. She smiled back like she was glad to see an old friend.

"You must be Francis."

"And you must be Cassie."

"That's me," she said, extending her hand confidently and smiling as they shook hands.

Durkin's ears detected a voice that was soft but sure of itself. His hands touched tough but tender skin. She smelled alive and natural.

"If you don't mind me asking, how'd you get those cuts on your face?"

Durkin had temporarily forgotten that bandaids covered half his face. "Oh," he said, gently tapping the largest bandaid. "A trooper used me as a piñata."

"It looks like they hurt."

"It's not too bad. My friends say I'm better looking with the bandaids."

Cassie chuckled. "Hop on."

Durkin looked at the seat. "I also injured my leg," he said with a twinge of embarrassment as he eyed the height of the seat.

"No worries," Cassie said understandingly. She hopped off the ATV and pointed to the steel bar designed for passenger's feet. "Put your left foot on that, and I'll help you up."

As he placed his foot on the bar, Cassie gently ushered Durkin's sore leg slowly over the seat. Her hands were strong and she moved with the confident, self-reliance of a woman who grew up surrounded by wind, waves and ice.

Durkin tried to mask his discomfort but despite his best efforts, a groan slipped through his lips as Cassie pushed his leg over the seat.

"You okay?"

"Absolutely," Durkin lied, unable to ignore the stabbing pain in his leg and ribs. "I'm good."

Cassie hopped back on the ATV. "Hold my waist."

Cassie rolled the throttle, churning up dirt and rocking Durkin off balance. He grabbed Cassie's waist as if he was holding on for his life. As he held on to her, he couldn't remember the last time he held a woman so close to him.

"Kyle said you wanted a tour of Grindstone. I'll give you a tour and then I'll take you back to Jolly Island where I stay." Cassie shouted over her shoulder. "It's only a few minutes ride. I take it that this is your first visit to Grindstone."

Durkin leaned into her back and shouted over the ATV's roar. "Yep. Are you a native?"

"Nope I'm not a Grinder. But I spent some of my summers here." Cassie slowed and stopped at a small, wooden building. "That's where my cousins went to school."

The small building resembled a modest house that had been expanded over the years. Durkin eyed the single story, wooden building that had all the marks of being shuttered for at least a decade.

"They had 12 students from first grade to eighth grade." Cassie pointed to the rear of the building. "The teacher lived in the back."

Cassie slid up and craned her neck to look back at Durkin. "When the quarry was running there used to be two schools on the island. But it got to be too small so they had to close it. It was the last one-room schoolhouse in New York State."

Durkin smiled with appreciation at Cassie's nostalgia for the island. "That's very cool. It sounds like you wished it never changed."

"Tempora Mutantur nos et mutamur in illis. Times change and we change with them," Cassie laughed before rolling the throttle open and racing down the dirt path. She assumed the role of a tour guide and commented on everything they passed. A Methodist Church, the general store that was converted to a multi-purpose hall that hosted dances, weddings, town meetings. She pointed to houses where her cousins lived. It was clear Cassie knew everyone on the island even though she only spent her summers there.

After driving for about a mile, she pulled into a winding road that cut under a canopy of hemlocks, spruce, cedar and pine trees that led to a dock. She pulled up to the dock and killed the engine. She motioned to a jet ski and the island across the way. "That's where I spend my summers. It's called Jolly Island."

Durkin smiled as he followed Cassie to the jet ski which she used to quickly whisk them across the sliver of river that separated the islands.

"Welcome, to my humble abode," she said with a glint in her eye after jumping off the jet ski. "I understand you'll be staying for the afternoon."

Durkin was unsure of how to respond. He certainly wanted to. He was captivated by the intriguing woman who drove an ATV, jet-skied and quoted Latin phrases. "I hope I'm not intruding."

"Not at all. It's nice to have a visitor. Stay as long as you want," Cassie replied as if she was genuinely enjoying his company. She then paused and stared at his bandages. "You need to make sure those cuts don't get infected," Cassie said as she leaned towards Durkin. "You got road dust in them."

Cassie then stepped back and seemed less than impressed by his bandages. "Who put those bandages on?" Cassie's tone made it clear that she didn't think an adult did it.

"I was in a rush," Durkin said with a flush of embarrassment.

"Come with me," Cassie said, taking Durkin by his wrist and pulling him into the house.

"Sit there," she ordered, pointing to a chair overlooking the river. She disappeared and in a few seconds returned with a brown-colored bottle and a box of bandaids. "This isn't going to feel great but it's better than having puss ooze out of your face."

Durkin chuckled as Cassie peeled the bandages off his face as he steeled himself not to react to the sting.

"Now hold still," Cassie said, dipping a swab into the bottle and wiping it onto an open cut.

"Ah!" Durkin hissed through gritted teeth as the iodine felt like acid burning through his face.

"Sorry but 'no pain, no gain.'" She gently dabbed another blotch of iodine on his wounds. "So what do you do for a living?"

Durkin groaned. "I'm a prosecutor."

Cassie stepped back and looked surprised that a prosecutor didn't have horns. "How long have you been doing that?"

"All my life."

"You must like it."

Durkin never examined his life's choice. He never wondered how his life would've turned out had he taken another path. Not once. Not even in a moment of idle daydreams. But now, sitting next to Cassie, he wondered if the other paths would have also left him single, without companionship.

"It keeps me focused," Durkin said smiling as he thought of his career that soaked up all of his waking moments for the past three decades.

Cassie meticulously pasted the fresh bandaids on Durkin's face. Once she was satisfied with her work, she said, "take a seat near the river, while I fix lunch."

Durkin's hunger was stirring so he welcomed the offer. "That would be great. What can I do to help?"

"Nothing. Now, get out of my way," Cassie joked, shooing him outdoors.

A short while later, Cassie carried out a tray of sandwiches and beers. "You look like a beer guy," she said with a smile. Durkin turned and saw that she had washed up and changed into a billowing blouse and shorts. Her long, muscular legs drew his attention. He was suddenly acutely aware he was alone on an island with an intriguing and great-looking woman.

"You look, er, comfortable," he said awkwardly.

Cassie set the tray down on a table between two chairs and plopped in the other chair. She twisted the cap off her beer bottle and held it up in the air to toast. "Here's to meeting you."

"Back at you," Durkin said with a slightly flirtatious ring. "I love your place." They clinked their beer bottles and their eyes met before quickly breaking off.

"It's not really mine. My family owns it but I'm the only one who uses it."

Durkin reddened as he suddenly was overcome with attraction for Cassie. It hit him with the same force as his revulsion for Rasmutin slammed him. What was going on? What was causing him to experience the waves of extreme revulsion and extreme attraction?

He sipped his beer and wondered if his interest in her was obvious. She was extremely friendly. Was it mutual? Maybe he had been out of circulation for so long he was unable to read a woman's signals.

"Sounds like you have the best of both worlds," he said clumsily, trying to mask his sudden awkwardness. "You get to live here and don't have to pay for it all."

"It is unless you want to change or remodel anything. Then it's a pain in the ass. There's five of us and there's at least six different opinions on every subject." Cassie laughed and took a small bite of her sandwich. She quickly chewed and swallowed.

118

Cassie pointed to an island straight across the river and looked as if she wanted to share a secret. "If I had all the money in the world, I'd never build a castle on the St. Lawrence River."

Durkin happily played along. "Okay, why not?"

"If you do, you're cursed."

"You believe in curses?"

"This one I do. The Thousand Islands are meant to be real. Ostentatious places are cursed."

Durkin took a swig of beer as his eyes twinkled with skepticism.

"No, it's true," Cassie insisted with a hint of amusement. "The grand hotels were also cursed. The T.I. Park Hotel burned down in 1890. The Columbian, built on the same ground, was even bigger. It had 200 rooms and it burned down in 1912. The Pullman Hotel across the way from T.I. Park burned down in 1904. They were all cursed."

"Or someone was collecting insurance money," Durkin replied with a chuckle.

Cassie laughed. "Maybe that too." She finished her beer and turned to Durkin with an apologetic air. "I have something to confess."

"I guess we all do," he said teasingly.

"No, I really do. Before you arrived, I looked you up. A little while ago I was pretending I didn't know anything about you but I did. I read up about your courtroom successes and then pretended like I didn't know anything about you. I'm a fraud."

"I'm just as much a fraud as you are," Durkin countered quickly. "I've been sitting here and not telling you how attractive I think you are."

Durkin's face exploded with shock as if the words just slipped out of his mouth. "I'm sorry if I sound too bold."

Cassie's face reddened. "No apologies needed. Everyone appreciates a compliment."

Durkin felt his face redden and his body pulse with desire. His head got light from the exhilaration of even thinking of being with her. "I hope I'm not coming off like a weirdo."

"No, you don't sound like a weirdo at all. You seem really nice."

As the two sat like awkward teenagers, they were interrupted by the ring of Cassie's phone. Cassie spied the name of the caller and answered. "Yep." She listened for a minute and then said, "I'll tell him." She stuck her cell phone back in her pocket. "Kyle will be here to pick you up in 10 minutes."

Ten minutes? Disappointment washed over Durkin's face.

"Kyle said to tell you, your friends told him that no one is going to visit your cottage on T.I. Park, whatever that means."

Durkin knew exactly what it meant. For some reason, the troopers weren't going to serve a warrant to force him to provide a swab of the inside of his cheek. He wondered what Rasmutin was up to and then turned his attention back to Cassie.

"I'm going to be at T.I. Park for a few weeks. I hope I can see you again."

"I'd like that. When?"

Durkin brightened. "How about tonight?"

A soft laugh escaped from Cassie. "That works, sure."

"Two cops I used to work with are staying with me but you'll enjoy their company. I think one of their girlfriends may be coming. We're just going to hang out and have beers and then throw something on the grill."

Before Cassie could respond, Kyle's Grady White appeared at her dock. He waved furiously like he was in a rush.

"You want to come back with us?"

Cassie's face looked as if she was wrestling with logistical complications as the wind picked up on the river. "I need about an hour. I'll jet-ski over."

"Great." Durkin felt the urge to kiss Cassie but he was keenly aware he was under the watchful eyes of Kyle. He stepped back and waved. "See you soon."

"Yep. See you soon." Cassie grinned like a smitten teenager.

*****

"Howdy," Kyle greeted Durkin as he stepped gingerly into Kyle's boat.

"How'd you like Grindstone and Jolly Island?" Kyle yelled over the roar of the wind.

"I really liked them. Beautiful," Durkin answered, thinking more of Cassie than Grindstone or Jolly Island. Kyle's face exploded in appreciation as if Durkin's compliments were directed towards him.

"How'd you like Cassie?" Kyle asked loudly, keeping his eyes pasted on the water ahead.

"She's a very nice lady."

"That she is. That she is," Kyle replied with a mischievous ring.

"Can you ride a jet-ski with this wind?"

Kyle motioned to the river, spurting with gusts of white. "This is nothing." Kyle increased their speed. "Cassie won't have a problem on a jet-ski," he said with a sly smirk.

A grin snuck out of the edges of Durkin's lips. The old cadger had an investigator's nose.

A few minutes later, Durkin spied PJ and DeMartin standing on the dock. Their rigid body language signaled they were filled with tension. Kyle piloted his boat gently against the dock and Durkin crawled out of the boat with the stiffness of a man who had just lost a fist fight.

"Thanks," Durkin said to Kyle as he sat, resting. Kyle's eyes widened as if his radar was on full-alert. He sniffed as if he detected adventure in the air and his expression changed to longing to participate in whatever was brewing.

"You want me to stick around? I'm happy to help out with anything you need."

Durkin pushed himself up and searched for a way to lessen the sting of his dismissal. Durkin reached in his wallet and pulled out a 100 dollar bill. "Thanks, I really appreciate the tour. I'll give you a call soon."

Kyle grudgingly accepted the money, still searching for a way to stay. Finding none, he said, "Okay. You gents have a good day."

The three men stood stiffly on the dock until Kyle put 50 yards between them.

"We had visitors," DeMartin said, breaking the silence.

Durkin drew a long breath as irritation leaked into his face. "Troopers?"

"Nope. Customs and Border Protection," PJ answered.

Durkin's face crunched up. "CBP?"

"Yup. They said it was just a random search."

The men stood in silence for a few seconds, knowing there was nothing random about a visit by the Customs and Border Protection.

"Random my ass," Durkin said, barely suppressing the growling anger brewing inside him.

"They knew exactly what they were looking for," DeMartin said. "They went directly to the boathouse."

The boathouse? Durkin's face crinkled as he stared at the boathouse. His face remained frozen for a long moment. Finally, his eyes widened and face dropped back in place. "Son of a bitch," he hissed, realizing what the CBP had come for.

Durkin replayed the mental scene of him peeling off the polo shirt he wore while riding the bicycle. He saw himself scooping up the shirt on the dock and him limping into the boathouse. He envisioned tossing the shirt on the rusty nail just inside the doorway. He hadn't given it a second thought until this moment.

"They came with all their cavalry," PJ said. "The boat had four, three-hundred horsepower engines. It was a floating rocket ship. They had three gun mounts for heavy firepower too. It was a pretty impressive show of force."

Like a dog with its hair standing up on its back, Durkin bristled at the description of the boat. For a long second, the men stood in silence.

"Pretty damn impressive," Durkin said sarcastically. "But not half as impressive as what I'll do to them in court." He cast his eyes out on the river and his thoughts turned to the Customs and Border Protection.

Formed in 1924, the then-sleepy agency originally focused on combatting smuggling through the porous Canadian border. It soon shifted its focus to the Mexican border and kept growing until its reach covered 7000 miles of border, 95,000 miles of shoreline and 328 ports of entry.

Then came 9/11.

Overnight, the CBP was tasked with defending America's borders from terrorists. New missions required new skills and an influx of unprecedented manpower. The CBP's personnel exploded to 60,000 agents, dwarfing the FBI's 19,000 and the DEA's 5000 agents. But the CBP's hiring frenzy put a premium on quantity over quality. The CBP skimped on background checks and training. Gang members, drug dealers and ex-convicts swelled its ranks and over 20 percent of border patrol agents had what were charitably known as "verifiable integrity problems."

"So they just landed and raided the boathouse?" Durkin asked as his eyes traced the path the agents took from the dock over to the boathouse.

"Pretty much," DeMartin answered. "The lead agent was a muscle-head with a buzz cut. You would've loved him."

Durkin forced a chuckle.

"He asked for the owner and we told him you'd be back shortly, hoping that would stall them." DeMartin paused. "It didn't. They played tough asses and ordered us to step back and not to interfere with the search. They went right to the boathouse and came out with your shirt like they knew it was there."

Durkin winced as he thought of his ripped shirt with his blood and DNA in the hands of the troopers. Rasmutin won round one, he said to himself. But it wasn't over. He'd get his punches in, he promised himself.

PJ exhaled like a punctured tire. "I tried to throw a wrench in their plans by telling them they needed a warrant." He drew a long breath. "They didn't go for it."

Of course they didn't, Durkin thought. He knew why.

The border exception.

The Supreme Court created an exception to the Fourth Amendment's prohibition against unreasonable search and seizures. The exception covers the border of the United States and grants federal agents wide latitude to stop and examine persons and property crossing into this country or near a border without any reasonable suspicion, probable cause, or warrant.

The border exception zone encompasses nearly two-thirds of the population of the United States, including cities such as New York, Seattle, Houston, Chicago, New Orleans, and Los Angeles, and entire states such as Maine, Florida, and Delaware.

The border exception allowed CBP agents to enter private property without a warrant within 25 miles of any border. In this zone, CBP is bestowed with extra-constitutional powers. Durkin looked across the river. They were no more than four miles from Canada.

"The lead agent was a cocky bastard," DeMartin offered. He pointed to the boathouse. "PJ told him that someone was using that the boathouse to live in."

PJ smiled. "It was a worth a try. You know, I said a man's home is his castle. He blew me off."

"But you got his attention when you pulled out that business card," DeMartin added.

A shadow of satisfaction crested over PJ's face. He pulled out an inch thick wallet bulging with business cards. He opened it and pulled out a battered CBP business card.

"I go pretty far back with the head of CBP's SWAT team. I told the agent I'm good friends with the guy and it's best to quit while he was ahead."

Durkin and DeMartin stared with amazement at PJ McLevy. How the hell was he on first name basis with the head of CBP's SWAT team?

"The CBP's Special Operations Group has snipers, hostage negotiation experts and SWAT teams with all the bells and whistles. I guessed that some of the agents dream of joining the elite team and having me call the leader and complain about them wouldn't help their chances."

Durkin scanned the horizon as if he was searching for troopers. "How do you think they knew where I put my shirt?"

PJ pointed to the sky. Durkin understood. CBP operates some of the most sophisticated reconnaissance drones in the world. Durkin gritted his teeth knowing that he wouldn't have a chance challenging the legality of the drones in court. The courts ruled that what a bird could see, a cop could see.

Durkin searched the sky as if every bird was a menacing drone. He peeled his eyes from the clouds and his face turned serious. The troopers were playing with fire. They couldn't piggyback on the border exception by outsourcing their investigations to the CBP. And he was sure that's what happened. And he was equally sure that he'd blow them up in federal court.

"They're playing hardball and we've got to swing back."

New York State Police Crime Laboratory
Biosciences Division
Albany, New York

No one seemed to notice the New York State Police's helicopter hovering in the sky like a kite, a 100 feet from the crime lab. Two troopers arrived in patrol cars, flipped on their emergency lights and blocked off the side road. When they secured the area, the pilot gave them a thumbs up sign before expertly guiding the copter to the ground.

Still no one gave a second thought to the swirl of wind or the screeching whir of the copter's blades that parted the grass and scattered leaves like a giant leaf blower. The lab was built next to the troopers' training academy and helicopters came and went all day, every day.

When the helicopter landed, a trooper, with mirrored glasses, gripping the side of his Stetson with one hand and carrying a black hard case in the other, hopped out. He crab walked until he was sure he was out of the blades' danger zone. Then he placed the case on the ground and kept his left hand on the brim of his hat as he shook hands with the other troopers. They exchanged a few pleasantries before the trooper picked up the case and hustled towards the entrance to the crime lab.

Still no one took any notice. There was nothing out of the ordinary. To a passerby, it was routine trooper business.

But it wasn't routine. It wasn't routine for Commander Igor Rasmutin to carry a hard case into the crime lab like he was carrying the nation's nuclear codes.

Two minutes later, Rasmutin sat in the crime lab's first floor conference room. The room was gray and besides the four government-issued chairs and small conference table, it was sterile. No white board, no mass produced artwork, no mirror.

Rasmutin looked to the door when he heard a slight, almost timid tap.

"Come in," he said with a twist of his face as if he disapproved at the feminine sounding knock. If you are going to knock, knock. He wiped his face clean of annoyance as Dante Russo opened the door and looked for permission to enter. Rasmutin waved him in and swung the hard case on the conference table. He extended his hand to Russo who was momentarily startled by seeing his reflection in Rasmutin's mirrored glasses. "Thanks for coming. This will only take a minute or so," he said as he shook Russo's hand firmly and motioned for him to take a seat.

"First, I want to stress that none of this is *sub rosa*," Rasmutin began.

Russo blinked trying to conceal the fact that he hadn't a clue what *sub rosa* meant.

"Director Chilletti is fully aware you and I are meeting here."

Russo nodded. Now he understood. The meeting wasn't a secret.

Rasmutin smiled under his mirrored glasses. "This is the sort of cooperation and teamwork that's been sorely lacking in the crime lab."

Russo smiled back, letting Rasmutin know his words were having their intended effect. "And I assure you this is not going to go unnoticed."

Not go unnoticed. It will be noticed. Recognition. Awards. Plaques. Photo and an article in the NYSP crime lab newsletter. Russo brightened as ego-satisfying endorphins pumped through his veins.

Rasmutin opened the hard case and pulled out a clear plastic bag that contained a green polo shirt wrapped in a smaller plastic bag. Russo stared at the bag that was sealed with official tape bearing bar codes that tracked the chain of custody from the Customs and Border Protection to Troop D's Alexandria Bay station and now to the NYSP's crime lab. But nothing in the chain of custody mentioned Commander Rasmutin.

"This is off the record, okay?" Rasmutin began. Russo's rapid head movement indicated that he agreed that whatever was said inside the plain, gray room, would stay there.

"This is the shirt that our prime suspect wore at the crime scene." Rasmutin sneered at the plastic bag. "I asked the guy if he would leave the shirt as part of our investigation. He started spouting off about his constitutional rights. What's that tell you, huh?"

Russo's face flexed in agreement. Only a guilty asshole spouts off about constitutional rights.

Rasmutin leaned towards Russo as if he was confiding a secret to a close friend. "The guy was a ball buster who claimed he was riding a bicycle at 4 a.m. in the middle of nowhere. Total bullshit." Rasmutin shook his head and his lips curled up with distaste. "A young, beautiful woman was brutally murdered. He…" Rasmutin stopped and acted as if he was reluctantly respecting the presumption of innocence. "Her head was crushed by rocks. Only a large man could inflict that kind of damage."

"Again," Rasmutin said, karate chopping the air. "This is strictly confidential and off the record, right?"

"Of course," Russo gushed. Rasmutin could trust him.

"Good, then since this stays between us," Rasmutin said, pulling a photo from his breast pocket. He handed it to Russo who accepted it with slightly trembling fingers.

"Oh, God," Russo gasped as his eyes took in the close-up of the victim's crushed skull. The blood, mud and fractured skull bones reflected the barbarity of the attack. He handed Russo another photo. Russo grimaced at the photo of the woman's nose bone torn from her face.

"My God, that's horrible."

"Only a monster could've done this," Rasmutin said as he snatched the photos back from Russo.

"Absolutely," Russo replied, shooting a hate-filled look at the evidence bag.

"I'm just sharing this with you because I was at the crime scene and I saw her crushed skull, up front and personal." Rasmutin sucked in a long stream of air as if his insides needed to be air-cooled. "You know, no matter how many years you do this, it doesn't get any easier."

Russo exhaled audibly in solidarity with Rasmutin. He felt the commander's pain. He then blinked and a sheen of confusion spread over his face as if he was suddenly confused about the purpose of the meeting. As if answering his unspoken question, Rasmutin tapped the evidence bag. "So can you expedite the test so we can nail this sick bastard?"

Rasmutin sounded as if running a DNA test was as simple as administering a pregnancy test bought at a pharmacy.

Russo looked inward, revealing he was having trouble formulating a response that would meet Rasmutin's approval.

"Listen, Director Chilletti has approved fast-tracking this," Rasmutin said, pointing back at the evidence bag as if he was annoyed the testing wasn't already underway. "But I'm a hands-on guy and wanted to speak directly with the guys in the trenches. I want to know I can count on you."

Russo deliberated whether he should share Chilletti's directive that another forensic scientist had to participate in all the tests the crime lab ran on the Wellesley Island murder and that forensic scientist would be Danielle

Keegan, a royal pain in the ass, who'd definitely slow down the tests by insisting they go by the book.

Suddenly, Russo beamed: he discovered the loophole in Cotton's directive. When he complained to Cotton that there'd be delays if he had to wait on Keegan, Cotton cackled. Russo could still hear the grating laughter coming from Cotton's mouth. Russo knew why she laughed. She couldn't fathom that Keegan, the indefatigable work horse, would slow down the plodding, dull-witted Russo. Cotton told him that he could do the tests anytime he wanted. Keegan would be there. The message was that Keegan works around the clock and, if anything, the tests would be slowed down by Russo's 9 to 3 schedule.

Russo's eyes darted to the wall clock. Keegan would be gone in a few hours. A smug look sprouted on Russo's face. "You can count on me."

*****

An uneasy sensation gnawed at Danielle Keegan all night. She tossed and turned and drifted in and out of sleep. After briefly dozing, she lay, wide-eyed, in bed trying to piece together the remnants of her dream. In her mind's eye, she saw herself running. She didn't know where she was or why she was running. But the wind was blowing. Keegan also recalled a mechanical throbbing noise. The other details of her dream were foggy, unretrievable. She shut her eyes and searched for what was fueling her strange dream.

Keegan flicked on her bedside lamp, making sure she didn't disturb Cajillion who slept, balled-up next to her. The light spilled over her bedroom which was decorated like a 13 year old girl's. Sparkly stars dangled from her ceiling. Spindly wooden chairs overflowed with stuffed animals; unicorns with oversized horns and rabbits with floppy ears and pink, girly nick-nacks cluttered the top of her dresser. Keegan didn't care if anyone thought it was weird for a 29 year old to fill her bedroom with stuffed animals and ceramic elephants. Screw them, she liked them. They made her laugh.

Unable to sleep, Keegan rose at 4 a.m., showered, dressed and drove through the all-night Dunkin Donuts drive-thru. She laughed to herself as she paid for her coffee and two jelly donuts. Drinking coffee was probably the most adult thing she did, she thought as she took her first sip and nibbled on her donut.

Ten minutes later she waved her ID pass over the black square next to the crime lab's front door. The automatic door swung open and she strode into the lobby. It was deserted except for a sleepy security guard behind the front desk.

128

His head rose and his red eyes gave the impression that his brain was too tired or too fried to acknowledge her arrival.

As she headed towards her office, the gnawing sensation that plagued her all night returned in full force. She stopped mid-stride and closed her eyes. She envisioned herself running through a field. It was windy. Bits of grass were being blown everywhere and she heard the loud, throbbing noise as if it was being piped in from an overhead speaker.

Keegan blocked out her disturbing dream and continued walking down the empty hallways. Ten steps from her office, she stopped abruptly, surprised to see a yellow stickie stuck to the door.

Keegan, I'm in Lab C. Join me when you're free. Russo

That piece of shit, Keegan exploded as she ripped the sticky note off her door. She pushed her door open and dumped everything she was carrying on a chair. Then she ran towards Lab C.

The lab's lights were on. This wasn't unusual. The lab was bathed in fluorescent light around the clock. But then her eye was drawn to motion. A technician in full lab gear was at work.

"You've got to be kidding me!" Keegan yelled. She raced to the changing room and slipped into lab gear as quickly as she could. She then burst into the lab.

The sound of her kicking the lab door open startled Russo. His head popped up and his rapid eye movement revealed his fear of being caught in the act.

Keegan's face screwed up as she scanned the lab. The son of a bitch ignored Cotton's directive to work together. There'd be hell to pay. What was he doing in the post room where the second half of DNA analysis is performed? There was no way he could have inspected the crime scene evidence, extracted the DNA from the evidence and prepared the reagents for the second steps. No way.

"What the hell are you doing Russo?"

Dante Russo shook his head as if Keegan asked a stupid question. "What does it look like I'm doing?"

Keegan scanned the lab's mini-sized test tubes and the sophisticated lab equipment that generated the human fingerprint from only a trace of DNA. There was no way he could've prepped the lab equipment properly, completed the painstaking documentation of every step and adhered to the established quality-control measures. No f'ing way.

"How long have you been here?"

How long? Russo rolled his eyes. That's another stupid question. What the hell does that matter?

Keegan gritted her teeth. Fine, you asshole. Every door is time stamped. Cotton can get the times when you stepped into the lab with a click of her key pad.

"You know Cotton directed me to work on this with you."

"This is a rush. I let you know I was working. If you have a problem take it up with Chilletti."

Keegan didn't respond. She'd let Cotton deal with Russo. "Bring me up to speed. What are you doing?"

Russo's shoulders sagged like he was protesting being forced to cooperate with a green rookie. "There's been a murder. We need to analyze DNA samples from the victim's clothes, swabs from her car and other stuff."

Keegan stepped back and tried to disguise her mounting concerns. "You're already running the samples in the PCR?"

PCR. Polymerase chain reaction.

Russo pointed to the PCR equipment that duplicated the DNA sample billions of times, allowing the technicians enough genetic material to analyze DNA strands.

"Yeah, I've been working for a while."

Keegan's face twisted up with disbelief as her eye fell on the clipboard. It indicated that Russo carefully captured DNA deposits from every item of the evidence that was submitted: DNA from a blouse, a pair of shoes, a skirt, a bra, panties, a purse, two cigarette butts and seven DNA swabs from various locations from a car. It also indicated that he painstakingly prepared the chemical solutions to release life's building blocks, quantified how much DNA was available for testing and now was amplifying the genetic codes.

It was impossible, Keegan thought. There was not a chance in hell he could've completed every painstaking task without cutting corners. On top of that, Russo was a moron. An ignorant, lazy moron. It would take him far longer than a qualified forensic scientist to properly run the tests.

"You weren't around so I had to work solo," Russo said, sensing her skepticism.

Keegan picked up the clipboard and dropped it on the countertop. "Are you saying you've completed all of these steps?"

Russo huffed. "Listen, I'm doing my job. I have to complete this ASAP," he said emphasizing the 'p' with a loud popping sound.

"I want to know exactly what you've done so far."

Russo rocked up and down on the balls of his feet like he was warding off the onset of a tantrum. "I'm going to have to ask you to leave."

Keegan ignored him. "What about the reference sample?"

"What about it?"

Keegan stared at him. Don't play dumb. A suspect's DNA was always analyzed separately from the crime scene DNA. Always. The risk of cross-contamination was too high.

"You've got to be kidding me," Keegan replied stonily. "Did you analyze the Person of Interest's DNA together with the DNA obtained at the crime scene?"

Irritation flooded Russo's face. He didn't need to be reminded about lab protocols by an impertinent and far younger employee. "I've got my marching orders."

"Who's telling you to march like this? Have you heard of the Texas Sharpshooter Fallacy?"

Russo rolled his eyes. There she goes with her smart-ass comments. Of course he knew about the Texas Sharpshooter fallacy. It was about a Texan who fired his rifle into the side of a barn and then painted a target around each of the bullet holes. When the paint dried, everyone who inspected the barn was amazed at his marksmanship. Every shot was dead-center.

"You know it's been proven that our minds naturally look for matches when we know the suspect's DNA before the crime scene DNA is analyzed."

"As I said, this is a rush."

"You can't rush DNA analyses."

"That's the problem with you, " Russo exploded. "If we did it your way, it would take weeks."

"It takes as long as it takes. What don't you understand about this? People's lives hang in the balance. Our results have to be accurate!"

Foam spittle appeared on the edges of Russo's lips. "In the real world, time is important. The troopers need the results and I busted my ass to get them what they need."

My ass, you did, Keegan thought. She glanced at the small PCR machine which repeated cycles of heating and cooling to separate the DNA. It would be running for 22 more minutes.

Then the only step left was to run the copied DNA through an analyzer that separates the DNA fragments. The uber-complicated computer programs would inform the analyst of the likelihood the suspect's sample was a match.

Keegan tried to calm herself as she decided she'd stay with Russo until the tests were completed. She considered calling Cotton. No, it was too early and what could Cotton do? The egg was already broken. She'd speak with Cotton in a couple of hours. Hell, Stephanie Cotton was going to flip out when she learns Russo ignored her orders. She's going to freaking flip out, Keegan repeated to herself.

"Do you want to stay around to see the results from the genetic analyzer?"

You smug prick, Keegan seethed. She pointed to a chair. I'm not going anywhere. Proceed.

CHAPTER FOURTEEN

Sam Rome parked his car next to the Thousand Islands Bridge Authority office which was located a stone's throw from the tollbooths. The building had the look of a house set back from the river which suddenly woke up one day and saw the entrance to a large bridge a hundred yards from its front door. In the backyard where the barbecue and swing set once stood, now contained an industrial garage that housed the bridge authority's equipment.

Rome opened his car door as if the movement required more energy than he possessed. He moved slowly, still recovering from parking himself on a barstool at the Clipper Inn from 8 o'clock until 2 in the morning. By closing time, Sam Rome was fast friends with everyone in the Clipper and stone-drunk.

When he reached the front door of the Bridge Authority's office, he knocked gently and pushed it open in one motion. Five feet from the door, a woman looked up from an old, gray desk that dated back to the bridge's opening and smiled as if she welcomed the interruption.

Sam instantly recognized the loneliness etched into the woman's face. He plastered a wide smile that had proven highly effective with single women over 50 and spied the name plate on her desk. Annamae Jones.

"Hello, Annamae."

The sound of her name caused Annamae's smile to widen. She blushed and asked herself if she knew the man who said her name in such a friendly manner. She felt her face warming as she searched her memory bank. She wavered. He looked somewhat familiar. Unsure, her smile morphed into an unsettled expression.

Sam smiled as he processed every detail of Annamae. No wedding ring. Her lonely eyes were a sign she was also not in a serious relationship or at least not a satisfying one. Her outdated hairstyle flagged she was in a rut. He guessed she had been in a rut for years.

He also bet Annamae was divorced.

Rome would've won the bet. Fifty-two years ago, Annamae Jones, was born Annamae Manley in La Fargeville, less than 10 miles away. She went to the central high school and when she was 19 years old she met Private Arlis

Jones, stationed at nearby Ft. Drum. After a whirlwind romance that consisted of four dates, two of which occurred at Blankey's bowling alley in Watertown, New York, she convinced herself that she loved Arlis enough to accept his marriage proposal. They were married in a civil wedding attended by two other people, none of which were family. Three months later the Army shipped out Arlis and his new bride to Fort Benning in Columbus, Georgia.

Annamae quickly got fed up with bad sex, her bad apartment and Arlis's bad breath. It took 7 months for her to come to grips with the fact that she was never in love with Arlis. The next day she took a bus to downtown Columbus and walked into the first attorney's office she found. Her mother wired $125 to the attorney and she filed for divorce.

Arlis didn't seem to care that Annamae was dumping him and keeping his last name. He didn't argue or beg her to stay. When she told him, he shrugged and opened up a bag of potato chips.

Annamae returned to La Fargeville and landed an administrative job with the Thousand Islands Bridge Authority sitting behind the old, gray desk from seven a.m. to two p.m. That was 32 years ago.

Sam reached into his back right pocket and dug out his wallet. With the flick of his right hand, he flipped the bill-fold open to show Annamae his shiny gold Massachusetts Bay Transportation Authority badge with a large "T" over a design of a vehicle that was half-firetruck and half-train.

"Sam Rome." Rome didn't mention the badge was from Massachusetts or that he no longer worked for the MBTA.

He didn't have to. He knew Annamae Jones was not going to scrutinize his badge. He had correctly pegged Annamae as the sort who naturally trusted people and she had no reason not to trust the slightly pudgy man with thinning hair who stood before her smiling.

Sam began with small talk. "You sure got a bird's eye view of the bridge."

Annamae smiled as she gazed out the window. "It's a beautiful bridge."

"I bet you know everything about the Thousand Islands Bridge."

Annamae's face burst with joy. She did. "Robinson and Steinman of New York City were the consulting engineers. Dr. Steinman was one of the leading bridge designers in the country in the 1930's."

"Is that right? Robinson and Steinman? You really do know everything about the bridge."

Annamae blushed and nodded. Hundreds of reports on every aspect of the bridge passed her desk every week. She could recite the length, the height, the type of materials and every detail about its maintenance.

Rome turned and directed his attention squarely on Annamae. "I hope you can help me."

From the gleam in her face Rome knew Annamae would do everything she could.

Sam lowered his voice. "I'm investigating the murder across the river," he said solemnly.

Annamae's face cooled. The news that a young woman was brutally killed just across the river terrified her. It was a single woman's worst nightmare. Annamae had driven on the same road at night more times than she could count. It could've been her, she thought. She shivered, thinking the murderer probably crossed over her beloved bridge.

"Could you tell me which toll collector was working the midnight shift two nights ago?"

Annamae twisted in her chair. "The troopers already spoke to Clifford."

"Yes, I know," Sam said, nodding as if he had recently spoken to the troopers. "But I'm investigating this separately."

"Oh, I see. It was Clifford. Clifford Putnam."

"Do you know how I can get in touch with Clifford?"

Annamae checked her watch. "He always eats at Rondette's before his shift. He'll be there at 7 p.m. like clockwork."

Rome nodded and looked out the window as if searching for Rondette's.

"It's on Route 12, towards Clayton. You'll find it on the right-hand side about three miles down the road."

A shadow of melancholy fell over Annamae's face as Sam rose from his chair. She searched for a way to extend their meeting. "You know, two waitresses also spoke with the troopers."

Annamae's tip perked Rome's interest. He sat down and fixed his warm smile on her. "I heard something about that," Rome said as his face crunched up as if he needed Annamae's assistance in refreshing his memory.

Annamae gushed, happy to oblige. "Betty Foyer and Suzanne Connolly. They're both waitresses and share an apartment over in A-Bay. If you want, I can get you their address."

"That would be a big help," Rome said, flashing a warm smile. Annamae sprang up and in a minute returned with a sheet of TIBA stationery with the waitress' address scribbled on it.

"Thank you," Sam said as Annanmae handed the paper to him. He then reached out and shook her hand, holding it two seconds longer than customary, as he smiled widely. "It's been really nice meeting you."

"Likewise," Annamae said with a mild swoon.

Sam took one step, stopped and turned back to Annamae. "Has Clifford worked as a toll collector for a long time?"

"Oh, no. He's only been here only about five years. He's a retired Watertown police officer."

"Oh, gotcha. Thanks again."

"He'll be wearing a TIBA baseball cap."

Sam nodded and headed out, making a mental note to himself not to wave his MBTA badge at a retired cop.

*****

Glimpsing at the diner's sign off Route 12, Rome slowed and pulled into the gravel parking lot. With a glance at Rondette's single story building, Rome guessed that its original owner built the circular building himself and, as business grew, cobbled on a rectangular extension. Judging from the wooden wheelchair ramps, Rome also figured a large portion of its clientele were gray-haired retirees.

Rome entered the main door and knew he had figured correctly. Canes were hooked to the back of the majority of chairs and walkers were parked in the corners. He nodded approvingly at the ship wheels and anchors nailed to wallpaper with lighthouses and trawlers. On the right side of the counter, a square-backed man in a plaid shirt, jeans and a baseball cap was reading the *Watertown Daily Register* as he nibbled on a french fry. Bingo, Rome said to himself. He'd bet a week's paycheck he was looking at Clifford Putnam's back.

Rome saddled up to counter and dropped into a stool, one over from the man. He beamed a smile and nonchalantly glimpsed at the man's hat. TIBA. Thousand Islands Bridge Authority. Bingo.

Clifford Putnam matched Rome's expectations. He had the plumpy body of an aging bachelor who ate cheeseburgers and french fries five nights a week, a friendly face and was about 68 years old.

Rome turned nonchalantly towards Putnam. "Cheeseburgers any good?"

Clifford Putnam looked up from the newspaper with a mouthful of cheeseburger. He gestured to Rome to give him a second, as he sped up his chewing and swallowed before answering his question. "I have one every day," Putnam said as he swallowed the last bits of his cheeseburger.

"A cheeseburger a day keeps the doctor away?"

Putnam chortled. "Something like that. I'm hooked on them."

Rome extended his hand. "I'm Sam Rome."

136

Putnam wiped his hand on a napkin and then shook Rome's hand. "Cliff Putnam."

Rome decided not to be coy with an ex-cop. Retired cops' noses were still keenly attuned to detect bullshit.

"That's what I guessed. Earlier today I was at the Bridge Authority's office. I spoke with Annamae. She told me that I could find you here."

Putnam's eyes narrowed with suspicion.

"I was with the Mass Bay Transportation Authority Police," Rome said, skipping over the fact that he job hopped through four other law enforcement agencies.

Putnam leaned back on the stool as he engaged his retired cop's mind. "Aren't you far from home?"

Sam chuckled. "Yeah, I guess I am. I've got friends in the area. I was up here on vacation and my curiosity is getting the best of me."

Putnam was either was satisfied with what sounded like half-truths or didn't care. He stabbed a french fry with a fork and stuck it in his mouth.

A stout, snow-haired woman in a stain-resistant waitress's uniform appeared. She held a pad and pen and was in a rush to take his order. "What can I get you?"

Rome pointed to Putnam's plate. "I'll have what Clifford is having."

The waitress shot a wary glance at Putnam as if her internal radar detected a con man. She looked away, scribbled in her pad, ripped a page from her pad and left it on the cook's ledge.

Rome resumed his conversation. "You must've been a cop."

"Annamae must've told you I was a cop."

Rome chuckled. Touche. "Yeah, she did. But I would've guessed it. You got a cop's face."

Putnam snorted. "I'm that ugly?"

"Ha! That's not what I said."

Putnam bounced on the stool as he chuckled. "But we know that's what you meant."

"No, I meant pretty-boy cops are only in Hollywood. I've got a cop's face too."

Rome knew Putnam was warming up but he needed another layer of small talk before he got to the point.

"What were your assignments throughout your career?" Rome asked, betting correctly that Putnam would welcome an opportunity to talk about himself.

"Just about everything. I started out in patrol. Then I worked in vice, robbery, K-9, juvenile and a few years with the Jefferson County Drug Task Forces. I liked patrol the best."

"Me too. That's where the action is."

Putnam resumed eating. It was the right time to get to the point, Rome thought. "I'm looking into the death of the girl on Wellesley Island."

The mention of the killing jolted Putnam's nervous system. "You mean the girl *murdered* on Wellesley Island?"

Rome nodded. That's right. She didn't just die. She was brutally murdered. "Do you remember when she passed through the tollbooth?"

Putnam wiped his lips with a paper napkin as if he needed to center himself before responding. "Sure do. I remember it clearly."

Rome nodded and bit his tongue. He'd let the silence prod Clifford to continue.

"I'll tell you what I told LeFleur and Parker," Putnam continued. "They're the troopers who came to see me."

Rome's head bobbed as if he was familiar with the troopers.

"It was little after four in the morning. 4:09 to be precise. This poor little thing drives up. She was half-scared to death. She looked like she was having a panic attack."

Putnam picked up his coffee mug and fixed his eyes on a decorative anchor on the wall as he arranged his thoughts. "I tried to calm her down. I joked that if she didn't relax, she'd drive off the bridge."

"She was that shook up?"

"Sure was. She was shaking."

"Did she say anything?"

Putnam turned as if he was about to deliver shocking news. "She asked me if it was customary for troopers to pull people over in the middle of the night for no reason." Putnam swiveled in the counter stool to see if anyone overheard him. He then fixed his gaze on Rome. "I told her no. I said some of the troopers are jackasses but I never heard of them pulling over young women just for kicks."

Putnam's face darkened as if overcome by a wave of guilt. "I lied to her. Every cop knew some troopers got their thrills pulling over young women. I heard that Hennigan did it all the time."

Rome drew a breath, knowing the cops instinctively cover for other cops. He had done it a hundred times.

"I knew better. I knew the rumors about Hennigan. He trolled the rest areas looking for women. He did stop women just for kicks. Maybe if I had

138

told her…" Putnam's voice drifted off. He shook his head and balled up his fingers as if he wanted to strangle the murderer.

"Did she say anything else?"

"She asked me if had a light. She pulled out a cigarette and her hand was shaking like a leaf. I gave her my lighter and it took her three tries to light her cigarette."

Rome's eyes pled for more information.

"I told her she'd be safe and there's nothing to be scared about around here." Putnam put his coffee mug down and exhaled loudly as if his emotions were welling up inside him. "Not in my wildest," Putnam stopped as if he was choking up. "I wished I hadn't misled her."

"You didn't. You never could've known she was driving into harm's way."

Putnam's face flashed with anger. "I sure as hell should've."

The waitress returned and set Rome's order on the counter. Her eyes sharpened as she saw Putnam's eyes welling-up. She turned angrily towards Rome as if he was the cause of Putnam's distress. Putnam shot her a quick look and shook his head. It's okay. It's not his fault.

"You want anything else?" the waitress asked snippily as if she did not like the stranger.

"No, this is perfect," Rome answered without taking his eyes off Putnam. "What did the detectives say when you told them this?"

"They didn't seem too interested in what I had to say," Putnam said with evident irritation.

"I am."

Putnam straightened and looked pleased that someone valued his thoughts. "A minute before the girl showed up at my tollbooth, Hennigan passed through in an unmarked car. He asked me if any of the brothers had crossed the bridge recently. I told him no. He didn't even waive goodbye. He just sped off like he was in an awful hurry."

"Do you know Hennigan?"

"Yeah, but not well. He grew up in Watertown."

Rome took a long breath as he processed Clifford Putnam's information.

"He always struck me as a strange bird," Putnam added, sounding as if he was talking to himself.

"You say that Hennigan drove up only a minute ahead of her?"

Putnam nodded. "Yep. He was in an unmarked trooper car. One of those muscle cars they drive and he acted like he was in a hurry."

Rome's face twisted up in thought. "Was it normal for Hennigan to cross over the bridge in the middle of the night?"

"That's exactly the point I made to the troopers. Troopers only cross over the bridge if there's an emergency. Hennigan was on interstate duty. He was supposed to be catching speeders on Interstate 81. What the hell was he doing on Wellesley Island at four in the morning?"

Putnam brought his coffee mug to his lips and muttered, "Doesn't sit right with me. That's exactly what I told the troopers. It doesn't sit right with me."

The waitress returned and glimpsed at Rome's untouched food. "Anything the matter with the cheeseburger?" There was a heavy trace of annoyance in her voice as if she took offense that someone didn't like her food.

"No, it's great. I'm just blabbing."

Rome dug two 20's from his wallet and dropped them on the counter. "This is for both of us." He pulled a napkin and scribbled his phone number. "If you think of something else, call me. I'll buy you more than a cheeseburger next time."

Putnam thumbed the napkin and looked amused. "This is your business card?"

"What can I say? I'm a poor ex-cop," Rome said with a laugh. He pushed himself up from the counter.

"Why don't you speak with him yourself?" Putnam asked.

"Who?"

"Hennigan."

"I'm not sure Hennigan would talk to a nosy ex-cop from Boston."

"He might if he doesn't know you're a nosy ex-cop."

Rome's eyes tightened as if he was trying to solve a riddle.

"Most nights he stops off at the Graveyard on his way home."

"The what?"

"It's an all-night dive that caters to guys on the graveyard shift. Cops, waiters, truckers and me. I usually stop in around 4:45 a.m.," Putnam said, sounding as if he could set his watch by his schedule.

Rome's face widened as he pictured the Graveyard in his head. He knew of at least six late night dive bars in Boston that fit the description. Dives that made their money by serving the nightcrawlers, alkies and deadbeats. He had spent a lot of time in them.

"Any chance I could buy you a few beers tonight in exchange for you introducing me to Hennigan?"

140

Putnam picked up his coffee mug deliberatively as if he was enjoying the moment. For the past five years, he was stuck in a rut. He lived a lonely and boring life, he told himself. Playing along with the Boston cop would at least spice up a night. Putnam smiled. "See you at the Graveyard."

CHAPTER FIFTEEN

Cassie tied her jet-ski up to the dock with the effortless efficiency of someone who has done it a thousand times. She reached down, grabbed a bag clipped to the back of the jet-ski and pushed herself up on the dock.

Francis Durkin had been keeping an eye out for her and limped down like a man with different sized legs to greet her.

"Glad you could make it," he said with a forced smile as he tried to jettison the thoughts of the Customs and Border Protection.

He was a poor actor. Cassie read his face and body language. "Is everything okay?"

Durkin's shoulders drooped. "We had some visitors." He pointed to the boathouse. "The Border patrol took the shirt I was wearing the morning the girl was killed."

"Huh?"

Durkin sighed and quickly recounted the story of how he rode upon the murder scene at Dewolf Point State Park.

"So why take your shirt?"

"They want my DNA."

A protective look washed over Cassie. "How the heck can they just march into your boathouse and take your shirt? Don't they need a warrant or something?"

"The CBP has different powers," Durkin explained. "My guess is that the troopers cashed in a favor with the border patrol. Somehow the troopers knew my shirt was in the boathouse." Durkin shot a disbelieving look towards the boathouse. "I'll leave that for another day," he said, already composing parts of his lawsuit in his head. "I'm glad you came."

"I'm glad I did too," Cassie smiled warmly at Durkin.

"Hello!" a voice yelled, interrupting him. Durkin turned and saw PJ and Angelo DeMartin standing next to a startlingly beautiful woman. "Madeleine just arrived," DeMartin announced.

Durkin ushered Cassie to the end of the dock. As he neared DeMartin's girlfriend, he counseled himself not to gawk at the beautiful professor. She was an absolute raving beauty, he thought as he approached Madeleine Marks. His eyes darted all around. Her legs. Her breasts. Her lips. It was as if her beauty caused his mental circuitry to malfunction.

"You must be Professor Marks," Durkin said warmly, trying his best not to appear stunned by her looks. He turned to Cassie. "This is my friend, Cassie."

Cassie smiled at Marks. "Hi, I'm Cassie Johnston. I'm also a professor," she greeted Marks warmly.

"Well, Professor Johnston," Durkin said, trying to make up ground with Cassie, "this is Angelo DeMartin and PJ McLevy."

Cassie greeted DeMartin and PJ with a full smile. "It's my pleasure." Just by looking at their faces, she knew she'd like them. Both PJ and DeMartin walked over and greeted her with a warm hand shake, taking care not to reveal their surprise at seeing Durkin with a female friend.

Cassie dug into her bag and pulled out a bottle of wine. "Here," she said to Durkin, "I hope you like wine."

"Love it," Durkin replied, genuinely appreciative. "Please, sit."

Durkin ushered Cassie to the chair as he finished setting the table. He poured her a glass of wine and turned on the boom box, signaling the party had officially started. Madeleine Marks and Cassie immediately found seats next to one another and began talking like old friends.

Durkin handed a beer to PJ and DeMartin. "Let's forget about the Border Patrol's visit." He glanced at the boathouse. "At least until tomorrow morning."

The men cracked the beer cans open.

"I'll drink to that," DeMartin said cheerfully. As they tilted the cans and poured the beer into their throats PJ's cell phone rang. He dug his phone out of his shorts and his expression turned serious.

"Yep," he answered. He nodded as he listened to the caller. "Okay. See you soon."

Durkin and DeMartin's eyes pried information from PJ. "That's Sam. Says he needs to meet with us. Says it's important."

"When?" Durkin asked.

"Now. It shouldn't take more than 20 minutes. He wants us to meet him at Hacker's. It's at the Thousand Islands Country Club. He says he can see from the restaurant if anyone is following us."

Cassie was eavesdropping. "It's not a problem." She turned and motioned to the glistening river and then to the bottle of wine. "We've got everything we need. Get going. We'll be right here when you come back."

"Definitely," Marks added. "This way we can talk about all of you without whispering."

Durkin grinned with appreciation. "Thanks. We'll be right back."

The men nodded and rose in unison like dazed combatants struggling with their battlefield injuries.

*****

Hacker's restaurant was like a worn-in couch perched above the Thousand Islands Country Club's pro shop. One side looked out on a marina and the other over a vast stretch of a scenic golf course.

The men clambered up the stairs and scanned the tables and bar stools as a cheery waitress scurried by with a tray of dirty dishes. "Take a seat and I'll be right with you."

"Much appreciated," PJ followed up with wink. The waitress smiled and as she turned her eyes snagged onto Angelo DeMartin. "Hi," she said as her cheeks flushed and she suddenly seemed unsure of where she was going.

"Hi," DeMartin replied warmly knowing PJ was going to mercilessly needle him over her reaction. PJ had an entire skit on how DeMartin's looks disoriented women.

Before the needling began, Sam Rome hooted and waved them over to the corner where he sat with a pitcher of beer and four glasses. The pitcher was already half-empty.

As they made their way to the corner, Rome peered out the window at the parking lot. A few golfers were coming and going, but he saw no signs of surveillance. Rome abruptly stopped as the waitress appeared. "Do you want to eat? We have our fish fry tonight." Her tone was friendly and voice bubbly as she shot a flirtatious smile at DeMartin.

"Just another pitcher of Yuengling," Rome directed.

"You got it," the waitress said as her eyes brushed over DeMartin on her way back to the bar.

Rome waited for the waitress to walk out of earshot. "I met with the toll collector who was on duty the night the woman was murdered."

Rome shared his conversation with Clifford Putnam ending with, "He doesn't think there was any reason for a trooper to be driving around the back roads of Wellesley Island in an unmarked car when he was supposed to be on I-81 catching speeders."

The waitress returned with the pitcher of Yuengling and milled around the table as if she had nothing else to do before she peeled herself away.

Rome began in a whisper and then his voice rose as the waitress moved further away. "I'm going to speak with the trooper who found the woman's body."

The men shot curious looks at him. "The tollbooth collector is a solid guy," Rome offered. "He's a retired cop." Their eyes bulged with interest. Go on. He then told him how he was going to go the Graveyard to try to speak with Trooper Hennigan.

"I also hear the troopers located a Boy Scout leader who was driving towards the bridge and saw a car with a spotlight next to the VW," Rome added. "The scout leader supposedly says he saw two people but since it was dark he didn't know if it was two men or a guy and gal. The problem is," Rome stopped and frustration sprouted on his face. "I can't get any details on the scout leader. I think once it got back to the troopers that I met with the toll collector and the waitresses, Rasmutin knows there's a leak in Albany and now information isn't freely flowing back to Albany."

Rome leaned into the table as if he wanted everyone to listen carefully. "I got in contact with an ex-FBI profiler. He's going to do a deep-dive on Trooper Hennigan."

"What do you have on him so far?" DeMartin asked.

"I hear he's a loner and a deacon in his church."

"A deacon?" DeMartin said with a mix of surprise and disgust.

"Yeah, he's a Catholic deacon at Sacred Heart church in Watertown. My guy tells me that Hennigan is a super Catholic type."

PJ eyed him for a clarification. "You know the type," Rome continued. "He probably carries rosary beads in his car and doesn't miss Sunday mass. He might even go to mass every day. Loves the smell of incense. Strictly follows the church's rule book. You know."

They nodded. They all knew the type. Then their expressions simultaneously turned sour. There was a jarring incongruity about a deacon and a trooper who was known to stop women at night just for kicks.

"He's also retiring," Rome added.

"Retiring?"

"Yeah. I hear he's got enough years to collect a full pension and said finding the girl's body was too much for him."

The waitress re-appeared. "You want another pitcher?"

"Yes, sweetheart," Rome said, handing the pitcher to her. "Keep them coming," he said with a folksy smile that bordered on a leer. The waitress laughed as she left like she was encouraging the leering.

145

"I've got another concern," Rome said as he sipped his beer and turned to Durkin. "I really think they're aiming their guns at you."

"Let them. They don't have anything."

"Maybe, but they could make your life mighty complicated."

Durkin shook his head in agreement. "Yeah, they can bust my balls but they're never going to charge me with anything. Never."

Rome rolled his eyes. "You're not being realistic. There's pressure building on them to name a suspect and you're the low-hanging fruit."

Durkin pushed back in his chair and fixed his eyes on his glass of beer. He couldn't process the possibility of being charged with murder. He opened his mouth but only a scared breath floated out.

Rome turned his chair around and leaned his chest into the chair's back. "As bad as it sounds, you have to think and act like you're a target." Rome pointed at Durkin. "I know you didn't have anything to do with the woman's murder."

Durkin rubbed his forehead as if hearing his name associated with a murder gave him a headache. "And believe me," Rome continued, "if I thought you were in any way involved, I'd tell you and the troopers."

Durkin had no doubt that Rome would do what he thought was right regardless of the political fallout. He was a bull in a china shop, but an honest bull.

"So what's next?" Durkin asked, sounding uncharacteristically vulnerable.

"I told you. I'm going to dig into Hennigan's background."

No one ventured to ask Rome about the details of his digging and Durkin knew a state's attorney shouldn't know the details.

"I'll need PJ's assistance with a few things."

PJ nodded. He was all in.

Rome let his words sink in and elicited their reactions. PJ and DeMartin stared soberly and nodded. They were all-in if there was going to be a fight. Durkin wore his courtroom straight-face that he trained himself to maintain in the wake of startling evidence. And he was startled.

Hearing nothing, Rome sprang to his feet. He snatched his glass, poured the remaining beer down his throat and put the glass down with a bang. "I'll be in touch."

Then he was gone. As he disappeared down the staircase, Durkin felt a strange uneasiness and wondered when he'd next see Sam Rome.

*****

146

As Francis Durkin made his way towards the dock sounds of friendly banter and splatters of laughter emanated from the table outside of the boathouse. He stopped and coached himself to wear a relaxed, carefree expression. But how could he? How could he block out the shock of hearing the cagey ex-cop from Massachusetts say he believed the troopers were building a case against him?

As he turned the corner, Cassie and Madeleine rocked with incapacitating laughter. Their eyes, wet with tears, brought a smile to his face.

"Sorry to see you guys don't get along," Durkin joked as he dropped into a chair as DeMartin and PJ followed him to the table.

The women smiled back. "Your ears must've been burning," Marks replied, holding her stomach. Durkin grinned and playfully patted his ears as if putting out a fire.

"I hear you have a photographic memory," Marks said as her laughter subsided.

Durkin shot DeMartin a sharp look. Was this part of his pillow talk? He then tilted his head as if he was embarrassed by talking about his powers of recall. "I'm not sure," he said humbly. "I can recall things I've read long ago. It comes in handy in court."

"Can you actually visualize the written word on the pages?"

Durkin walked over to the table and poured himself a glass of wine. "I really don't think about it," he said humbly. "It just happens when I'm thinking about a case."

Marks squinted skeptically. "I have a colleague at Fairfield University whose speciality is eidetic memory. He says the classic photographic memory ——where someone can look at a piece of paper and later on see it in your head——doesn't exist."

"He may be right," Durkin shrugged, sipping his wine with air of dismissiveness. "I'm sure he knows way more about photographic memories than I do."

"Have you heard of Harry Lorayne?"

Durkin nodded as he sipped his wine. "Yeah, he's the guy who could memorize a telephone book and recite hundreds of people's names in an audience."

"I've heard you have similar powers in a courtroom."

Durkin stiffened and was conscious not to react awkwardly. "I'm able to see legal cases in my head."

"Only legal cases?"

Durkin stopped and laughed lightly. "No, but for most of my life I've only been reading legal cases."

"How long can you recall the document after you've seen it?"

Durkin shrugged as he coached himself not to show his growing unease at Marks's persistence.

"There's no recorded case of a person being able to recall everything he's read," Marks said.

"Really? I wasn't aware of that." Durkin nodded and touched the tip of the wine glass to his lips. Okay, noted. Let's move on.

Marks looked intently at him, ignoring Durkin's obvious desire to switch subjects. "I'd love to introduce you to my colleague," Marks said. "He'd find you fascinating."

Durkin softly chuckled. "No, he'd think I'm a fraud. I don't know what type of memory I have. I just know it helps in a courtroom."

DeMartin read Durkin's body language and pushed himself to his feet, intent on changing the subject. He picked up a bottle of wine. "Who wants a touch more of white?"

Marks smiled and held up her glass. "Please," she answered as she suppressed the urge to ask another question about Durkin's famed memory. Another time. Another place, she said to herself as she sipped the wine.

The rest of the evening went smoothly as laughter continued through the meal.

As darkness began to fall on the river, PJ pulled two cigars from his shirt pocket. "I'm going to take a walk around the park. Anyone want to join me?"

Walking in his moon boot was the last thing DeMartin wanted to do, but understood PJ was artfully giving Durkin and Cassie a chance to be alone.

"I'd love to," DeMartin said with feigned enthusiasm.

"Me too," Marks added with a tipsy giggle.

Durkin waved tiredly as if he was waving to guests he thought would never leave. The men stood, pecked Cassie on the cheek and whispered jokes at Durkin's expense into her ear. Marks squeezed her hand. "It's been great getting to know you."

Cassie beamed as the three faded into the darkness. She turned and met Durkin's gaze. For a long second, their eyes fixed on each other like they were viewing classic used cars for sale; overlooking the blemishes, dings, and cracked upholstery consistent with their mileage.

"You had an adventurous day," Cassie said as the wind carried the aroma of unseen cigars back to the boathouse.

He nodded and shifted the attention to Cassie. "I'm a little embarrassed I didn't know you were a professor."

"I'll give you a pass this time," Cassie smiled teasingly. "We did just meet."

Durkin grinned. "But it doesn't seem like that."

Cassie returned the smile. "I know what you mean. It doesn't."

They held a long, warm look, on one another. "So what do you teach?"

Cassie swiveled around and gazed at the brilliant moon's reflection on the river. "American History. I'm a professor at St. Lawrence University in Canton, New York."

"Where'd you——-"

Cassie interrupted, anticipating his next question. "I went to Northwestern undergrad and got my Ph.D at the University of Chicago."

Durkin couldn't contain his surprise.

"You're surprised that an ATV riding woman hails from academia?"

Durkin smiled. "Nah, I had you nailed as a Ph.D from Chicago the second you quoted Latin."

They both laughed.

"I'm not stopping with the questions," Durkin said as a burst of intense attraction shuddered through him.

"Fire away."

"What was your dissertation on?"

Cassie enjoyed his genuine interest.

"The forgotten eagle," she said with a twinkle.

"The what?"

"There's a wonderful poem in his honor." Cassie shifted in her chair as if she was slightly self-conscious about reciting a poem.

Sleep softly, eagle forgotten...under the stone.

Time has its way with you there, and the clay has its own.

Cassie blushed. "It's a lot longer but I won't bore you."

"You're definitely not boring me. Who's the forgotten eagle?"

Cassie picked up her glass of wine and sipped it. "Have you ever heard of Altgeld?"

Durkin's eyes widened. "John Peter Altgeld?"

"You know about Altgeld?" Cassie asked excitedly.

Durkin suddenly looked as if he feared his budding romance would be still born. He was sure they held unalterably opposing views on Altgeld. A liberal college professor and a law-and-order prosecutor had no chance together. They viewed the world from opposite vantages.

"Altgeld was a former governor of Illinois," Cassie continued.

"Yeah, I know who he was," Durkin sighed. He had to come clean. "I recreate the Haymarket massacre trial in my Advanced Criminal Law class."

"Altgeld pardoned three of the men convicted in the trial."

"Yes, he did," Durkin replied, his tone pregnant with judgement.

The Haymarket riot.

A light drizzle fell on the night of May 4th,1886 in Chicago. It was slightly after 10 p.m. in the waning moments of a labor rally. The rally was peaceful, but the memories of violence and death at another labor rally only a few days ago gave the air the feeling of crackling kindling waiting to burst into a roaring flame.

The leaflets that publicized the Haymarket rally called for revenge for recently martyred labor supporters. REVENGE! WORKINGMEN! TO ARMS! ...If you are men... you will rise and destroy the hideous monster that seeks to destroy you. To arms, we call you, to arms!

Then the police appeared. One-hundred and eighty Chicago policemen marched in military formation into Haymarket Square. A sergeant ordered the crowd of several thousand labor supporters to disperse.

The crowd turned a deaf ear to his order.

The police began to march towards the crowd. As they neared, a round bomb with a fuse, flickering like a lit fire cracker, sailed into the evening sky.

The bomb landed in the middle of the police. There was a fraction of a second delay and then the bomb exploded, instantly killing a policeman. Six other policemen would later die from their wounds.

Then all-hell exploded. The police unleashed a torrent of over a hundred bullets from single-shot hand guns. Enraged, the police then fought with clubs and guns.

When the melee finally subsided, hundreds of wounded men lay scattered across Haymarket Square.

The police unleashed a furious manhunt for the bomb-thrower. Raids. Beatings. Interrogations. When the frenzied hunt ended, hundreds of anarchists, labor organizers and agitators filled Chicago's jails.

But the bomb-thrower was never caught.

The State's Attorney charged eight anarchists and labor leaders with murder.

Jurors were hand picked and the trial was conducted by a judge bent on a conviction.

The men were convicted; seven were given the death penalty; one a 15 year sentence. One of the convicted anarchists was proven to be a bomb-maker. Before he was sent to the gallows, other bomb makers smuggled explosives into his jail. He stuck a blasting cap into his mouth and lit the wick. He blew half his face off and suffered tortuously for six hours before succumbing to his wounds.

Before the hangman got to the rest of them, the governor commuted two sentences, from death to life in jail. After their legal appeals were exhausted, five anarchists were dressed in hoods and the hangman slipped nooses around their necks. When the hangman gave the orders, they dangled from ropes until dead.

"No one ever knew who threw the bomb, right?" Cassie asked, fully knowing that the police never identified the bomb-thrower. It was at night and the bomb flew from the middle of a large crowd.

"No one was ever charged with throwing the bomb but historians have their theories."

"If I remember correctly, the men were convicted of conspiracy to murder. Right?"

Durkin smiled. Who's playing coy now? "Technically, they were convicted as accessories before the fact. I think there was something like 69 charges in the original indictment."

Something like? Durkin knew every detail of the trial. The anarchists were convicted of aiding and abetting the conspiracy to kill the policemen. Under the law it didn't matter if the bomb thrower was never identified. The jury, the trier of fact, determined that the bomb-thrower was part of the conspiracy and tossed the bomb as part of the conspiracy to kill the policemen.

Durkin closed his eyes as the 1848 case of *Regina v. Sharpe* ran through his head like a thread of ticker tape. *He who inflames people's minds and induces them by violent means, to accomplish an illegal object, is himself a rioter, though he take no part in the riot.*

"It was a miscarriage of justice," Cassie added with the confidence of a mathematician describing a simple equation.

Durkin took a deep breath. He knew most of academia viewed the Haymarket Square trial as a calamity, a travesty of justice, a legal lynch mob. But he saw it differently. Very differently. Yes, he knew the jury was cherry-picked and the defendants deserved separate trials. But he also knew the defendants petitioned the court to have the first judge removed on the basis he

151

was prejudiced against the defendants. The defendants succeeded and were rewarded with having a hanging-judge appointed. The judge they had removed later wrote that the trial was a travesty. The defense attorneys screwed up. They couldn't complain about the hanging judge.

Durkin also knew the evidence was overwhelming against several of the men. Bomb making materials were found in two men's homes. The trial proved that others incited men to violence.

Durkin felt a pang of panic. The night was being derailed by their positions on a practically ancient event. They probably couldn't even agree on its name. Depending on one's world views it was called, the Haymarket Tragedy, the Haymarket Affair, the Haymarket Riots, the Haymarket Massacre, the Haymarket Incident.

For decades, a statue of an old-time policeman with a raised hand commanding law and order stood at the Haymarket Square until one day a trolley driver intentionally crashed into it because he was sick of looking at the statue. The statue was repaired and moved to a park but it was repeatedly vandalized. It had to be moved to the safety of the Chicago Police headquarter's lobby.

"Altgeld was a former judge and examined the trial transcript in detail," Cassie said, sounding as if she was navigating treacherous waters. "He knew the judge did everything in his power to convict the men and a sham jury deprived the men of a fair trial."

Durkin took a sip of his beer to mask his feelings. He held the beer can over his face and took a longer swig. He definitely didn't want to wade into the contentious waters.

Cassie sat back in her chair. "When Altgeld was Governor he aspired to be a Senator. And he knew he'd get murdered politically if he pardoned the three anarchists. It wasn't an easy decision. He wrestled over it and studied the trial transcripts carefully. But he knew the men got railroaded and his conscience wouldn't allow him to let innocent men rot in jail."

Durkin nodded.

Cassie raised her wine glass as if toasting to her hero. "When he signed the pardons he signed his political death warrant. That was an act of political courage."

"Then why'd he do it?" Durkin asked, despite having a fully formed opinion about Altgeld's motivations.

Cassie eyed Durkin curiously as if suddenly sensing the brilliant lawyer was baiting her.

"Well, what attracted me most to Altgeld was his courage. He's famous for saying that he did it because it was right."

"It sounds like you have a healthy skepticism that politicians won't always do what's right."

Cassie burst out laughing. "Yes, you can say that. How many politicians will make a career-ending decision just because it's the right thing to do?"

Durkin nodded. She was right. He hadn't met one yet. Suddenly the vibe changed. Maybe it was the laughter. Maybe it was the wine. Maybe it was the moon. Whatever it was, their differences no longer seemed to matter.

"Can I read your dissertation?"

She studied his eyes, trying to see if he was serious. He looked sincere. "Sure, it's titled, John Peter Altgeld: an American political hero. I have to warn you, it's full of wonky political science lingo."

"I'm used to legal wonkiness," he replied as his eyes drifted into the darkness over the river and his prosecutor's brain began processing the day's events. Then he abruptly ended the processing as if he didn't want to spoil the moment.

"You're thinking about the troopers, aren't you?" Cassie asked, sensing his mood change.

"I'm usually the guy on the other side. It's unsettling battling with law enforcement."

"I bet it is."

"But let's forget about it until the morning."

Cassie smiled warmly. "I've only known you for a short while but something tells me that you're not the type who is able to just switch off your brain. I'm betting you haven't stopped thinking about your battle with the troopers since I got here."

Durkin returned the smile. Cassie had his number. Francis Durkin never could compartmentalize or switch off his brain. He couldn't ignore a nagging problem. No, the problem would knock around in his brain until it was resolved. It was just the way he was wired.

Cassie poured herself another glass of wine. She poured the wine a half inch to the top of the glass as if to say she wasn't rushing off in the middle of the night on a jet-ski.

"There's a lot about you on the internet," she said with a sly grin.

The internet. Durkin's mind raced. There were hundreds of articles about his courtroom victories in state and federal courts. There also was an equal number of blogs, posts and articles excoriating him for his tough-on-crime stance. There was more than enough written about Francis X. Durkin to turn off a bleeding-heart liberal.

"I have to warn you. Some of it is probably true," Durkin replied with a tired laugh.

"Did you really get blocked from being a cop because you were too smart?"

"You dove deep," he laughed.

"Is it true?"

Durkin's mind flashed back to 35 years ago. He saw himself sitting in a gym lined with desks taking the police entrance exam. Then he envisioned a young version of himself and his attorney sitting in the Second Circuit courtroom. His attorney stood at a podium and argued that the state couldn't discriminate against Francis Durkin simply because Mr. Durkin's scores were too high.

Durkin's shoulders drooped as he relived the moment when he heard that the three judges ruled that the state had not discriminated against him because it had a legitimate reason to exclude him from the pool of applicants: it was reasonable to expect a man of his intelligence to get bored and quit the force. It seemed odd to him that after a lifetime he still pulsed with emotion when he thought of how the same court ruled that others, who scored poorly on tests, were discriminated against when they were excluded from consideration for promotions. The Second Circuit ruling certainly shaped his world view, he thought to himself.

"Why didn't you become an FBI agent?"

"I always wanted to be a local cop. I don't know why, but I did. In an odd way, it turned out to be a blessing in disguise. I wouldn't have become a prosecutor if the door to becoming a cop didn't close on me."

Cassie scooted her chair closer to him. "Can I ask you a personal question?" she asked before she took another sip of her wine.

"Something else you found on the internet?" Durkin reddened with anticipation of her question. "Fire away."

"Why didn't you ever get married?"

Durkin let the question linger before answering. "I guess because I never met the right person."

Durkin challenged himself; was he telling the truth? Had he ever searched for the right person? His life had been dedicated to prosecuting the vilest criminals. He hadn't any time to share a life, he thought. But then he wondered if that was really true. Most of his fellow prosecutors were married.

They found the time. Maybe the truth was that he never really wanted to find the right person.

He had some female companionship but it was basically just sex. There'd be dinner, drinks, small talk and he'd go back to her house. He'd be gone by the morning and see the woman in a few weeks if she hadn't met someone who was looking for a serious relationship in the mean time.

"What about you?"

Cassie smiled. It was a fair question; she opened the door to the subject. "I came close once but I broke it off. A couple months before the wedding, I realized I wasn't getting married for the right reasons." She belly laughed as if her brush with marriage still amused her. "I realized I was getting married because I was sick of eating alone."

"I'd like to see you again," Durkin said abruptly.

"Are you sending me home?" Cassie leaned towards Durkin and put her hand on top his.

"Absolutely not."

Cassie leaned in and kissed Durkin. "That's what I was hoping you'd say."

Durkin felt like his head was exploding with glorious emotions as their lips met again. He leaned back in his chair and marveled at the beam of moonlight glistening across the St. Lawrence River as his mind and body tingled with the anticipation of sex.

CHAPTER SIXTEEN

JB Alexander's thoughts were fixed on his next article about Irene Izak's murder as he pulled up to the Thousand Islands Bridge tollbooth at 4:15 a.m., almost the exact time Irene Izak passed over only days ago. The bridge was lit up and deserted.

"What the hell are you doing here at this hour?" Clifford Putnam asked in a froggy voice as he slid open the tollbooth window.

Putnam knew JB. JB would take every opportunity to shoot the breeze with cops. On the street. At a diner. Anywhere. Putnam was one of the rare cops who understood crime reporters had a job to do even when their stories reflected poorly on the cops. It wasn't personal.

For a split-second, JB thought about dodging the question but JB knew Putnam's cop nose could detect a lie a mile away. "I'm just going over to Dewolf Point State Park to see for myself what it was like at four in the morning."

Putnam shook his head. Better you than me. He'd rather stay in the comfort of his tollbooth.

"Are the troopers getting anywhere?" Putnam asked, hungry for gossip.

"The troopers tell me they have promising leads but won't be specific. They're extremely tight-lipped. They're supposedly having a press conference later today."

Putnam's face scrunched. It didn't sit right with the retired cop but he wore a restrained expression. "Do you get the feeling they're looking at everyone?"

JB paused and dissected the question. "They're looking at the prosecutor from Connecticut pretty intensely."

Putnam sniffed as if he detected something disagreeable in the air. "Yeah, that's what I hear too. I also heard that McClusky was here yesterday driving around with Hennigan as they reconstructed the path Hennigan said he took when he drove over just ahead of the woman."

JB and Putnam met each other's eyes. "Is that normal for a D.A. to do?" Putnam asked.

JB raised his eye brows. Was McClusky working with Hennigan to nail down any loose ends in his alibi?

"Nothing's making sense right now," JB said with a head shake.

For a second, Putnam considered telling JB about the ex-cop from Massachusetts who was poking his nose into the murder. He then decided to skip it. He was looking forward to meeting Rome at the Graveyard in less than an hour and JB could ruin his fun.

"No, it doesn't appear to be making sense," Putnam agreed.

JB gave a tired wave and slowly pulled out of the tollbooth. He wondered what Irene Izak was thinking as she ascended the bridge. How did she feel when her car filled with the humming of her tires as she drove over the steel grates? Was she scared? Was she looking in her rear-view mirror for signs of danger? As she reached the bridge's apex, did she think danger laid ahead?

JB drove off the bridge and took the first exit. As he pulled up to the stop sign, Wellesley Island was draped in darkness except for the faint glow of a street light hanging off a telephone pole. The quiet, desolateness of the island hit him. It must've hit Izak, he thought as he started up and his headlights sliced across jagged rocks and trees as he turned left and drove down the dark road.

As his car tires crunched over bits of gravel, JB rehashed Francis Durkin's story. How probable was it that a middle-aged guy would be riding his bike in the middle of the night on a sleepy island? He turned over Durkin's words in his mind, looking for inconsistencies under each one. JB looked around at the dark, uninviting road. Who rides a bike on a deserted and pitch-black road at this time?

It wasn't a crime to ride a bicycle at night but it sure wasn't normal either, JB said to himself as he switched on his high beams as he came to a bend in the road. He continued down the dark road and made a mental note to check if Francis Durkin's bicycle had a light.

JB parked in the small rest area near the entrance to the state park. Nothing on the road suggested that it had been the scene of a vicious murder. He shined his flashlight on the guardrail and stopped and listened to the sounds of a thousand birds chirping. The leaves rippled and the thin branches swayed but everything sounded in harmony.

JB continued to ask himself questions.

Was her heart racing when the killer approached her? It had to be. It was only her and the killer. She was defenseless. The killer had to be big. Yes, he had to be a big man. There was no way the savagery was inflicted by a woman, JB concluded.

The coroner's preliminary report listed the cause of death as blunt-force trauma. He cringed, recalling the coroner's description of her wounds. Her nose bone was pushed to the other side of her face.

Standing in the dark, JB bet the killer didn't come here to murder Irene Izak. He bet he came for sex. He bet something then went wrong. Terribly wrong and a large man with a short fuse and a propensity for violence, snapped. He bet she was killed in a wild outburst that took less than 10 seconds.

JB continued to make bets. If she was killed in a spasm of madness, he bet the killer first struck her with his hands and then used something hard to smash her head in. He bet the killer's hands were bruised.

As he stared into the darkness, the mind-numbing violence, the brutality, the sheer evil of the attack, struck JB. Only a monster could've crushed the young woman's head. This was the work of a psycho. He had written about sick molesters, abusers and sadistic bullies. But somehow this was different. Crushing the skull of a defenseless woman was pure evil.

JB stepped back and stared at the asphalt. Was this the spot where the woman's life ended with a cataclysmic blow?

JB's breathing sped up. He shined his flashlight into the woods. He wasn't sure what he was looking for. He was just spooked. A muddy path where the cops and ambulance crews trod to the body was still visible. One good rainstorm and every trace of her murder would be erased for eternity.

He followed the muddy footprints down the small hill and tried to gauge where he had stood two days ago. It was too dark for JB to get his bearings. He followed his flashlight's beam, comforted by the fact that the morning sunlight would soon peak out from the clouds.

The woods were thick with brush and saplings. Every two feet a thin tree sprouted from the ground. He navigated his way through the dense brush and stopped, unsure if he heard something or it was the twigs snapping under the weight of his feet. He clicked off his flashlight and listened as he felt his heart pound.

JB thought he heard the snap of a thin branch. Then nothing. It was impossible for anything or anyone to take a step in the woods without making noise. His heart raced in the dark. What the hell was he thinking when he decided to re-enact Izak's last steps? What if the murderer returned? Would he strike again?

JB suddenly thought his breath sounded like loud wheezing, loud enough for anyone to hear. He froze for a minute, careful not to make a sound. He only heard the nocturnal sounds of the woods. But then he was sure he heard something snap. He replayed the sharp, cracking sound over in his mind. It wasn't a twig. A snapping twig has a distinct sound to it. This was different. He was sure it was a branch.

After a long minute, JB wondered if he was needlessly panicking. Anything could have caused the noise. Dead branches crack on their own. Wind. Gravity. But he couldn't turn on his flashlight: he'd draw attention to himself. But who was he afraid of? He couldn't just stand there. He had to move, do something.

JB took a small step. The leaves crunched under his feet but he somehow avoided snapping a branch with his first couple of steps.

He picked up his pace and headed towards his car. That's when he heard the crack of a branch. He was sure it was a crack of a branch and it was nearby. He was sure it wasn't a dead branch falling. He was sure it was the sound a foot makes when it steps on a thin branch and it was right behind him and whatever it was, it was close and getting closer.

JB took off running. Small branches battered his face as he ran through a patch of saplings. He ran about 10 feet and then his right foot tripped on something hard. A root or a rock. He was airborne. Uncontrollably helpless and airborne, falling to the ground littered with rocks and sharp branches. He instinctively covered his face just as he hit the ground with a painful thud. His left shoulder screamed as it landed on something hard. Sharp and hard.

JB screamed in raw agony. He could've broken his left shoulder, he thought. He tried to muffle his groans but the pain was too much. Moans seeped out of him.

He rolled to his right side and looked up at the woods from a worm's eye. Everything seemed higher and denser. He listened for footsteps. The woods' sounds seemed livelier but he didn't hear footsteps approaching him. He laid still. Perfectly still. Nothing. He reached with his right hand for his flashlight that rested on the ground. Just the slight movement caused him to cry out in pain. Damn, he never experienced red-hot pain like this.

He ran the light beam down his body, expecting to see a piece of bone jutting out of his shirt. His shoulder screamed but there was no bone jutting through his skin. He could barely move his arm. He self-diagnosed. It probably wasn't broken. Maybe something was torn. A tendon. Muscle? Whatever it was, it hurt like hell.

That's when he saw it. Next to his right foot, was a crumpled newspaper softened by dew and beginning to decay. He shined the flashlight on it. It was a definitely a newspaper. Not a full newspaper but maybe two or three sheets of a newspaper. JB clawed his way over to the papers and scooped them up with the tips of his fingers.

That's when he saw it.

Blood.

A dried red blood stain smeared in the shape of a palm. The paper was bent as if someone had wiped blood from their hands and then shoved the newspaper under a clump of dried leaves.

JB struggled to his feet and picked up the edge of the newspaper with his thumb and index finger. The early morning light bled through the woods allowing him to get his bearings. He spun around and spied the guardrail through a small clearing in the woods. In the dark, he had become disoriented and ran away from the entrance to the park. He turned and walked gingerly towards the entrance, cradling his left arm.

JB deposited the newspaper in the back of his car and checked his watch. 5:22 a.m. The pain in his shoulder was excruciating. He was in too much pain to drive. He dialed 911.

Trooper Andrew Loughlin, the baby-faced rookie, arrived with a screeching stop. He looked around the entrance to the Dewolf Point State Park with disbelief. What the hell was going on? It was the second time in two days he was called to an emergency in the deserted area.

Loughlin pulled up to JB's car and shined his patrol car's spotlight on JB as if he posed a danger.

"Jim Breen," JB moaned with a weak wave with his right hand. *"Watertown Daily Register."*

Loughlin exited his patrol car with his right hand on his revolver. JB was visibly in distress but his training told him to treat every call as a potential ambush. Loughlin relaxed when saw both of JB's hands."Are you okay?"

JB shook his head. No, he was in mind-numbing agony.

"Where did it happen?"

JB gestured with his head. In the woods. The trooper stared off into the woods and then turned back to JB. Was he attacked? Did he fall?

JB winced in pain, too embarrassed to admit he got spooked and tripped on a root running from the wind.

Loughlin's eyes tightened as they touched on JB's injured arm and then scanned the woods. "What are you doing here?"

"I'm doing some background research for a story," JB wheezed.

"And how'd you hurt yourself?"

"I tripped on something."

"Okay, wait here."

160

Twenty minutes later, an ambulance roared up next to the trooper's car. Two EMTs, one wide shouldered and weighing 300 pounds and the other a tall drink of water, jumped out of the ambulance, instantly recognizing JB. They played in the same softball league. Drank beers together. JB had interviewed them for a story a year ago.

The larger, husky EMT, was Bear Jones. The tall, skinny one was Lionel Medoc.

Bear Jones was careful not to move JB. He asked all the right questions. Where did he hurt? What happened? Did he hit his head? Medoc took his blood pressure and shined a light in JB's eyes.

Nothing was broken but his shoulder was separated. Bear Jones gripped his arm and gently rotated his left arm. "This is going to hurt and then it will be fine."

JB braced himself. Bear Jones ran his fingers over his left shoulder's socket and then twisted his arm in one quick movement. JB screamed as a blinding pain tore through his body and then, almost instantly, receded.

JB sat, relieved the acute pain was replaced by a manageable throb. "Thanks, Bear. You're a life-saver."

Lionel pointed to the ambulance. "JB, you need to come with us."

"I'm okay, Bear did the trick."

"The pain is going to return," Bear replied forcefully. There was no waver to his voice. He was sure it was going to come back with a vengeance. It always does. "You need to keep your shoulder immobilized."

"I got some tylenol," JB replied. He checked his watch. He had a deadline and he was starting to agree with Larry Costello. He was sitting on a national story.

"I've got to get back to work," JB said with the tone of man who couldn't be persuaded otherwise.

Bear shook his head and huffed off to the ambulance with his body language screaming, don't say I didn't warn you.

A few seconds later, Bear returned with a sling. He carefully pulled it over JB's shoulder and gently slid JB's left arm into it.

"Thanks, man. I'll see you at the softball game."

"You'll be watching from the sidelines for a while," Bear replied with a grin as he tapped JB on his right shoulder and nodded to Medoc to pack up.

JB plopped down in his car, thankful that if he had to hurt a shoulder, he hurt his left one. At least he still had the use of his right hand. With a slight nod to Loughlin, JB started his car and began driving towards the bridge. As the bridge came into view, he suddenly remembered the bloody newspaper sitting on his back seat. In the blinding pain he forgot to tell Loughlin about the newspaper.

He crossed over the Thousand Islands Bridge and headed to Troop D's barracks. JB exited his car and carried the two sheets of newspaper between right forefinger and thumb as if they contained deadly toxins. He used his right shoulder and feet to wedge the barracks' front door open.

He stood for a moment, gathering himself before stepping towards the protective glass. JB didn't recognize the trooper on duty, figuring the guy was one of the troopers he heard were shipped into Albany to help with the investigation.

"I found this not too far from where the woman's body was found."

The trooper stared at JB's sling and his eyes then traveled to the dirt on JB's clothes. "What did you say?"

Breen huffed with the dreaded feeling he brought work to a man who was allergic to it. "I'm Jim Breen with the *Watertown Daily Register.*" JB listed to his left as if he was a sinking boat. He motioned to the newspapers pressed between his fingers. "I just found these not far from where the murdered woman was found."

The trooper sprang to his feet and his confused expression turned to disbelief. "You said you found that where?"

"I just told you," JB said as the throbbing in his shoulder intensified. "Shouldn't you put these in a plastic bag or something?"

The trooper raised his hand. Wait there. He opened a closet and returned with a clear plastic bag and slipped on a pair of blue, rubber gloves. As JB extended the newspaper towards the trooper, he suddenly remembered to take a photo. He grappled with his phone with his right hand and clumsily snapped photos of the newspaper before he handed them over. "Here you go."

The trooper slid a piece of paper and a pen under the security divider. "Write your name and phone number." His tone was not unfriendly but it wasn't what JB expected. He expected a hint of gratitude. Hell, he separated his shoulder finding the bloody paper, he groused as he scribbled his name and phone number.

Before he put the pen down, another trooper entered the barracks with an elderly priest. The priest's face was wracked with anguish. His eyes were glassy and seemed to be disconnected from his brain.

JB instantly knew he was looking at the murdered woman's father. He had heard her father was a Ukrainian priest from a religious Order that allowed priests to marry. The trooper led the man to a government issued

162

chair and whispered something that JB couldn't hear before exiting, leaving the grieving man alone in the small lobby.

JB pushed the paper with his details under the glass and approached the priest.

"Excuse me sir. Are you Irene Izak's father?" he asked even though he was sure of the man's identity.

The man's neck craned upwards, revealing eyes glazed with sadness. His head barely nodded as if unable to find the words to answer.

"I'm very sorry for your loss. My prayers are with you and your family."

Fr. Izak's eyes flickered like an old bulb. The man who dedicated his life to administering to the needy was going to need prayers. Lots of them.

"I'm Jim Breen with the *Watertown Daily Register*. I'm writing a story on your daughter's murder. Would you be able to describe your daughter in a few words?"

Fr. Izak's face shattered. He sank his face into his hands and mumbled something that sounded like, "he won't meet with me."

JB crouched next to Fr. Izak and gently placed his hand on his shoulders to comfort the grieving father. "I'm sorry. I didn't hear you."

"He won't meet with me," he repeated, sounding as if he was stabbed in the chest.

"Who won't meet with you?"

Fr. Izak sniffled loudly. "The trooper."

"The trooper?"

Fr. Izak slumped under the weight of his grief. "He found my daughter's body and he won't meet with me. Like any father, I have questions." Fr. Izak was on the verge of tears. "He should meet with me."

"Breen! You're not helping things!"

JB looked up and recognized Trooper Frank Connelly. Connelly was known to JB. Known to be a tough ass who had no time for reporters. They had crossed swords a few times over the years.

JB stood and grimaced as blinding pain shot through his shoulder. He paused for a long second. "Father Izak says that Hennigan won't meet with him."

"That's none of your business," Connelly snapped.

"Don't you think Hennigan should meet with him out of common decency?"

Connelly gritted his teeth and pointed to the barrack's front door. "You need to leave."

163

JB held his ground, betting that Connelly wouldn't use force against a man in a sling. "I have every right to interview the father of a murder victim, especially when a trooper won't even talk to him."

Connelly's face turned beet red. He was about to tell Breen that Breen's rights didn't extend to the barracks but reconsidered. "I've been speaking with the man for two hours," Connelly hissed.

"That's great but he wants to speak with Hennigan since Hennigan found his daughter's body."

Connelly gritted his teeth and moved towards JB with the force of a snow plow. A foot away he suddenly slowed and steered JB out the front door. When the front door closed, Connelly jabbed his finger at JB. "Everybody reacts differently to death!"

Connelly then stopped abruptly. "Is this going to be in the papers?"

JB considered his reply, knowing he needed to win over Connelly. "Not if you don't want it to be."

"I don't!" Connelly's words crashed like the blade of a guillotine. "Since this is off the record, I'll share with you that Hennigan can't handle meeting her father. I've been trying to convince him to speak to the poor man for two hours. He just won't."

"Why the hell won't he?"

"My guess is he's suffering from sort of PTSD. Have you ever been the first to find a dead body?"

JB had. When he was fourteen, he saw a car stuck in a hedge. Its engine was running. He looked inside and saw a man slumped over the steering wheel. JB could still hear the radio playing and the hum of the engine. He reached in and turned the engine off and then checked the man's pulse. His wrist was cold and clammy.

"Listen," Connelly said, stabbing his finger at JB, "He told me he can't get the girl's bloody face out of his head. I'm not going to sit in judgment of the man." His tone indicated that he was telling JB, he shouldn't either.

"Okay, I won't say anything about Hennigan to Fr. Izak. I'll just get a few quotes about his daughter."

Connelly considered barring JB from the barracks. All he had to say was that JB was bothering a grieving man and he acted out of humanitarian considerations. But that would probably result in a hostile story. And Connelly knew Rasmutin would chew his ass out if he got negative press. Connelly sighed. "Make it quick. The man is in a bad place."

CHAPTER SEVENTEEN

A pungent aroma hit Rome the second he stepped into the Graveyard. He instinctively covered his nose as he searched for the source of the obnoxious smell. He spied a yellow mop bucket near the door with a mop stuck into it next to a wet spot on the floor.

Rome was sure he knew the source of the putrid odor as his nostrils detected a sharp ammonia scent barely covering a sharper scent of vomit. He envisioned an over-served guy barfing his guts out before he made it to the door. Judging by the wet floor, he figured he just missed the guy.

Rome stepped away from the mop bucket and scanned the bar. The rest of the bar was pretty much as he envisioned. It was frozen in time. Mid 60's or thereabouts, Rome guessed, judging by the hair styles of the locals in the black and white framed photos that hung crookedly on the walls. Fifty year old tin signs advertised Genny Cream Ale, unfiltered Camel cigarettes and extinct brands of whiskeys.

A large juke box cast an orange fluorescent glow on the corner of the bar. Country music pumped in from unseen speakers and a tired pool table with a torn felt cover sat in the corner of the bar.

When the creaky front door closed, a few of the regulars turned and cast unfriendly stares upon Rome. He avoided eye contact and quickly spied George Putnam sitting in the corner of the bar with his back against the wall as if he positioned himself to keep an eye on the entrance. The barstool next to him was empty and he was chatting with a guy slumped on the bar, pulling at the threads of his frayed baseball cap like they were worry beads.

Putnam grinned broadly and waved Rome over like he was greeting a lifelong friend.

"Billy!" Putnam rang out as Rome neared the empty barstool.

Billy? Was Putnam tipsy or was he going overboard play-acting? Rome shook Putnam's hand and Putnam drew him in for a hug. He was definitely over doing the play-acting, Rome thought as his chin pressed against Putnam's shoulder.

Putnam pointed to the guy in the frayed baseball cap. "Kenny, this is Billy. I've known Billy since he was this high," Putnam said, holding his hand an inch over the bar stool. Rome shuddered, thinking Kenny would ask a question about how they knew each other. Kenny just mumbled something that sounded like a greeting and turned his attention back to his Genny Cream Ale.

Putnam signaled to Rome to take a seat as the bartender plunked down a bottle of Miller High Life in front of Rome. "I told him that was your beer," Putnam said, gesturing to the bartender whose face was covered with a three-day stubble and dried skin that looked like brittle layers of a croissant.

"Mac Evans," the bartender said, extending his hand to Rome.

"Ah, I'm Billy," Rome replied, sounding like he needed more time to get used to his new name. Evans's hand felt like rough sandpaper. Mac held on to Rome's hand and flicked his ear, making it clear he wouldn't let go until he told him his full name. Rome hesitated for an awkward second, unsure of what to say. "Carter," he finally said.

Mac's face widened. "Carter? Like Billy Carter, the president's brother, the peanut farmer?"

Rome nodded. He didn't know why he said Carter. The name just popped into his head. "Yep. Like the peanut farmer."

Evans smacked his chest as if trying to kick-start his heart. He then bent over in a fit of laughter. It was the funniest thing he heard all night. Billy Carter. The peanut farmer. When his laughing fit slowed, he blew his nose in a bar napkin and wiped his tears with his apron. "Nice to meet you, Billy Carter," he said before moving on to another customer.

"You've been good?" Putnam asked, sounding like he was trying to make small talk.

"Yeah, same old, same old."

Before Putnam manufactured more small talk, the creaky bar door announced the entrance of another customer. A second later, Trooper David Hennigan entered, wearing street clothes. Every one of his moves was mechanical as if he was on auto-pilot, tracing his former footprints from the doorway to his seat at the bar. Before Hennigan sat down, Mac Evans had a Seven & Seven waiting for him. Hennigan grunted an acknowledgement for the drink and Evans moved on after tapping his knuckles on the bar in lieu of a verbal greeting.

Hennigan plunked himself on a barstool and sipped his drink. He lowered his eyes to the bar as if mentally burrowing into a safe harbor. Then, as if his internal radar system sensed an intruder, he raised his head and scanned the bar. His eyes moved on from the regulars and then stopped abruptly on Rome.

He noted how George Putnam was animatedly speaking with him like Rome was an old friend.

Hennigan nursed his drink and settled into his early morning routine. He ran through the night's events. All the talk was about the murder and how Rasmutin was telling anyone who'd listen that the prosecutor from Connecticut was his chief suspect.

"Hey, I'm Billy," a voice interrupted Hennigan's thoughts.

Hennigan swiveled towards Rome as if he was slowly coming out of a trance. He eyed Rome with suspicion. He was too slick and cocky for his liking.

Rome slid on to the barstool, one over from Hennigan, holding a folded newspaper in his hand. "I don't want to bother you but I was talking to Clifford," Rome said with a friendly air. He turned and pointed to Putnam who waved back at them. "He says you were the trooper who found the young girl on Wellesley Island."

Hennigan shot a suspicious look at Rome.

Rome tapped the newspaper with his fingertips. "The D.A. sure gave you a helluva of a compliment." Rome unfolded the newspaper and tapped it as he read it. "Trooper Hennigan's diligent discovery of the crime had been a great assistance to the investigation."

Hennigan sat, frozen-faced, unsure of whether a friend or foe sat next to him. For a long second, Rome stared back with a questioning look.

Rome abruptly broke off eye contact. "The shit you guys deal with is incredible," he continued. "I just wanted to say hi and thank you for doing a damn tough job."

Rome dropped a ten dollar bill on the bar. "Mac, the trooper's next one is on me."

Hell, he knows Mac, Hennigan thought as Clifford Putnam raised his glass as if toasting Hennigan from afar.

Hennigan lowered his guard. "Thanks," he said, extending his hand. As the men shook hands, Rome said, "You don't get many murders around here, do you?"

Suddenly Rome's "pahk the kah in Hahvahd Yahd" accent grated on Hennigan's ears. Why had he not noticed it before?

"Where are you from?"

"Charlestown."

Hennigan eyes indicated that either Charlestown didn't register with him or he couldn't understand Rome.

"It's in Boston. Just came down to see Clifford for a day or so." Rome didn't want to dwell on his relationship with Putnam. It was too easy to slip up if he started spinning lies. "You don't get many killings in these parts do you?"

"More than you think," Hennigan replied, leaning over the bar as his spine bent like a fishing pole. "This is hunting country and a lot of farmers and soldiers have assault rifles stashed in their homes."

"That makes sense," Rome said in a casual tone intended to induce Hennigan to continue speaking.

"Yeah, there was a fucking soldier who shot his wife 12 times and then killed one of ours who was the first on the scene. It happened right here in Theresa." Hennigan pointed to the wall as if Theresa was located right outside the Graveyard. "It's just a couple of towns away."

Hennigan lifted his glass to his lips, "This area may not have any big cities but it's a lot more dangerous than you think."

"Yeah, I'm sure," Rome said with a rising concern that he was running out of time. "You got any leads on who killed the girl?" Rome interjected, afraid Hennigan would go off on a tangent about other local murders.

"You know, that prosecutor's alibi makes no sense to me," Rome continued.

Hennigan's eyes widened as if the words were soothing to his ears.

"Who rides a bicycle at four in the morning? I mean for God's sake, how stupid does the guy think you guys are?" Rome added.

Hennigan visibly relaxed as he twirled his plastic straw like he was stirring Durkin's words around in his head.

Rome rapped his knuckles on the bar. "I mean, I can see a guy riding a bike in the dark if he was some sort of Olympic cyclist or something. But I saw the picture of this guy. He's about 40 pounds over weight. No, he wasn't riding his bike for exercise in the middle of the night. Not a chance."

Hennigan smiled for the first time since he entered the Graveyard. "That fucking guy. He's a piece," Hennigan slowed as he mentally auditioned his next words. "He's a piece of work."

"He did it," Rome said with a wisp of beer-fueled certainty. "Yes, I guarantee he did it. No one just rides a bike and stumbles upon a woman in the middle of the night. No sir-ree. That guy did it."

A smile squirted out of the sides of Hennigan's lips before dissolving into the look of a man weighed down by troubles. Rome detected the sharp and sudden change in his mood. He knew he didn't have much more time before Hennigan slid off the barstool and called it a night.

Rome eyed Hennigan as Hennigan looked for answers in his drink. He jiggled the ice in his drink and looked up at Rome. "Yeah, that cocksucker probably did it."

"I hope you nail that bastard."

Hennigan wiped his mouth with his sleeve and readied to leave. "We will," Hennigan said, standing.

"Can't I buy you a drink?" Rome said, pointing to the bill he tossed on the bar.

"Thanks but I'm beat. Maybe some other time."

"You got a rain check." Rome hesitated and then added with a tinge of caution, "The paper says you stopped the girl on 81 before she was murdered."

Hennigan didn't say anything. He just nodded as he zipped up his jacket.

"And then you found her with her head crushed in." Rome shook his head. "So fucking sad." He studied Hennigan's reaction as Hennigan visualized Irene Izak's limp body and crushed skull.

Hennigan shook his head. "I'm too old for this," he said with a tired release of air as he headed shakily to the exit.

"Take care," Rome called out as Hennigan reached the door. Hennigan raised his hand but didn't look back. Rome and Putnam watched Hennigan exit as rays of sunrise shot through the darkened bar, signaling to everyone left in the bar that they missed the opening of another day.

Rome sauntered back to the bar and plunked himself in the stool next to Putnam.

"What do you think?" Putnam asked.

Rome rubbed his eyes to ease the pain in his burning eyes and gathered his thoughts. Then he looked up at Putnam. "The murder investigation smells worse than this joint."

Putnam let out a hoot and gripped the side of the bar for support. When he settled himself he drew a deep breath. "I can't see them going after one of their own." Putnam shook his head. "Nope. My guess is that prosecutor from Connecticut is going to get a whole lot of attention."

Putnam checked his watch. It was time for him to call it a night. He sloshed the last ounce of his beer around before tipping the can sharply over his lips. He slid himself off the bar stool and shook Rome's hand. "Good luck."

"Thanks. I'll probably need it."

Twenty minutes later, Rome laid on his motel bed in his street clothes as he mind raced and adrenaline pulsed through his veins. He was sure Hennigan killed Irene Izak but how he could prove it?

CHAPTER EIGHTEEN

Francis Durkin woke to the comforting feeling of a warm body next to him. Cassie's steady breathing rekindled distant, long forgotten, happy memories.

For the most part, his memories of women in his bed were foggy and distant. His relationships had come in spurts and lasted until the day it became obvious to the women that Francis Durkin was married to the state's attorney's office. Then it was only a matter of time until the women exited his life.

Cassie was sleeping on her side and Durkin maneuvered out of the bed as gently as he could, trying not to wake her. The mattress sagged under his weight and the floorboards creaked as he hobbled towards the bathroom like a man with a sore back.

Durkin slid on a pair of baggy gym shorts and a rumpled polo shirt. He exhaled heavily as he ran his eyes over his bedroom. In the darkness of the night when they crept up to his bed, he hadn't given the room's condition a second thought. Now, as daylight crept through the windows, he felt a tinge of embarrassment over the dirty clothes and shoes strewn on the floor.

Hell, how could he have planned for this? A day ago, he didn't have a ray of hope of finding a date and now an attractive woman was in his bed. And it wasn't just any woman. There was something palpably different about this woman.

Durkin watched Cassie's chest gently rise and fall with her slow breaths and for the first time in a long time felt self-conscious of his appearance. He eyed his clothes and patted his gut. He then patted the bandaids on his face. The touch of his bandaids triggered a soft laugh. Maybe Cassie stayed the night because she couldn't see how ugly he really was, he laughed to himself as he pushed the bedroom door open as quietly as possible and left.

PJ sat alone on the porch, staring across the river as the sun's rays began to dance on its surface. He was lost in far-off thoughts when he turned towards the staircase's creak. When he saw Durkin standing at the bottom of the staircase, his face broke out in celebratory cheer. Miracles happen.

Durkin muffled a laugh. Men never grow up, he told himself.

PJ followed Durkin into the kitchen and remained beaming. No words. Just a shit-eating grin pasted on his face. Durkin fixed his eyes on the coffee machine. He wasn't going to talk about Cassie. It's too early in the morning and he's too damn old to share any details about his sex life.

"Morning," PJ finally broke the silence, smiling brightly with the appreciation of a fan.

"Morning."

Durkin feigned interest in the stream of coffee filtering into his cup. "Shut up," he snorted as the men burst out in hushed laughter. Men never grow up.

To fill the time and calm his nerves, Durkin flittered around the kitchen. He swept the floor and tidied the area. Twice. Then he started breakfast. Bacon, pancakes, eggs. Then he waited and drank another cup of coffee.

Durkin finally heard DeMartin, Madeleine Marks and Cassie rumble down the stairs together in a jumble of conversation and laughter. When they turned the corner, he could see Cassie dressed in a fashionable shirt and matching shorts. For a second, confusion washed over his face: Cassie had no clothes when she arrived on her jet-ski. Then it dawned on him; Madeleine had lent her the clothes.

"Morning," Durkin said loudly as if the boom of his voice was set off by an explosion of nerves.

"Good morning," Cassie smiled. She eyed the kitchen. "You've been busy."

"Chefs work while their customers sleep."

Durkin and Cassie eyed the other in hope of divining a hint of the other's feelings. Both smiled widely. She seemed happy, free of regret. Maybe he was kidding himself? Maybe he was seeing what he wanted to see? Maybe he was interpreting every smile or grin in an unrealistically positive light?

Maybe. Maybe not.

He brushed off the rush of emotions and stirred the pancake batter, regretting he had let his dating skills rust.

The breakfast was a blur; coffee, pancakes and laughter. When they finished, Madeleine stood and announced, "I've got the dishes."

"Let me help you," Cassie said, rising and picking up her plate.

"Nope, I got this," Madeleine replied, taking the plate from Cassie. "Last night you said you were going to show Francis the Bathhouse shoals." Madeleine Marks said with a teasing wink.

Cassie smiled and the women exchanged a look of women who instantly bonded. Maybe their similarities drew them together. Both had earned Ph.D's. Both were professors. Both were women with relationship voids in their lives.

Durkin stood. "Yeah, you promised," he said, hoping to coax her outside.

"Okay, you got it." Cassie looked out the porch. "It's just down there."

Durkin and Cassie descended the front steps made from slabs of pinkish granite from Picton Island, a nearby island.

"She's great," Cassie said, referring to Madeleine. "Have you known her long?"

"I met her the same time as you."

"She's beautiful."

"Yep, she is." Durkin was about to tell Cassie he thought she was also beautiful but he held the words back. Instead, he reached out and held Cassie's hand. In the daylight, on the small paved road in front of the Victorian cottages with brilliant gingerbread trim, his action seemed more tender, more personal than even spending the night with her.

For an instant he just held her hand and hoped that her fingers would grip his. A slight, gentle touch was all that was needed. In this nano-second, the state's attorney felt more vulnerable than he had ever been. Then he felt a charge of relief as she squeezed his hand.

"I'm really glad I met you," Durkin said with a note of 'better late than never'.

"Me too," Cassie said. "Where have you been all this time?"

Durkin squeezed her hand and began walking, hand in hand, down the road.

They walked quietly for the time it took to pass three cottages that lined the road headed to the river's edge. "Do you know what the first thing I thought of when I woke up this morning?" Cassie asked.

Durkin snorted. "You probably asked yourself what the hell did you do?"

Cassie laughed. "Besides that. I was thinking what you would have done if you were beamed back in time to the Haymarket trial."

He felt a pang of alarm. The Haymarket trial. Was it just a matter of time before their vastly different outlooks on the world drove an irreconcilable wedge between them?

Durkin held her hand gently, consciously trying to maintain his grip pressure. "You're asking to see if the man you slept with last night is the charming guy you hope he is or if he's actually a right-winged ogre?"

Cassie chuckled. "Maybe. Maybe it is some kind of sly compatibility test."

"And we'd be compatible if I said what?"

"Your honest opinion."

Honesty. How many times had Durkin witnessed honesty crater relationships? Durkin nibbled on his bottom lip, wondering if he could risk the consequences of honesty. Could he ever be honest about how he viewed cop killers? It was his job to slay them in court. Could he be honest enough to tell her that he thought the world would be a safer place if they brought back the death penalty?

Then he thought of the Haymarket bombing.

The anarchists' bomb fragments tore through a policeman, killing him instantly. He could cite the policeman's name; Mathias Degan. Six other policemen, names long forgotten to history, died of their wounds within six weeks. Sixty other cops suffered serious wounds. No, Francis Durkin knew he couldn't be brutally honest about how he felt about the anarchists who organized the Haymarket meeting, advocated violence against cops and armed men with bombs. No, he could temper his honesty but he was sure complete honesty would kill their budding romance.

Cassie's fingers slid out of Durkin's as she waited for his response.

"In 40 years," Durkin cut himself off in mid-sentence. "No. In my whole life, I've never been so forcefully attracted to anyone. Not even close."

His admission brought a smile to Cassie's face as she waited to hear his stance on a practically ancient murder trial.

"I know you admire John Peter Altgeld. Hell, there's a lot to admire about him."

"Did you know the Cook County State's Attorney was from around here?" Cassie asked as if she was temporarily letting him off the hot seat.

Durkin grinned. He had to admit that wasn't one of the thousands of the esoteric facts of the trial that were crammed in his head.

"Julius Grinnell was born in Massena which is just down river." She pointed to the American channel. "If you jumped in there you'd float to Massena."

"A local, huh?"

"Yep. He studied law in Ogdensburg and then moved to Chicago around 1870." Cassie's expression changed abruptly as if her mood was changing in anticipation of what she was about to say. "Even though Grinnell was a local guy, I can't agree that he was justified to try the men for murder."

Durkin's face twisted as she placed him back on the hot seat. He had studied the trial. He knew all of its harsh realities which clashed with the popular narratives.

174

"There was a lot wrong with the Haymarket trial but I would've tried some of the men."

A bewildering look spread across Cassie's face. "The Haymarket trial was a miscarriage of justice. Eight anarchists were tried for the murder of a policeman. Only two were even at the scene of the murder and the police never even proved who threw the bomb that killed the officer."

"There certainly was a lot wrong with the trial," Durkin began softly, "but some of the men were guilty for the death of the cops."

"How can you say that when no one even identified the bomb-thrower?"

Durkin's head bobbed understandingly. She raised a good point but she needed to hear him out. "A person can be convicted of conspiracy to murder even if they don't know who eventually committed the murder."

Durkin searched for the best to explain the law. He pulled up the mental file of *People of Illinois vs. August Spies, et al.* "Okay, suppose a person who I'll call A, instructs B to hire someone, who'll I'll call C, to kill D."

Cassie's head bobbed as she concentrated. A tells B to hire C to kill D.

"So, B, on A's instruction, hires C, whose identity is unknown to A. C then kills D and C's name never becomes known to the State. Under the law, A is guilty as an accessory before the fact for the murder even though the State and A didn't know who actually committed the murder."

Cassie digested his words. Intuitively it made sense. If A directed B to hire C to kill D and A and the State didn't know who C was, A should still be guilty of conspiracy to murder.

"But there was no proof that the anarchists instructed anyone to kill the police."

Durkin raised his finger in mild objection. "The prosecution only needed to prove there was a conspiracy and the bomb thrower was part of their conspiracy."

"That was impossible to prove."

"No, that's why we have juries. The prosecution offered evidence that some of the defendants were involved in bomb-making. On that point, the State's proof was rock solid. The prosecution proved the bomb that killed the policeman was similar to the ones that the bomb maker made."

"Is that enough to convict men of murder?"

"Not by itself. But the prosecutors added evidence that the defendants distributed the bombs at their meetings which proceeded the Haymarket massacre. The defendants organized the Haymarket meeting and the bomb was thrown from where the defendants had gathered. There was more than enough facts for a jury to find that the bomb-thrower was part of their conspiracy."

"The jury was a sham."

"Why?" Durkin asked sounding like he would have a counterpoint to whatever she said.

"It's on the record that most of the jury members had a bias against anarchists."

Durkin shrugged. What right minded person wouldn't be biased against anarchists? "Anarchists advocate taking our private property and putting it into a fund for the common good of society. Theft is a crime. It's not surprising that most men would be prejudiced against anarchism, which is the same thing as being prejudiced against crime. Is it improper to appoint a juror who is prejudiced against murder or rape on a trial involving murder or rape?"

"I think it is."

"Okay, but the law allows it."

"The jurors in the Haymarket trial were incredibly biased."

"But not as much as everyone thinks."

Cassie seemed stunned by his stance.

"Listen," Durkin said, taking Cassie's hand in his. "I've read a hundred law review articles on the Haymarket trial. They gloss over or never mention that 981 men were called as prospective jurors. It took three weeks to interview them all and settle on a 12 man jury. The defense only needed a single juror to hold out."

Cassie wore the look of the unpersuaded.

"Seven hundred and fifty-seven prospective jurors were excused for cause." Durkin looked almost embarrassed for quoting the exact figures. "That means the judge agreed with the objections raised about those men. A 160 men were excused by the defense and the prosecutors excused 52. Eleven of the twelve jurors were accepted by the defense. There was only one juror who was shoved down the defendant's throat and the Illinois Supreme Court reviewed that juror and found he was not objectionable."

"It's universally accepted that the jury was stacked against the defense."

"The jury pool was tainted because the bailiff rounded up men who were sympathetic to the prosecution. That's true. But the defense attorneys agreed to have 11 of the 12 jurors sit in judgment of their clients. There also was an iron clad charge of inciting a riot."

"They incited the crowd to take action against serious injustices."

"It didn't stop there. The anarchists called for revenge and issued a call to arms. If you are men you will rise and destroy the hideous monster that seeks to destroy you. To arms, we call you, to arms! It's pretty clear they were advocating violence."

"So were they prosecuted for their beliefs in anarchy?"

"No. They were prosecuted for incitement to violence. He, who inflames people's minds and induces them to accomplish an illegal object, is himself a rioter, even though he takes no part in the riot. I know you don't want to hear this but history shows most of the Haymarket defendants incited violence, were part of an illegal armed militia and built over 50 bombs that they planned to use against the police."

Cassie's eyes wandered over the children splashing about in the river. Finally, she said, "There's a strong stream of thought that if the police hadn't acted like a goon squad and raided the meeting the killings never would've taken place."

"Who knows? I think eventually there would've been bloodshed. The industrialists were squeezing the workers and it was just a matter of time before the workers would push back. It was a very volatile time."

They both soaked in the peacefulness of the river, a world away from strife.

"Did I pass your compatibility test?"

Cassie smiled meekly. "No, but you passed a more important test. Honesty." She reached over and kissed Durkin on his cheek. Francis Durkin silently felt relief that he hadn't shared all his raw emotions regarding cop killers and wondered if that would've been a deal breaker.

Durkin broke off the hug. "There's something I want to ask you."

"Fire away."

Durkin itched his neck as if his nerves kicked in. "I was asked to give a lecture back in Connecticut." Awkwardness bled into the normally fearless prosecutor's voice. "I was just thinking, you might have time to join me."

Cassie's face exploded in a wide smile. "When is it?"

"Tomorrow."

"I'd love to but I," she froze her sentence as she struggled to sync her desires and words. "I'll have to move some things around but I think I can do it." She paused and looked tenderly at Durkin. "How will you introduce me?"

"I guess I'll say you're Cassie Johnston."

Cassie laughed heartily. "They won't ask any questions?"

"I'll let everyone else worry about that."

"When are you going?"

"I'd like to be wheels up at 5:30 a.m. which would put us in Connecticut late morning. There's a reception at 5 p.m. and I speak at 6 p.m. I warn you. It will be wonky, legal speak."

"I'll just strike back with wonky political science speak."

Cassie bubbled excitedly. "Let me go and I'll see if I can arrange a few things."

The professor and prosecutor walked back to the cottage, hand-in-hand.

CHAPTER NINETEEN

New York State Police Crime Laboratory
Biosciences Division
Albany, NewYork

Even Danielle Keegan, who normally was indefatigable, was dragging. She dipped her head and performed a tired neck-roll and stifled a yawn as she finished the last steps of sanitizing the lab. She stepped back and wrinkled her nose. She detested the smell of the industrial disinfectants which burned her nose hair and made her wretch.

She dropped a used towelette in the garbage and eyed Russo angrily. Ever since he fed the DNA data into the analyzer, he sat and stared at the machine as if it required chaperoning. He hadn't lifted a finger to wipe down the shields or counters. It was standard protocol but he acted as if he was above the menial, mind-numbing tasks that were part of a forensic scientist's job. She was sure he was the sort of asshole who let the dirty dishes stack up in the sink until the entire kitchen smelled. What a tool, she said to herself with a shake of her head.

The analyzer erupted in a high-pitched whir, signaling it finished analyzing the DNA data, causing Russo to pop up from his seat and race to the report that the analyzer began spitting out.

Keegan had never seen him so eager about anything. He was the epitome of a lazy, civil servant who punched the clock. What prompted the sudden enthusiasm for his work?

Russo eyed the report with the zeal of a high school senior opening a college's admission letter. Keegan wanted to review it but that would involve standing next to Russo. It could wait. Russo's eyes widened and then his head bobbed. Whatever he eyed, it agreed with him.

He handed the report to Keegan. Her eyes darted over the report and her experienced eyes saw immediately that the suspect's DNA matched the DNA found on the body of the victim. She wouldn't want to be the suspect's defense attorney, she thought to herself. The science was damning.

"You can't discuss this with anyone outside the lab," Keegan hollered as Russo began to rush towards the exit holding a copy of the test results. He mumbled something incoherently.

"Russo!" Keegan screamed. The ferocity of her scream caused him to halt in his tracks and turn around.

"Did you hear me? This has to be peer reviewed and then a senior manager has to sign off on it before you can speak with anyone. Those are the strict protocols. You got it?"

Russo stood frozen, expressionless as if he didn't understand English.

Keegan trembled with tired, pissed-off energy. "Do you understand?"

"You're an insufferable scold," he hissed.

Keegan's face bunched up until she looked like she was squinting. Scold? Insufferable? Someone fed him the line, Keegan seethed. She was sure that he wasn't smart enough to come up with the line on his own.

"Answer me. Do you understand?"

Russo shook his head. Get a life. He then pushed his way through the lab's door.

The prick is going to tell someone, she said to herself. She was sure. Keegan knew it in her bones. She pressed a button on the analyzer and another copy of the test results spit out of it. She snatched the report and headed to see Cotton. Maybe Cotton can scare Russo straight.

She eyed the lab report once more. The chance of a random person's DNA fingerprint matching the crime scene's profile was one in ten billion. One in ten billion. A billion times beyond a reasonable doubt, Keegan thought. Whoever Francis Durkin was, he was in a heap of trouble.

CHAPTER TWENTY

Durkin sat in a wicker chair perched on the edge of the dock. He wore his white floppy hat and sunglasses as if he was hiding from the prying eyes of a satellite orbiting over the Thousand Islands. Behind his sunglasses, his eyes followed the white spray lines behind motor boats that sped across the river. For a few seconds, he waxed philosophical, thinking that most men's lives were like the watery foam; they were born, lived and left the world without a trace. He was probably going to be as impactful as the foam on the water, he said to himself as a bout of self-pity crept in.

He gazed downwards at the yellow notepad on his lap. He had written a handful of illegible notes regarding the legal claims he'd bring against the Customs and Border Protection: he'd roast them for conducting an illegal search and seizure on behalf of the NYSP. Durkin grinned, sure once he got his legal teeth into the lawsuit, he'd have the CBP attorneys squirming in federal court.

Durkin dropped the notepad on the dock as if he was suddenly bored by charting his legal revenge. He eyed the glittering river and his thoughts turned to how fast and how hard he was falling for Cassie. His passion for her seemed to control him. Did he even know her? He felt like a stalker when he googled her and read her biography on the St. Lawrence University website.

Durkin's thoughts came to a sudden halt as his eyes detected a figure approaching. The sun shined directly into Durkin's eyes. All he could see was a silhouette of a thick-shouldered man lumbering up to him with a mixture of urgency and agitation. As he neared, Durkin could make out that the man's muscular hands, rounded shoulders and wispy hair belonged to Sam Rome.

Durkin waved softly as the serious look on Rome's face came into focus. "Everything good?"

Rome scanned the area. "Can we talk?"

Durkin looked to down the empty dock. "Sure."

Rome looked eager to talk. "There's been some developments." Without providing a hint of the developments, he flopped down into the chair next to Durkin. "I told you I was going to speak with a FBI profiler about Hennigan."

Durkin nodded. He remembered.

Rome pulled out a folded piece of paper from his back pocket. It was folded in squares and he meticulously unfolded it. "Well, I passed as much information as I could find on Hennigan to the profiler."

Durkin nodded. He was all-ears.

Rome hesitated as if he wasn't sure where to begin. Then he said, "Hennigan is the sort of guy who likes command and control structures. You know, the ones with hierarchies and strict authority," Rome said as his nose curled up with disdain for rigid organizations. "Hennigan found the structure he needs in the state police and the Catholic church."

Durkin nodded. He could buy that.

"He took courses and trained for four years to become a deacon," Rome continued. "If his wife dies before him he can't remarry and has to remain celibate for the rest of his life."

Rome's face exploded with revulsion as he thought of a life without sex. "He's also what the profiler called Radical Traditionalist Catholic."

"A what?"

"Radical Traditionalist Catholic. He calls it a RTC." Rome shook the folded paper as if it held a gems of information. "He rejects the Second Vatican council which opened up the church. He prefers the Latin Mass and hates the popes who've tried to modernize the church like Pope John and Francis."

Durkin shot a puzzled look at Rome. Where was this heading?

"Hold on. He also holds very conservative views towards women and probably has some strange fetishes."

"Like what?"

"Like he could get aroused just at the sound of high heels clinking on a hard surface."

Durkin rolled his eyes, commenting on Hennigan's fetishes. Rome straightened up as if was coming to his main point. "So I got thinking. What would a Radical Traditionalist Catholic deacon do if he murdered someone?"

Rome was too excited to wait for Durkin's reply. "An RTC would run to confession, right?"

"Makes sense."

"It did to me." A heaviness crept into Rome's voice. "I need some advice."

"What sort of advice?"

"Legal."

"I'm not in private practice. I'm a state's attorney."

"Yeah, but you're on a sabbatical," Rome countered quickly as if he anticipated Durkin's response.

For the second time in two days, Durkin's instincts rebelled against taking on private clients; even temporary clients. Sure he was technically permitted to so during his sabbatical but it could surely turn messy. But he felt like an undertow was pulling him under the water and he had to take a risk. "The moment I return to Connecticut, I can't be your lawyer."

"That's okay. I just want to be covered by the attorney-client privilege when we talk."

A smirk leaked out on Durkin's face. "What do you know about the attorney-client privilege?"

"I know if you're my attorney, anything I say can't be used in court."

"It's not that simple. There are exceptions."

"Like?"

Durkin straightened in his chair and looked around at the river. "If the purpose of getting legal advice is to help you plan or commit a crime, what I tell you wouldn't be covered by the attorney-client privilege. That's called the crime-fraud exception."

Rome rubbed his chin. "You said if I was *planning* to commit a crime."

"Yep, the crime-fraud exception only applies to on-going or future crimes, not past ones."

"So if I discuss past crimes, you couldn't say anything?"

"Yep. But you need to understand I can only be your attorney for a very limited time."

"You're still hired," Rome replied, lowering his voice. He paused for dramatic effect. "My hunch paid off."

Durkin's face twisted. "Your hunch about what?"

"If the FBI profiler was right, I asked myself what would a Radical Traditionalist Catholic do if he murdered someone?" Rome's eyes sparkled excitedly. "He'd seek redemption through confession, right?"

Rome slapped his knee. "I knew I was right." Rome punched his right fist into his left palm.

Confusion washed over Durkin for a long second before his eyes widened as if he just solved a vexing problem. He then shut his eyes as if a migraine was coming on. "Did you do what I think you did?"

A shit eating grin spread across Rome's face.

"You taped Hennigan's confession to a priest?"

"It was easy but I had to confess my sins to get into the confessional," Rome laughed as he pulled a miniature recorder from his front pocket. He looked around to make sure no one was in earshot and began to press the 'play' button. Durkin grabbed his hand. "Wait!" Durkin had to think through the legal ramifications of hearing a taped confession that was illegally obtained.

Durkin knew he had to tread carefully. He could be subpoenaed about the contents of the tape. Durkin released Rome's hand. "Just tell me what you heard."

Rome smiled broadly, happy to share his secret. "He talked like he had a bad dream. He said he blacked out and just woke up and found Irene Izak's bloody body at his feet. The scumball even lied in his confession!"

Rome sneered. "You know when I knew he did it?" Rome asked rhetorically. "I knew he killed the girl when I heard the shithead refused to meet with the victim's father."

Rome's face flushed. "Can you imagine how badly her father was hurting? All he asked to do was to meet with the trooper who found his daughter's body. Only a guilty man would refuse to meet with the dead girl's father."

The men sat in silence for a long spell. Finally, Rome asked, "So what's the best way to leak the tape?"

Durkin stiffened as he analyzed the legal issues.

"I know what you're thinking," Rome said with a cocky ring.

"You do?" Durkin said, sounding amused that Rome thought he could read his mind.

"Yeah. You're worried I'll go to jail for taping Hennigan."

"Yes, and you should be too. It's a felony, punishable by imprisonment up to five years in prison for recording a conversation without one of the parties consent."

"Come on," Rome hissed. Be serious.

"In New York, you can tape a conversation that you're having without telling the other person but you can't tape two other people speaking without letting them know."

Rome waved his hand dismissively. "If it took me going to jail to put this piece of shit away, I'll happily do it."

Durkin shook his head. "It's not that simple." Durkin paused dramatically. He pointed to Rome's tape recorder. "That tape will never be admitted as evidence in a criminal trial."

A confused grunt erupted from Rome. "Come again?"

"It's called the priest-penitent privilege."

"Huh?"

"The privilege is six hundred years old and dates back to English common-law which shielded priests from having to divulge a confessor's communications. It was rooted in the Catholic faith's Sacrament of Penance. The law held that the sacred rite would not be compromised by earthly legal procedures."

"And that still applies?"

"Well, England dropped the priest-penitent privilege when Henry VIII broke with the Catholic church. And since English common law served as the basis of early American law, the privilege was not originally recognized in the U.S. At least until 1812."

Rome grinned, knowing a legal history lecture was coming as Durkin assumed his professorial airs.

"*People v. Phillips*," Durkin began. "A Catholic in New York City confessed to a priest that he had stolen jewelry. The Catholic priest absolved the confessor of his sin and instructed the man to return the goods to the owner. When the court ordered the priest to divulge the name of the confessor, he declined, saying he would prefer instantaneous death over breaking the sacramental seal of the confessional."

"He'd preferred death?"

"That's at least what he said. His lawyer was a guy named Sampson. Sampson was an Irish-Protestant who was disbarred and banished from Ireland for demanding equality for Catholics. Sampson argued that the court had to recognize the priest-penitent privilege if it was going to recognize the American's constitutional guarantees of religious freedom and equality. The government argued that recognizing a privilege that could be conferred only on Catholics violated the Establishment Clause that kept the 'state and church' separate in the United States."

Rome shrugged. The People's argument made sense to him. Why should one religion be treated differently than others?

"In 1812, in New York City the mayor sat on what was called the general court. Mayor De Witt Clinton held that Irish Catholics were protected by American laws and were entitled to the full and free exercise of their religion. He ruled that a priest didn't have to breach the sacramental seal of confession." Durkin grinned. "He also probably also took notice of how many Irish-Catholic voters were walking around New York City."

"So we could use the tape if Hennigan wasn't Catholic?"

"No. The priest-penitent privilege morphed into the clergyman privilege, the minister privilege, the rabbi-privilege. It's recognized in every state and federal court."

"There's got to be an exception."

Durkin smiled. Rome thought like a prosecutor. There's an exception to every legal rule. But Durkin shook his head. "Unfortunately, there's none here."

"There's got to be."

"There was a case where cops got a warrant to tape the conversation between a murder suspect and a priest in prison."

"Okay," Rome said with rising hope.

"The priest, Father Matriatis, went to state court to get the tape destroyed. The judge told him to pound salt. He then went to federal court and the district judge told him the same thing. He appealed and the Ninth Circuit sided with him. The court ruled that anything said to a priest or minister that was part of a confession, even a murder confession, should be excluded from a court."

Rome squirmed with frustration. He bit his thumbnail and breathed heavily. "If I leaked the tape to the press at least the truth would come out."

"Who cares about the truth if justice won't be served? It won't be admitted into evidence."

"At least it will clear your name."

"I'll be cleared soon enough," Durkin said with wavering confidence.

Rome broke off eye contact and took in the beauty of the river.

"What?" Durkin asked.

Rome turned back to Durkin with the face of man who regretted being the bearer of bad news. "I heard that your DNA was found on the woman's body."

"That's not possible."

Rome tilted his head and furrowed his brow. It's not only possible. His source inside the troopers was sure of it.

"If so, it's faint, trace DNA that the EMT or trooper transferred to her body."

Rome shook his head. "Nope. I don't have the facts but I heard the superintendent of the troopers was told that there's strong evidence you were in direct contact with the woman." Rome paused for a long moment and then lowered his voice. "I wouldn't be surprised if they arrest you soon."

"Arrest me?" Durkin felt as if he was going to vomit. "What's soon?"

Rome shrugged. "Who knows? A day or so. I don't think any sooner than that."

"That can't happen," Durkin objected, immediately regretting that he sounded like a kid protesting that life's not fair. But this was worse than unfair. He was getting railroaded. Set up. His life was crashing down on him.

He'd have to take a leave of absence from the state's attorney's office and he'd be barred from teaching his law classes.

"I think I should release the tape to that reporter."

Durkin shook his head. No. "Believe me, the tape can never be used in a criminal trial. We have to find another way."

Durkin sighed and rubbed his face as if hoping he could rub his troubles away.

Rome quickly pushed himself up from his chair as if propelled by the force of a brilliant idea. "I'm going to try something. It's a long shot but it might work."

Durkin held up his hand as if he was instructing Rome not to speak. There were certain things he couldn't hear about and he suspected Rome's long-shot plans were one of them.

"I won't release the tape now," Rome said. He pointed at Durkin. "But if you get arrested…." He intentionally didn't finish the sentence. He didn't have to. He flipped his hand as if the gesture counted as a wave and walked back to his car.

Durkin inhaled deeply and twisted his lips. There'd be a shitshow if he got arrested and then the tape of Hennigan's confession was released. A complete and utter shitshow, he said with a gush of frustration.

CHAPTER TWENTY ONE

JB's car lights cut across the back of the Price Chopper supermarket like a spotlight sweeping prison walls. With his left arm in a sling, he turned the steering wheel gingerly and his car lights slowly sliced across the bottom half of a row of tractor trailers unhitched from their cabs. Standing alone, the trailers looked oddly incomplete; like headless horses.

He came to a stop, put his car in park but kept the engine running. He scanned the lot. Nothing moved. The early morning had a quiet, eery feel to it.

A sudden shiver seized JB. It was too quiet. Too deserted. He expected to see Commander Rasmutin sitting in his trooper's car with its engine running. Rasmutin had stressed the need to be on time. Now, at four in the morning, he was on time but Rasmutin was nowhere in sight.

A hot fear pulsed through JB's body. He sensed something wasn't right about the murder investigation but never felt threatened as he dug into the story. But he did now. It was the fear that investigative reporters in Mexico must feel, he thought. Fear of physical injury. In Mexico, reporters were routinely murdered, but not here, JB thought as if trying to reassure himself. But no matter how hard he tried, every cell in his body screamed that he was in danger.

JB's thoughts raced. No one knew where he was. No one knew what he was doing. No one knew who he was meeting. JB gripped the steering wheel with his right hand and he was about to pull away when a hard rap on the passenger's window caused his heart to skip. A guttural sound of raw panic shot out of his throat as his eyes turned towards the window, expecting to see the barrel of a gun.

Instead, he saw a large face wearing mirrored glasses staring through the passenger's side window. Commander Rasmutin stared at him with a bemused grin. For a few seconds JB stared, open-mouthed, at Rasmutin in a fixed, catatonic state, unable to speak.

Rasmutin rapped on the window a second time with a tinge of impatience. Startled back into action, JB's fingers found the controls and lowered the passenger window.

Rasmutin grinned. "Sorry I scared you," Rasmutin said with a demented chuckle. It was then that JB noticed that Rasmutin was in street clothes. He was one of those law enforcement officials who looked wildly out of place in civilian clothes.

"What are you doing?" JB asked, unable to mask his fear.

Rasmutin understood. He had scared the hell out of the reporter and was out of uniform. "I needed to make sure you were alone."

JB scanned the parking lot. It was still deserted. There was no sign of Rasmutin's car and JB had no idea how Rasmutin had snuck up on him.

JB felt another surge of panic overwhelm him. "I told my editor I was meeting you," JB lied. His voice was flat and hollow as if he was talking into a PVC pipe.

A wave of anger washed over Rasmutin. "You said this was only going to be between you and me."

"I said it would be off the record."

Rasmutin's lips tightened.

"My editor will honor my promise to keep this meeting off the record."

Rasmutin stepped back, gripped the edges of his mirrored glasses and then slid them off his face. His black eye seemed to cut through JB like an evil laser. Rasmutin bore his tormenting eye into JB and methodically slid his mirrored glasses up and down the bridge of his nose. He then leaned into JB's car and handed JB a piece of paper. JB flipped on his cell phone's flashlight and examined the heading: New York State Police Crime Laboratory. It was stamped "draft." He ran his eyes over the report.

Item #	D19S433	vWA	TPOX	D18S51	AMEL	D5S818	FGA
6-S2	11, 12, 14,	15, 16, 18	8, 9, 11, 12,	14, 17,	X, Y	9, 10, 12, 13	21, 23, 26
6-S3	11, 12, 13, 13.2, 14, 15.2	14, 15, 16, 17, 18	6, 8, 9, 11, 12	13, 14, 17, 20, 21	X, Y	10, 12, 13	21, 23, 24, 25, 26, 29,
DURKIN	12, 14	15, 16	8, 9	14, 17	X	10, 12	21, 23

RESULTS OF EXAMINATION CONTINUED:
Identifiler Alleles Detected (continued)

"The left column lists the evidence. Item 6-S2 is her dress. 6-S3 is her shirt." Rasmutin pointed to the vWA loci column. "See the 15 and 16?" He then pointed to Item 6-S2 in the left column. "That's Durkin's DNA taken from the shirt he was wearing the morning he was supposedly riding his bike."

He ran his finger from Item 6-S2 over to the vWA column. "15,16." He then touched the column for each DNA address and then back to Durkin's loci. At every DNA location, Durkin's numbers matched.

"It's a perfect match across the board. Can you see that?"

"I'm not an expert in reading lab reports," JB replied.

"None of us are," Rasmutin replied testily. "That's why we have forensic scientists." He pointed to the bottom of the report. "Did you see what the lab said about the match?" He flipped the paper over and eyes raced to the findings.

"A billion to one odds." Rasmutin grinned slyly. "That's the same damn odds that the prosecutor was innocently riding his bike around at four in the morning."

JB balled up his right fist and blew into it as he processed Rasmutin's words. "Why are you sharing this with me?"

Rasmutin anticipated the question. "Because that Connecticut state's attorney is exerting political pressure to get us off his trail."

JB recalled his conversation with Durkin. Durkin seemed pretty even-keeled for a guy who had his face ripped up by state troopers. He didn't strike JB as man capable of a heinous crime.

"Who's he been talking to?"

Rasmutin hadn't anticipated JB's follow-up question. Rasmutin diverted his eyes and his voice waffled like a man concocting a lie on the fly. "It's been going on at high levels. His boss and our Superintendent have been talking."

Why was the normally tight-lipped, hard-ass trooper, suddenly playing nice with him, JB asked himself. Rasmutin read his mind. "No man is above the law. Especially a smart-ass lawyer who likes to bully people with legal arguments."

JB eyed Rasmutin, searching for the truth. Why was Rasmutin so eager to leak the lab report?

"If you write a story that the state's attorney's DNA was found on the woman's body, they can't ignore it. McClusky will have to press charges."

JB's eyes darted back to the lab report. This is exactly what his editor had been harping about. This would be a national story. The *Watertown Daily Register* would be the first to break a story about a state's prosecutor murdering the young woman. For an instant, JB pictured his byline plastered all over the national press. And there were whiffs of scandal; the state's attorney was vacationing with the youngest Public Valor Medal of Honor recipient in history. He envisioned the picture of Angelo DeMartin receiving the medal from President Obama on the front page. Yes, it had all the ingredients for a blockbuster story.

JB's breathing slowed. He shook the lab report and wore the expression of a man who wasn't making any promises.

"Will this be in tomorrow's paper?"

JB shrugged. There was plenty of time to have a story ready for the next day's paper but a lead story had to reviewed by multiple editors. It takes time.

"This will be front page, right?"

"That's not my call," JB said, striking the tone of a humble reporter. But JB was sure it would be a lead story and splashed across every national paper. *New York Times. Washington Post. L.A. Times.* Yes, he was holding a winner in his hand he thought, as he battled to conceal his excitement.

Rasmutin suddenly turned dark. "Everything is off the record, right?"

"Everything we spoke about here is off the record."

"And no one will know I gave you the lab report?" Rasmutin's words sounded more like a threat than a question.

"I'll write that the DNA report came from an anonymous source."

JB paused and then remembered something he wanted to ask. "What about the bloody newspaper I found?"

Rasmutin's face wrinkled and his right cheek vibrated as his brain formed a response. He pulled back a few inches and adjusted his mirrored glasses. "Oh yeah. That was nothing. Turned out to be animal blood."

"Animal blood?"

"A kid could've wrapped up a dead raccoon or something in the newspapers. Who knows? But it was definitely not human blood."

"You have a lab report on that?"

JB thought he detected Rasmutin blinking under his mirrored glasses. "Yeah, I could get you it if you want."

JB nodded. "Yeah, that would be good. Thanks."

Rasmutin pulled back from the car and then stood, sentry-like, as if he was dismissing JB.

JB got the message. The meeting was over. He put his car in drive and rolled out of the dark lot as his car beams raked the back of the square, industrial building and the headless, steel horses.

*****

Sam Rome vibrated with nervous energy as he followed JB's car from the Price Chopper to the entrance to I-81, heading south towards Watertown.

Out of desperation, Rome decided to trail Rasmutin. He had trailed cops before in Boston. Once when his nose told him a high ranking Boston cop was dirty, he followed the cop around the clock. Two days later, the cop led him to a late night rendezvous with the mobsters. In less than a week, Rome had everything he needed to nail the dirty cop.

Rome also detected an ethically rancid odor emanating from Rasmutin and his sources inside the New York State troopers all told him to keep a close eye on Rasmutin.

So he did.

For the past day, Rome followed him from a far. In the last hour, he tracked Rasmutin from his house to Price Chopper. When Rasmutin drove around to the back of the supermarket, Rome broke off the tail and circled the building on foot. For 10 minutes, Rome peered into the darkness and searched for Rasmutin. He disappeared. There was no sound or any movements, just the sound of wind blowing over steel containers.

Five minutes later, a car drove into the back of the lot and parked with its lights and engine on. That's when Rome detected a man's shadow moving slowly towards the car. He was sure the large, muscular shadow was Rasmutin's.

Rasmutin hesitated and scanned the area before knocking on the car window. Rome heard muffled words but he was too far away to see who was in the car or read the license plate.

Rome broke off his surveillance and hustled back to his car that he parked in a gas station. For ten minutes, he went through the motions of cleaning his windows, over and over, with a squeegee. He dropped the squeegee in the pail the moment he saw the car roll out of the back parking lot. Then he followed it to I-81, heading south towards Watertown.

The car drove for 25 minutes and exited at Arsenal Street in Watertown. The quiet street glowed with the neon signs of all-night gas stations and chain stores whose economic life depended on nearby Fort Drum.

Rome was sure whomever was driving, had no inkling he was being tailed as he followed from a distance. The car continued for a mile and then turned onto Washington Street and parked in a parking lot behind a square building.

A hundred yards away, Rome killed his lights, pulled to the side of the road and exited his car without a sound. From behind a tree, he spied the car parked under a streetlight that illuminated a parking sign. Parking Reserved for Employees of *Watertown Daily Register*. All violators will be towed.

The car's interior lights went on as if the driver was reading something. A minute later, the lights went off and he heard the opening and closing of the car door. When the man emerged from the car the glow of the street light illuminated his face. Rome instantly recognized the face from the papers; James Breen Alexander.

Why was the troop commander holding a clandestine meeting with the reporter? Rome then shook his head and grimaced as the answer came to him.

*****

JB sat under the glare of his desk lamp, the only source of light in the deserted newsroom. As he twirled a pen with the tips of his fingers he felt his heart pound and the wetness of droplets forming on his forehead.

His sensory explosion was ignited by the euphoria of knowing he had a chance to pen a national, block-buster article that could change the trajectory of his career. It could be his spring board to the big time.

But his euphoria was chilled by a nagging sensation that something wasn't quite right. He couldn't put his finger on it. What was it? Why was Rasmutin so eager to share the information with him? The tight-lipped trooper never contacted him before. Hell, he was the last cop he'd ever guess would leak information to him.

But should he care? His eyes dropped to the copy of the lab report. It was stamped "draft" but everything looked legit. He scanned the letter head. New York State Crime Laboratory.

Staring at the report, JB recalled reading about Virginia cops who used fake crime lab reports to pressure suspects to confess.

The Virginia cops would point to the lab's test results. Look. The lab found your DNA on the gun. Your DNA was found in the bedroom. Your DNA was found in the car. The DNA report proves you were at the crime scene. You can admit to the crime or go to court and the DNA evidence will prove your guilt. No jury is going to believe you over a DNA report. You're going down. Confess and make it easier on yourself.

It was an aggressive tactic but not against the law. When the Virginia cops' tactics came to light, civil rights groups and defense attorneys ranted and raved. Unfair. Unethical. Unbecoming of law enforcement. But the tactics weren't illegal. Deception was a part of law enforcement's playbook. The Virginia cops were just being creatively deceptive. The cops took a heap of shit and promised not to do it again.

JB dismissed his concern that Rasmutin was pedaling a fake lab report. No, two forensic scientists' identifying numbers were listed on the bottom of the report. It had to be legit. Rasmutin would never pass on a fabricated lab report.

JB sat up and positioned himself next to his desktop. With only his right hand, he began pecking away at the keyboard. This was his chance.

*****

Two and a half hours later a red-eyed JB stared at his story that he typed with only his right forefinger. It beamed back at him from his computer screen. He knew it was going national. He felt it in his bones.

[DRAFT] CONNECTICUT STATE'S ATTORNEY DNA FOUND ON VICTIM [DRAFT]

By James Alexander Breen

High ranking law enforcement officials have confirmed that DNA tests link State's Attorney Francis X. Durkin to the murder of Irene Izak, the 25 year old woman killed on Wellesley Island, NY.

Durkin was apprehended at the scene of the crime shortly after the victim's body was located but was released at that time. Sources, who have requested to remain anonymous since they are not authorized to discuss the on-going case, claim that the DNA tests performed by the New York State Police Crime Lab provide incontrovertible evidence that Durkin was in close physical contact with the victim shortly before her body was discovered by the troopers. Sources indicate that the odds the DNA matches someone other than Durkin are one in six billion. One anonymous source commented that the odds were also one in six billion that Durkin was innocently out for a bike ride at four a.m. when he happened upon the crime scene.

JB stopped reviewing his draft and wondered why he wasn't more stoked over his potential blockbuster. He should be on fire; working off adrenaline. But he wasn't. He was becoming more deflated as the morning wore on.

He printed out a copy of his draft and headed upstairs to Larry Costello's office. He sauntered through a floor of abandoned cubicles and pushed the staircase door open and climbed the stairs. As soon as he emerged on Costello's floor, he saw Costello through his glass walls holding his morning coffee. Costello paced behind his desk with his eyes glued intensely on his speaker phone. After listening for a few seconds, Costello became animated and barked into the phone.

JB's ear couldn't decipher Costello's muffled words but his eyes could read the irritation sprouting on Costello's crimped face. He curled his lips, exposing his teeth as if threatening to bite the phone. He then pointed his finger at the phone as if he was reasoning with a boss who held a very different opinion. A second later, Costello's forefinger punched a button, killing the call.

JB considered giving Costello time to cool off. But he didn't have the luxury of time. The story had to be vetted and JB knew Costello would bring in Y.A. Weeks, the Register's long-time city editor, to get his read on the matter. He always did.

JB waited a few seconds and the gently knocked on Costello's office door. Costello looked up and let his puffed up cheeks deflate like a popped balloon before signaling to JB to enter with a tired finger motion.

JB entered and handed Costello his copy. Costello stared at JB's sling and was about to ask him what happened when the headline caught his eye.
CONNECTICUT STATE'S ATTORNEY DNA FOUND ON VICTIM

JB watched Costello's eyes dart back and forth as he devoured the story. When he finished, he looked energized and free from nagging business concerns.

"Is your source a senior trooper?"

JB nodded. Yep.

Costello studied JB's face as he considered pressing him for more details. That's when Costello first noticed that JB sprouted the tell-tale signs of pulling an all-nighter. There were rings around his eyes, his hair was matted and his clothes hung limply on his body.

"Why would the troopers leak the lab report to me?" JB asked Costello.

Costello itched his nose as if he also detected a strange aroma. He then shrugged. "They're under immense pressure to charge someone with the murder. Maybe someone wants to show the world they're making progress."

The men pressed their lips together as their heads bobbed. It's plausible.

"Should we run this by Y.A?" JB asked.

Costello scrunched his lips together as he considered the question. Y.A. Weeks.

Y.A. Weeks was named after Yelberton Abraham Tittle, a Hall of Fame quarterback who ended his career with the New York Giants. Y.A.'s dad was a fanatic Giants fan and had no misgivings about naming his son Yelberton Abraham after his all-time favorite player.

Now, long after Yelberton Abraham Tittle was dead, Yelberton Abraham Weeks was the senior man in the paper and a font of knowledge which Costello routinely drew on.

Costello shrugged. It certainly couldn't hurt. He pushed a button on a speaker phone. Y.A. answered immediately as if he was waiting for the call.

A minute later, Y.A. Weeks strode through Costello's office doorway. He wore an orange polyester shirt and a black tie that looked like he kept it perpetually knotted so he could slip it over his neck rather than go to the trouble of tying it every morning.

"Jeez, what happened to you?" Y.A. asked, eyeing JB's sling.

"I tripped."

Y.A. and Costello waited for more details. When Costello realized none were coming, he handed Y.A. the copy. Before he set his eyes on it, Y.A. settled in a chair, crossed his legs and propped the paper on his knee as if it was his portable reading stand. Then his eyes went to work.

For the next 60 seconds, his face remained expressionless even when his eyes re-read sections of the article. Finally he relaxed and directed his attention to JB.

"Can we get some background on these lab tests?"

"Background?" Costello said, sounding frustrated at the prospect of a delay.

Weeks kept his eyes trained on JB. "If I'm reading this right, this lab report points the finger squarely at that prosecutor from Connecticut."

"That's a fair reading," JB replied.

"What if there's an explanation why his DNA was found on the body other than he killed her?"

Costello shook his head dismissively. "How can we confirm the results without compromising JB's source?"

Weeks drew on his five decades of experience. "No one would raise an eyebrow if JB made some calls to the crime lab to dig up some background information on a DNA report."

JB's heart jumped. Why hadn't he thought about that? A year ago, he had gone on four double dates. The woman who worked at the state police's crime lab was paired with his buddy. They were fun enough but the double dates fizzled. One day, the girl stopped calling him and he never bothered to call her. The fun just fizzled.

The woman who worked in the lab had a nerdy streak but JB was attracted to her self-deprecating humor. He also remembered she was wicked smart.

"I know someone who works in the lab," JB announced. "She's a forensic scientist in Albany. I can give her a call."

"This is something you need to do face-to-face," Y.A. said. His advice was issued with steely, no-nonsense authority.

Costello glanced dramatically at his watch and pointed to JB's copy. "We don't have time for him to drive to Albany."

"We don't have an option. We can't get this wrong." Y.A. countered like a wise old man offering sage advice.

Costello dropped into his chair. He wasn't happy but he knew Y.A. was right. They couldn't just report the results without any background information. The Register would be professionally humiliated if it got the facts wrong.

"I'll get on it," JB said, nodding to Y.A. as he quickly exited Costello's office. In the stairwell, he pulled out his cell phone and dialed Danielle Keegan.

*****

A flicker of excitement pulsed through Keegan as she saw JB's name flash on her cell phone. More than once she wished she had been paired up with JB instead of his friend.

"Hey, JB," Danielle answered with a spring to her voice.

"Hey," JB said, sounding as if he was unsure of what to say next. "I'm sure you're surprised to hear from me. I hope you're well."

Danielle's face reddened. "Yeah, I am. I hope you're doing okay too."

"Yeah, I am." JB paused, testing his next words in his head. "Hey, I'm wondering if you can do me a favor?"

"Sure."

"Well, I'm working on a story and it concerns a DNA lab report. I wonder if I can bounce a few things off you."

Before Keegan had a chance to utter her confidentiality spiel, JB added, "It's just general questions. Nothing specific to any case."

"Oh, in that case, sure. Shoot."

"Would you be free for dinner?"

"Tonight?" Keegan's voice pulsed with excitement.

"I know it's last minute."

"No, I can," Keegan interrupted as she leaned into the small mirror propped on her desk. Her hair was atrocious, she thought. "I can meet you around 7:30," she said, giving herself ample time to get ready.

"Great. How about the steak place we went to?" JB asked.

"Maloneys. Love it."

"Okay, see you then."

"Perfect," Keegan said more breathlessly than she planned.

CHAPTER TWENTY TWO

As Francis Durkin reached the apex of the Thousand Islands Bridge he struggled to mask the emotions swirling inside of him. It was a churning, suffocating feeling of being hunted.

His thoughts turned to his favorite plaque that the Fraternal Order of Police awarded him that quoted Lord Maitland.

He who breaks the law has gone to war with the community; the community goes to war with him. It is the right and duty of every man to pursue him, to savage his land, to burn his house, to hunt him down like a wild beast and slay him; for a wild beast he is; not merely he is a 'friendless man' ,he is a wolf.

Yes, for the first time in his life he felt like a wolf on the run. Durkin envisioned himself being pulled over on the highway or led off the stage in handcuffs. He was sure Rasmutin would maximize the press coverage of the arrest. What better venue than an audience of hundreds of lawyers and prosecutors?

Durkin could hear the champagne corks popping at the Criminal Justice Commission. His enemies would be ecstatic. And even if he never got convicted, his life as a prosecutor would be over. State's Attorneys don't recover from murder charges.

His intense emotions caused red blotches to form on his cheeks. As he began the descent on the bridge, he gripped the steering wheel as he spied a helicopter hovering over the treetops. It was too far away for him to see if it was a State Police helicopter but just the sight of it triggered a rush of nerves. He could feel his face warm as he thought of the eyes in the sky bearing down on him.

Durkin sucked in a long breath through his nostrils. He urged himself to relax. Besides, Rasmutin didn't need a helicopter to track him. Rasmutin could track him through ALPRs.

ALPRs.

Automatic License Plate Readers were strung up all along the interstate highways. Durkin knew ALPRs captured thousands of license plates every second, even those speeding under the electronic readers at over a 100 mph. The ALPR's instantly relayed the data at the speed of light to super computers that searched for hot plates; license plates cops wanted to track.

Durkin knew the law. He knew that the law related to ALPR's upheld the principle that when a person knowingly exposes himself to the public he forfeits his Fourth Amendment protection. And now he was driving on a public highway, knowingly exposing himself and his license plate to anyone he passed. No, the law didn't shield him from the scrutiny of the ALPRs.

He considered avoiding the license plate trackers. He could wind his way through he back roads that traversed through the rural towns of Northern New York. But that would add two hours to the journey and besides, there was no guarantee that a local cop with nothing better to do, wouldn't shoot him with a portable license plate reader at a sleepy intersection. No, there was nothing he could do. He cursed Rasmutin, knowing the trooper didn't need a search warrant to track him and probably already loaded his license plate into the hot plates list and knew he was heading south on I-81.

"You seem distracted," Cassie said as they rolled off the bridge and onto the mainland. As he began to reply, Durkin suddenly stopped as if his thoughts were too jumbled to voice.

"Is everything all right?" Cassie traced his eyes to a trooper's patrol car parked on the median, aiming a radar gun at on-coming traffic in the other direction.

Durkin tried to sprout a wide, carefree-looking grin. His cheeks mashed up awkwardly as he realized it was futile to try to mask his surging emotions.

"You're reading me right," Durkin said with a release of air. "Listen," he began tentatively, keeping his eyes trained on the road. "You and I have become extremely close in record time. I feel I can be honest with you even at the risk of sounding like a nut job."

A soft laugh escaped from Cassie. "Honesty has its risks."

Durkin chuckled. How true. "I have this," Durkin paused, searching for the right word, "premonition—that I'm going to be arrested."

"There's probably a good reason for your premonition."

There was, Durkin sighed to himself. It was actually more than a premonition, he thought as he wished he could share Rome's warning that he'd be arrested.

"I've heard some things through the grapevine," Durkin continued. "But they don't add up. At this stage, Rasmutin would need the District Attorney to sign off on the arrest. There's just plain not enough evidence."

"We both know there are rogue prosecutors out there."

Durkin grew quiet, seemingly mesmerized by the white lines threading the middle of the highway shooting by at 75 miles per hour. He filed his thumbnail over his front bottom teeth, thinking that Cassie was right. Dead right. Sadly, there were rogue prosecutors out there.

"It would take an extremely rogue one to press charges against me."

"We both know there are extremely rogue ones out there. What about the Duke lacrosse case?"

Durkin released his left hand from the steering wheel and stretched his fingers as wide as they'd go. Cassie struck a nerve. Durkin's face convulsed as he pulled up his mental files on the Duke lacrosse case.

Michael Nifong. The mere mention of his name made Durkin ill. To Durkin, Nifong was a criminal who lied and perverted the law to advance his career. Seduced by the glare of the national press, Nifong whipped up the racial hatred that lies right below the surface in so many people.

Nifong suppressed exculpatory evidence. Nifong lied to the judge and lied under cross-examination. Durkin shook his head to himself. Nifong was a horrible beast who would ruin innocent people's lives because it could improve his career.

"It was a travesty of justice but the DNA tests eventually cleared the lacrosse players," Durkin said quietly as he sped up and passed a slow moving car. "Thankfully, Nifong was disgraced and stripped of his law license." Durkin suppressed his opinion that Nifong was a piece of crap who should have spent years in jail.

"The troopers don't have any evidence I was even near the body, let alone committed the murder."

"Then why is your gut telling you that you'll be arrested?"

Durkin's eyes widened. Cassie struck another nerve.

"Gilchrist."

"Pardon me?"

"Joyce Gilchrist," Durkin replied.

"Gilchrist worked for the Oklahoma City PD crime lab. She testified as a forensic expert in over 3000 cases and played a part in 23 death penalty cases, 11 of which resulted in the defendants receiving the ultimate penalty. She lied through her teeth about the DNA evidence to convict people."

Cassie leaned over and squeezed his arm. "You're not going to get railroaded by a Nifong or a Gilchrist."

The comfort of her touch lingered long after she released her hand.

"Why don't you practice your lecture on me?" Cassie asked in a playful way, hoping to lift Durkin's spirits.

"That'd be hard," Durkin said with a sheepish grin, "since I have no idea what I'll be saying."

Cassie's eyes widened. "You haven't written your lecture?"

Durkin let out a rambling laugh. "I never do. I usually try to get a bead on the crowd and then speak about whatever will rile them up the most."

Cassie shook her head in disbelief. She couldn't fathom delivering an extemporaneous speech in front of a large audience. She prepared meticulously for every one of her classes before 20 students.

"Want to be a guinea pig?"

Cassie laughed. Sure, why not?

"I may discuss the Terrance Police case. I'm sure you've never heard of it," Durkin said. "Hardly anyone has."

Cassie shook her head. No, it didn't ring a bell. "I'm all ears."

"Well, the criminal's name was Terrance Police." Durkin paused and peered down a small road behind a crop of bushes and trees where state police with radar guns lurked. As they passed, his shoulders relaxed as he saw an empty road as they sped by. He turned back to Cassie. "The crime occurred in Norwalk which is a city not far from Fairfield back in Connecticut."

He trained his eyes on the road and continued. "A woman parked her car at about 1:40 in the afternoon in a shopping center parking lot. It was a busy area. Cars were everywhere. No one should be in danger." Durkin inhaled deeply as if the thought of a wolf on the loose enraged him.

"She got out of her car to walk her dog and began to text someone. While she was looking at her phone a man suddenly attacked her. The guy forced her inside her car. He demanded her money and jewelry. Then he shot her."

Durkin paused as they passed another secluded area where state police routinely hid from speeders. It was also empty.

"He shot the woman?"

"Yeah, he shot her. The bullet penetrated her abdomen, ripped through her uterus and her small intestines."

"That's horrible."

"Yeah, it was. Bleeding, she handed over her rings and iPhone and the bastard ran off across Connecticut Avenue, a busy street and then ran behind a

Best Buy store. The woman staggered out of her car and yelled she had been shot and passersby called 911."

Durkin sucked in a long breath of air. "The woman went under emergency surgery and survived."

"Did they catch the shooter?"

"Well, that's what I may talk about. Three days after the shooting, police officers returned to the site of the shooting and traced the perpetrator's route."

"Three days?"

"I'm not sure why it took so long but once the cops returned they found the perp's sweatshirt, the gun he used to shoot the woman and the woman's Kate Spade iphone cover. However, for a host of reasons, the perp was not readily identified."

Durkin stared at a trooper's car that had pulled a car over and sat with its lights flashing on the side of he highway. He instinctively slowed and checked his speed. He was going 73 mph in a 65 mph zone. He was fine.

Durkin shot a glance at Cassie who stared back with interest. Continue.

"The cops released pictures of the perp and got DNA fingerprints from the sweatshirt and gun. They searched the DNA in something called CODIS; which stands for the Combined DNA Index System. It's a national database of DNA profiles from convicted felons."

Durkin paused as if he had forgotten an important point. "Every person convicted of a felon has their DNA entered into CODIS. There's a good chance that a guy sick enough to shoot a woman in broad daylight would have his DNA listed in CODIS."

"I'm guessing that wasn't the case here."

"Nope. And it gets crazier. A few days after the cops released the photos of the suspect, a woman called with a tip that the shooter was a guy named Terrance Police. The cops ran a background check on Police. He'd been convicted multiple times for robbery and has been a suspect in many other robberies so his DNA had to be in CODIS. But there wasn't a match. The cops figured it wasn't him because the computers weren't matching his DNA to the DNA found on the sweatshirt and iPhone case."

"Sounds like you're going to tell me there was a mix-up."

Durkin squeezed the steering wheel and blew a gust of anger. "That's a nice way of putting it. The Department of Corrections royally screwed up. They checked a box that Terrance's Police's DNA had been uploaded in the DNA databank but it was never submitted. It was a complete, utter, incompetent screw-up and no one was ever held accountable."

Durkin trained his eyes on the road hoping to shield the rage he felt every time he thought of Terrance Police. Did some lazy state employee just check a box instead of uploading the prisoner's DNA in CODIS? Was it gross incompetence? How many other felons' DNA fingerprints were missing from the system? He shook his head as he thought of how many times a clerical error allowed a wolf to be released.

"How'd they finally catch him?" Cassie asked as if she wanted to pull Durkin away from his angry thoughts.

"There was a five year statute of limitations and after almost five years, Terrance Police had not been identified. Since they were closing in on the five years, the cops tolled the statute of limitations by getting a judge to sign a John Doe arrest warrant."

"John Doe?"

Durkin tapped the steering wheel. "The Fourth Amendment requires that an arrest warrant describe the person to be arrested with 'particularity'. In legal parlance that requirement is known as the Particularity requirement."

Durkin slowed and took the exit for I-90 which cut across Central New York. As he eyed the sign for I-90 East, he saw he was holding Cassie's attention.

"What did the Founders mean when they required an arrest warrant to describe the person with particularity?" he asked rhetorically. "Remember, the Founders didn't say that the police had to use the accused's name. All the police had to do was describe the person with particularity. An arrest warrant could say a caucasian man, approximately 50 years old, with a hawk shaped nose and a jagged scar running from the left side of his mouth to his ear. The Constitution requires the police to use identification that can, on its face, zero in on a particular person. That's all."

Durkin scrutinized the highway as he arranged his thoughts. "Let me step back. The issuance of an arrest warrant stops the statute of limitations from ticking. And all the Fourth Amendment requires is that an arrest warrant describe the person to be arrested with particularity."

Durkin then wagged his right forefinger like it was a gun and he was searching for someone to shoot. "With the development of DNA evidence, virtually every court in the country agrees that a DNA identifier is sufficiently particular to identify a person in an arrest warrant even though a DNA code is just a jumble of letters and numbers on paper. Everyone has a unique DNA jumble of letters and numbers."

Durkin covered his mouth as he coughed. He eyed his rear view mirror and pulled over in the right lane to let a pick-up truck roar by him.

"DNA is like a human bar code. And the courts have said we can use a human bar code to satisfy the Fourth Amendment's particularity requirement. So if we have a bad guy's DNA and for some reason we don't know the perp's name, we can substitute his DNA code for his name. Once that is issued, the statute of limitations stops running."

Durkin ran his hands through his hair and seemed to need to continue with his explanation. "Now let's go back to the vicious crime that Terrance Police committed. The forensic lab found saliva on the perpetrator's sweatshirt. They found DNA on the gun the police linked to the shooting. They found DNA on the victim's iPhone cover. The cops then identified the perp by his DNA code in the search warrant."

Durkin paused as his eyes traveled to the rapidly approaching Automatic License Plate Reader spread over both sections of the interstate. A few days ago, he wouldn't have given it more than a passing glance. Now he glared at it as he passed under it as if he was in a hostile stare-off with Rasmutin's evil eye. Fuck you, Rasmutin.

As they cleared the ALPR, Cassie asked, "So what was the problem?"

"There shouldn't be any, right?" Durkin replied. "Wrong. Our highest court had a lot of problems because the DNA evidence was something that's called 'trace DNA'. Trace DNA is picked up on an item by touching the object or even touching a person who then transfers the DNA to the object."

"Is that what the state police tried to get from you at the barracks?"

Durkin's eyes lit up. He hadn't said a word to Cassie about how the state police tried to surreptitiously obtain his DNA when he went to their barracks. He was sure DeMartin whispered the story to Madeleine Marks and Marks, in turn, whispered to Cassie. He sucked in a mouthful of air and made a mental note to speak with DeMartin later.

He returned to his story. "Based on another tip, the cops got a search warrant to compel Terrance Police to give them a DNA sample."

Durkin blew a gust of frustration and raised his forefinger in the air, "One," he said, "the lab found his DNA on the sweatshirt he discarded after he shot the woman." He raised two fingers. "Two. The trace DNA on the gun he used to shoot the woman matched his DNA." He raised three fingers. "Three. The iPhone case which he stole from the woman the day he shot her, contained his trace DNA."

Durkin shook his head vigorously to demonstrate the degree of his disagreement with the Connecticut Supreme Court's decision. "There was not a trace of doubt about his guilt. He pleaded guilty and began serving a 5 to 10 year sentence for shooting an innocent woman."

Durkin took a deep, fortifying breath. "Unfortunately, Terrance Police never received justice."

Durkin tapped the steering wheel as the car's speed increased to 82 mph. "The criminal," Durkin said with a forceful tap, "the man who beyond a shadow of a doubt shot a woman at close range and inflicted trauma to her uterus and intestines, was permitted to appeal the legality of his arrest and conviction."

Durkin wagged his finger at an imaginary audience. "Our State Supreme Court held that Terrance Police—the slime ball with a violent rap sheet—had his Constitutional rights violated because the John Doe arrest warrant didn't identify him with sufficient particularity."

"I'm not following."

"The DNA found on a few items like the iPhone cover, contained DNA from multiple people, including the victim. The court claimed that since the DNA fingerprints in the arrest warrant were made up of several people, those DNA codes were not particular enough to identify Terrance Police. It's utter nonsense. The Connecticut State Supreme Court set Terrance Police free."

Durkin kept his eyes trained on the highway and shook his head in frustration. "The stinking decision makes no sense. The DNA fingerprint substitutes for a name. The cops used the DNA fingerprints from several people in the arrest warrant because that was the DNA found on the evidence. When the DNA is compared to the suspect's, there was an absolute match. Worst thing was that the decision was unanimous."

Durkin shot Cassie a glance. "And, of course, a unanimous decision looks solid to the world since they assume a wide diversity of judicial minds weighed in on the subject, right?"

Durkin shook his head as if telegraphing the correct answer to Cassie. "No. What's the value of an unanimous decision if there is a very narrow range of judicial thinking? Terrance Police's DNA sample matched the DNA on the gun, the sweatshirt and the iPhone case with scientific certainty." Durkin sped up as he became more animated.

"I begged Roslyn to appeal the case to the U.S. Supreme Court because it concerns the Fourth Amendment's Particularity requirement." His nostrils flickered. "She doesn't have the stones."

"Would you mind if we stopped at the next rest area?" Cassie asked, pointing to a sign that warned that the next rest stop was in 36 miles.

"Of course," Durkin said with a trace of an apology for not asking her if she needed to take a nature break. He steered the car onto the off-ramp and into the half-full parking lot. For the past hour, Cassie's distractions worked: Francis Durkin had forgotten he was in law enforcement's crosshairs.

*****

Francis Durkin pulled into his driveway. His home was a tasteful gray colonial with sharp, V-shaped turrets on a quiet neighborhood lined with other tasteful colonials all built about a hundred years ago.

Durkin was overcome with jitters as he killed the engine. In the 27 years he had lived there, he had taken other women to his home. But Cassie was different. She mattered. It was bad enough that she occupied the other side of the political spectrum. What if she found something patently disagreeable about his home? It would be two strikes against him.

"This is my humble abode," he said, pointing through the car window.

Cassie studied his house like she was absorbing a painting. "I love it. It's got character."

Damn, she knew the right thing to say, he thought as he opened his car door. He checked his watch. They had two hours before they had to leave for his lecture. Two hours alone, he thought as his heart skipped like a young man with the prospect of losing his virginity.

Durkin carried their luggage to the front door and fumbled with his key ring. He set the luggage down and inserted a tarnished copper colored key into the doorlock.

"Entre vous," he said playfully as he swung the door open. Before the door swung fully open, a stench of rotting fish and toxic chemicals assaulted their noses.

"What the hell?" Durkin shouted as he covered his nose. He signaled for Cassie to remain outside and then raced inside. After two steps inside, he knew the source of the noxious fumes. He had tossed two servings of Kimchi in his garbage a week ago. It had fermented in the heat of the garbage can that he asked his neighbor to drag inside to his kitchen. The smelly microbes were like a runaway test tube, doubling in size every day.

"You keep your garbage cans in your kitchen?" Cassie asked, coming up from behind him. She pointed to the two green plastic bins in the middle of his kitchen. Durkin opened his windows and dragged the bins outside as if they were on fire.

"It's a long story," he said, covering his nose. He rushed into the bathroom and emerged with a can of Lysol as if he was carrying a fire extinguisher. He filled the air with a thick, scented cloud until the can was spent.

"Let's go out on the patio," he said with a tinge of embarrassment. Cassie followed him quickly to evade the odor.

"Listen," Durkin began as they sat on the black iron chairs on his small patio. "I got wind that troopers were going to rifle through my garbage, looking for my DNA." Durkin wore a meek expression. "I wanted to bust their chops so I asked my neighbor to bring the garbage inside. I forgot to ask him to move it back outside. That's the long and short of it. The good news is the horrible smell is dissipating."

He detected a shimmer of concern in Cassie's eyes. "Listen, I know it sounds strange but when I found myself as a target I instinctively wanted to punch back."

"Is that why you asked Kyle to give you the tour of Grindstone Island?"

Durkin nodded. "Yep. I thought the troopers were going to serve me with a warrant to force me to give them a DNA sample. I decided I wasn't going to make it easy for them so I went off to see Grindstone and Jolly Island." A sly grin spread across Durkin's face. "I'm glad I did it. I wouldn't have met you otherwise." Durkin left his voice drift off.

Cassie leaned over and kissed Durkin. "If it's safe to return, I want a tour of your house."

Durkin grabbed Cassie's hand and gave her a quick tour of the floor level that still stunk of rotten kimchi. They walked through the small kitchen, the small dining room and the mid-sized family room. She studied every one of the framed law enforcement citations that lined the walls. She complimented the original formica in the bathrooms and the classic paneling in his studio. Classic. He liked her description of things that looked exactly the way they did a quarter century ago when he bought the house.

A gust of nerves whipped up in Durkin as he climbed the staircase. He showed her his guest room, a room crammed with law books and files and then pointed to his bedroom.

He stepped inside and met Cassie's eyes. With magnetic passion, they kissed and lowered themselves on to his bed. Francis Durkin felt a rush of passion he had never felt before. He fumbled with her shirt's buttons and then fumbled with his belt buckle. He was all fumble but he was more excited than he could ever remember.

*****

The doorbell sent a shiver through Durkin as he glanced at Cassie who faintly stirred in her sleep. Durkin slid out of bed, pulled on his pants, threw on a shirt and began buttoning it on his way down the stairs.

Durkin reached his front door as the second ring filled the house. It was a muted, almost soothing ring but he cursed the interruption which pulled him away from napping next to Cassie. He spied through the peephole and saw a fish eyed view of Alex Phillips waiting patiently outside his door. Phillips looked uncomfortable and shot a furtive glance at the road as if he was looking over his shoulder to see if he had been tailed.

For a second, Durkin wondered why his second-in-command was standing outside his door and then he remembered. He had told Phillips to meet him at his house if he needed to speak to him.

Durkin finished buttoning his shirt and then tucked in his shirt a second time for good measure before he opened the door.

"Hondo," Durkin said with a tired smile as he ushered Phillips inside. Before Phillips had a chance to reply his nostrils flared with distress. "What's that?"

Durkin sniffed. The stench of rotten kimchi and Lysol still hung in the air. "It's the stench of a bad decision."

Phillips's eyes searched for clarity.

"I got my neighbor to pull in my garbage cans. I forgot they were full of kimchi."

Phillips broke out in a wide grin as he held his nose.

"Let's go out on the patio," Durkin said.

While the men sat in the shade, Phillips looked relaxed, ready to converse now that he was out of the reach of the offending odor. "How are you doing?"

Phillips's question yanked Durkin back to reality. His chest felt heavy and constricted. Where should he start? He wished he could start by picking Phillips's rock-solid legal brain. He wished he could have the benefit of Phillips's take on the admissibility of Hennigan's taped confession if the tape was leaked to the press.

But Durkin could never share the secret that Sam Rome had illegally recorded Hennigan's confession to a priest. It wasn't a matter of trust. Durkin trusted Phillips more than anyone else in the state's attorneys office but Phillips was sworn to uphold the law. If he told him about the confession, Phillips would have to report the felony.

"What's on your mind?" Durkin asked, knowing Phillips wouldn't have shown up at his house unless he had something important to discuss.

"The office is buzzing," Phillips began. He pointed to Durkin's kitchen. "Word leaked that the troopers were asked to rifle through your garbage." Phillips grew serious. "There's some other crazy rumors flying around."

Durkin's eyes widened. "Okay, I'm going to bite. What are you hearing?"

Phillips lips tightened as if he was afraid the truth would crush Durkin.

"For God's sake. You can tell me."

Phillips scratched his cheek as if attending to an imaginary itch. "Francis, you know that there are people who would love nothing more than to dance on your grave."

Durkin sighed, imagining the gleeful faces of his enemies dancing around his tombstone. "I didn't become a state's attorney to win popularity contests."

Phillips nodded. He understood. "Roslyn came to see me."

Durkin's eyes bulged with curiosity.

"She asked me if you contacted me. I didn't lie. I told her, no." Phillips grinned. "It was the truth. I contacted you." The two litigators laughed. Roslyn screwed up. She should have asked if Phillips had spoken to Durkin.

"She then started asking me about your dating habits."

"My dating habits?"

"It was weird. She asked me if you went to men's clubs."

"Un-fucking believable," Durkin said, blowing a gust of frustration as he ran his fingers through his thinning hair. The Chief State's Attorney was essentially asking his top assistant if Durkin was twisted enough to arrange to meet a young woman in a parking area for sex.

"So, what did you tell her?"

"I told her we had a professional relationship. We rarely go drinking after work but I didn't think so."

It was true. Durkin and Phillips were extremely close. Phillips was Durkin's protege. But besides holiday office parties, they rarely mixed their professional and social worlds.

"Hey, it's going to turn dark before the sun comes out again," Durkin said.

Phillips stared, wide-eyed at Durkin. What was he saying?

"I'm pretty sure I'm going to be arrested."

Jagged lines of disbelief began cutting across Phillips' face until he looked like a cracked porcelain plate. He held the expression for a long count and then stared, slack-jawed at Durkin. Durkin had never seen the injured expression on Phillips's face.

"Maybe even tonight."

Additional cracks rippled across Phillip's face.

"Listen, I'm getting railroaded."

Phillips shook his head in disbelief. Railroaded? Phillips was a seasoned prosecutor and knew bad cops and bad prosecutors once in a blue moon railroaded innocent people. But it was rare. Extremely rare. But no one railroaded a state's attorney. Durkin was essentially saying the New York State Troopers were framing him. It was an intellectual leap that Phillips had a hard time taking.

Durkin read Phillips expression and resisted the urge to tell Phillips about Hennigan's confession. He was bound by the attorney-client privilege.

"You've got to understand," Durkin began with the heaviness of a man whose professional stature was being chiseled away in front of him. "This guy Rasmutin is a nasty character. He's not above playing dirty." Durkin was suddenly aware he was sounding desperate and weak.

"I give you my word. I had nothing to do with the woman's murder. The facts will come out."

"You know I'm in your corner."

"I know, but right now my corner is not a good place to be."

"I get it." Phillips's words were wrapped in the sadness of a man accepting the fact that he was turning a page in his life. Phillips had hitched his wagon to Durkin's star. For a decade, he basked in the glow of Durkin's success. Hell, he knew he generated a considerable amount of the wattage that shined on Durkin. He accepted his role and his ego didn't demand to share the limelight because they had an unspoken agreement that when Durkin finally departed to academia or became a judge, Durkin would use all his political juice to get Phillips appointed as state's attorney.

If Durkin got arrested for murder, he wouldn't have an ounce of political juice. If Durkin was arrested, there was a good chance Phillips would be sidelined and he'd never climb above an assistant state's attorney. As it was, he didn't check most of the boxes for new state's attorneys. He was white and male. The appointments were going to anyone except white males and if his decade of labor and glory at Durkin's side didn't put him in the pole position for the top spot, he was going to finish his career on a slow boat to nowhere.

Phillips rose and wobbled as if he suddenly realized his ties to Durkin were more a liability than an asset. "Be good," he said, shaking Durkin's hand.

"Be good," Durkin replied, pulling Phillips tightly to him.

CHAPTER TWENTY THREE

A warm wave of paranoia washed over Durkin as he watched men and women in business suits emerge from their cars and head towards the entrance to Quinnipiac's Law School. Was it a larger crowd than usual? Had word leaked through law enforcement channels that he was being arrested? Was this the place that the State's Attorney Francis X. Durkin was going to take an ignoble fall?

"Would you give me a second," Durkin said to Cassie, pointing to his cell phone. She read the stress on his face, nodded and stepped out of the car.

Durkin hit his speed dial and PJ answered immediately. "Have you heard anything?"

"Hold on, let me put Sam on the phone," PJ said, soberly. Durkin heard the crackling sound of the phone being handed to Sam.

"Francis," Sam began in an apologetic tone. "We were going to call you when the meeting is over."

"What meeting?"

"There's a meeting going on in the superintendent's office in Albany."

"Huh?"

"It's a meeting with all the top brass."

"What's the meeting about?" Durkin regretted allowing desperation to leak into his voice.

"Everything is hush-hush but I'm pretty sure it's about DNA tests."

Durkin's chest heaved. "What about the tests?"

"I heard Rasmutin personally delivered evidence to be tested at the crime lab," Rome said, sounding like he considered that an ominous sign. He pulled a train of air through his nostrils and decided to be fully transparent. "My gut tells me they're making damn sure the DNA tests justify arresting you."

Durkin's felt a shot of electricity surge through his body. His worst nightmare was coming true.

Rome recognized the sound of fear over the phone; the sharp intake of oxygen followed by a sudden contraction of throat muscles.

"I should know something soon." Rome paused, trying to think of something reassuring to say. He drew a blank. His source inside the troopers HQ had drawn a bleak picture. There were rumors that the DNA tests placed Durkin at the center of the crime scene. There were rumors that the District Attorney was drawing up an arrest warrant. There was nothing to be optimistic about.

"As soon as I hear anything, I'll call you."

Durkin sat in silence. At least he knew why he hadn't been arrested yet: the troopers were going over the DNA tests with a fine-toothed comb. But he also knew that once they were done, the hammer would fall.

"Whatever you do, don't release that tape," Durkin said, still concerned that releasing the tape would jeopardize convicting Hennigan.

Rome pointedly ignored him. "I'll let you know as soon as I hear anything."

"Thanks," Durkin said in the distressed voice of a man watching his career slide into a ditch.

Durkin killed the call and exited the car. He hugged Cassie tightly against him as if trying to draw strength from her.

"Is everything okay?"

Durkin nodded like a man who knew a dark fate awaited him. He forced his chin up. "There's nothing new. Let's go."

As Cassie and Francis passed through the entrance to Quinnipiac's Law School, a man wearing a blue, pin-striped business suit, spotted Durkin. He rushed down a short flight of stairs and greeted Durkin with a gush of enthusiasm.

"State's Attorney Durkin," the man boomed as if the louder he spoke, the warmer his reception. The man was Gerard Oliphant, the head administrator at the law school. Oliphant's bald head shined brightly as if it was illuminated by a bulb, positioned just under his scalp. He extended his hand to Durkin. "Thanks for coming in on your sabbatical."

"No problem," Durkin said, shaking Oliphant's hand. He turned to Cassie. "This is my friend, Cassie Johnston. She couldn't pass up the opportunity to hear me wax eloquently."

Oliphant missed the humor and shook Cassie's hand warmly. "It's a pleasure. Thank you for coming."

Oliphant pointed to the atrium, just outside of the auditorium, where a large crowd milled about. He eyed his watch as if he had an obsession for punctuality. "I'll show you to the stage now since we're running late."

213

Oliphant escorted Cassie and Durkin through the large crowd while Durkin nodded at familiar faces, slowed and shook a few hands while never completely stopping. Quickly scanning the crowd, Durkin recognized six state's attorneys, a handful of judges and at least two crime reporters. He made eye contact with a few and greeted them with nods as he wondered if they heard rumors he'd be arrested. His face warmed as his paranoia heated up.

Two Connecticut troopers stood like stone-faced sentries at the entrance to the auditorium. Durkin stopped, which caused Oliphant, who had been gently guiding him by his arm, to be yanked to a stop. Durkin fixed his eyes on the troopers. He had never seen troopers lined up on both sides of an entrance to the auditorium. They were waiting to arrest him. Durkin was absolutely sure of it. That bastard, Durkin muttered to himself, cursing Rasmutin.

"Is something the matter?" Oliphant asked.

Durkin exchanged a knowing glance with Cassie. It's happening. Prepare yourself. He issued a blanket instruction to his vitals, his heart, his pulse, his diaphragm, to remain steady and under control. He promised himself he was going to be dignified throughout the most debasing moment of his life.

"No, it's nothing," he said to Oliphant. What else could he say? Your speaker was about to get arrested for the brutal murder of a young woman?

Durkin summoned the nerves to start up again, walking slowly towards the entranceway with the unsteady gait of a man walking to the gallows. If he was going to be arrested, there was nothing at this stage he could do about it. Dignity was paramount, he reminded himself again. Smile. Shake your head lightly and smile.

Durkin slowed as he neared the troopers. To his visible surprise neither of the trooper's expression changed as their eyes passed over him. As he passed unimpeded, he released a heavy breath that sounded like he popped to the surface of water after holding his breath.

"Francis!" Durkin turned to the familiar sounding voice. Roslyn Jones smiled, noting to herself that Durkin looked like he had just seen a ghost. She was going to comment on his expression but was startled to see a woman standing next to him. Her eyes pried an introduction from Durkin.

"Roslyn Jones this is my friend, Cassie Johnston."

Roslyn Jones studied Cassie like an older sister, sizing up whether the woman was good enough for her brother.

"Nice to meet you," Cassie said warmly as she confidently held out her hand to Jones.

"Likewise. It's always nice to meet a friend of Francis's."

Cassie flashed a weak smile, unsure of whether there was a hidden message in Roslyn's greeting.

Jones turned all business. "Would you mind if I talk shop with Francis for a moment?"

"Of course not. I'll go find a seat," Cassie said, flashing Durkin a warm smile before walking away.

Knowing she only had a few seconds, Jones got right to the point. "What are you going to speak about?"

"It's in the program," Durkin parried.

Jones held up the program. A photo of Benjamin Cardozo, the famous white haired, Supreme Court Justice, adorned the cover. Next to Cardozo was a decade-old photo of Durkin, standing in front of the U.S. Supreme Court building. The court's impressive white granite columns seemed to infuse Durkin with power and prestige. He had more hair and carried around far less weight. Durkin was also smirking because he had won a resounding court victory over his long time nemesis, the ACLU.

"All it says is that you're going to address criminal law issues."

"Yep."

"Francis, don't touch *State v. Police*."

"Tell me you'll appeal and I won't breathe a word about Terrance Police tonight."

Roslyn stepped back and eyed him with a strained look. "You know it's complicated."

Durkin stared at her like he could see right through her. It's only complicated if you make it complicated. He held his stare for a moment. "You know it should be appealed. The court got it wrong and you should be appealing the constitutional issue to the U.S. Supreme Court." Durkin tapped his photo on the program. "You know I'd win."

"This is not the time for a debate," Jones replied curtly.

"Okay," Durkin said with a short rush of air that signaled he was amenable to change the subject. "Have you heard anything from Superintendent Crowley?"

"No. Should I have?"

Durkin weighed whether to share his belief that he'd be arrested soon. Should he warn Jones that her star prosecutor was about to be escorted off the stage in handcuffs? Durkin's nervous system went into overdrive.

"Are you okay?" Jones asked as Durkin's face turned white and droplets of sweat leaked from the fissures in his forehead.

"I'm fine," he replied unconvincingly. "Just pre-game nerves."

"You don't look fine and you've never been nervous speaking to anyone."

Gerard Oliphant who had been standing a respectful distance away, cleared his throat loudly. "Professor. I beg your pardon but we have to begin."

"Yes, of course," Durkin answered. He stepped close to Jones. "I'll speak to you after my lecture."

Roslyn studied his face as worry sprung on hers. "Yes, and speak about something besides Terrance Police," is all she said before she turned to find her seat in the front row next to a bevy of assistants.

The stage was empty except for a podium positioned on the left side. In the middle was a chair, a small table that held a pitcher of water and a glass. Oliphant pointed to the chair. "I will introduce you and then you can take it from there."

Oliphant's eyes searched Durkin for a trace of papers or notecards. He eyed the outside of Durkin's jacket pocket, looking for a lump of papers. His eyes darted to the back of Durkin's pants, expecting to see papers stuck in his back pocket. Finding none, he shrugged to himself and approached the podium.

The auditorium was at full capacity and slowly quieting as Oliphant beamed from the podium. He tapped the microphone to get their attention.

"Good evening," he began as the suits still standing took their seats. "Tonight it is my distinct honor to introduce you to Francis Xavier Durkin, Connecticut's State's Attorney from the Judicial District of Fairfield."

Oliphant beamed at Durkin as the crowd further quieted. "We are honored that Francis Durkin is also an adjunct professor of criminal law at our law school. This semester he has agreed to deliver three speeches on issues related to criminal law. The subject he selects is entirely his choice."

Oliphant grinned nervously knowing that while Durkin was free to express his opinions on any topic, the law school would catch the blowback for anything controversial Durkin said. "Professor Durkin has been described as an intellectual tour de force," he began with a gush. Oliphant paused and ran his eyes over the audience while sporting a broad smile. "He earned that lofty description for his peerless track record before the United States Supreme Court and his record in Connecticut's criminal court system."

Oliphant shook his head as if awed by Durkin's courtroom record. He then pushed the piece of paper away from him as if signaling that he was ad-libbing. "His adversaries in court have been known to say going up against Francis Durkin is like playing chess against a super computer."

Oliphant glanced at Durkin to see if his flattery hit the mark. Seeing no reaction, he then read Durkin's biography verbatim from the program and seemed disappointed when he finished. With a wave of his right hand, Oliphant signaled to Durkin. The floor is yours.

For a long second, Durkin sat as if unsure of what to say. He looked at the crowd as if searching for the answer. As the seconds ticked by his eyes glazed as if he was drifting into deep, solitary thought. Then, as the awkwardness of his silence crested, he reached down to the glass of water and took a sip. He stood deliberatively and tapped the microphone attached to his lapel.

Durkin scanned the audience as if looking for inspiration to choose a topic. Then he saw Representative Stephon Stratsberg, co-chair of Connecticut's Judiciary Committee by the doorway. He was sure that Stratsberg stood by the door to draw attention to himself.

As far as Durkin was concerned, Stratsberg had forgotten that the state was supposed to wield the sword of justice. Instead Stratsberg led the charge to reduce felonies to misdemeanors. Now the criminals had their wrists slapped for possession of illegal guns, car jackings, even assault. There was no deterrence. No fear of the law. And of course, crime sky-rocketed and teenagers were recruited by gangs to steal cars since there was no meaningful penalties for juveniles. They'd be released immediately and their records would be wiped clean.

Durkin credited Stratsberg for his role in selecting his topic with a nod in his direction. "The criminal is to go free because the constable has blundered," Durkin boomed to a sea of smiles. Judging from the facial expressions, he guessed 90 percent of the audience recognized Benjamin Cardozo's famous quote.

People v. Defore.

Cardozo's decision in Defore allowed evidence, which had been seized illegally by the police, to be introduced in criminal trials if it shed light on the guilt of the defendant.

"In 1925, a New York City police officer arrested John Defore for stealing an overcoat. The arrest took place in the hallway of a boarding house. After Defore was arrested and without permission from Defore or obtaining a search warrant, the police officer searched Defore's room. The officer found a blackjack which was illegal to possess pursuant to New York's penal law."

Durkin assumed the air of a law professor with legal theories bubbling in his head as he strolled across the stage. "The arrest was illegal. This point was uncontested. The officer did not see Defore steal the coat and had no basis to arrest him other than his suspicion that a poor man in a boarding house had no other way to procure a new overcoat other than by stealing it."

He stopped and commented on the officer's logic with a shrug of his shoulders. "The officer also did not have probable cause to believe an illegal weapon would be found in Defore's room." Durkin wiggled his right forefinger in the air as if to warn the audience against rushing to judgment. "Now, by a show of hands, how many in the audience feel that illegally obtained evidence—in this case the blackjack—should be suppressed and not allowed to be used as evidence against Defore?"

A majority of the audience's hands shot up. Durkin pointedly glanced at the doorway and saw Rep. Stratsberg with his arm stuck straight up in the air.

"That's what I thought. That's the law of the land and is, as most of us know, known as the Exclusionary Rule," Durkin said, drawing up his nose as if the law of the land smelled to him. "The states were force fed the Exclusionary Rule in 1960 with the Supreme Court's decision in *Mapps v. Ohio* which held that the Fourth Amendment barred illegally obtained evidence in all—state and federal— criminal cases."

Durkin sprouted the same smirk that he wore in the old photo in front of the U.S. Supreme Court. "When Cardozo issued his decision in *Defore,* only 14 state courts held that illegally obtained evidence could not be admitted as evidence against a defendant. So most state courts had ruled that evidence; no matter how it was obtained—legally or illegally—could be used in a criminal trial if the evidence shed light on the guilt or innocence of the defendant. Those courts held that the most important thing was the guilt or innocence of the defendant, not how the evidence was procured."

Durkin's face grew serious as he returned to the *People v. Defore.* "Cardozo wrote that the question is whether the protection for the individual would be gained at a disproportionate loss of protection for society if illegally obtained evidence could not be used against defendants."

Durkin walked over to the small table and picked up his glass of water and sipped it. He then raised his glass. "It's a balancing act. How much weight should be given to Defore's Constitutional rights and how much weight should be afforded to the protection of society?"

Durkin shook his finger as if admonishing those who felt Defore's interests were paramount. "Cardozo noted that if the defendant's rights are to be held to be more important than society's, then a body which was discovered by an illegal search could be ignored and a murderer could be set free if there was no other evidence linking the suspect to the murder. The stark madness of allowing such a travesty was clear to Cardozo in 1926 and the madness of it is just as clear today."

Durkin took a seat and for an instant, gave the impression that he was done. The audience stirred as if they had been cheated out of the price of admission. It was precisely the reaction that Durkin sought. He exhaled deeply and sprung to his feet.

"For decades, the medical profession believed that taking two aspirin a day had salutary effects on a person's health. But then a modern study of the medicinal effects of aspirin turned the accepted medical wisdom on its head. We now know that taking two aspirin a day can hurt us." Durkin paused and smiled widely. "The field of criminal law would be well advised to similarly re-asses the merits of the Exclusionary Rule. So-called established wisdom needs to be revisited."

Durkin saw a palpable scowl roll across Stratsberg's face. Good, Durkin thought. He was getting his intended reaction.

"Every man and woman in this room knows there is nothing in the Constitution that says that evidence secured in violation of the Fourth Amendment can't be used in criminal trials."

Durkin provocatively pointed to the crowd. "And many of you know that lawless countries as England, have not adopted the Exclusionary Rule." He drew a breath and let his sarcasm float in the auditorium like a slowly dissolving wisp of smoke. He then sat down looking as if his legs needed a rest.

"How often have we heard the worn out argument that if it wasn't for the Exclusionary Rule there'd be no deterrent for the police to respect the Constitution and we'd devolve into an authoritarian state?"

Durkin scrunched his face as if he was shocked by the idiocy of his own question. "Today, the Exclusionary Rule is accepted as a bedrock of judicial wisdom. Its intellectual foundations are almost never questioned."

Durkin scooted to the edge of his chair. "It is time to question whether Benjamin Cardozo in 1926 or the Warren Court in 1960, got it right."

He leapt to his feet as if suddenly re-energized. He tried to read the audience's reaction. A few heads nodded in agreement. Others stared back with disagreeable looks that shouted they'd never agree on anything with Francis Durkin.

"Benjamin Cardozo's warning has come true: murderers have gone free because the prosecutors have been deprived of using clear-cut evidence of guilt because a judge, bound by the Exclusionary Rule, has ruled that it was obtained in contravention of the Fourth Amendment. I had to sit and suffer the indignity of seeing more than one ruthless killer walk out of court because of the Exclusionary Rule."

Durkin made a pecking motion with his forefinger as if he was pointing at every member of the audience individually. "Are you safer because of the Exclusionary Rule? Is society better off because of the Exclusionary Rule?" Durkin's pace increased and he shook his head demonstratively. "You're not. Society isn't. No one is better off for the simple reason that murderers murder. Rapists rape. Thieves thieve and those people should not walk the streets free because a cop obtained evidence of their guilt illegally."

Durkin threw up his arms as if he was reading the minds of some of the audience. "One aspect of the penal system is retribution; society taking retribution against offenders. Society has the obligation to seek retribution for the victim."

A bearded man in an olive colored khaki suit stood and wore an aggrieved look for having to wait so long to share his thoughts. He cleared his throat. "I'm Benjamin Cox, a defense lawyer in Connecticut. I've sat here listening to you and," Cox paused, "I'm in utter disbelief. You sound as if you'd like to put our criminal justice system back in the stone age."

A ripple of laughter rolled over the audience, causing Durkin to reflexively flash a defensive smile. The man looked familiar but Durkin couldn't place his face.

"Pitting the state against an individual is not a fair battle," Cox continued. "The Exclusionary Rule is crucial to balancing the power imbalance in court and holding the police accountable."

"What about the victims? What balance is offered to them? They see criminals walk free because evidence of guilt is tossed out of court because of the Exclusionary Rule."

Cox began to respond but Durkin cut him off. "Can we agree that the Founders of our nation didn't create the Fourth Amendment to protect criminals' rights?"

A smattering of applause rippled over the audience.

Cox sputtered. "The Fourth Amendment was designed to protect everyone's rights."

Durkin shrugged disagreeably. "Then it's failed because it doesn't protect victims' rights."

"You advocate reactionary positions. You also incorrectly imply there's a correlation between the severity of penalties and crime rates."

Durkin smiled. He loved the rush of legal debates. "Do people speed on highways where the speed limits are strictly enforced?"

The audience shook its collective head. Durkin was right. Drivers kept close to the speed limits if they thought there was a good chance a cop with a radar gun was hiding in the bushes.

"And what happens on the road if drivers know there's no penalties for speeding?" Durkin paused. "I'll tell you. Drivers would go over a 100 miles per hour, endangering everyone on the road. Without strong deterrents, it's human nature for people to ignore the law. That's a fact."

Cox countered strongly. "If that were the case, we'd still have the death penalty."

The death penalty. Cox's mention of the death penalty triggered Durkin's memory: Cox led the Connecticut Network to Abolish the Death Penalty. It was a sore spot for Durkin. He fervently believed in the death penalty. An eye for an eye. But he lost the battle in front of Connecticut's State Supreme Court.

And now he knew where Cox was headed. There was no evidence that the death penalty deterred murderers.

Cox pounced precisely as Durkin anticipated. "You know there's no evidence that the death penalty leads to less murders."

Durkin exhaled audibly. He had heard it all before. "Maybe not but most victim's family believe that justice is served by the death penalty."

Oliphant walked to the middle of the stage and pointed to a person already holding a microphone and waiting to be addressed. "Let's take another question." He then pointed to a woman waiting to be recognized.

"I'm Kate Shelden with the *Hartford Courant*. Do you have any comment on Connecticut's Supreme Court ruling in *State v. Police*?"

The veins in Durkin's neck bulged. It was as if the reporter tossed bloody meat to a shark. Roslyn Jones glared at Durkin. Stop, you fool. Say "no comment." Say it's under review and just take another question. Roslyn's leg muscles began contracting involuntarily as stress flooded her body. She steadied herself and instructed herself not to visibly react as she felt the heat of eyes on her.

"I'll just say that our highest court's decision put an attempted murderer, with a rap sheet longer than your arm, back on the streets. Do you think Connecticut is a safer place with him roaming the streets?"

Durkin stared out at the audience. He saw some commotion at the back of the room. His heart skipped. For the last 45 minutes he was too focused on his speech to think about his impending arrest. Now, the fear of the professional embarrassment, the raw indignity of being carted away in handcuffs, came rushing back.

It was the moment that Rasmutin planned. Connecticut troopers would march in and cart State's Attorney Durkin off the stage in handcuffs. He'd be on the front page of the national papers with his hands cuffed.

Two men began to walk, side by side, down the center aisle towards the stage. Durkin inhaled deeply as if he was attempting to sustain the oxygen levels in his brain. Durkin felt his chest pound. He actually felt his heart muscles beat. He could hardly breathe, let alone speak. He gripped the arms of his chair and brought his glass of water to his lips to mask his face.

As the men reached the tenth row he could see the men were dressed in suits. He was sure they'd send uniforms to get him. It was much more dramatic. Troopers, clasping handcuffs on the state's attorney in militaristic uniforms. They took another step and then slowed and dropped into two open seats. Just two suits.

Gerald Oliphant strode to the podium looking as if he was concerned about Durkin's health.

"Thank you very much Professor Durkin. Your passion is extraordinary. We all look forward to your next talk in the Benjamin Cardozo Criminal Law series." He turned to the audience. "Professor Durkin will be on hand for the next hour or so if you want to speak to him in the reception hall." He turned back to Durkin and began clapping. "Thank you for your insights."

The audience clapped on cue and Durkin's chest sagged with the relief of a man who dodged a bullet. He waved lightly in response to the audience's applause as he felt his heart rate slow. Then, for the next hour, he exchanged small talk with a horde of suits.

CHAPTER TWENTY FOUR

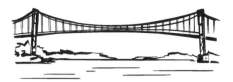

Commander Igor Rasmutin woke up an hour earlier than he usually did. When he awoke, he didn't rise groggily and slowly summon the energy to shake the cobwebs of sleep off that normally gripped him in the morning. No, this morning he woke, fully charged and alert. His customary morning scowl was replaced with a sly grin.

Rasmutin showered, shaved and inspected his uniform to ensure that its creases were razor sharp. His uniform was immaculate and he knew once he wrapped it around his body, he'd radiate a command presence. But just for good measure, he plugged in his iron and shot an extra puff of starch on his collar. This morning, he'd look his best he assured himself.

As he sipped his first cup of coffee, he used his trooper-issued phone to check his official emails. A NYSP automatic tracking alert told him Durkin's car was detected on I-90, heading back from Connecticut. Rasmutin smiled as he envisioned Durkin arriving back at the Thousand Islands and seeing the morning's *Watertown Daily Register*. Rasmutin chuckled. Durkin is going to shit his pants.

Rasmutin then checked an email from the sergeant at the barracks that listed all the arrests and tickets issued during the night. His eye skipped down the email, looking for anything that referenced Irene Izak's murder. The last line of the email caught his eye. The superintendent requested copies of the polygraphs administered to Hennigan. Rasmutin tightened. He knew having Senior Investigator Cordon administer the polygraphs would raise flags in Albany but that was better than having some unknown yahoo administer the test, he thought. You'd never know what you'd get. Now he'd get a few annoying questions from Albany but nothing he couldn't handle, he assured himself as he finished the last slug of his coffee.

Rasmutin's usual 20 minute drive to the 1000 Island Bait store took only 15 minutes. As he entered the store, he stopped and scowled under his mirrored glasses at the cashier. The guy's age was obscured by a tattoo of an ancient warrior on his right cheek. His rumpled t-shirt was decorated with a skull pierced by a Bowie knife. His hair was spiked and ears pierced.

Rasmussen's nostrils flared. The punk rock style offended his eyes. On any other day, Rasmutin would find a way to get the guy's name or license plate and run a background check on the puke. He'd find a way to bust the guy's balls. But not today.

Today, Rasmutin picked up a copy of the *Watertown Daily Register,* making sure not to shift his mirror glasses to its cover. Every one of his movements was designed to appear routine and mechanical. It was just an ordinary day. Rasmutin dropped a dollar on the counter and waved his hand nonchalantly. "Have a good day."

"You too," the cashier replied, happy to see the intimidating trooper leave.

Rasmutin folded the paper and tossed it on his passenger seat as if he had little interest in it. He started his patrol car up and drove across the street to the empty North Country Welcome Center parking lot.

He parked where he could observe traffic in and out of the lot and picked up the newspaper. His eyes darted across the front page, carefully scanning the headlines. Confusion splashed over his face. His eyes tightened and his thick eyebrows contracted like a furry worm. The paper crinkled in his angry hands as he searched for JB's byline. Nothing. He tore the newspaper open and scanned every page with a growing fury. There was nothing about the murder investigation. He smashed the newspaper, contorting it to a crumpled paper ball.

"What the fuck!" he screamed as he flung the newspaper into the passengers's seat. His body vibrated and then he punched the passenger seat with such force that the car rocked. He gritted his teeth and every one of his muscles constricted into a tight, angry lump as he dug out his cell phone and tapped a name in his directory.

JB answered on the second ring. "Breen," he said in a sleepy voice.

"You said you were going to publish the article!" Rasmutin hissed with the heat of a blow torch.

JB emitted the sounds of a man quickly waking. "We have to verify some facts." JB groaned at the knifing pain in his shoulder as he pushed himself up in bed.

"What's there to verify? I gave you a copy of the lab report."

"It's my editor's call," JB pushed back.

"I could have given this to the *Times Union,*" Rasmutin growled. "Hell, give me one good reason why I shouldn't do that right now."

"This shouldn't take long," JB said, clearing the last threads of sleep from his throat.

"It better not!" Rasmutin barked as he killed the call.

JB pressed his shoulder against the headboard and eyed Cajillion, Danielle Keegan's small kitten, curled up on the rumpled sheets where Danielle Keegan had slept.

He eyed her bedroom full of girly, pink and purple stuffed-animals. He smiled to himself. Her nerdiness was endearing. He leaned against Keegan's light pink headboard and thought about their dinner. They hit it off immediately. She treated him like a wounded warrior when she saw his arm in a sling. He complimented her new haircut and started with light flattery. He told her he thought forensic science was exciting and under-appreciated. He then skillfully pushed her science button. "How does DNA fingerprinting work?"

Keegan's eyes lit up. "After all my years in the lab, I'm still in awe at the process. Did you know that 99.9 percent of DNA sequences are exactly the same in every human being?"

JB's eyes widened. No, he had no clue.

"The small fraction of DNA that's different allows us to do DNA fingerprinting."

"So how do you get a DNA fingerprint?"

Keegan beamed. "It's mind boggling how efficiently DNA is packed into our cells. If our DNA was stretched out it would stretch over 10 billion miles. Enough to stretch to Pluto and back."

JB shook his head. That's long.

"We can even replicate a sample so we can run complex tests on it."

"You what?"

"We replicate them. DNA is helix shaped. Like a ladder. You've seen the sketches of a twisted ladder, right?"

JB nodded. Kind of.

"Well, there's a process that breaks apart the sides of the ladder, copies them and then pairs them back together. Then it breaks the ladders apart again, repeats the process which doubles the amount of the DNA. There's practically no limit to the duplication process."

Keegan looked disappointed to see JB's eyes glaze over. She cleared the plate and utensils in front of her as if she needed an open space to explain DNA fingerprinting for dummies. "We all have genetic markers. Think of the genetic markers as houses located in a planned development. You know, the kind of almost identical houses that line block after block."

JB nodded as he envisioned a split level housing development right outside of Watertown.

"Now, think of each one of those houses as subdivided, like a two family house. Are you with me?"

JB's face bunched. He was just barely hanging on.

Keegan pushed on. "At the crime lab, we look for at least twenty DNA addresses. Now, our mother and father give us something called alleles. There's different alleles at each address. Think of these as windows in each subdivided house."

JB looked on with growing confusion.

"Stay with me," Keegan said with a smile. "Just think that everyone has a different number of windows in each subdivided house. So, if a person has what I'll call 16 windows on one side of the house and 15 windows on the other side of the house, the DNA test will show that they have 15 or 16 at that DNA address. Everyone's alleles vary at each address."

"Are you following me?"

The glaze in JB's eyes turned to a high sheen.

Keegan grabbed a napkin and dug out a pen from her pocketbook. She scribbled furiously for a moment and then passed the napkin to JB.

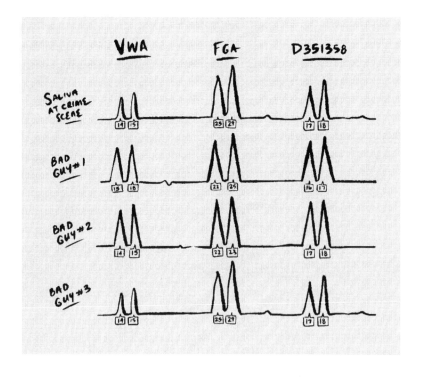

"You see those spikes?"

JB tapped the spikes on the napkin to confirm he was following her.

"Well, those are electropherograms that show the DNA profiles. As I said, think of them as the windows in the subdivided house."

Keegan pointed to the napkin. "Once you get a match on 20 genetic markers you have a very high probability that the DNA matches the guy. There could be only a one in an octillion or a one in a sextillion chance the DNA belonged to someone other than the suspect. Do you get it?"

JB picked up the napkin and marveled at Keegan's enthusiasm for science. He barely understood her but her passion was contagious.

"Look at Bad Guy #3," Keegan said. "His genetic address, if you will, matches up with the DNA addresses of the hypothetical saliva. See?" Keegan pointed to the numbers next to Bad Guy #3 and then pointed to the numbers on the saliva at the crime scene. "This is a gross simplification but you get the idea, right?"

JB didn't but he thought it was time to broach the subject about Rasmutin's lab report. "Do you think a draft lab report can be relied upon?"

Keegan stiffened and her eyes became like lasers, penetrating his eyes and reading his thoughts.

"I'm speaking hypothetically," JB stammered under the heat of her glare. JB's face reddened as Keegan placed her elbows on the table and rested her face in her palms. She had read JB's article on the murder on Wellesley Island. She knew Russo had rushed the DNA test at the troopers's request. She instantly saw right through JB and was sure he was poking around for information about the draft DNA report.

"Yes, let's keep this hypothetical," Keegan said with a grin of a chess player one move away from checkmate. "Would it be easier to use a case like the recent murder of the woman on Wellesley Island?"

JB stared back at her with a flustered look.

"To answer your question," Keegan continued, "you have to be extremely wary of draft reports. I'd proceed with extreme caution."

Extremely wary. Extreme caution.

"Listen," Keegan added. "Forensic scientists work with petri trays, microscopes and miniature plastic tubes. It's very easy to contaminate the tests. In fact, it's very hard not to contaminate tests. Especially if someone doesn't know what they're doing."

Keegan paused and envisioned Dante Russo, who she considered the poster boy for incompetence. "And even if the test isn't contaminated, a microscopic DNA sample could be mixed with something that distorts the tests. I'd be very cautious about drafts."

JB's thoughts were jumbled. He considered coming clean with Keegan but he knew she'd press him on who gave him the draft report. She might even report him. It could turn ugly, fast, he concluded. No, he couldn't admit he had a copy of the draft DNA report.

Their eyes locked and Keegan would bet a cajillion dollars that JB had a copy of the draft DNA report in his pocket.

"As I said, I would never rely on drafts of lab results," Keegan repeated herself to drive the message home. "Managers often point out errors. It happens all the time. I'd be extremely wary."

Keegan couldn't be any clearer, JB thought. Something was wrong with the DNA test Rasmutin leaked to him. He excused himself and called Larry Costello. Costello was furious. JB had never heard him curse before. And he didn't just curse. He let a string of expletives fly. When Costello calmed down, he pressured JB to edit the story and emphasize that the lab results were only draft results. JB held firm. He reminded Costello that a reporter's reputation was all he had. He could never be sullied. He reminded him of Sabrina Erdley's article in *Rolling Stone* magazine about a gang rape at a University of Virginia fraternity. It hadn't been vetted and Erdley and *Rolling Stone* cut journalistic corners. But it was sensational so *Rolling Stone* rushed it to print.

The article landed with a bang. The UVA president instantly suspended all fraternities. All were guilty upon an accusation of the horrendous charge. The Charleston PD opened an investigation. Every UVA fraternity brother was put under the microscope and drew scorching national scorn.

But under the stress of the investigations, the truth leaked out. Erdley's story began unraveling. The accuser lied to win a man's affections. Defamation lawsuits were filed and settled for millions. And in the end, Sabrina Erdley and *Rolling Stone's* reputation lay in tatters.

"I'm not going to be another Sabrina Erdley," JB told Costello. He held the line. "And you don't want to lose your job for making the Register look like the *Rolling Stone*."

Larry Costello hung up the phone just as abruptly as Rasmutin. In the last 8 hours he hadn't made any friends, JB thought as he rolled out of Keegan's bed. Then he corrected himself as Danielle Keegan returned, carrying two cups of Dunkin Donuts coffee and jelly donuts. He had made a friend.

CHAPTER TWENTY FIVE

A car's front tire scraped against the curb in front of the Sacred Heart Church in Watertown, New York. The original Gothic-styled church burned to the ground decades ago and was replaced by a sharp-edged, brick building.

From inside the car, PJ McLevy and Sam Rome eyed the church nervously, wary of the reception awaiting them. The men gathered themselves with a let's-get-on-with-it burst of energy and exited the car. Halfway to the church's front door, Rome stopped at a statue of the Virgin Mary with "Our Lady of the Sacred Heart" chiseled into the bottom of its granite base. Rome eyed Virgin Mary adorned with a crown and cradling baby Jesus with a crown of his own. His eyes fell on baby Jesus. To Rome, the baby looked more like a small, unhappy man wearing a crown than an infant. He studied the baby Jesus's eyes for a long second. The unhappy man with the crown just stared off into the distance as if he refused to recognize Rome.

Rome moved on and pulled the heavy church's door open to the sticky sound of rubber weather-stripping pulling apart. He held the door open and motioned for PJ to enter first. As their eyes adjusted to the darkness, a dour-looking woman in a smudged apron, stopped what she was doing on the altar and eyed them suspiciously. Her hair was balled up in a bun and Rome guessed she was about 65 years old. Over her shoulder, he could see a priest arranging gold chalices on the altar.

The woman picked up a rag and wiped her hands as she walked down the aisle towards the men. The men began to detect the smell of wood polish as her oval shaped face came into focus. Rome recognized the look. Her face was lined with Eastern European deprivation. She had scraped for everything she had and never had much.

The woman stopped a few feet from PJ and Rome and continued wiping her hands on the rag as the scent of wood polish grew stronger. She then blinked rapidly as if she smelled a cop and the odor triggered unpleasant memories.

An awkward silence hung over them until the men realized she had no intention of offering a greeting.

"We'd like to speak with Father. Patrick," Rome said, pointing to the priest on the altar. The woman eyed the men with the hostility of an overprotective gatekeeper.

"Who wants to see him?" she demanded in a gruff, foreign accent that Sam guessed was either Polish or Ukrainian.

"Tell him Sam Rome wants to see him," Sam replied in a tone that suggested she was supposed to recognize his name. She didn't. For a split second she considered asking PJ his name before she concluded one name was sufficient. She turned and walked down the aisle and whispered to the priest. The priest looked up at the two strangers at the back of his church as he listened to the woman. He nodded as she finished and then set a chalice down on the altar before strolling to the back of the church.

"I'm Father Patrick." His voice was steady but guarded as if he was taking the woman's advice to be wary of the men. Father Patrick O'Brien was 47 years old and had spent the last 6 of them tending to the Sacred Heart Church's flock. His face was drawn as if constant worrying had caused his metabolism to operate in perpetual overdrive.

Rome studied O'Brien. He had seen thousands of similar pasty-white faces in Boston whose boyish freckles had aged into brown flecks which now courted melanoma.

Rome extended his hand warmly. "Sam Rome, Father."

Rome's manufactured warmth had no effect. The priest shook his hand mechanically and assumed a look of a man in a rush.

Rome began haltingly. "We're here for some spiritual advice," Rome said unconvincingly.

Fr. Patrick O'Brien scrutinized the men. His tense face made it clear that he didn't believe they were seeking spiritual counseling. "What is bothering you?"

"Well, we are friends of the family of the woman who was murdered on Wellesley Island a few days ago," Rome said.

O'Brien shuddered. It was a slight, almost imperceptible reaction but their cops' eyes caught the infinitesimal eye dilation and rabbit-like flare of his nostrils. It was enough. Rome and PJ were sure they had struck a nerve.

"What's the spiritual component of your inquiry?" O'Brien asked, regaining his priestly composure with a deep pull of air through his nostrils.

"We don't know how to proceed and as a man of God we are hoping you can help us."

Fr. Patrick glared at Rome as if he had a bitter taste in his mouth. Red blotches brightened and then faded on his face.

"Spare me your lies," Fr. Patrick hissed as if he had run out of patience.

"Did you know the woman's father is a priest, just like you?" PJ asked.

Fr. Patrick's face crunched with disgust as if he saw through PJ's effort to play on his sympathies.

"He's a priest in the Ukrainian orthodox church. And a very terrible man crushed his little girl's skull."

"Why are you telling me this?" Fr. Patrick spit out without an ounce of compassion for the woman.

Rome decided to go for broke. "We were hoping that since the girl's father is a priest you would consider telling us what you know about the murder."

"Why would I know anything about the murder of a girl on Wellesley Island?" O'Brien said, turning and pointing to the church door as if to say Wellesley Island was hundreds of miles away.

"Do you?" Rome asked with the sound of man that knew the answer.

"Do I what?" Fr. Patrick snapped.

"Do you know anything about the murder of Father Izak's daughter?"

"I don't like your question. It's pregnant with accusation."

"I'm not accusing you of anything," Rome replied calmly.

"You're certainly accusing me of knowing something," Fr. Patrick seethed.

Rome fought the urge to blurt out that O'Brien was a lying sack of shit. He wanted to scream that he had a tape of Hennigan confessing his murder to him. He wished he could play the tape and watch O'Brien squirm.

"People come to you all the time to seek your advice. Maybe you heard something, that's all."

Fr. Patrick turned and shot an alarmed look at the woman on the altar. Her radar worked properly. The men brought trouble. He peeled his eyes off her and turned back to the men."Why haven't the police contacted me if I know anything?"

"I can't answer that," Rome replied. He deployed a soothing voice. "Father, we are just talking to you now. If I mentioned to you that I had murdered someone, and it's not part of a confession, you'd be free to share this information with the police, right?"

O'Brien bubbled with fury. The men were treading on the sacred sacrament of confession. "You're smearing an innocent man with your questions. Defamation is a very serious crime."

"You seem very upset. Is there anything you want to tell us?"

"Tell you?" Fr. Patrick asked as if revolted by the question. "You are strangers who are insinuating things without a shred of evidence. Have you no shame?"

"Covering up for a murderer is a serious crime," Rome snapped.

"This conversation is over."

PJ and Rome exchanged disbelieving looks. Their effort to leverage a holy man's compassion was a complete bust.

Rome took one more swing. "Do you really think you can cleanse a murderer's soul by telling him to dedicate his remaining time on earth to God's work?"

Fr. Patrick's eyes vibrated with shock. That's precisely what he directed Deacon David to do. His look turned to a mix of fear and confusion.

Fr. Patrick's lips quivered. "Get out!"

The woman in the apron scampered towards the men holding her cell phone in the air like she was threatening to toss a hand grenade at them. "Father Patrick, would you like me to call the police?"

Fr. Patrick looked at PJ and Rome as calling on them to answer. "Do you want us to call the police or are you leaving?"

PJ tugged on Rome's arm. They were well past the point of diminishing returns. The visit had been a flat-out train wreck.

The men exchanged disgusted looks before PJ and Rome shook their heads and started for the door.

"I wanted to break the puke's face," Rome said as they reached their car.

"We knew it was a long shot," PJ rationalized. "We had to try something. It wasn't too preposterous to think that a few drops of humanity would leak out of a priest."

"Yeah, but I thought at least he'd give us something when he heard the girl's father was a priest. He didn't give a shit about Irene Izak or her father."

"Yep. He doesn't give a shit."

PJ fell into the driver's seat and started the car. "Now what?"

Rome didn't hesitate. "We don't have a choice." He paused and gazed at the modest houses built around the church. "There's only one thing we can do."

CHAPTER TWENTY SIX

PJ McLevy dug his knuckle into his eye socket to relieve the burning sensation. The feeling of burning eyes triggered long buried memories of lying motionless for hours as he stalked his prey. He began as a Marine sniper, training his eyes on his enemies in the jungle. Then as a cop, draped in camouflage, he watched bad guys selling drugs, selling guns, selling stolen car parts, selling young boys and girls. Silently waiting and watching others, he had always felt comfortable, always felt at home, stalking and then pouncing at precisely the right moment.

At this moment, his whole body was stiff as if he was a wet rag, thrown in the back of a trunk and forgotten. His muscles ached each time he shifted his body. Undercover surveillance is a young man's game he sighed, knowing he was too bull-headed to ever hang up his spurs and leave the game to the young. No, he was content knowing he'd leave the earth playing the game, somewhere, sometime.

He picked up his binoculars and trained them at Troop D's barrack's rear door for the hundredth time that night. He had a perfect view of the rear exit but he hadn't seen Trooper David Hennigan come and go as he expected.

PJ inhaled deeply in a primal effort to feed oxygen to his brain. He'd need it to get through the night. He held his breath for a four count and then exhaled loudly.

As the air escaped from him his phone rang. It was an unlisted number but that was not unusual since most of the calls he received were from burner phones.

"Yeah," he said, sounding like a 68 year old man who had sat for the past 8 hours in the front seat of a car.

"Hennigan was out on sick leave. He's returning today. He's on the 7 a.m. to 7 p.m. shift, not the 7 p.m. to 7 a.m. shift."

The voice didn't identify himself. It didn't need to. He recognized Sam Rome's voice instantly.

"You know why his hours changed?" PJ asked.

"Nope. A buddy checked the trooper's personnel system. There's no reason listed."

PJ grunted as he asked himself what was behind the change in Hennigan's schedule. He checked his watch. Hennigan should be arriving shortly.

"Okay, the show should get on the road soon." He hung up without saying anything more. PJ was always succinct, saying as few words as possible on a phone.

Five minutes later, David Hennigan pulled into the back of the barracks in his personal car. It was a black, nondescript Buick four door sedan. He stepped out of the car wearing his uniform and entered the barracks from the rear door.

PJ picked up an encrypted radio transmitter. "I got him."

A tired, "Roger" answered him. PJ started his car and stretched his arms to help revive his energy. He wanted to stretch his legs but he couldn't take the chance of being detected. It was his Marine sniper discipline. An almost super-human self control was wired into his genes. In his prime, PJ could go a day without peeing and four days without eating. He knew he wasn't in his prime but he also knew the troopers' morning briefing wouldn't take more than 10 minutes as he stretched his limbs in the front seat.

A few minutes later, Hennigan exited the barrack's rear exit with another trooper. They exchanged a few words and then separated as they proceeded to their patrol cars. The other trooper was faster. He started his car and sped off as if he was already chasing a speeder.

Trooper Hennigan checked his cell phone, adjusted some dials on his dashboard computer and then slowly exited the parking lot, driving slowly as if he was still easing his way into the day.

"Coming your way," PJ radioed. "He's driving out now."

"Roger, I got him."

Hennigan drove a short way on Rte. 12 and then entered the on ramp to Interstate 81 going south, towards Watertown, just as PJ and Rome had bet.

Rome spotted the NYS trooper patrol car a quarter mile away. He began pulling slowly towards the on-ramp, timing his entrance so he could slide undetected behind Hennigan.

"I'm on his tail," Rome radioed from four car-length's back.

For the next five minutes, Hennigan drove only slightly above the speed limit but as the cars ahead of him saw the trooper's car approaching they pulled into the right lane and let him pass. He proceeded for another mile and then signaled that he was getting off at Bradley Street in Watertown.

Hennigan drove over the highway crossroad and immediately circled back on to I-81 going Northbound.

"He's getting back on 81. I'm going to pull off and let you advance."

"I've got a visual," PJ replied as he exited 81 and drove over the crossroad. He entered the highway and sped up to catch up to Hennigan as Rome circled back and drove well behind PJ.

"He's turning into the rest area just north of Bradley Street," PJ radioed with a burst of excitement as he watched the trooper's car turn into the slip of land that curved off the highway. It was exactly the sort of rest area they had hoped for. No food. No bathrooms. Only two picnic benches and a garbage can. Best of all it was deserted, PJ thought as he slowed and entered the rest area 10 seconds after Hennigan.

PJ parked 30 yards away from Hennigan who positioned his patrol car so he could shoot his radar gun through the trees at unsuspecting cars.

A minute later, Rome pulled in and parked five spots away from PJ. Both men eyed Hennigan who fired his radar gun at on-coming cars with the familiarity of a man who shot over a 100 thousand cars in the course of his career.

"There's no time like the present," Rome radioed. PJ flashed a thumbs up sign and readied himself as Rome stepped out of his car holding a small tape recorder in his hand. As Rome walked towards Hennigan, his heart rate sped up and he could feel his hands moisten. He knew anything could happen and if it turned violent it would turn very violent, very quickly. Rome heard PJ's engine start up and begin to roll into position.

Rome instructed himself to slow down to avoid alarming Hennigan as he neared the patrol car. He couldn't afford spooking him, he reminded himself.

Sam Rome didn't have to worry. Trooper David Hennigan was trained to be alert against ambushes. From 20 feet away his peripheral vision detected Rome approaching his passenger door. Hennigan swung into defensive action. He was right handed. An attacker would have the jump on him if he started firing from the passenger's window. He'd be dead before he could get his gun out.

Hennigan popped open his door and climbed out of the car, looking over the patrol car at Rome as if it provided a safety barrier. "Can I help you?" he asked with a mix of annoyance and apprehension. Then he stiffened. The round face, covered with thinning hair looked familiar. The longer he set his eyes on the guy, the surer he was that he knew the guy. But Hennigan's brain failed to connect the face to a name or a place.

"Yes, officer," Rome said with a respectful ring. "Can you help me listen to this?"

Hennigan's face tightened as his brain discharged warning signals. In his 22 years on the force, no one ever approached him and asked for him to listen to anything. Who was this guy? Where did he know him from? His hand instinctively slid down to his pistol grip.

Rome's experience kicked in. He read the danger alerts surfacing on Hennigan's face and saw Hennigan's right hand slide towards his gun. He slowly raised his hands to signal that he didn't offer a threat. "I'm just going to turn this on."

Rome clicked the 'play' button and set the tape recorder on the roof of the patrol car.

"Bless me Father for I have sinned. It has been two weeks since my last confession."

Rome clicked the recorder off. There was a second delay and then Hennigan let out a deep gurgling sound as if his brain was firing instructions to speak, breath and swallow simultaneously.

Rome clicked the recorder back on. The sound of a man sobbing filled the air. The intensity of the sobs rose and fell and then petered out. The crying was followed by sniffling and then the sound of a man wiping his nose with his sleeve.

"It wasn't me," the voice said through a splatter of wet sniffles. "I was there but it wasn't me!"

"Was this the woman who was killed on Wellesley Island?"

The man on the tape sounded as if he was choking on his tears. "Yes, Father, but I don't really remember what happened."

"Tell me as best you can," the priest's sober voice instructed.

"I had no control of myself. I don't know what happened. My memory is blank like it was erased." Loud sniffling followed. "I just found myself standing over her body with my flashlight in my hand."

The man let out a snot-and-tears gasp. "I think I killed the woman."

"You think?"

"I mean," the man said as if he was unsure of what he meant. "I think I killed her but it was like an out-of-body experience. It was like some evil force controlled my body. Like I was possessed by the devil. Do you know what I mean?"

Rome clicked the recorder off and stared at Hennigan. He signaled for PJ to drive behind him and get out of the car.

Hennigan pulled his gun and trained it on Rome's head. "Give me that," he snapped, pointing to the recorder. Rome calmly shook his head. Nope. That's not how it was going to go down. He defied Hennigan by slipping the recorder into his front pant's pocket. He then slowly turned and pointed to PJ who stood between his car and Hennigan recording everything on his cell phone.

Hennigan froze, unsure of what to do. Should he kill them both? He could say he was attacked. Just as he considered shooting them, PJ raised his revolver in the steady, cool fashion of an experienced cop. The strange looking older man had the confident air of an expert marksman, Hennigan told himself. If he started shooting they'd shoot back and he'd be dead, Hennigan reasoned. Worse, the recording of his confession wouldn't be secure.

Hennigan slowly lowered his gun and secured it in his holster. He then scanned the area to see if anyone had seen him point his gun at the man standing on the other side of his patrol car. A handful of cars sped by on the Interstate but the rest area was still deserted.

"What do you want?" Hennigan's words rang with desperation.

"Money."

"Money?" Hennigan said, sounding as if he was unfamiliar with the word.

"I don't give a shit you killed that woman on Wellesley Island," Rome said coldly. "But I do care about money," Rome delivered in his best low-life impression.

"You bastard," Hennigan hissed. "How much?"

"Fifty grand."

Hennigan shook his head vigorously. "I'm a trooper. Where the hell am I going to get that kind of money?"

"That's your problem," Rome barked cold heartedly as he channeled all his contempt for Hennigan into his character. "Don't get confused. This isn't an offer. It's the price for your freedom."

Hennigan stepped back from his car and tried to remember how he knew the guy who was shaking him down. From where? In the swirl of stress, he still couldn't place the face in across from him. "Where do I know you from?"

Rome shook his head. Forget about that. We don't have the time.

"I don't have 50 grand."

Rome spun around and shot a look at PJ. "Can you believe this guy?" He turned back to Hennigan. "This isn't an offer. It's a demand."

"Forty grand."

Rome shook his head as if he couldn't believe a man would haggle over the price of his freedom. "You cheap son of a bitch. Okay, 40 grand." Rome took a step towards his car.

"Wait! How do I know you didn't make copies of the tape?"

Rome and PJ anticipated the question. "There's only one copy. You'll get the original and the copy when we get the money."

"How can I trust you?"

Rome stared at Hennigan with contempt. "I know if I cross you, you'll kill me so I'll be motivated to honor our deal."

Hennigan looked partially satisfied with Rome's answer. The guy with the familiar looking face was right; he'd kill him if he ever threatened his freedom again. He then rubbed his face as if he wished he had other options.

"You're a lucky bastard," Rome added.

Hennigan didn't look like he felt lucky. He looked as if his life was crashing down on him. "How do we do this?"

"You have until 12 a.m tomorrow night to get the money."

Hennigan instinctively began to protest but Rome's intense glare shut him down. "Drive to the entrance to the walkway of the Thousand Islands Bridge. Come alone and don't bring a gun. Men with guns will search you. If you are carrying, the deal is off. You'll never see me again but I guarantee you'll hear the tape. So will others."

Hennigan's chest heaved as if he was on the verge of suffering a panic attack. "What if I need more time to raise the money?"

"Then you'll have a big problem." Rome paused for effect. "12 a.m. at the base of the walkway to the bridge on the mainland side. You'll have one chance. Don't fuck this up."

Rome turned and walked to his car without glancing back at Hennigan.

"Where do I know you from?" Hennigan yelled after him. Rome didn't turn around but he visualized himself sitting on the barstool at the Graveyard next to Hennigan.

Rome got in his car, started his engine and pulled out of the rest area without glancing back at Hennigan. PJ pulled out behind him.

Just as they planned.

CHAPTER TWENTY SEVEN

Hennigan sat in his patrol car for the next 15 minutes staring blankly ahead, oblivious to the traffic racing by 20 miles over the speed limit. He felt nauseous like he was on the verge of vomiting. He opened his window and dry heaved.

Where did he know the bastard from? His body shook as his mental search for the familiar looking face took a crazed, out of control turn. His mind was ablaze. All he knew was that there was no way he could finish his shift. He started up his patrol car and drove in a fugue of despair, mentally assembling the lies he was going to toss at his supervisor. He'd claim he was suffering from food poisoning. He ate something rancid. What? Fish. Sashimi. Where? He bought the sashimi at the Price Chopper a week ago. He forgot that he had left it in his car. He'd say he puked twice already and had a bad case of the shits. He'd remember to gag violently in the barracks.

He drove back to the barracks and spit in his hand to wet down his hair. His frothy saliva added to the natural sweat that trickled off his forehead and into his eyes.

Hennigan opened the barrack's rear door unsteadily and entered like a drunk staggering into a bar. He instructed himself to shake like a leaf as he entered the supervisor's office. His supervisor took one look at him and ordered him to go home as if he was afraid Hennigan was contagious.

*****

Hennigan lived in a plain, ranch-style house on the outskirts of Sackets Harbor, a small town on Lake Ontario where a military base once guarded the Great Lakes. He purchased the modest house 10 years ago. He painted it white 8 years ago and the harsh winters wore away the paint, leaving patches of wood exposed like holes in an old man's trousers.

Hennigan stumbled into the kitchen which had the musty smell of a room whose windows had been nailed shut. He leaned against the sink and dropped his face into his hands.

"Are you okay?"

Hennigan looked up at his sister wrapped in a threadbare, terry cloth bathrobe.

Camelia Hennigan was a frail woman whose face bore the scars of childhood trauma that followed her into adulthood. Her eyes now glowed like the eyes of a patient charting her escape from a psych ward. Her spine arched like a branch after an ice storm giving her the look of someone 20 years older than her 42 biological years.

There was never any discussion of whether or not Camelia would live with Hennigan. Where would she go? She had no other place to live. The strange, brooding woman would be living on the streets if it wasn't for her brother's support. Camelia arrived 10 years ago and rarely left her room and it was even rarer for her to leave the house. Camelia was devoted to him: she was his rock-solid confidante and he could share things with her he couldn't share with anyone else.

He leaned over the sink and heaved as if he was about to vomit. Camelia rushed to the sink and poured him a glass of water. She handed it to her brother and waited patiently by his side. He sipped the water and slowly regained the strength to stand on both feet without the support of the counter.

Hennigan then told her about his encounter at the rest stop. When he finished, his shoulders heaved as if he was on the verge of hyperventilating.

Since Hennigan confessed that he murdered Irene Izak to her, Camelia hadn't slept more than two hours a day. Now, the news of blackmail caused her survival instincts to kick into overdrive. Her forearms swelled as her blood pressure rose to dangerous levels pushing her narrow arteries to their breaking point. Her eyes dilated and beamed with the desire for revenge.

She stepped back and snapped her head forward. "As for the cowardly, the faithless, the detestable, as for murderers, the sexually immoral, their fate will be in the lake that burns with fire and sulfur. It will be their second death!"

Hennigan took another sip of water, unfazed by Camelia's biblical outburst. He was used to it. For the past decade, she routinely broke out in crazed, biblical verse. In the kitchen. Watching television. In the car. She'd just start spewing passages from the Old Testament.

"I don't know what to do," Hennigan said. His voice was hollow and sounded as if he was talking to himself.

"You should've killed them," Camelia Hennigan hissed like a snake.

Hennigan's face cracked with stress. "I couldn't just shoot them at the rest stop."

"Yes! You could have." Camelia slapped her barefoot against the cracked tile floor. "You could have said they attacked you and you had no choice. Remember," she added, shaking her bony forefinger at him, "sometimes it is necessary to take a life because we live in a world of sin."

Hennigan shook his head vigorously. "There could've been witnesses!"

Camelia shook her head dismissively. Her younger brother was lost and needed her wisdom.

"You've got to kill them." Camelia spit her cold edict out with absolute certainty.

David Hennigan straightened slowly until he stood rigid as a board and stared disbelievingly at his sister.

"The Bible says we live in a 'kill or be killed' world," Camelia yelled. "Sometimes we must kill to survive."

Hennigan stared at Camelia as she quieted and lowered herself into a chair as if her outburst had drained her of energy. Her eyes were glossy and distant and her lips moved as if she was conducting a hushed conversation with an invisible person.

"She was a harlot!" Camelia spat. "The woman used her sexual wiles to ignite your lust. Lust is every man's weak spot! You were the victim."

Camelia Hennigan closed her eyes and imagined the patrol car's flashing lights as her brother pulled the woman over on Interstate 81. He was just doing his job! The woman flirted with her brother and she tempted him into a rendezvous over the bridge. She was familiar with the dark, out of the way roads that led to Canada and knew the perfect spot for a tryst. Yes, her brother was weak and putty in her hands once the slut triggered an arousal.

Camelia shouted like a crazed evangelical minister. "And God looked upon the earth, and, behold, it was corrupt! For all flesh had corrupted his way upon the earth."

Camelia was certain of the facts. When her brother met the young woman in front of Dewolf Point State Park, he had time to cool off and realized that the slut was pulling him down the path to a fiery afterlife. He found strength and refused the slut's entreaties.

The woman reacted like a wild, spurned woman. She threatened to lie and tell the world that Trooper David Hennigan tried to rape her unless he satisfied her. The slut threatened everything that her brother had worked for. His job. His pension. His reputation. She pushed her brother beyond the breaking point. It was her fault he crushed her skull with his flashlight.

Camelia mumbled unintelligibly. Then she yanked a paper napkin out of the holder and blew her nose loudly.

"If a thief is found breaking in and is struck so that he dies, there shall be no bloodguilt for him." She dropped the dirty napkin on the kitchen table. "You do not have bloodguilt."

Hennigan's glazed eyes stared at his sister. She spoke as if someone was speaking through her.

"A little while and the wicked will be no more …," she mumbled and quieted. Then the ferocity in Camelia's eyes intensified. It was as if a car's high beams kept getting brighter and brighter until they were blinding to oncoming traffic. "You've got to kill them."

As his sister's words hung in the air, David Hennigan began to think a godly force was speaking through his sister.

"What do you mean by *them*?"

"Start with Father Patrick."

David Hennigan stepped back and braced himself against the kitchen counter.

"Are you sure?" Hennigan asked in a soft tone that hoped she was sure.

"I told you that you didn't need to speak to that Catholic priest! What you did wasn't a sin! It was justifiable!"

Hennigan's head rattled, unsure of what to think or say.

"Who else besides me knew you confessed to that Father Patrick?" Camelia asked.

Hennigan stilled as he replayed her question over in his head. He received the Sacrament of Penance the day after he killed Irene Izak. He had told only Camelia about his confession. No one else. He was sure of it.

Hennigan pinched his forehead. After he killed Irene Izak, he was consumed with the terror that his soul was forever lost and he'd burn in hell. Hennigan became desperate for forgiveness. Desperate to regain a path to Heaven.

Camelia warned him not to utter a word to anyone; especially a Catholic priest. But Camelia was a crazy, born-again Christian. What the hell did she know about the absolution of the soul?

Hennigan leaned against the kitchen cabinets and thought of the healing powers of Fr. Patrick's holy words.

God, the Father of mercies, through the death and resurrection of his Son has reconciled the world to himself and sent the Holy Spirit among us for the forgiveness of sins; through the ministry of the Church may God give you pardon and peace, and I absolve you from your sins in the name of the Father, and of the Son and of the Holy Spirit.

Camelia's eyes shined even brighter. "There is a time for everything and now is the time to kill," Camelia growled through a stream of spittle. "You need to kill the priest and then the blackmailers."

Hennigan's voice cracked. "I can't kill a priest."

"He turned on you! He taped your confession."

Hennigan stared at the kitchen floor and tried to assemble his jumbled thoughts. A few days ago, he pleaded with Fr. Patrick to hear his confession. The sound of his own desperation was still fresh in his mind. He saw himself enter the Sacred Heart Church. He heard the creak of the entrance door opening and the hollow, echoey sounds of his footsteps in the empty church. He saw the empty pews. He was sure he was alone with Fr. Patrick when he received holy absolution. All was forgiven. His soul was cleansed.

Hennigan looked up from the floor. "I only told you and Father Patrick."

"Exactly," Camelia hissed loudly.

"Exactly what?"

"Do you remember calling Father Patrick?"

Hennigan nodded. Of course he did. He was tormented. He remembered his hand shaking as he held his cell phone. He was almost too shaken up to talk.

"The second you asked Father Patrick to hear your confession he knew you killed the woman."

Hennigan's face twisted, causing a squirt of doubt to eke out of his eyes.

"Father Patrick is a smart man," Camelia argued. "He could hear the fear in your voice. He knew you were the trooper who found the body. He doesn't live in a bubble! He heard the rumors that a trooper killed the girl. He connected the dots!"

Hennigan's face froze as he replayed his call with Fr. Patrick. He could hear the panic in his own voice. He was on the verge of tears. Camelia was right. Fr. Patrick recognized the tremors of guilt on the phone. Fr. Patrick knew he had killed the woman before he confessed his sins. He was sure of it.

"Father Patrick would never break his vows and reveal the content of the confession," Hennigan said with an anguished breath. "I'll stake my life on that."

"Your life!" Camelia erupted. "Your life is over unless you wise up!"

Camelia seethed with anger. Anger towards God for allowing the devil to tempt her brother. Anger towards the priest who betrayed her brother. Anger towards the evil blackmailers.

243

"Father Patrick was the only person who knew you were going to Sacred Heart to confess the murder. He taped the confession!"

Camelia's words hit home. Hennigan couldn't find a single weak spot in her argument. He couldn't find a single point to refute. He played the blackmail tape over in his head. There was no doubt it was his voice. He had forgotten his exact words but when he heard them played back he was sure it was his voice. He was also sure that the other voice belonged to Father Patrick. There was no doubt in his mind the tape was genuine.

"But it doesn't make any sense," Hennigan blurted. "Why would he do this to me?"

"You're a deacon! No priest can have a deacon who committed a mortal sin. He has to get rid of you."

Hennigan punched the kitchen table, sending the sugar bowl crashing to the floor. "Why would he blackmail me?"

"He wants you out of his church and he found others to do his dirty work."

Hennigan slumped into a kitchen chair as Camelia's words slowly settled in his head like silt slowly settling on the floor of a lake. He sat still as his brains filtered his murky thoughts. As he gripped his forehead, everything suddenly became clear. Camelia was right. A godly voice was talking through her.

"Father Patrick is like Judas. He betrayed you," Camelia added.

Hennigan ran his thumbnail over his front teeth as he considered his next moves.

"You have to kill all of them," Camelia pressed on.

CHAPTER TWENTY EIGHT

David Hennigan paced back and forth from his stainless steel sink to his small, formica surfaced kitchen table for over an hour. His eyes glistened like a rabid raccoon. His breathing sounded like a rush of wind through a small pipe.

He rested against the edge of the kitchen sink and pawed at his temple as if hoping his fingertips would extinguish his anguish. "Hell," he said, loudly exhaling. "Camelia is right."

Hennigan's eyes darted to the 1950's vintage clock with crooked hands that circled around the yellowed clockface with an electric moan that grew louder each year. It was too early to call Fr. Patrick. He'd call him in two hours.

Hennigan suddenly exploded with rage. He kicked a hole in his kitchen cabinet and punched the air wildly before pounding his chest over and over until his energy depleted. Who were the guys blackmailing him? How did Fr. Patrick know them?

He'd get his revenge, he seethed through gritted teeth. They'd regret the day they thought extortion would work with him. Hennigan kicked the cabinets again, shattering another panel.

Hennigan racked his brain. Where had he met the blackmailer? He was sure he had seen him somewhere. But where?

Hennigan slumped in a kitchen chair, exhausted. He knew he should get some sleep but his brain was on fire and his chest heaved like an overheating engine. No, he'd just wait in the kitchen and call Fr. Patrick in two hours.

*****

Hennigan slammed his cell phone on the kitchen table the third time his call went directly to Fr. Patrick's voicemail. He then picked the cell phone up and pressed the edge of it against his teeth as if he wanted to sink his teeth into it.

The ring startled him. His spine straightened like he was jolted by an electric current as he eyed the phone vibrating in his hand. He took a deep, fortifying breath to avoid sounding like a bottle rocket. "Good morning, Father," he answered so softly he sounded slightly medicated.

"Deacon David, I see that you've been trying to reach me." Fr. Patrick's voice was laced with mild irritation. One call would have sufficed.

"Yes, Father. Thank you very much for returning my call." Hennigan paused and tried to regulate his breathing by sucking a long train of air in and out of his nostrils. He began shakily. "I'm in need of the Sacrament of Penance."

Silence. Hennigan could hear Fr. Patrick thinking. Just days ago Fr. Patrick heard Hennigan's shocking confession. Now Hennigan could almost hear Fr. Patrick asking himself if the Hennigan committed another mortal sin.

"I really must see you," Hennigan added, pleadingly. "There are things on my mind."

For a split second, Fr. Patrick considered telling Hennigan about the two men who came to the church asking questions about the murder on Wellesley Island. But he reconsidered. Hennigan was far too stressed. He'd tell him when he next saw him face to face.

Fr. Patrick had heard thousands of confessions. He recognized the tone of a troubled conscience, an unbalanced mind. He was sure he was hearing one now. "Deacon David, the Lord knows you were sincere when you confessed your sins. You have been absolved of guilt. Your soul has been cleansed."

"Please Father," Hennigan begged. "I need the spiritual cleansing that only absolution provides."

Fr. Patrick blew a weary gust through the phone. "The Lord can be reached through prayer."

Hennigan moaned as if he was an addict badly in need of a fix.

"I have a very full schedule today," Fr. Patrick replied. "What about first thing tomorrow morning?"

"It can't wait."

"Deacon David, I have to officiate a funeral this morning," Fr. Patrick sighed as if he was miffed his parishioner had chosen an inconvenient time to cross over to the other side. "Then I have to drive to Rochester. I'm afraid I won't be able to hear your confession today."

"You have to." Acute desperation bled through Hennigan's voice.

"As I said, I have to drive to Rochester and I won't be back until quite late."

Hennigan tightened. He couldn't wait a day. He'd go mad. "I'll meet you when you come back," Hennigan blurted, sounding like a man at his wit's end.

Fr. Patrick blew a short breath of frustration into the phone as he ran through his schedule. Dinner would be over at 7 pm. He'd be back in Watertown about 10 pm. "I guess I could see you around 10 p.m."

Hennigan puffed with relief. "Thank you very much, Father," Hennigan whispered into his cell phone. "I will see you at 10 p.m."

"God be with you, my son. I will meet you at the confessional," Fr. Patrick said before ending the call.

As Hennigan sat with Fr. Patrick's words echoing in his head, it suddenly hit him! He pulsed with energy as he remembered where he had seen the blackmailer. The Graveyard! The guy was with Clifford Putnam! He came over and spoke to him at the Graveyard! The bastard even bought him a drink. Hennigan shook with energy as he played back the scene from the Graveyard in his head. The blackmailer was definitely the guy with Putnam.

For a minute, Hennigan sat staring off into space. His forehead tightened as he concluded that Putnam was connected to the blackmailers. Hennigan rubbed his forehead and revised his plan. It would be an active night.

CHAPTER TWENTY NINE

Ten hours later, David Hennigan sat in his car in the corner of Rondette's diner parking lot. He checked his watch. He had about three hours before he'd meet Fr. Patrick, he thought as his eyes fixed on the diner's front door. Hennigan wore a patient, determined look of a man who was prepared to wait for as long as it took.

It didn't take much longer. Hennigan's heartbeat accelerated as he saw Clifford Putnam emerge from the front door. Putnam stopped and extracted the last Life Saver from his pack and seemed to draw satisfaction from rolling the aluminum foil wrapper in the tips of his fingers as he studied the dark rain clouds hovering over him. It's going to pour at any moment, Putnam thought as he gazed up at the threatening clouds.

Hennigan stepped out of his car, readying himself to call out to Putnam. He had practiced how he was going to act surprised to see Putnam. Then he'd tell him he had something to show him in his car. He was sure Putnam would take the bait, especially if it started to rain.

"Put—," Hennigan sputtered and stopped himself as a pick-up truck on a jacked-up chassis swerved into the parking lot, kicking up a cloud of dust and gravel. The noise of its tires grinding over the gravel drowned out his aborted call. As the dust cloud slowly dispersed, Clifford Putnam stood rigidly at the diner's entrance wearing the look of an ex-cop who wished he was still on the force.

The driver, a guy, about 20 years old, recognized the body language of a pissed off ex-cop. The driver waved apologetically and pointed back to the road as if saying the diner appeared quicker than he expected.

The guy's wave didn't melt Putnam's icy stare but a smattering of thick rain drops spurred Putnam to move. He shook his head and began hustling, stiff-legged to his car. He ducked into his car as fat rain drops began to darken the gravel lot. He started his engine and drove slowly to the edge of the parking lot, before pulling onto the two lane asphalt road that was quickly becoming spotted with rain drops.

Hennigan cursed his bad luck as he waited for two cars to pass before heading out in pursuit of Putnam. As he accelerated, the sky darkened and his car was buffeted by wind gusts as a barrage of large rain drops descended upon it. Visibility plummeted to zero as the rain pounded his car. He flipped on his wipers to maximum speed and the frantic swooshing and rush of water under his tires now added to the storm's menacing chorus.

With his wipers at full speed, Hennigan could see only about 10 feet ahead of him as sheets of blurry rain slid down his windshield. Hennigan slowed and his trooper's training kicked in. He had driven countless times through winter whiteouts and blinding rain storms but he never felt comfortable in them.

Hennigan growled as he switched on his car's lights and fixed his eye on the yellow line that ran along the right-hand side of the road. His heart rate rose as he slowed his car to about 20 miles per hour, searching for cars which may have pulled to the edge of the road.

The rain continued to pound his car for another minute. Then the rain turned from a downpour to a steady, heavy rain, bringing a smeary visibility to the road. Hennigan immediately spotted Putnam's back wheels shooting a cloud of road spray as he barreled towards the Thousand Islands Bridge.

Hennigan accelerated as he quickly considered his options. Even with the steady rain, Rte. 12 was too busy for him to force Putnam off the road. Too many eyes. But the cover of rain would give him a chance to intercept Putnam in the Bridge Authority's parking lot before Putnam punched in for work.

Only a single car separated him from Putnam's as they continued along the road with the sound of his windshield wipers swooshing back and forth at a frantic speed. Then he saw Putnam's right signal light flashing. Hennigan knew immediately that Putnam was stopping at the 1000 Island Bait Store. Putnam's brake lights lit up as he slowed and then turned into the Bait Store's parking lot.

The rain had cleared the parking lot and a gaggle of tourists without umbrellas stood in the doorway trying to muster the courage to sprint to their cars under the soaking rain fall.

Putnam drove to the far end of the parking lot and parked right around the corner of the building. It was perfect, Hennigan thought as he drove past the Bait Store and circled back to the parking lot. As he rolled into the lot, he saw Putnam closing his umbrella and duck into the store.

Hennigan swung into action. He parked, killed his engine and pulled his umbrella from his back seat. He then scanned the parking lot through the blurry rain covering his windshield. No one was around. It was perfect, he repeated under his breath.

Through the smudges of rain on the windshield Hennigan saw a man with an umbrella heading towards Putnam's car. Now was his chance. He might not get another, he thought.

Hennigan opened his car door and umbrella in one smooth motion.

Putnam did not see Hennigan. His attention was fixed on his fingernails as they dissected the end of a new roll of Life Savers. Holding the umbrella on an angle, he stopped as he wedged his thumbnail under a Life Saver and flicked it over his bottom lip, in one smooth motion.

As the familiar peppermint taste hit his tongue, he looked up and saw Hennigan standing two feet away. Startled, he cried out, "Hennigan!"

"Putnam," Hennigan replied coldly, indicating that their meeting wasn't a chance encounter.

"Why the hell are you standing in the rain?" Putnam asked nervously, unsure of what to say as his cop's radar kicked in.

Hennigan deliberated whether or not to coax Putnam into his car with a ruse or just utilize brute force. Force won out.

Hennigan pulled his Sig Sauer 229 pistol from his waist band. Putnam's eyes widened. He recognized the gun. He carted around an earlier model on his waist for most of his career. He was also acquainted with its devastating effects on the human body.

"You and I need to talk," Hennigan said with a wave of his gun.

"I'm on my way to my shift," Putnam replied, knowing his words would have no effect on Hennigan.

Hennigan tilted the umbrella to cover his gun as he pointed it at Putnam's head. "Get in my car. This will only take a second." Hennigan's sharp tone made it clear there'd be fatal consequences for non-compliance.

Putnam's eyes scanned the parking lot, silently praying a tourist was watching them. His prayer wasn't answered. The rain-splattered parking lot was deserted.

Clifford Putnam took a slow step towards Hennigan's passenger seat knowing if he was going to stay alive, he had to comply with Hennigan's order. He collapsed his umbrella and slid into the passenger seat. In a flash, Hennigan was sitting across from him in the driver's seat with his gun trained on him.

Hennigan started his car and pulled back on Rte. 12 as Putnam cradled the roll of Life Savers in his palm. He considered asking Hennigan if he wanted one but reconsidered. "Where are we going?" Putnam asked as Hennigan entered I-81 heading south and quickly accelerated to 75 miles an hour.

"I told you. We need to speak."

The men drove in silence until Hennigan turned on his blinker and pulled off at a rest stop. The stop was deserted except for a tractor trailer parked near the exit. Hennigan was sure the driver was asleep in the bunk behind the cab and wouldn't take any notice of a car seeking refuge in the rain.

Hennigan put the car in park and leveled a death stare at Putnam. "Who is the guy who you brought to the Graveyard?"

Putnam hesitated for a minute as he constructed his response. Hennigan was trembling. He knew if he lied he'd get a bullet in his head. "You mean Billy?"

Hennigan's hand shook as he pointed the gun at Putnam. For a split second, Putnam was sure that Hennigan would pull the trigger in an explosion of anger.

"Whoa!" Putnam said. "Okay. Okay. Put that thing down, would you?"

Hennigan only glared at him.

"He's an ex-cop who is investigating the murder of the woman on Wellesley Island. That's all I know."

Hennigan wasn't buying it. His eyes darkened.

"The guy came looking for me because I was working the tollbooth the night," Putnam hesitated, taking a small breath. "The night you found her body."

"What did you tell him?"

Putnam shrugged as he tugged on a thread of hope that Hennigan would let him go once he got the information he wanted. "I said the woman was a basket of nerves when she pulled into the tollbooth. That's all I said."

Hennigan glared at Putnam. "So how did he get to the Graveyard?"

Putnam sighed. That's easy. "I told him if he wanted to speak to me I would be there after work. He met me. When you walked in he went over to talk to you." Putnam shrugged. That's all there was to it.

Hennigan's eyes tightened as he questioned himself if Putnam was lying or not.

"Listen, that's the truth," Putnam said, answering Hennigan's look. Hennigan stared out the blurry windshield. He replayed the scene of meeting the guy at the Graveyard over in his head. He couldn't recall entering the Graveyard. His mental reel started with him sitting at the bar and the guy approaching him. He remembered his first reaction. He didn't like the guy. Too slick. Too cocky.

Hennigan turned sharply to Putnam. "You're a lying sack of shit."

"I don't know the guy! I met him twice." Putnam's tone pleaded for his life. Hennigan gritted his teeth and shook his head. He was not going to commute Putnam's death sentence. He jabbed the barrel in Putnam's ribs. "Get out of the car."

"Hennigan, don't do anything you'll regret."

The ring of Putnam's cell phone beat Hennigan to his reply. "Don't answer it."

"It's the bridge. I'm sure they're calling me. They'll be looking for me."

"Give me your phone."

Putnam slowly dug into his breast pocket and handed over his phone. Hennigan turned it off and set it down on his dashboard. "Now get out."

Putnam's eyes and voice filled with fear. "You got the wrong idea about me. I didn't do anything to you."

Hennigan was unmoved. Putnam pushed the door open, opened his umbrella and stepped into the rain. The splattering of the rain seemed far louder and his umbrella wobbled from the force of the wind.

For a long second, Hennigan stayed in the car, sparking hope in Putnam that Hennigan would just drive off in the pouring rain. But Putnam's cop instincts told him otherwise.

That's when Clifford Putnam decided he wasn't going to just stand in the rain like some defenseless schmuck. He'd take action. He spotted the tractor trailer. There had to be someone in it. He started running as fast as his old man's joints would go.

Putnam didn't hear Hennigan's door open or the slap of Hennigan's shoes in the puddles as Hennigan closed in on him.

But Clifford Putnam felt the agonizing, white-hot pain of a bullet ripping through his rib cage. He fell to his knees and held his stomach as the bullet tore through his heart's ventricles. His body convulsed twice and then he collapsed, faced down on the asphalt in a clump.

David Hennigan walked up to Putnam's lifeless body as blood formed a pool around his chest. He aimed the gun at Putnam's head. "You lying sack of shit," he said, squeezing the trigger.

Hennigan spun around and checked the rest area. There were no passing cars. No one was in sight. There was no movement from the tractor trailer at the end of the rest stop.

Hennigan grabbed Putnam's ankles and dragged his body behind a tree. He raced back to his car, not noticing the pack of peppermint Life Savers sitting in the middle of the road. He just knew he needed to get into dry clothes and the night was just starting.

*****

For the past four hours, Hennigan sat in his car, parked a 100 yards from the entrance to the Sacred Heart church. He slumped as low as possible in his seat to avoid detection by any passersby. But there were none. The wet and darkened streets were cold and deserted.

Hennigan bid his time and stared at the entrance of the church like a hawk stalking its prey from afar, still and intense. He only moved when he saw the lights of the familiar looking car rake across the side of the church. The lights switched off and he saw the silhouette of Fr. Patrick walking towards the church, carrying his vestments draped over his arm like a member of a marching band would carry his uniform after a tiring performance. Fr. Patrick pulled out a set of keys, opened the church door and entered.

Hennigan scanned the neighborhood one last time. There was no one in sight as he exited his car and headed towards the church. With each step, his breathing accelerated and heart pumped faster. With each step, he felt his scalp muscles tighten as if Camelia's orders were burrowing deep inside his head.

He opened the heavy church door and when his eyes adjusted to the darkness he saw Fr. Patrick sitting in the front pew. He seemed to be meditating as Hennigan approached and lightly scuffed his shoes on the tiles to announce his arrival. Fr. Patrick shook himself back to consciousness, turned and nodded as if there was nothing unusual about meeting someone alone at 10 p.m. in the church. He patted the pew, directing Hennigan to sit next to him.

Hennigan sat. There was a long silence as Fr. Patrick mentally prepared himself to absolve Hennigan's sins for the second time in a matter of days. He reached over and squeezed Hennigan's hand. "You have come for a confession."

Hennigan pulled back his hand. Was Fr. Patrick offering to hear his confession, face-to-face?

Fr. Patrick sensed Hennigan's unease. "It's perfectly all right to confess your sins directly to me. All the early confessions in the church were done this way." Fr. Patrick's voice was soothing, as if trying to calm a spooked horse.

A face-to-face confession was not part of Hennigan's plan. His face exploded with discomfort. "I'd prefer the sanctity of the confessional."

Fr. Patrick grimaced as he pushed his tired body up from the pew. "That's perfectly fine."

Fr. Patrick set off towards the confessional in a slight huff. When he reached it, he struggled opening the small door and held the back of his neck as he ducked under its small doorway.

Fr. Patrick clicked on a small light that cast a shadow between the thick screen that separated him from the confessor. He slid the divider panel open. Hennigan then entered the confessional and knelt on a padded kneeler six inches from the screen. Fr. Patrick leaned so close to the screen that Hennigan could feel the priest's breath.

"Welcome my son. I know you are burdened by a great sin but your soul has already been wiped clean by the Sacrament of Penance."

"Thank you Father, but I seek further reconciliation with the Lord," Hennigan said in a low, pious voice.

"As you wish. I am a conduit to the Lord."

"I have a question for you," Hennigan said, suddenly changing his tone.

The wooden chair creaked as Fr. Patrick adjusted himself. He had a long day. He was there to listen to a single confession, not to talk.

"Would you ever share my confessional secrets?"

Fr. Patrick's chair creaked louder as if his body was shocked by the question. "Never. That's a grave sin," he answered stiffly.

"Do you know that only the Pope can forgive a priest for revealing the details of a confessor?" Hennigan asked.

"I'm aware of that," Fr. Patrick responded with an air of confusion. Where was Deacon David headed? "It's the gravest sin a priest could commit. I'd be excommunicated if I revealed your confession. As a deacon, you know the Seal of Confession is inviolable."

Hennigan's heavy breath streamed through the confessional screen. "Is it a sin to tape a confession?"

"Of course it would be," Fr. Patrick snapped. "Deacon David, what is troubling you?"

Hennigan's ear was tuned to weed out lies from the truth. Fr. Patrick's tone was weak and wavering. He was sure Camelia was right. He was sure Patrick was lying. The mother fucker was lying, Hennigan screamed to himself.

Hennigan pulled his gun from his leg holster. The 7 inch, Sig Sauer P229, weighing almost 2 pounds, felt solid in his hand. He disengaged the safety switch and bounced the gun in his palm. He then pointed it at the silhouette of Fr. Patrick's temple.

Ten inches from his temple and Fr. Patrick did not flinch. Of course, he didn't, Hennigan thought. He couldn't see the gun. He'd shit in his pants if he saw a Sig Sauer pointed at his skull. One squeeze of the trigger and he'd obliterate the lying, deceitful priest's skull.

"Deacon David, what is weighing on your conscience?"

That's when Hennigan heard Camelia's command echo in his head.

You've got to kill them. All of them.

"Father, I forgive you for your sins."

"What?"

Fr. Patrick began to say something else as Hennigan pulled the trigger. The blast echoed through the confessional and hung in the church like vibrations from a loud gong. The force of the bullet exploding through Fr. Patrick's skull splattered blood and brain tissue through the confessional screen and on to Hennigan's face and hands.

As the echo of the gun shot slowly faded, Hennigan remained kneeling. He didn't wipe the specks of blood or brain from his face as he stared at the hole in the confessional shield. He waited a minute and then blessed himself.

"My God, I am sorry for my sins with all my heart. In choosing to do wrong and failing to do good, I have sinned against you whom I should love above all things. I firmly intend, with your help, to do penance, to sin no more, and to avoid whatever leads me to sin. Our Savior Jesus Christ suffered and died for us. In his name, my God, have mercy."

Hennigan blessed himself again. In the name of the Father, the Son and the Holy Spirit and pushed himself off the kneeler and opened the confessional door.

There was no movement. No sounds. No sign anyone heard the gun blast.

He stepped out and entered the part of the confessional reserved for the priest. Fr. Patrick's body was slumped against the wall and a steady trickle of blood dripped from the hole in his head. Hennigan didn't seem to notice the gobs of the priest's brain splattered everywhere as he rifled through Fr. Patrick's pockets. Keys. A few bits of paper. No tape recorder. He then ran his hands over the brain-splattered walls, searching for wires or a microphone. Nothing.

"Damn," Hennigan cursed as he wiped Fr. Patrick's brain matter on his sleeve. He was sure he'd find evidence of his duplicity. He glanced contemptuously one last time at the priest's body, knowing Fr. Patrick committed the worst sin imaginable for a priest. Fr. Patrick O'Brien would rot in hell Hennigan told himself.

Hennigan stuck his gun back into his concealed holster and casually wiped his face with his shirt as if he was wiping ketchup off his face. He then walked slowly to the church door. He cracked it open to see if anyone was outside. The rain soaked walkway was still deserted. Hennigan was sure the thick wooden church door had muffled the gun shot.

Hennigan reminded himself to walk casually, almost stroll, just in case anyone was watching. He lowered his head as a car neared. It kept a steady speed and drove past him. Hennigan hustled to his car feeling confident no one detected him as he pulled away from the church.

He was wrong.

CHAPTER THIRTY

Sam Rome and PJ McLevy knew they had rattled David Hennigan. They also knew a rattled man makes mistakes. They were banking on Hennigan making the mistake of saying too much so they'd have a confession that would be admitted in court. It was a long shot but it was their only shot.

But they also knew a rattled man could go off the deep end and try to end his anguish in a blaze of gunfire. And Rome and PJ McLevy knew if David Hennigan went off the deep end, he'd be aiming his gun at them.

As he waited in camouflage, PJ reminded himself he had trained for these sort of moments all his life. He endured the grueling training of a Marine sniper. He endured years lying in wait, wearing a meticulously designed ghillie suit that allowed him to blend seamlessly into the jungle landscape. He endured severe deprivations for days at a time. He was ready, he told himself, trying to pump up his sagging confidence.

PJ McLevy needed to shore himself up because cracks in his confidence were setting in. He was 68 years old. He reluctantly acknowledged to himself that he didn't have the same energy, the same focus or the same reactions he had as a Marine or a cop. PJ sighed as he patted his gun. That's why he was taking precautions.

The sound of tires crunching gravel in the distance drew PJ's attention, causing him to scamper off into the darkness.

A car's headlights sliced through the darkness as it entered the North Country Welcome Center parking lot and drove down the road that led to the Thousand Islands Bridge's walkway. It rolled to a stop next to a 'No Parking' sign, the headlights shut off and the driver killed the engine. "Game time," PJ whispered to himself as he felt the sensation of adrenaline surging through his body.

The driver's door opened and PJ observed Hennigan's silhouette exit the car, carrying a small gym bag. Hennigan walked in the direction of the bridge. So far, so good, PJ thought behind the protection of a tree. Hennigan walked another 10 feet when PJ pressed a remote control that lit up a four foot long sign in Hennigan's path. As planned, the bright light startled Hennigan. He stopped in his tracks and then spun around, searching the area. Seeing no one, he approached the sign.

Take off your jacket and raise your hands in the air.

Hennigan frantically searched for the eyes he knew were trained on him. Seeing only darkness, he dropped the gym bag at his feet and slowly complied, taking off his light jacket and raising his hands in the air.

From his cover, PJ inspected Hennigan closely, knowing there was no room for error. He saw Hennigan's hands were empty. PJ McLevy then emerged from behind the tree and approached Hennigan from behind.

"Don't move. Keep your hands in the air," PJ said in his stern cop voice.

Hennigan kept his hands in the air but craned his neck to see the man behind him. "What the hell?" he said as he set his eyes on a man wearing a ghille suit constructed of artificial green pipe. The guy looked like he was dressed in an exotic Halloween costume.

"Turn around," PJ ordered, pointing his gun at Hennigan. Hennigan didn't comply and for a long second, PJ examined Hennigan's face. Was he looking at smeared specs of blood? Hennigan was disheveled as if he had been in a fight or gone on a drinking binge? He leaned in and sniffed. He didn't detect alcohol.

"Turn around," PJ ordered forcefully.

Hennigan slowly complied.

"I'm going to pat you down. If you're clean, you can meet the man on the bridge and the transaction will be done."

Hennigan kept his hands in the air as PJ patted his arms, his torso, his inner legs. PJ knew Hennigan could be hiding a razor blade or ice pick but Rome could handle himself in a knife fight. PJ was searching for a gun. Hennigan was clean.

PJ opened the gym bag and ran his hands over the inside. All he felt was cash neatly stacked and wrapped. Fresh cash from a bank.

Satisfied, PJ pointed to the bridge. "You'll find your contact in the middle of the bridge. It will only be you and him. Do your business and then return to your car. We'll never see one another again."

Hennigan shook his head and emitted a grunt. "You want me to walk all the way to the bridge?"

"I'm not going to give you a lift," PJ replied sharply. "Now get going."

Hennigan set off for the bridge.

"He's on his way," PJ radioed when Hennigan was beyond earshot. "No gun but keep an eye out. I could be wrong but it looks like he's got blood on his neck. Keep your guard up."

DeMartin and Rome replied in unison. Roger. They got it. A man who may have blood on his neck is approaching them.

Hennigan reached the bridge's walkway that ran from one end of the bridge to the other. He stopped and peered at the bridge's arches, decorated in a string of lights. This is the last act of a three-act play, Hennigan thought to himself. Two down and one to go.

As Hennigan made his way across the bridge, DeMartin swung into action. For the past 30 minutes he stood half a mile away at the other end of the bridge's walkway. Now he slowly walked, stiff-legged, in his moon boot, towards the middle of the bridge; towards Hennigan.

Hennigan walked a 100 yards before a tractor trailer roared by causing the suspension bridge to sway and creak under its weight. The thundering noise slowly subsided as it rolled off the bridge. Then the bridge fell quiet again.

A little further up, Hennigan stopped and put his hands on his knees as if to signal to anyone watching that he was pausing to catch his breath. He was sure more than one person was watching him as he peered down into the black expanse below. A green and red navigation light indicated a freighter was heading down river, coming from the Great Lakes and headed to the Atlantic. From the bridge, it looked like a floating wedding cake.

Rome saw Hennigan's shadowy figure as he climbed up the walkway with a bag in his right hand.

So far, so good, Rome thought as he reached into his pocket and pushed the "start" button on the recorder in his pocket. He had practiced what he was going to say for the past hour. Based upon the FBI profiler's report, Rome was sure he knew what would trigger Hennigan and trick him into confessing to the murder. "I got a visual," Rome whispered into his radio.

Hennigan stopped again and his shoulders drooped as if he was catching his breath again. He bent over like an out of shape man who just finished a sprint.

Rome was too far and it was too dark to see Hennigan smiling like a man who out-witted his opponent. Before he withdrew the cash from the bank, Hennigan crossed over the bridge and on his return made an emergency stop to check on his tires. He moved too fast for anyone to see him tape the gun under the bridge's railing as he knelt next to the tire.

Now, out of sight and in the shadows of the bridge's lights, Rome couldn't see David Hennigan reach over and dislodge the gun taped to the underside of the railing. All he saw was a shadow, stopped on the bridge.

"He's stopped," Rome whispered nervously as he eyed him suspiciously.

"Watch him carefully," PJ radioed back.

Hennigan slid the gun into his waist band and continued on with laboring steps as if he was an out-of-shape hiker.

"He's moving. We're good."

A minute later, Hennigan reached the apex of the bridge. He stopped and gave himself a moment to catch his breath.

He recognized Rome, the guy from the Graveyard. Putnam's guy. He smiled slyly thinking of Putnam's body stashed behind the tree at the rest stop. This guy would soon be joining Putnam and Patrick in Hell, he thought.

"Here's the money," Hennigan said, dropping the bag at Rome's feet. Rome eyed the bag with his street-wise caution. That's exactly where'd he place the bag if he was going to try to get a drop on a guy, Rome thought. The second he bent over to pick it up, he'd be exposed.

"Is it all there?"

"Count it."

"No. I want you to count it," Rome said, kicking the bag back to Hennigan.

Hennigan shook his head. It wasn't going to happen.

Rome and Hennigan were in a stand-off on the Thousand Islands Bridge, neither sure what to do next.

The money didn't matter, Rome concluded. What mattered was getting Hennigan to talk.

"You're a lucky son of a bitch," Rome spit out.

"That's easy for you to say. It's not your money."

"No, you're lucky because you got troopers covering for you."

Hennigan gritted his teeth and looked as if he wanted to tear Rome to pieces. "You don't know jack-shit."

"What do you have on Rasmutin? Why's he protecting you?"

Hennigan began to shake like an earthquake was brewing inside of him. That's exactly the reaction Rome wanted. He wanted him rattled and excited, in the state of mind to shoot off his mouth.

"A blind man can see you killed the woman. You pulled her over on the highway. You exchanged small talk and shined your flashlight into her car. The light shined over her breasts and you got excited. You made some dirty comments and when you saw how you flustered her, you got even more turned on."

"As I said, you don't know shit."

Rome knew he hit a nerve. "When she drove away you were standing in the road with a hard-on. You jumped back in your car like a dog in heat. You knew where she was going so you raced ahead and waited for her to drive into your trap. This time you were salivating for sex."

"Shut the fuck up!"

Rome planned to rattle him until he snapped and he was definitely on his way to snapping. "You ordered her out of the car. You tried to seduce her. When that didn't work, you pleaded with her. When that didn't work, you tried to scare her. But that didn't work. Nothing was working and you were overheating."

Hennigan shook.

"You dragged her into the woods and tried to rape her. When she still resisted you snapped and crushed her head with your flashlight. Didn't you?"

"That's not how it went down," Hennigan exploded. "She slipped and hit her head."

Rome's face twisted. "She slipped? Tell it to the jury, you sick fuck."

Hennigan spat at Rome with a hot, fiery rage. He then pulled a gun from his waist band and aimed it at Rome's head. "You're a dead man."

"Put the gun down." Rome was sure that he was a goner but he knew PJ and DeMartin were listening and they needed to know Hennigan was armed.

Hennigan aimed the gun at Rome's head. "Who the fuck are you?"

"Take it easy. Put the gun down."

"I'll put a bullet in your head if you don't start talking." There wasn't a hint of a bluff in Hennigan's voice.

"I'm an ex-cop. I was vacationing up here when I read that a woman was murdered. It's obvious to me that you killed her. It's also obvious that the troopers are covering for you. I just want to benefit from it."

Hennigan shoved his gun into Rome's face. "How do you know Father Patrick?"

Hennigan shook like he was ready to snap. Ready to pull the trigger and blow off his head. Rome searched for a way to calm Hennigan. If he could buy time for PJ and DeMartin to make their way to the top of the walkway maybe he had a chance. Maybe.

"Why did Fr. Patrick give you the tape?"

Rome reminded himself that he was recording every word. He couldn't tell Hennigan the truth. If he lived, he'd be embroiled in investigations if anyone learned he bugged the confessional.

"I have what you want in my side pocket," Rome said as steadily as possible. He held his hands out and then looked for Hennigan's approval to proceed. Hennigan signaled with his eyes. Go ahead but you're dead if you play any games.

Rome slowly reached into his side pocket and pulled out a package the size of a thin deck of cards. "Here. Once you go, you'll never see me again."

Hennigan snatched the package from him and stuffed it in his pocket. He then stepped towards Rome and pressed the end of his gun into Rome's forehead. "This is the last time I'll ask you. How the fuck do you know Father Patrick?"

Rome knew the left side of his skull would be scattered over the St. Lawrence River if his next words even had a whiff of bullshit.

"I don't."

Hennigan took a step back and wore a confused look. "Then how'd you get the tape?"

Rome squirmed, reminding himself that his life would end if his words didn't ring true. "You're a deacon. I knew your murder would eat at your conscience. Your guilt would be like acid burning through your soul. It's easy to predict that you'd run to confession."

"What are you saying?" Hennigan yelled.

Rome tensed. In a flash he assessed the consequences of his next words. If he told the truth, he'd risk prison. If he lied, a bullet would tear through in his head. Prison beat a bullet.

"Yeah, I wired the confessional."

David Hennigan's face turned ashen. "Fr. Patrick had nothing to do with the tape?"

Rome scrunched his lips and shook his head. Nope.

Hennigan stepped back and lowered the gun as he digested Rome's words. Could Camelia have been wrong? Could he have killed an innocent man? An innocent holy man? Hennigan's eyes blazed as if his world was beginning to unspool.

He pointed the gun up at Rome's face. "Get over the railing."

"What?"

"You heard me! Climb over the railing! I want you where you can't get a jump at me."

Rome glanced down at the dark expanse of the St. Lawrence River. A moonbeam rippled down the center of the channel as a freighter's lights beamed in the distance.

Rome turned back and took stock of Hennigan. The trooper was more than rattled; he was on the verge of snapping. If he didn't follow his orders, he was sure Hennigan would shoot him, point blank in his head.

Rome gripped the railing and swung one leg over and then the other. He shoved his feet on top of a beam and held on for life as he peered down at the shining water below that would be like hitting asphalt if he lost his grip. As Hennigan swept the bridge with his eyes, it suddenly dawned on him why PJ had nagged him about wearing a carabiner on his belt. At first, Rome blew him off but the old Marine sniper persisted. You never know when you'll need a carabiner. You'll just need it, PJ said as he thrust carabiners at DeMartin and him. Rome didn't argue. He just accepted the metal clip that PJ told him to connect to his belt. Thank God for the carabiner Rome thought as he slid the carabiner over a half inch-wide steel wire that ran up to a support beam.

With the click of the carabiner, Rome eyed the river below and his thoughts flashed to a lecture about jumpers from the Golden Gate bridge. Every cop in Boston had to attend the lecture. In his mind's eye, he could see the cop in front of the class room. The cop was clean shaven and spoke like a guy who went to a prep school; far too polished for Rome's taste. But somehow, as he peered down at the black water below, he recalled the polished cop's words.

More people jumped from the Golden Gate Bridge than any other bridge in the U.S. Something like 750 people had jumped to their deaths from the Golden Gate Bridge. The number boggled Rome's mind. The Golden Gate Bridge had become a magnet for the desperately depressed.

It took only four seconds to free-fall from the Golden Gate Bridge to the water. The bodies picked up speed and hit the water going 75 miles an hour. The impact was like getting blasted by 15 thousand pounds per square inch.

The internal injuries were horrific. At impact, a jumper's ribs were shoved like spears through his spleen, lungs, and heart. His backbone would snap and livers would be torn apart. The San Francisco coroner unpacked shattered sternums, clavicles, pelvises, necks and skulls a couple times each month. Rome recalled the cop saying one jumper hit the water face first. Her face was ripped away leaving just facial bones.

Rome stared down at the water about 150 feet below. He figured it would take about three seconds to hit the water and calculated that he'd be going at least 60 mph at impact. If he fell, at least he'd die instantly he thought as he

263

turned his attention back to Hennigan, making sure his eyes did not draw Hennigan's attention to the men he silently prayed were coming to his rescue.

Hennigan kept his gun trained on Rome as he scanned the walkway coming up from the mainland. He relaxed for a second not seeing a sign of anyone.

Rome stared at Hennigan. He was looking at a sick, deranged man at the end of his rope. He had to find something to keep him speaking. Anything.

"See that water down there?" The men glanced at the darkness below that flickered with the bridge's light beams.

"Do you know who St. Lawrence was?" Rome didn't wait for a response. "He was like you."

"Like me?"

"Yeah. You're a deacon. He was a priest." Rome pointed to the water. "And you know what happened to him? He was burned on the rack on the order of a crooked Pope. Burned alive."

Hennigan's face scrunched as if disgusted by the mental vision of burning flesh.

"Yep. A corrupt Pope ordered St. Lawrence to give up the church's money. St. Lawrence defied the Pope and distributed money to the poor. The Pope went batshit and ordered St. Lawrence to be roasted on a spit like a piece of meat."

Hennigan sneered at Rome. Why the fuck are you telling me this?

"You need to put the gun down and confess your sins or you'll roast in Hell forever."

The conversation had taken the turn Rome wanted. He could see the wheels turning in Hennigan's head. He was sure he'd have his confession if he stayed alive another couple of minutes.

"In 1973, Pope Paul VI promulgated the Decree on the Rite of Penance," Rome shouted.

Hennigan stilled as if the mention of the Pope deserved his attention.

"In a time of crisis or imminent death when there's not a confessor you can receive the sacramental grace of Penance if you just confess your sins to God."

Hennigan's body stiffened as he pointed the gun at Rome and looked up at the sky like he was speaking directly to God. "It was an accident."

Hennigan pointed his gun at Rome's head. His eyes told Rome he was about to die.

"Drop the gun!"

The voice sounded as if it belonged to a powerful cop. It also sounded like a last warning.

Hennigan froze and considered his options. If he gave himself up, he'd live the rest of his life in prison for killing Irene Izak, George Putnam and Father Patrick. The life of a trooper in a state prison would be worse than death, Hennigan thought. If he swung around, he'd catch a bullet. Either way, he'd be dead. He eyed Rome who clung on to the bridge rail. He was the primary source of his torment. If he was going to die, he was going to take Rome out with him.

Hennigan's eyes blazed as if his self preservation was no longer a concern. Rome recognized the look. He was sure he was going to die.

Hennigan pulled the trigger.

A powerful gunshot slammed into Rome's chest, tearing his hands from the railing and sending him into the darkness. Another gunshot quickly followed and Rome felt a hot stinging sensation in his calf.

Then another shot rang out.

On the bridge's walkway, Hennigan's right hand was limp and bloody. He staggered and fell to one knee.

"Don't move!" DeMartin's loud, angry voice yelled out as distant police sirens filled the air.

Hennigan was not going to follow orders. He pulled himself to his feet and leaned over the walkway. His face burst with surprise at seeing Rome dangling from the bridge. He cursed Rome's fortune and wished he could shoot his tormentor who swung below him. He then realized he didn't need a gun. He'd push him off. He charged Rome.

"Don't!" the same, deadly serious voice rang out from behind him. He turned in the direction of the voice. In the darkness, all Hennigan could see was a bulky shadow of pipes. He took another step towards Rome. Another shot rang out.

Hennigan's left hand exploded as a bullet tore through his hand where his thumb joined with his wrist.

With his two useless hands, Hennigan searched for the man who blew his hands apart. But the shooter was gone without a trace. His eyes then dropped to his mangled hands. Both were obliterated. He was shot by an expert marksman, Hennigan thought as he slumped against the bridge's railing.

Hennigan swayed as if both of his hands were severed from his arms. He glanced over the bridge as a freighter's bow began to pass under the bridge so closely it looked as if the top of the freighter would scrape the bottom of the bridge. Hennigan pressed his forearms against the bridge rail and looked at DeMartin who trained his gun on him from 15 feet away.

"Fuck you," he yelled as he pushed himself over the bridge's top railing with his arms.

As Rome dangled over the bridge, he saw Hennigan's body cascading towards the black water. He must be going 65 mph, Rome thought as he watched Hennigan free-fall through the night sky.

Rome heard a loud snapping of bones as Hennigan's body crashed against the freighter's side and toppled into the darkness. Rome pictured Hennigan's ribs slicing through his lungs and heart and his bones shattering like pieces of a broken china.

The next sounds they heard were sirens screeching towards them as police cars roared up the bridge and skidded to a stop. It sounded like 50 troopers cars arriving in a screech of rubber and wailing sirens.

"Don't move!"

"Get your hands up!"

DeMartin raised his hands to the sky. "He needs help," he yelled, signaling with his chin towards Rome who dangled helplessly from the bridge.

CHAPTER THIRTY ONE

PJ McLevy's plan called for him to be sipping Francis Durkin's scotch at 2 a.m. and then to be resting comfortably in bed a half an hour later.

But his plan had gone terribly awry. For the past two hours, he had been floating in the St. Lawrence River and his energy reserves were rapidly depleting.

McLevy had been trained to survive for long periods in rivers and swamps behind enemy lines with little sleep or food. But that was half a century ago and now his body felt a waterlogged beachball.

As he floated just above the surface of the river, his thoughts drifted to the reasons behind his misfortune. He had meticulously planned three escape routes from the Thousand Islands Bridge. Two hours ago, he was sure that one of the three routes would have led him to a path back to Durkin's cottage.

The first escape route was simply to drive away from the North Country Welcome Center. But that route had been obliterated by the swarm of cops arriving at the bridge quicker than he anticipated. There must have been six deputy sheriff cars parked at the base of the bridge's walkway alone.

PJ's second plan was to walk back under the bridge, hike through the woods to an RV community a quarter mile away where he left a getaway car. That route was now blocked by two teams of troopers with yapping blood hounds.

The third route was to cross the half mile-wide American channel. He hadn't planned on swimming. His plan was to be pulled by an underwater scooter he purchased a day ago at a local diving center and buried at the base of the bridge.

When he reached the base of the bridge, PJ saw that his third contingency was blown up as well. He hadn't figured on the rapid response by the state police's marine division. Their search lights lit up the area and he couldn't reach where he stashed the underwater scooter without being discovered.

McLevy's only shot at escaping was to locate the snorkel and fins he buried not far from underwater scooter. He crawled on his belly a 100 yards and located them under a pile of dirt. He slipped the fins on and bundled Hennigan's tote bag and his camouflage under his arms.

As he crept into the reeds, he assessed the strength of the river's current and temperature of the water. It was about 57 degrees Fahrenheit, he guessed. He was lucky, he thought. If it was it March or early April the water would be 35 Fahrenheit and he'd be dead in less than 30 minutes.

With his body's temperature hovering around 98 Fahrenheit, McLevy knew he could ward off hypothermia for about two hours before his body temperature dropped below 95 F. He knew the cold water was sucking the heat from him 25 times faster than if he was standing in the open air. He knew he'd first lose dexterity in his fingers and then his arms would go numb. He also knew he'd need a miracle to survive.

As he waded his way into the river, he cursed himself for not anticipating the trooper's marine division's fast response time. The patrol boat was under the bridge in less than 8 minutes after receiving a call about a shooting on the Thousand Islands Bridge. He also cursed himself for not figuring on the possibility that Hennigan would squirrel a gun and knife away on the bridge. The sick bastard was far more cunning than he had figured.

The trooper's patrol boat was joined by the Customs and Border Protection and Coast Guard vessels. He also hadn't figured on 10 spot lights slicing through the river or the divers quickly entering the river in a feverish search for Hennigan's body. With shocking speed, crews dropped anchors and shined powerful spot lights on the river making it look like a late night highway construction area.

Now, hours later, McLevy clung to a clump of tree roots on the other side of the river as his body shook uncontrollably. He had crossed the American Channel and reached the edge of Wellesley Island. His chest heaved as he assessed the slope of the bank. It was too high to ascend. Where would he go anyway? Cops with dogs were swarming both sides of the bridge. He'd be detected in minutes; walking on the streets, dripping wet and carrying two bundles.

Hennigan's bag of money began to feel like a lead weight. He knew he had to jettison it but he also knew it couldn't be discovered. It would open a Pandora's box. No cop or prosecutor would buy their story the blackmail ruse was used to draw Hennigan to the bridge. Extortion charges would certainly follow.

PJ leaned into the river bank and ran his hand down a spindly tree root. He sucked in a mouthful of air and ducked under the water's surface. Four feet under, he found what he was looking for. A gnarly, inch-thick outgrowth that bent upwards would act as a hook for Hennigan's bag. It wasn't perfect but it would have to do, PJ thought as he hooked the handle over the twisted root. The bag was dark and hopefully would blend in with the silty river floor. All he could do was hope.

Unsure of his next steps, he swam away from the direction of the lights, staying as close to the water's surface as possible. He soon slowed and treaded in the cold water. His hands and feet were killing him. He curled his toes and clenched his fists to try to get the blood flowing in his extremities but nothing relieved the intense pain.

As search lights continued to crisscross the river, McLevy figured it was at least three miles to the tip of Wellesley Island and another mile to the safety of Durkin's boathouse. It was all against the current. He checked his watch and grimaced as he reached the obvious conclusion. He'd never make it. He'd drown long before he swam another mile.

McLevy's confidence flagged. In the hundreds of life-or-death situations he endured, a surge of adrenaline would always imbue him with super-human powers that allowed him to endure extreme pain and power himself to safety. He never panicked or questioned if he'd survive. Never. Until now.

PJ kicked his flippers and slowly drifted towards a boathouse about 50 yards away, careful to minimize the ripples in the water. As he neared the boathouse, a moon bean illuminated the inside of the crumbling structure. He felt a ripple of hope-driven strength as he spied old kayaks, paddle boards and a sunfish.

His hopes were immediately dashed by the sounds of loud voices and the sight of flashlight beams bumping up and down in the darkness. He knew they were cops, going boathouse to boathouse, along the river.

PJ put on his snorkel and ducked under water and headed for a buoy up river, knowing if he didn't reach it, it would be his end. Fighting for his life, he kicked his fins and willed himself onward.

Twenty minutes later, he gripped the bottom rung of the steel ladder but his fingers could not bend. With frozen fingers he pulled the carabiner that dangled from his waist and, in one last gasp of energy, clicked it on the bottom rung of the ladder. He then pulled a plastic bag from the zipped pocket on his shorts. Holding it above the water he slid out his cell phone and dialed it. One ring. Two. Three.

"Yeah," a sleepy woman's voice answered.

"Cassie, this is PJ. I need to speak to Francis." PJ's frantic, desperate tone yanked her from sleep's grip. Even with his life on the line, McLevy knew he couldn't call the state's attorney. The call would be traced. It would be like pulling Francis Durkin into the cold, deadly waters with him.

A few seconds later, Francis answered groggily, "Durkin."

"Francis. It's PJ."

"What's up?" He could hear Durkin instantly breaking sleep's hold, adjusting to the moment.

"I'm in the river and I need help."

"I can pick you up in my cousin's boat."

"No, the troopers and Coast Guard will catch you. You're probably under surveillance anyway. Somebody else," PJ's words drifted off as both men instantly thought of the same man.

"I'll call Kyle," Durkin said. "Where are you?"

PJ was prepared. "I'm hanging on to buoy marker 210. It's just up river from the bridge." His voice quivered, leaving no doubt he couldn't hang on much longer as he watched the boats buzz with activity under the Thousand Islands Bridge. High wattage search lights shined down from poles on the boats reminding PJ of a high school stadium lit up for a night football game.

"I'm calling now."

PJ stuck the cell phone back in the plastic bag and clung to the mile marker as the neurological effects of the cold water set in. He shivered and his teeth clattered uncontrollably. His mental abilities seemed to sputter like his brain was short-circuiting. In spurts of clarity, he knew his bodily fluids were congealing. He knew his blood was turning thick and gooey and his heart was pumping in overdrive to force the thicker blood through his ventricles. He also knew with the extreme loss of body heat his brain was being deprived of oxygen. He knew he'd soon lose the ability to think and communicate.

His arms and legs felt like dead appendages as they barely responded to his brain's commands. As his eyes tried to focus on the bright lights under the bridge, black drops descended over his irises as if he was caught in a dark rain storm.

For the first time in his life, PJ McLevy felt despair overtake him. He had battled despair thousands of times. But he always gritted it out and never allowed himself to lose. Now his thoughts turned to how far his body had lost its resilience. He once was invulnerable, breaking pain-enduring records. Now he felt aged, right down to his cellular structure. His tendons and ligaments had lost elasticity. His joints ached and his bones seemed frail as if they lost half their density.

PJ McLevy knew he only had minutes left and it would take Kyle far more than minutes to find him. He closed his eyes and drifted into unconsciousness.

*****

270

PJ would never remember being tugged from the water. A force tried to lift him and then dropped his body back into the water like a lobster trap that had been checked and re-set.

Kyle Johnston cursed the carabiner that PJ attached to the buoy's ladder. It may have saved him from drowning but now it was preventing Kyle from saving his life.

Kyle secured the boat to the ladder and pulled PJ's body closer to slacken the line and then, in a burst of energy, unhooked PJ from the ladder. As he gathered the strength to pull him from the river, the sound of a power boat startled him. The roar of boat engines signaled a speed boat was quickly approaching. He turned and saw a trooper's boat rapidly closing in on him.

Kyle snapped PJ's carabiner around his rubber bumper and dropped it over the side of his boat as a powerful spotlight sprayed him from the other side. The large engines quieted as water splashed against Kyle's fishing boat.

"What are you doing here?" an irritated voice yelled.

Kyle Johnston was wired to meet aggression with aggression. He glared at the two troopers for a long moment and then said, "What's the problem? I fish here all the time."

The trooper ignored him. "What's under the canvas?"

"Hell, if I show you, will you get off my ass?"

The troopers didn't answer. They just stared at the canvas. Move it now. Kyle grunted with displeasure as he rolled the canvas sheet in a ball, revealing tackle boxes.

"There. It's not a crime to carry two tackle boxes, is it?"

The troopers eyed his boat suspiciously.

"You want to see anything else?" Kyle asked defiantly.

The troopers' angry eyes stared back at him. Normally, his wise-ass tone would result in the troopers performing a safety check. They'd meticulously check the life preserves, flares, horns and first aid kits. They could find a violation when they wanted to.

Now they wanted to but they didn't have the time.

"Move on. You can't fish here," a trooper's angry voice snapped.

"I can't fish where I want?"

Pause. "You need to move on."

"You want to see my fishing permit?"

A loud groan erupted from deep inside of the trooper. He was bone-tired and not going to put up with Kyle's horseshit. "A quarter of a mile around the bridge in both directions is a crime scene. That means it's off limits for fishing." The trooper paused and let his words sink in. "If you don't comply, we'll arrest you."

Kyle tilted his head and stretched his jaw bone as if trying to re-align it.

"Are you moving?" The voice was tense and no-nonsense.

"All right, all ready." Kyle sat on down on his seat and motioned to the bridge. It was lit up and buzzing with activity. "What's going on at the bridge?

Silence. The troopers weren't going to share information with a pissant like Kyle. Move on.

"Okay. Suit yourself. I'll move upriver even though the fishing ain't shit up there."

"Start moving or you'll be arrested. You understand?" The trooper waited with his eyes glued on Kyle. Get moving. Now.

Kyle fed gas into his idling motor and began motoring slowly upriver, making sure he didn't expose PJ to the troopers' line of sight. When he was 20 yards away, the trooper cut off his angry surveillance and the troopers' patrol boat headed back to the bridge with a powerful burst of their three engines.

Kyle put his boat in neutral and began drifting. He picked up a rod and went over to the side of the boat, hoping that from afar, it would look as if he was working on a snagged line.

He immediately saw that PJ's head was above water but he was hardly breathing. And Kyle knew he couldn't pull him up without drawing the trooper's attention. Kyle quickly set his plan of action in play. He'd continue up river and when he was out of sight, he'd pull PJ aboard.

Kyle leaned over the side of his boat and yelled to PJ. "Hold on! I'll have you out of the water in a jiffy." He didn't wait for a response. None was coming anyway. PJ was dragged through the water as if he was an unconscious water tuber hanging on to a slow moving rope.

When they neared the lighthouse, Kyle slid the engine in neutral and grabbed PJ's arms. He undid the carabiner and gripped PJ by his armpits and pulled him up as if he was pulling a net full of fish. He struggled with the dead weight of PJ's body. He almost dropped him back in the water before he summoned all his the energy for one powerful tug. He knew he didn't have the strength for a second try.

Like a power-lifter, Kyle expended all his energy in one explosive burst, grabbing PJ's belt and pulling him over the side of his boat.

Thank God, PJ was still breathing, he said to himself as he detected PJ's faint heart beat. Then he saw that PJ's fingers were stretched as far as possible from each other. Kyle instantly recognized the full-claw; the sign of devastating cold ravaging a body.

"I can't move." The words dribbled out of PJ's mouth as if propelled from his subconscious.

"I got you now," Kyle said with the reassuring tone of a medic who knew the clock was ticking on PJ's life.

Kyle wrapped PJ in a work-blanket and grabbed a thermos of tepid coffee. He poured a half cup into the plastic top and nursed PJ to drink. PJ's lips barely moved at the touch of the warmth.

Kyle powered his boat, unsure of his destination.

*****

"Thank God," Kyle gasped at the sight of Cassie waiting on her dock as he neared Jolly Island. He had no idea that she sped there on her jet ski after Durkin called him. All she had was a hunch; a hunch that Kyle would need a place to bring PJ and Jolly Island was better than most. Her hunch paid off.

Kyle tossed her his boat's line and she quickly tied the bow of the boat to her dock cleat as Kyle secured the stern line. She then hopped into the boat and examined PJ. He looked like a wrinkled corpse with rigor mortis.

Cassie recognized the glassy look of a dying bird, in his eyes. She grew up hearing stories how islanders perished after falling through the river's ice as they traveled back and forth to the mainland in the winter. She knew she had to get PJ out of the cold and out of his clothes before the last bit of life drained out of him.

"Get the wheel barrel," she shouted. Kyle leapt out of the boat and in half a minute was standing on the dock holding the two wooden arms of her wheel barrel. He jumped back in the boat and together they hauled PJ's inert body to the edge of the boat and then, as if he was a sack of potatoes, rolled him on the dock and scooped him into the wheel barrel.

In less than a minute, they were inside her cottage and PJ's body laid on her bed. Without a word passing between them, Kyle cut his clothes off and Cassie wrapped his naked body in woolen blankets.

"I'll get some tea," Cassie said as her thoughts turned to the dangers PJ faced. In the next 10 minutes, she'd know if PJ would live or die. She was petrified of mismanaging the inevitable onslaught of after-drop; the continual cooling the body undergoes when it's exposed to extreme temperatures. She knew if she moved him too much or tried to warm him up too fast, his heart would get smashed with a rush of cold blood that would surge from his limbs back to his core. His heart would be jolted so violently by the cold blood it would be thrown into ventricular fibrillation, an electrical storm that would

273

trigger a massive heart attack in a strong and healthy man. She looked at PJ. He was anything but a strong and healthy man. He wouldn't be able to withstand the shock of even mild after-drop.

Cassie ran into the kitchen and called Sadie Delany, Grindstone's island's resident medical guru who attended to all of the islanders' medical needs. Sadie answered on the second ring. She shook off her grogginess and assured Cassie she'd be over as fast as her jet-ski could take her to Jolly Island.

Cassie returned in two minutes with a luke warm cup of tea. She gently pressed the cup to PJ's lips. PJ lips moved like a fish left for hours on a dock. Cassie prayed for Sadie to hurry.

CHAPTER THIRTY TWO

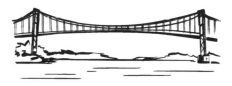

The sun's morning rays pierced the dusty gray clouds as Durkin rolled off the Thousand Islands Bridge and headed towards the troopers' barracks. When he pulled into the barracks, he saw the small parking lot and grassy area around the normally sleepy, square shaped barracks had been transformed into a buzz of activity. Troopers hustled in and out of the State Police mobile command post set up next to the barracks. In the corner of the lot, three television crews broadcast from temporary towers.

Durkin parked on a patch of grass near the edge of the road and walked, eyes-forward, as if he was afflicted with tunnel vision. At first, none of the troopers noticed the middle-aged guy in street clothes with bandaids plastered on his face. But as he neared the barrack's entrance, one-by-one, the troopers stopped in their tracks and trained their eyes on him like lasers. Francis Durkin felt the heat of their glares but kept his eyes fixed straight ahead and walked expressionless towards the door.

He entered the barracks and strode to the bullet-proof partition with a purposeful gate; trying to exude the image of a man on a mission; a man who didn't give a shit about what anyone thought of him.

Behind the glass, two middle-aged troopers with mid-level authority talked to one another in low whispers. They both turned and set their eyes on Durkin at the same time. In the same flash, their faces conveyed their shared dislike for the man on the other side of the bullet-proof glass.

"I'm here to see Sergeant Angelo DeMartin," Durkin said in a crisp, official tone.

The troopers' faces tightened. The one closest to Durkin sniffed and then said, "It's not visiting hours."

Durkin shook his head and his facial expression made it clear that he considered the trooper a moron. "I'm not visiting." His eyes darted to the trooper's name tag. Mason. Durkin's glance made it clear that he was filing Mason's name in his memory bank. "I'm Sergeant DeMartin's attorney. Trooper Mason, are you going on record that you're not permitting Sergeant DeMartin to see his attorney?"

The two troopers sneered in sync and conferred in low whispers. The shorter one then shook his head in agreement and walked off to a conference room. Durkin could see him softly tap on the door and then enter.

A second later, the door flung open and Commander Rasmutin sprang out of the room. Rasmutin's face flushed and he coiled his body as if preparing to lunge at Durkin like a hungry and agitated caged lion. The skin tightened around the side of his eyes and Durkin knew Rasmutin's eyes were bulging under his mirror glasses. Every other fiber in his body was taut, on the verge of snapping.

Rasmutin relaxed a notch as he sensed the presence of someone by his side. Durkin noticed Rasmutin's reaction and turned his attention to the man next to Rasmutin. Durkin knew the trooper's military insignia identified him as a colonel; Rasmutin's superior officer.

Rasmutin turned and whispered to the senior trooper in a low voice making it obvious whatever he had to say was only for the senior trooper's ears. The senior trooper nodded and then Rasmutin gave the signal to admit Durkin. The mid-level troopers reacted to the order with the same expression; they didn't like the directive but would comply. The shorter trooper pressed a button which triggered the clatter of a metal lock opening.

Durkin pushed through the barrier and locked eyes with Rasmutin. For a split-second, the combustible tension threatened to ignite. Then, as if he suddenly remembered the presence of the high-ranking trooper behind him, the snarl on Rasmutin's face faded and he jabbed his finger in the direction of the conference room.

Durkin understood: his client waited behind the door. He quickly opened it and entered. Inside, Angelo DeMartin sat across from two serious-faced, plainclothes troopers. Durkin recognized one: Parker from his last visit to the barracks. The detectives looked startled and sprang to their feet at the sight of Durkin. The flash of concern morphed into confusion when they saw Rasmutin and the high-ranking trooper enter behind Durkin.

Durkin flashed a look at DeMartin; don't say anything. DeMartin nodded reassuringly. He wouldn't open his mouth. No, for the past two hours DeMartin sat on a metal chair wearing the uncomfortable look of a cop not willing to answer a single question until his attorney arrived.

For a brief second, Durkin experienced a strange, out of body sensation. Here, the life-long, fire-breathing prosecutor, was playing the pain-in-the-ass defense attorney, poking his thumb in the eye of law enforcement. The role was jarring and distasteful but Durkin reminded himself it was only temporary.

"What can we do for a state's attorney from Connecticut?" the high-ranking trooper asked in an even tone, not aggressive but designed to convey that Durkin held no sway in Northern New York.

All eyes turned to Colonel Robert Welsh. Durkin guessed Welsh was in his late forties, probably a high-potential candidate poised to someday lead the state police.

He was right. Welsh had been on the state police's fast track for the past 10 years. He was easy going and down to earth but possessed a steely determination to do whatever it took to get the job done.

Welsh ran his eyes over Durkin and DeMartin as if he was familiar with the men's backgrounds. He was. For the last hour, Welsh had poured over the files on Francis Durkin and Angelo DeMartin. He had watched the Jihadist Boyz Youtube video three times where Sergeant DeMartin rescued a fellow cop in a blaze of gunfire. He was impressed by what he read about both men.

"I'm here in the capacity as Sergeant DeMartin's lawyer."

Rasmutin exploded. "A state's attorney is acting as a defense attorney?"

Welsh shot an angry look at Rasmutin. Be quiet. He'd do the talking. All of it.

Durkin shook his head dismissively and directed his attention squarely on Welsh. "Have you charged Sergeant DeMartin with a crime?"

"Not yet," Welsh replied breezily as if to say that could change if Durkin pushed him too far.

Durkin pushed gently. "If he's not charged with a crime, then he can go."

Welsh's head bobbed in a friendly manner as if encouraging Durkin to lower the temperature in the room. "State's Attorney Durkin, you know full well that we can detain someone for a reasonable period while we gather the facts about a crime."

Durkin knew better than anyone that Welsh was correct. While cops weren't allowed to hold a suspect indefinitely, they weren't required to catch-and-release either. Durkin knew if the troopers had reasonably suspected Angelo DeMartin had engaged in criminal activity they could detain him while they conducted their investigation. Durkin also knew the courts declined to put limits on how long the police could detain a suspect. It was case specific.

And in this case, DeMartin had been detained for less than 8 hours. He was found on a bridge's walkway after a shooting. The detention time so far wasn't close to being unreasonable.

Durkin tacked to firmer legal ground. "What crimes are you investigating?"

Welsh motioned to the open chair next to DeMartin. "Please, take a seat so we can go over some important points."

Durkin considered rejecting Welsh's offer but something about Welsh's folksy, down-to-earth, style connected with him. After he appeared to weigh his options, Durkin pulled out a chair at the end of the table and sat. Welsh then took a seat in the middle of the table, happy to cede Durkin the symbolic leverage of sitting at the head of the conference table. The only man who remained standing was Rasmutin who stood, arms folded, like a snarling bouncer, glaring at Durkin from across the conference table.

"What crimes are you investigating?" Durkin asked again.

"Let's start with the easiest. Trespassing."

"That's all you've got?"

An even-keeled grin sprouted on Welsh's face. "No, as you probably guess, we're looking at much more serious charges. There was a shooting on the bridge and at least three homicides occurred last night. We think they're connected." Welsh drew a breath as if giving Durkin time to contemplate the potential charges his client faced.

Durkin zeroed in on Welsh. "You know who killed Irene Izak and we all know that the same man killed the priest and the tollbooth collector."

Durkin let his words settle in before plowing ahead. "There's no reason to detain Sergeant DeMartin. He didn't have anything to do with the murders."

The room filled with heavy breathing as Welsh considered Durkin's words. Welsh knew he was dealing with a brilliant prosecutor; a man whose legal reasoning was likely already three steps ahead of him. Without looking at DeMartin, Welsh asked Durkin, "Is your client willing to tell us what happened on the bridge?"

Durkin scratched his cheek as if he was buying time to compose his reply. He sought to come off as cooperative but firm. "Sure." He paused for effect. "But under the circumstances, we're only going to speak with your Internal Affairs division."

Durkin turned to Rasmutin who glared back at him from under his mirror glasses. "You've got rot in your house. Every thing pointed to Hennigan but your boys were doing handstands to avoid investigating him. There wouldn't have been any other murders had the troopers just done their job."

Rasmutin's cheeks turned beet red. He opened his mouth as if he'd lash out at Durkin but constrained himself—barely. Durkin instantly knew he had the emotional advantage and now was the time to exploit it.

"How often does a Commander personally deliver evidence to the trooper's crime lab?"

Welsh shot an incredulous look at Rasmutin. Was it true?

Rasmutin quaked and began to rock on the balls of his feet as if an uncontrollable firestorm was brewing inside of him.

Durkin read him like a book. His next words were crafted to provide a spark. "It's a crime to cover up a murder."

Rasmutin shook like he was battling to contain himself. He rocked unsteadily as if the rage was shooting up from his toes. Then his legs began to vibrate as if the rage was rising through him. When the rage seemed to boil up to his shoulders, he exploded.

Rasmutin launched his muscular body at Durkin with the force of a linebacker. His shoulder caught Durkin in his chest, slamming Durkin into the floor with a loud crash as the conference table toppled under Rasmutin's weight. Before Durkin recovered from the hit, Rasmutin unloaded a flurry of punches to Durkin's rib cage. For a split-second, Durkin felt as if he was in mortal danger as he felt the excruciating pain of Rasmutin's fists raining down on him like sledgehammers. The man was terrifyingly strong.

Finally, he sensed a flurry of arms and legs above him as if he was lying in the center of a school yard brawl. A second later, he heard a loud thud as the two detectives and Welsh pushed Rasmutin against the wall and forcefully restrained him.

Welsh's face tightened to the breaking point as he glared at Rasmutin. Rasmutin's glasses had fallen off in the scuffle and he scowled at Welsh through his dead, black eye.

Welsh was unmoved. He fixed his eyes on Rasmutin's dead eye. You fucked up big time. You're going to pay dearly for the outburst. He then turned to the detectives who each clung to one of his arms. "Get him out of here!"

The troopers held Rasmutin tightly by his arms as if they expected Rasmutin to charge Durkin. Rasmutin tensed his muscles and gritted his teeth as he cursed Welsh through his dead eye.

"Get him out of here!" Welsh yelled again. The detectives tugged at Rasmutin's arms, unable to shield their amazement at Rasmutin's raw strength, knowing there was little they could do to prevent another attack on Durkin. To their relief, Rasmutin relaxed his muscles and pushed the detectives' arms away as they ushered him out of the conference room.

Welsh hurried over to Durkin who was splayed on the floor like a battered lamp. Welsh and DeMartin stood over Durkin for a few seconds, searching for the right body part to lift him up. Without exchanging words, they directed one another to hook their arms under Durkin's armpits and pulled him onto the only chair still standing.

Welsh then picked up a chair and fell into it, shutting his eyes as if overcome with a severe migraine. In the blackness of his thoughts, he envisioned years of his life being consumed by reports, depositions and courtroom testimony over the violent explosion he just witnessed. He opened his eyes to confront reality.

For a few seconds, the men sat in a fatigued silence.

"Are you okay?" Welsh finally panted, sounding genuinely concerned as DeMartin screwed off the cap of a bottle of water and held it towards Durkin. Durkin's eyes took a second to focus on the bottle and his rib cage was too battered for him to reach for it. He sat still and gathered his strength like a guy who got the worst end of a bad bar fight. Bandaids dangled from his face and the scabs on his face dripped blood. His shirt was torn and his hair disheveled. His movements were constrained by knifing pain.

Durkin drew a breath and accepted the water bottle gingerly. Like an old man in a desert, he pulled the bottle to his lips and sipped the water. He placed the bottle back on the table and seemed to go over a mental checklist of his body parts. He stretched his ribs. They hurt but he didn't think they were cracked. Check. He moved his arms. Sore but responsive. Check. He rolled his wrists. Check. He rubbed his neck. Check. He massaged his kneecaps. Check. He was in dire pain but everything seemed to work.

"Looks like most of my parts still work," Durkin wheezed. He raised his right forefinger. "Just give me a second."

"Okay," Welsh said, blowing a gush of exasperation. "I'll be right back."

Welsh stepped out of the room and returned a minute later with an arm full of first aid equipment: ice packs, bandaids, antiseptic pads and packets of Tylenol. He spread the first aid material on the conference table like it was a peace offering.

"Can I get you guys a coffee or something?"

DeMartin and Durkin, shook their heads. No, they were good.

Welsh picked up two overturned chairs and took a seat across from Durkin. "Then, I'll start by apologizing for Rasmutin's outburst."

Welsh shook his head as if there were no words to adequately capture Rasmutin's conduct. "But if you're okay, I'd like to get back to a few questions about what went on around here over the past week."

Durkin ripped open an antiseptic towelette and dabbed his face. He unsuccessfully masked the sting of iodine and examined the blood on the towelette. He then sensed the weight of the bandaids dangling off his face. His fingers plucked them off and he dropped the bloody bandaids on the conference table. He then eyed Welsh. "That's the second time in a week I've been roughed up by one of your troopers."

Welsh pressed his lips together. He knew Hennigan's report that Durkin posed a threat at Dewolf Point State Park was bullshit. There was nothing he could say.

"You know I'm going to have a field day in court." Durkin pointed to the two surveillance cameras. "Make sure that you preserve those tapes."

Welsh continued nodding, trying to wear the look of an unconcerned man who would be passing on the problem to someone else. But he was concerned. The whole pile of shit was going to fall right on his desk and consume the next couple years of his life.

But right now, Welsh had to press on. "Can I ask you a few questions?"

Durkin continued to dab his face and nodded. Knock yourself out.

"Can you shed some light on how a tape of Hennigan's confession found its way to a reporter?"

Welsh eyed both DeMartin and Durkin as if he'd accept answers from either of them. Both men just shook their heads. Welsh was unsure of their message. Was it, no, they couldn't shed light on the tape or no, they wouldn't share any information about the tape?

"The reporter says the tape of Hennigan's confession was delivered anonymously to him," Welsh said in hope of spurring a comment from either Durkin or DeMartin.

Durkin's brain sent a buckshot command to his heart, his eyes, his cheeks, lips and nostrils not to spike with emotion as he thought of Sam Rome delivering the tape to the reporter. His only outward reaction was two blinks. But two quick blinks were enough for Welsh's trained eye to know Durkin possessed the answer to his question.

"I'm going to cut to the chase. Have you ever heard the tape?"

Durkin's lips pressed together and slid a millimeter to the left. Again, Welsh detected the minute change in Durkin's emotional state.

Durkin inhaled loudly. "No. No, I haven't." He kept his eyes trained on Welsh as if to prove he was telling the truth. He was. When Rome came to tell him about Hennigan's confession, he stopped Rome from pushing the 'play' button on his recorder. He had never actually heard Hennigan's confession.

"But if there was a tape of Hennigan's confession," Durkin said with the ring of a man who knew there was, "the crime is solved."

Welsh stared at Durkin for a long moment. He decided not to share that James Breen, the reporter from the *Watertown Daily Register*, provided the state police with a copy of the tape and it was in the process of being authenticated by a forensic audiologist. He also wasn't going to share that he listened to it along with Detectives Parker, LeFleur and Rasmutin. Everyone but Rasmutin was sure it was Hennigan's voice.

"Can you shed any light on who taped the confession?"

"That I can't help you with," Durkin said sharply. Welsh winced at his lawyerly response. Can't help you? Was he saying there was a legal, moral or professional reason prohibiting him from assisting the troopers or did he plain not know who taped the confession? Knowing the video tape of their conversation was rolling, Welsh decided not to press Durkin.

"Well, then do you know anything about the murder of Father O'Brien?"

Both Durkin and DeMartin shook their heads firmly. They could take an educated guess who pulled the trigger but they had nothing to share about the why, how and when Fr. Patrick O'Brien was murdered.

"This is the first I've even heard about it," Durkin said. He was being honest. In the frantic mid morning hours of coordinating PJ's rescue, he hadn't listened to the radio or eyed his cell phone for news.

"He had his brains blown out in his confessional about two hours before Hennigan reportedly took a header off the Thousand Islands Bridge."

"Hennigan was a deacon at the same church, right?"

Welsh nodded slowly.

"That's interesting," Durkin said. "But as I said, this is the first I've heard about the priest's murder."

Welsh's head bobbed. He believed him. Maybe it was Durkin's tone or maybe it was the look in his eyes. Whatever it was, Welsh accepted it with a sigh. "Okay, then, tell me why you think charging Sergeant DeMartin with trespassing is chicken-shit."

Durkin sipped the water from the plastic bottle. He then sucked in a deep breath. "He can't be charged with trespassing."

Confusion splashed across Welsh's face. "No? The bridge was closed to foot traffic."

"Sergeant DeMartin went on the bridge with the intent to arrest Trooper Hennigan."

"With all due respect," Welsh countered, "a Bridgeport, Connecticut cop doesn't have any authority in upstate New York."

"He doesn't need any," Durkin said, rubbing his neck. "He was making a citizen's arrest."

"A citizen's arrest?" Welsh searched Durkin's face for a sign he was joking. He couldn't find a trace of humor.

"New York Penal Law, section 35.20."

Welsh's face seemed to freeze. Durkin was actually citing from the NY Penal Law?

"New York law allows a private citizen to use force in making an arrest or preventing an escape. New York's penal law also authorizes a private person to use physical force to effect an arrest or prevent an escape of someone he reasonably believes to have committed an offense and who in fact has committed such offense."

Welsh studied Durkin as if astonished by Durkin's photographic memory.

Welsh picked up a water bottle, slowly unscrewed the top and took a long swig. "Weren't your," he paused and carefully selected his words, "weren't your clients doing a lot more than making a citizen's arrest?"

Durkin shrugged and deflected the question. "From what I know, it was a legal citizen's arrest."

Welsh leaned towards Durkin. "Really? Some ordinary folks might not think that your clients and Hennigan just met up randomly at midnight on the Thousand Islands Bridge."

Durkin nodded. Yes, he could see how ordinary folks would think that.

"A lot of people, including me," Welsh continued on, "are wondering why Hennigan would meet a retired cop from Massachusetts and a famous cop from Connecticut on the Thousand Islands Bridge at midnight."

Durkin dabbed his open scab with a clean towelette. "I don't have the answers for that." Durkin turned and eyed DeMartin as if signaling him not to supply any answers. "I just know that if a person has reason to know that law enforcement is intentionally failing to do its job he can take reasonable steps to make a lawful arrest."

Durkin dropped the towelette on the conference table. "And I certainly can make a good case that the state police weren't doing their job here."

Welsh made a face that indicated he couldn't argue. "Yes, someone is going to have to answer a lot of questions." And everyone knew the 'someone' was Rasmutin.

"You'll probably find many of the answers in Hennigan's confession."

Welsh remained expressionless as he considered Durkin's words. Yes, there was no doubt that Hennigan brutally murdered Irene Izak. There was no doubt that he killed Fr. Patrick O'Brien and executed George Putnam at the rest stop on I-81. There would be official investigations that would take another year but those crimes were solved as far as he was concerned.

But Welsh had other concerns. Days ago, he concluded that Rasmutin must have known that Trooper David Hennigan committed the murder. Worse, he was coming to believe Rasmutin actively covered-up the crime. Now he was hearing rumors of a shitshow at the troopers' crime lab in Albany.

Welsh swallowed hard as he thought of the political shock waves that would ripple down from the Governor's office when the truth of Irene Izak's murder leaked. The state police's reputation would be shattered. Could a law enforcement organization recover from covering up a murder committed by one of its own? Welsh sighed audibly as he thought of getting swept out of his office in the tsunami whipped up by the political scandal. Welsh knew that when a scandal turned rancid, the only political move was to clean house. Everyone in a senior position would be ushered out of the state police.

Welsh expelled a long breath. This certainly was not how he envisioned ending his career. "This is a cluster fuck," he finally said with a rush of air. He wore an expression that he regretted giving voice to his thoughts. But his back was against the wall; he had no choice.

"Yeah it is. And it's only going to get worse," Durkin replied, rubbing his ribs. "You've got to bring in your internal affairs to finish the investigation."

Welsh nodded somberly. He had already reached the same conclusion. He also needed time to refine his strategy. Too much was riding on his next steps not to carefully plan everything.

"Are you going to charge Sargeant DeMartin with a crime?"

"We haven't decided yet."

"Well, under the circumstances, don't you think it's appropriate that you release him?"

Under the circumstances? Did Durkin mean since the commander of the barracks beat the shit out of him, the least he could do was to release his client pending further investigation?

"Will you give me your word that you'll both come back later today?" Welsh deftly appealed to Durkin's sense of honor.

Durkin pushed himself up unsteadily as the pain from Rasmutin's crushing blows pulsed through his body. He braced himself against the table and gathered himself. He then stood on wobbly legs and shook Welsh's hand. "You've got my word."

*****

Francis Durkin and Angelo DeMartin limped past a cordon of troopers who glared menacingly at them. Their glares were fueled by the rumors that

284

continued to leak from the barracks; the Connecticut cops robbed and threw Trooper Hennigan over the Thousand Islands Bridge. The Connecticut cops assassinated George Putnam. District Attorney McClusky was only hours away from charging the Connecticut state's attorney with the murder of Irene Izak.

The only eyes that weren't shooting darts at Durkin and DeMartin belonged to James Alexander Breen. JB's eyes were circled with tired rings. He looked like a war correspondent who hadn't slept in days.

Less than 12 hours ago, JB drove to the Sacred Heart Church to follow up on an anonymous tip that Fr. Patrick O'Brien knew who killed Irene Izak. Instead of eliciting a news-worthy quote he walked into a bloody murder scene. The mental visions of Fr. O'Brien's brains splattered on the confessional walls still made him gag. And he was now part of the story. His quickly unfolding national story.

Then there was the killing of Clifford Putnam. He hadn't been allowed to approach the crime scene and inspect Putnam's body. The troopers had set up a tent around his body to block everyone's view. The only thing he got was an off-the-record quote that it looked as if Putnam was executed at the rest stop and his body was dragged behind a tree and left in a heap like a discarded tire.

JB caught troopers' searing glares aimed at Durkin and DeMartin and he caught up to them as fast as he could walk in his sling. He intercepted the men just as they reached Durkin's car.

"Sergeant DeMartin" JB said, slightly out of breath. "Can you tell me what happened on the bridge?"

Durkin interceded with a raised hand. "I'm sorry, Mr. Breen. There's an investigation going on and we can't discuss it until it's over."

JB stopped and examined Durkin's battered face. He was sure Durkin looked worse than the last time he saw him."What happened to you?"

"You know, the state police got a little rough with me."

"Again?"

"Once is plenty," Durkin answered in a deliberatively vague fashion and pointed to JB's sling. "What happened to you?"

"An occupational hazard. I tripped while investigating a story," JB said, purposely omitting any connection to Dewolf Point State Park. "Now, getting back to the bridge—"

"Sorry, you have to ask the troopers," Durkin interrupted.

A wave of disappointment splashed over JB's face. "Can you at least confirm that Trooper Hennigan was on the bridge last night?"

Durkin wore a pained look as he shook his head. "Sorry. Talk to the troopers."

A larger wave of disappointment splashed across JB's face. He had hoped for more than boilerplate bullshit from the famous state's attorney. As if retaliating for his disappointment, JB asked, "Then can you comment on the reports that the troopers are investigating you?"

The question caught Durkin off-guard. He took a moment before he answered. "I know the troopers were looking at everyone who was in the vicinity of the murder." Durkin shrugged. "I came across the murder scene and called 911. The troopers naturally needed to check me out. That's standard. I think the troopers will now confirm that I'm not a suspect."

JB was sure Durkin was no longer a suspect. He had listened to Hennigan's confession at least 20 times. But JB knew there were loose threads; threads that could make intriguing, national stories for months to come. But he still needed crucial facts to weave a block-buster story. "Can you comment on how your DNA was found on the victim's body?"

Durkin paused as if he was startled by the question. "I can't. There's no legitimate reason for it to be there. I never came in contact with the victim or the murder scene."

"I've been told by a reliable source that your DNA was found on the victim's body."

"Let me guess," Durkin replied with a roll of his eyes. "Your reliable source is a trooper. "

"I can't comment on that."

"No, I'm sure you can't. But the credibility of the source matters."

Durkin was about to comment on the credibility of the state police when he remembered that every word would likely end up in print. He changed tacks. "Listen, about a week ago, I was riding a bike and came across a crime scene. Everyone knows that. There's been a whirl of events since that time. And I'm sure the troopers will be releasing information on who murdered the woman shortly. I'll happily speak with you after the troopers release their findings."

JB stuck his pad and pen into his back pocket. He was experienced enough to know he wasn't getting anything of value from Durkin. "Okay. I look forward to it."

The men nodded at one another. Until later. Durkin and DeMartin climbed into Durkin's car. No one spoke until they were out of the troopers' parking lot as if afraid the troopers employed long range listening devices.

"Is PJ back?" DeMartin asked as he mentally replayed the scene on the bridge after Hennigan dove off the bridge. The loud noises; the search lights, the sounds of barking dogs and the roar of marine vessels scouring the water below, all flooded back into DeMartin's head.

"I'm told he's going to be fine," Durkin answered as he envisioned PJ wrapped in blankets on Jolly Island. "He had an eventful night. I heard it was touch and go for a while."

DeMartin sat silently. Touch and go? He had grown intensely close to the odd looking, eccentric cop with a heart as big as Montana.

"I'm looking forward to seeing him," was all DeMartin could say before a wave of emotion engulfed him.

"You'll have to wait a bit. He's thawing out at Cassie's cottage."

Thawing out? "How long was he in the river?"

Durkin's face bunched. He couldn't share what he knew with DeMartin. He then let a long sigh escape as he thought of the legal shoals ahead of him, knowing any prosecutor worth his salt would charge him as an accessory after the fact for aiding PJ's escape and 20 other crimes if the facts ever came to light.

"I'm not sure," Durkin sighed in a tone that signaled it was a long time.

"How did PJ get away?" Durkin asked.

DeMartin shook his head. "He's like Houdini." His thoughts flashed back to the bridge. "After Hennigan jumped, I saw PJ moving towards Rome in a camouflage suit that completely blended into the bridge. Same color, shapes, everything. PJ leaned over the bridge and Rome tossed something to him. PJ took my gun and Hennigan's gym bag which I'm guessing had the money."

"Money?"

DeMartin explained that to make it look like blackmail they demanded 40 thousand dollars from Hennigan. Durkin winced as if he was coming down with a headache.

"Sam and PJ's plan was to get Hennigan to confess. It was a long shot but we had no other option."

Durkin nodded as he focused on keeping his car in the lane as an eight wheel truck thundered past them.

"What about Sam?"

"He's in the local hospital."

DeMartin nodded pensively as he flashed back to Hennigan shooting Rome. There were two shots. He was sure one hit Rome in the chest. When Rome fell backwards into the darkness he was sure he witnessed Rome's death. It wasn't until he saw PJ yelling over the bridge that he realized Rome was still alive.

Durkin slowed at the bridge's tollbooth. "By any chance, did Hennigan say anything before he jumped?" Durkin's tone indicated that he didn't think there was any chance but he had to ask.

"He was raving about something right before he jumped."

DeMartin remembered Hennigan shaking his right hand as if it was on fire. He had a strange look in his eye as if he was running a cost-benefit analysis on living or dying. In a nano-second, Hennigan looked as if he had concluded the costs of living were too high: the rest of his life behind bars was a price he wasn't willing to pay. He stopped and shouted and then, without the use of his hands, Hennigan crawled over the bridge's railing.

"What was he raving about?"

"I heard him say something like 'bless me father for I have sinned'. He peered over as a freighter crossed under the bridge and pushed himself over the railing."

DeMartin relived the scene of Hennigan's body shooting towards the freighter crossing under the bridge. The last thing he saw was Hennigan's body smack against the freighter and tumble to the side.

Durkin pulled up to the tollbooth and waited for the gate to rise after E-Z Pass electronically deducted the toll. Durkin slowed at the section of the bridge's walkway that was still closed off with police crime tape and imagined what had transpired only hours ago. He looked up and down the river from the perch of the bridge. He guessed he could see 10 miles in both directions.

The men were interrupted by Durkin's cell phone. He didn't recognize the number. It could be anyone and right now he didn't want to speak to anyone, let alone a reporter, a crank or someone from his office. His phone buzzed again. Hell, it could be important, he reconsidered. And if it's not, he'd just hang up.

"Durkin," he answered plainly as if nothing out of the ordinary had taken place over the past 24 hours.

"State's attorney Durkin, it's Paula Mucci."

Durkin shot a look to DeMartin like a strong headache was coming on, as he shuddered at the thought of the fiery defense attorney's temper.

"What can I do for you?"

"I've been trying to reach Angelo DeMartin but he's not picking up his cell phone."

"He's right here. I'll hand him the phone." He turned to DeMartin. "It's Attorney Mucci."

DeMartin's eyes widened and he signaled for Durkin to cover the speaker. "I forgot to tell you," he whispered. "I knew Rome would be in trouble so I used one of my calls to arrange for Paula to represent him."

Durkin shook his head as if his headache was worsening and handed the phone to DeMartin.

"Hi Paula," DeMartin said in the friendliest voice he could muster. He listened for a few seconds and shot a weary glance at Durkin. Durkin was sure Paula Mucci was ranting about him.

"Okay, thanks. I'll be at Francis's cottage in a few minutes. Come on over after you speak with Sam. Give him my best."

DeMartin smiled meekly as Mucci told him that he and Durkin weren't on the same team in this matter. He ignored her. "Call me when you know about Sam's condition."

DeMartin placed Durkin's cell phone on the console and chuckled. "My mild-mannered attorney is never boring."

"Does she know I acted as your attorney this morning?"

"Nope," DeMartin replied. He winced at the thought of Mucci's reaction once she learned of it.

The men chuckled as if they just dodged a bullet as they headed off the bridge and towards the Thousand Island Park.

"She's on her way to meet Rome at the River hospital in Alexandria Bay. She'll meet us at your cottage afterwards."

Durkin nodded. "When she comes, she can resume her duties as your defense counsel."

"With everything swirling about you, you may want to retain her also," DeMartin said.

As much as Durkin wanted DeMartin to be wrong, he had to admit to himself that DeMartin was probably right. He knew only a fool acts as his own attorney. But he also knew a state's attorney who wanted to remain one would be a fool to retain a defense attorney.

"We'll see," Durkin said vaguely as he weighed which course to take.

CHAPTER THIRTY THREE

River Hospital
Alexandria Bay, NY

For the first time in 9 hours, Sam Rome was alone. He rested his head on the crisp hospital pillow case and closed his eyes.

Rome wasn't tired. He shut his eyes because he detected a change in the tenor of the whispering outside his door. His cagey cop's ears recognized the sound of other cops' voices speaking with the doctors. He could recognize their low, serious voices anywhere. He was also sure the cops outside his room weren't coming to wish him a speedy recovery.

Rome peeked through his eyelashes. The room was small and sterile but he had a stunning view of the St. Lawrence River. The River Hospital was built on prime real estate and Rome figured he had the best view from any hospital in the world.

He quickly shut his eyes as his ears detected a door knob turning and three sets of feet walking gently on the linoleum floor. The cops mumbled to one another and one of the men sniffled loudly and cleared his throat. The sounds were the sounds a person makes at a counter when they think the cashier is in a nearby room. It could be scuffing feet or gently placing a set of keys on the counter. Gentle, unobtrusive sounds, designed to announce their presence.

But Rome was in no mood to assist the cops. Rome played possum, lying with his eyes shut, trying to regulate his breathing to mimic a man deep in sleep as he fought off the urge to laugh.

One of the cops produced a loud, artificial cough laced with impatience. Rome didn't move. Instead, he found humor in feigning sleep.

"Sam Rome?" a forceful, no-nonsense voice rang out.

Rome stirred, imagining himself emerging from a deep sleep. "Huh?" he uttered sounding half-drunk. With his eyes still closed, he filled his lungs to the max. He held the breath for a long count and then fluttered his eyelids as he exhaled. He took three seconds to focus his eyes on the men standing by his bedside.

Rome rubbed his eyes as he gazed at the men. All of them sported short hair and looked like straight-laced types. Rules guys, Rome thought derisively. He lived to break the rules.

"Yeah?" Rome said throatily as if he had no idea why the men stood in his room.

"I'm Lieutenant Roberts with the New York State Troopers," one of the rules guys said, flashing a badge. He then motioned to a square-jawed rules guy to his right. "This is Lieutenant Williams." Then he swiveled to his left. "This is Sergeant Dicks."

Rome kept the back of his head on his pillow and nodded passively, as if he hadn't yet concluded if the troopers were friend or foe. But he had. He knew he was amongst foes.

"We'd like to ask you a few questions," Roberts continued, trying to guess the level of cooperation he would get from Rome. His instincts told him not to get his hopes up.

Rome leaned up and wore an impish grin, despite trying to look like he was still trying to break from sleep's clutches. "Given the gravity of what transpired on the Thousand Islands Bridge, I think it's prudent to wait until my attorney arrives before I submit to questioning."

The troopers faces simultaneously twisted as if they suddenly detected a repulsive odor.

Given the gravity?

Of what transpired?

Prudent?

Submit to questioning?

The asshole is fucking with us, they all thought. The troopers stared at Rome as if they were itching to smack him around.

Lieutenant Roberts smacked his lips together as he composed his response. After a slight delay, he asked, "You're a Boston cop, right?"

Rome was sure the troopers were fully versed in his background. He was equally sure none of them were impressed by it. "Yep. Went to Fenway High School. Associate of Science degree in Criminal Justice from Bunker Hill Community College."

"Impressive," Roberts deadpanned.

"Any of you boys Sox fans?"

291

Roberts glared at Rome. What a dick. "We are hoping that since you're a cop and all, you'd be willing to help out with our investigation."

Rome's thoughts flashed back to the Thousand Islands Bridge. He was in excruciating pain, dangling from a carabiner that connected his belt to a steel wire. PJ leaned over the edge of the railing. "Give me the tape," PJ called out. Rome used the last of his energy reserves to fish the small recorder from his back pocket. He remembered telling himself that he'd have only one chance to toss it to PJ. If anything, throw it too far, he told himself.

He tossed it up and PJ snatched it from the air. As PJ stuffed the recorder in his pants, he yelled for Rome to throw him his bullet proof vest. There was no chance he'd be able to rip the velcro patches apart and toss the heavy vest up to Rome. None.

That's when Rome saw a parade of headlights racing over the bridge. Then PJ was gone. A few seconds later, the bridge was swarming with troopers and deputy sheriffs.

Rome's mental reel ended. "You can definitely count on my cooperation," he replied in a manufactured sleepy voice.

A slight flicker of relief rippled over Roberts' face.

Rome then produced a pained expression. "But we're are going to have to wait for my attorney to arrive."

Rome pressed his wrists together as if gesturing that his hands were tied.

Roberts ignored him. "How many men were on the bridge last night?"

Rome twisted his face, hoping to convey the message that it pained him not to be able to speak with the troopers.

"Can you at least tell us who shot you?"

Rome sighed loudly as if saying the hiss of air would be his only response.

"What were you doing hanging off the side of the bridge with a bullet in your leg?"

Rome shook his head and pressed his lips together.

"You're sure acting like you have something to hide," Sergeant Dicks interjected with the hope he'd get a rise out of Rome.

His hopes were realized. "I heard a rumor that the troopers were covering up a murder on Wellesley Island. Any truth to that?"

Dicks' face reddened. He stiffened and looked like a kid on a playground preparing for a fist fight.

Lieutenant Roberts intervened. "We're here to investigate what happened on the bridge."

"Well, while you're at it you may want to look into who killed Irene Izak and who covered up for the murderer."

"Thanks for the suggestions," Dicks snapped.

Rome straightened and look energized. He was in his element; jousting with other cops. "Well, since you're open to suggestions, I suggest you investigate why no trooper zeroed in on Hennigan even though every piece of evidence pointed directly at him."

"That's rich coming from you," Williams interjected. He was the only trooper who hadn't spoken and he sounded as if he reached the limit of his patience. "You're a third rate, busted-down cop and you have the balls to offer suggestions to us? How many times have you been cashiered out of an agency?"

Rome sat up and pointed his finger aggressively at Williams. "Even sharp bloodhounds like you boys should've smelled something rotten on Wellesley Island."

"Oh, my nose works just fine," Lieutenant Roberts said, trying unsuccessfully to remain calm. "And right now I smell manure. You know, manure with a strong ammonia and hydrogen-sulfide odor."

Roberts pointed to Williams. "John here grew up on a farm. You recognize the smell of shit, don't you?"

Williams nodded. "Sure do."

"What's the worst smelling shit?" Roberts asked Williams, sounding as if they had rehearsed a monologue.

"Chicken and turkey shit are bad," Williams replied. Williams panned the room as if he was picturing the animals on his boyhood farm. "Cow shit can also be real bad. The smell can make you choke. But the worst—eye watering bad shit— comes from hogs."

"Is it as bad as what you smell in this room?" Williams asked.

"No, I'd say this smells even worse than hog shit."

Rome clapped three times. "Bravo. Very entertaining. You should take that act on the road. You'd give everybody another reason to laugh at the New York State troopers."

Roberts faced flashed with anger. "How many men were on the bridge?"

"For the record, this is the second time I advised you that I will speak to you only in the presence of my attorney."

The troopers and Rome engaged in a stare down. "And, given your agency's cover-up, I'm only going to speak with your Internal Affairs unit when I do speak."

The troopers shuffled awkwardly. "We're with Internal Affairs," Roberts said crisply.

"Funny how you forgot to mention that when you introduced yourself, eh?"

The sound of the hospital door swinging open drew everyone's attention as a woman in a blue pants suit burst in with a gust of energy. She looked like a walking coat hanger holding her jacket and juggling her purse and leather briefcase.

"This interview is over," the woman announced, sounding badly out of breath. The woman was Paula Mucci, the fire-breathing defense attorney from Bridgeport, Connecticut.

The troopers held their ground, unimpressed with Mucci.

Mucci set her bags down on an empty chair. "Out! I'm going to confer with my client."

Rome's eyes twinkled. Angelo DeMartin told him about Mucci's legal bouts with the FBI. She was far younger than he expected but DeMartin assured him she had brass balls and could go toe-to-toe with any prosecutor.

"Who are you?" Roberts asked plainly.

"Well, as we all know, I don't have to identify myself," Mucci said, establishing her authority over the room. "It's enough for you to know that I'm a licensed attorney who represents this man," she said, pointing to Rome.

For a second, Roberts looked unsure of to respond to the woman he was quickly finding to be insufferable.

"You're his attorney but you're not going to identify yourself?"

Mucci suppressed her grin. She didn't want to go on record that she refused to identify herself to law enforcement. "Paula Mucci. Attorney Paula Mucci."

Roberts exchanged looks with the other two troopers. This is bullshit. Total bullshit. He then pulled out his business card and handed it to Mucci. "I expect a call from you shortly."

As Mucci took his card he extended his palm outwards to her. Give me your business card. Mucci dug a business card from her purse and slapped it in his waiting palm. Roberts' eyes darted to his business card and then back to her like he was instructing her to call him soon.

"I'm not making any promises."

Roberts pressed her business card between his thumb and forefinger and then brushed his palm with it. He was about to say something but pulled his words back into his mouth. He nodded and exited with the other troopers behind him.

CHAPTER THIRTY FOUR

Madeline Marks and Angelo DeMartin sat in awkward silence, staring off into the river. When they did speak it was small talk. A comment about the weather, a boat or the beauty of the river. DeMartin couldn't take a chance and say anything about what took place on the bridge and Marks was smart enough not to ask about why he spent the night at the state police barracks. Neither mentioned PJ, Rome, Clifford Putnam, Father O'Brien nor uttered a word about Trooper David Hennigan.

"Hello!" a woman's voice yelled out. DeMartin and Marks turned to the direction of the voice and saw Paula Mucci marching towards them. The woman looked incredibly out of place in her business suit and high heels as she traipsed down to the dock slinging her soft leather briefcase over her shoulder.

As Mucci neared, DeMartin pushed himself out of his chair and wobbled towards her, hobbling along in his moon boot. Gathering his balance, he assumed the introductory duties. "Attorney Paula Mucci, this is Professor Madeleine Marks."

The professional women assessed one another with cordial smiles and, in the blink of an eye, concluded there'd be little chance of becoming friends. Mucci eyed Marks and guessed the beautiful professor was more than just a friend of Angelo DeMartin's.

"First time in the Thousand Islands?" Madeleine asked as everyone found a seat and Mucci placed her briefcase on the dock.

"Yes. I've heard of the Thousand Islands but I have to admit I never knew where they were." Mucci's eyes scanned the river and over to Pullman, Maple and Grenell islands. "It's a beautiful area."

"How's Sam?" DeMartin asked with a hint of impatience.

Mucci's head gently bobbed as her defense attorney's instincts kicked in; she had trained herself to share as little information as possible in the early stages of an investigation.

"He'll be fine." Her tone signaled she wasn't going to share more; especially in Marks's presence.

"Attorney Mucci!" Durkin rang out in a loud, artificially cheery voice as he descended the stairs, carrying a tray of appetizers and trying his best to minimize his limp.

"Welcome," Durkin said as he neared the table. He set the tray down and noticed that Paula Mucci had lost the baby weight that came with the birth of her baby boy 6 months ago. But he wasn't going to touch the topic with a barge pole, acutely aware that an innocuous compliment could be twisted and come back to haunt him.

"Can I get you something to drink?" Durkin asked with a hospitable ring.

"No, I'm all good," Paula replied in a tone that left the impression she felt accepting a drink from the state's attorney would cross a relationship line that she didn't want to cross.

Mucci turned to Marks. "Would you mind if I steal Angelo for a moment?"

"No, of course not," Marks replied with a smile. She waved to DeMartin softly as he and Mucci headed off towards the cottage.

Five minutes later, Durkin's cell phone rang. He answered, nodded and killed the call. "Sorry, I have to abandon you," he said to Marks. "I've been summoned," he said, flicking his head towards the cottage.

Durkin rolled his eyes and stood with the look of a man preparing himself for an unpleasant encounter. He sighed as he shuffled off, grimacing from the pain shooting from his rib cage.

When he entered the cottage, he found Mucci and DeMartin sitting at the kitchen counter. Durkin walked into the kitchen and stood across the counter. He nodded slightly, signaling Mucci had the floor.

Mucci's face contorted as she wrestled to mentally assemble her question without smothering her words with emotion. She exhaled strongly. "Can you kindly explain how you came to represent my client?"

Durkin's eyes tightened. Here we go. Durkin took a deep breath. "Your client retained me for a particular matter," he said as calmly as possible. "He has that right."

Mucci stared at Durkin. That's all he was going to say? Durkin stared back sternly. Yep, That's all.

Mucci made small chopping motions with her hands. "I've never heard of a state's attorney taking on personal clients."

Durkin's lips moved but he pulled back his words. It wasn't any of her business but there wasn't any need for a knock-down, drag-out fight. "I can take clients while I'm on my sabbatical."

Mucci pressed her palm to her face as if applying an ice-pack to a bruise. "Nothing is making sense."

Durkin's blank stare offered little help.

"As I understand it," Mucci began attempting to sound uncharacteristically meek, "you are a suspect in a murder investigation."

"You understand wrong," Durkin snapped with an indignant flash. He immediately regretted the heat in his voice. "Listen, as you can imagine I'm a bit sensitive about the issue. A trooper confessed to killing the woman. The confession was caught on a tape. My guess is that there will be a public announcement very shortly."

Mucci exchanged a puzzled look with DeMartin as if she was considering whether or not to share an important secret with Durkin. Her eyelids fluttered and then she pressed her eyelids closed for a second before opening them and fixing her eyes on Durkin.

"I just came from seeing Sam Rome. When I left the River Hospital, one of the troopers was waiting for me in the parking lot. He said their divers haven't found Hennigan's body. He was cute and wondered why only Rome and Angelo claimed to have seen him jump. I got the impression they think DeMartin and Rome' story is pure bullshit."

Durkin shrugged. Where should he start? "Did Rome say anything about the taped confession?"

Mucci squirmed. What her client told her was privileged and she wasn't sharing what transpired between her and Rome.

"I took on Sam for a client as well," Durkin said slightly above a whisper.

"You've got to be shitting me," Mucci growled. "You set up your own private defense practice up in the Thousand Islands?"

Durkin wasn't going to get in to it with Mucci. "Hennigan's car was in the tourism parking lot. They know Rome didn't shoot himself and they know that Hennigan killed the priest. Everything was coming crashing down on Hennigan. It's not surprising he took his own life."

"Maybe, but that doesn't mean that you're cleared as a suspect."

Durkin made a steeple with his fingers and rested his lips atop them as he mulled over Mucci's comment. His thoughts shot back to his conversation with Welsh. Welsh never acknowledged the tape. He just stood, stone-faced and listened to Durkin. Hell, maybe he read Welsh wrong. He then thought about Rasmutin shouting that the tape didn't clear him.

"Do you know something, I don't?"

"No. I'm just reading the tea leaves. They're very confusing to say the least."

Mucci's right, Durkin thought. Everything was confusing but he was sure the tape would clear him. Durkin shook his head. "Believe me. The tape clears me," he said as he considered the evidentiary arguments for admitting an illegally taped confession from a dead man to a dead priest, into a court of law.

"The tape will surface and it will clear me. I'm sure of it," Durkin said, sounding as if he was trying to convince himself. He paused and then said, "Right now, I think we need to get our strategies aligned."

"Strategies? My strategy is to not let my clients speak with these cowboys. They'd love to rope them into a conspiracy to obstruct their murder investigation or some other bullshit charge."

"They don't have anything on Angelo or Sam."

"No? What's this little issue of 40 thousand dollars?"

Durkin shot a stern look at DeMartin. Why the hell did he tell her that?

"And by the way," Mucci added quickly, "how far did you think your citizen-arrest theory would go in a courtroom?"

"I'd be happy to help you with it," Durkin said, allowing a hint of snarkiness to leak into his voice. "But right now, we're all better off if we coordinate our strategies."

Mucci stood and looked as if she was about to dispense bad news. "State's Attorney Durkin, your interests are not aligned with my clients' interests. You know better than anyone that if the troopers want to nail you, they'll squeeze Angelo and Rome to get to you."

DeMartin interjected. "So we'd be fools to let the troopers divide us."

"That may sound honorable to you but a young woman has been murdered. A priest has been murdered. I hear that a tollbooth collector was executed gangland style. The trooper who everyone thinks was behind all the killings is missing and presumed dead."

Mucci paused to give the men a chance to point out any factual errors. Hearing none, she pressed on. "The troopers are not going to just let everyone drive back to Connecticut and forget about what went on at the bridge. Even if they know Hennigan killed the young woman, they're going to be under intense pressure to charge someone with a serious crime."

Durkin stepped back and rubbed his chin as he assessed the legal landscape.

"My advice to my client," Mucci said, shooting a quick look at DeMartin, "and to you," she said, turning back to Durkin, "is to say nothing at this point. Nothing."

"I told Welsh that we'd return to the barracks today."

"You said what?" Mucci's face became stuck in a pose of extreme shock. "Angelo is not returning to the barracks."

Durkin's face reddened. "Listen, counselor. They weren't going to let Sergeant DeMartin go unless I gave my word we'd return voluntarily. They could have continued to hold him. You know that."

Mucci stood firm. "I'm not going to allow it."

The state's attorney and defense attorney stared icily at one another. Finally, Durkin said, "Fine. I'll call Welsh and tell him that you've taken over as Sergeant DeMartin's attorney. I'll tell him that we'd like to meet with him without your client. Will that work for you?"

Mucci considered Durkin's suggestion. She took a deep breath and nodded as she exhaled a stream of frustration. "You shouldn't be meeting with the troopers."

Durkin shook his head dismissively: the young defense attorney hadn't earned the legal stripes to dispense legal advice to him.

Mucci sighed. Have it your way but you're making a mistake. A colossal mistake, she thought as Durkin pulled his cell phone from his pocket and walked outside.

*****

"You gave me your word you'd return here today." Welsh's voice pulsed with stress and anger.

"I know," Francis Durkin replied. "Sergeant DeMartin has a new attorney and we're just asking if we could meet you without the clients."

Durkin held his cell phone away from his ear as if he expected Welsh to explode. Instead, Welsh's quiet anguish flowed through the phone. He didn't know what to say.

"The reason I'm calling you is so you're not blindsided. I wasn't going to just show up without Sergeant DeMartin."

"Listen, I did you a favor. If you weren't a prosecutor, I wouldn't have done it. I trusted you."

"I know. I appreciate the professional courtesy. When I got back to Wellesley Island, I met with his attorney and she is firm about not letting you speak with her client. I didn't know she was even representing him when I spoke with you. That's the truth." Welsh's labored breathing flowed through the phone.

Durkin filled the silence. "I met the reporter from the *Watertown Daily Register* when I left the barracks. He implied that he's going to run a story about Hennigan's confession."

"I can't comment on that."

"No, I imagine you can't. But you know there'll be a shitshow once the story hits."

"As I said, I can't comment on that."

"Fair enough. Do you still want to meet?"

"Yes. I still want to meet you," Welsh said, sounding as if he had a specific subject he wanted to discuss.

"And Sergeant DeMartin's attorney?"

"Nope. Just you. I'll call you within the hour." Without another word, Welsh abruptly ended the call.

CHAPTER THIRTY FIVE

New York State Police Crime Laboratory
Albany, New York

Stephanie Cotton and Danielle Keegan entered the lab covered, head to toe, in full disposable lab gear but their eyes, accented by the hair coverings and the masks, glistened with cold determination.

The two forensic scientists made a beeline to Dante Russo's workspace. When they reached it, Cotton stopped and glowered at Russo.

Russo's mouth hung open. He blinked nervously as if knew Cotton had discovered his darkest secrets. He coughed and uttered, "Assistant Director," like he was uttering "not guilty" to a judge.

Cotton's tight face spied Russo's computer screen that identified genetic markers in graphic form. She brushed past Russo and sat down behind the computer. Her intense eyes narrowed as she began scrolling through the DNA profiles. After reviewing the graphs for a minute, she set her eyes on Russo who blushed under the heat of her gaze.

"Francis Durkin was identified to you as a person of interest before you completed your initial tests, correct?"

Russo swallowed hard as if he feared being drawn into a trap. "I'm not sure."

"When did you first hear his name?"

"I have to check my notes."

Cotton pressed on as if she was unconcerned Russo was lying through his teeth. "Did you determine the likelihood that the suspect's DNA matched the DNA found at the crime scene?"

"I didn't determine it. The computer did."

Cotton tilted her head. Cute, she thought. "Yes, but its conclusion is based on the samples you analyzed, correct?"

Russo shot a pained look at Keegan as if he was asking her to throw him a lifeline. Keegan's eyes stared back coldly. She was going to happily sit back and watch him drown.

"And the computer determined, based on the DNA samples you analyzed, that the chance a random person's DNA matched the DNA found on the victim was one in a billion, right?"

Russo ran Cotton's question through his head several times before nodding. "I guess so," he said meekly as if he was terrified his words would incriminate him.

"And the DNA sample was in sufficient quantity and not degraded in any fashion?"

"I believe so."

With her eyes riveted on the computer screen, Cotton pointed to a graph. "Then where's the victim's DNA?"

"Huh?" Russo replied, leaning closer to the screen.

Cotton pushed her chair back from the screen. "This is the DNA profile found on the person of interest's shirt. Where's the victim's DNA?"

Russo's eyes widened in surprise. "I don't know. How would I know that?"

Cotton used the computer mouse to flip through each of the DNA profiles. "There's not a trace of the victim's DNA on Francis Durkin's shirt, is there?"

Cotton itched the bridge of her nose. "The woman was brutally murdered with a blunt instrument. If the suspect bashed the woman's head in, wouldn't there be a trace of her DNA on his shirt?"

Russo's shoulders tightened. "How would I know?" he repeated louder. "I just conduct the lab tests, I'm not an investigator. You know that."

"You don't think it's odd? A bell didn't go off in your head that something was wrong?"

"He could've changed his shirt," Russo said as he searched for plausible explanations. "The troopers may have seized the wrong shirt. Who knows? That's not my job."

Cotton pursed her lips and nodded as her expression coarsened. "The troopers' report noted the suspect wore a green polo shirt with a tear around the buttons at the crime scene." Her eyes danced to Keegan and then to Russo. "The DNA sample was taken from a green polo with tears around the buttons, right?"

"We just tested the shirt sent to us," Russo exclaimed, sounding like a defense attorney refusing to admit or deny anything.

"Who opened the evidence bag containing the green polo?"

"We did."

Cotton's voice and body stiffened. "There's a notation that you opened the bag. There's no *we*."

Russo wobbled as he was having difficulty breathing.

Cotton turned to Keegan. "Were you in the room when the evidence bag containing Francis Durkin's shirt was opened?"

Keegan shook her head emphatically. "No."

Russo's face drained of color. "Everything is noted in the report. I have nothing to hide."

Cotton squeezed her eyes shut as if Russo was insulting her intelligence. "Why, then, did you violate protocol and open the evidence bag alone?" Cotton asked as she opened her eyes.

"To confirm the texture."

Cotton's nose twitched as if she detected a strong scent of bullshit. "I see. Did you note the texture on your notes?"

Russo reddened. "I don't know. I may have. What are you getting at?"

Cotton chose her words with precision. "I'm perplexed why the victim's DNA is not on the suspect's shirt. You found his DNA on the victim in multiple areas but none of her DNA was found on his clothes. No blood. No saliva. Not a single skin cell from the victim." Cotton paused. "Does that make any sense to you?"

Russo pointed his finger at Cotton. "You keep saying the same thing. I don't know what you're implying but I don't like it."

"Didn't it seem odd that the rocks you tested didn't have any of the person of interest's DNA on them if he supposedly used them to bash her head?"

"I just analyzed the samples that were delivered to me. This conversation is making me uncomfortable."

Cotton stood and peered down at Russo. She didn't give a shit about Russo's discomfort. "Did you release the draft results?"

"Are you asking me?"

"Yes, of course, I'm asking you," Cotton snapped. "I've got my eyes glued on you. Who the hell else would I be asking? Now, answer the question!"

"What do you mean by 'release'?"

"Did you discuss the test results with anyone not employed by the lab?" Cotton's tone had the ring of a cold and steely executioner.

Russo shivered like a cornered rat. "I was asked about our preliminary results. So I shared the draft analysis. I told them it was preliminary and couldn't be relied upon."

"Who did you share it with?"

"Our clients! That's who. I don't like what you are insinuating."

Cotton had enough. She motioned to the door. "Leave everything as it is. Some people want to speak with you."

Russo's eyes pleaded for an explanation.

"I suggest you don't bullshit them like you just did to me."

Russo hesitated and then sprang to his feet. "Director Chilletti is going to hear about this."

"Oh, yes, she will."

Russo walked briskly to the door and when he swung it open, he found two uniformed troopers and a man in a black suit blocking his exit. They had the cold, muscular air of hit men.

"Mr. Russo, I'm Detective Shapiro with the Internal Affairs division," the man in the black suit said.

"I didn't do anything wrong," Russo sputtered.

Shapiro nodded. That's good. "Then you don't have anything to worry about." He pointed to a small conference room across the hallway. "Let's talk in there."

Russo pulled off his hair covering and mask and reluctantly allowed himself to be ushered into the conference room. As he fell into a metal chair, he didn't notice the room was fitted with surveillance cameras in the corners. Shapiro sat down across from him and the uniformed troopers remained standing like vigilant prison guards.

"Assistant Director Cotton was asking me crazy questions," Russo began, sounding aggrieved.

"Like what?"

"She's implying that I manufactured DNA results."

"Did you?"

Russo's eyes darted around the room as if he was searching for a plausible answer. "It's not a crime to contaminate a sample. It happens all the time. I can guarantee Cotton and Keegan have done it!"

Russo trembled. "If it was a crime to contaminate a sample, everybody in this building would be locked up."

"No, you're absolutely correct," Shapiro said matter of factly. "But don't you think it's a crime to intentionally rig a DNA analysis?"

Russo sank into his seat. "Do I need a lawyer?" Russo began sweating as if he was suddenly coming down with a fever.

"That depends."

Shapiro pulled an index card from his shirt pocket."We have evidence you took the DNA of a suspect and placed it on the victim's clothing. Isn't that like pasting a fingerprint from an innocent man on a murder weapon?"

Beads of sweat appeared on Russo's forehead. He wore the face of a caged man, knowing his only exit was blocked. There was no escaping Shapiro.

Shapiro placed a small laptop on the conference table. He opened it up and tapped the keyboard. He then spun it around so Russo could see it. A frame of a video clip was frozen on the screen.

"You recognize where this was taken?"

Russo stared at the screen. It was an overhead surveillance shot of the laboratory they had just left. He recognized the top of his head in his lab coat and goggles. Russo nodded and breathed heavily as if bracing himself for a blow.

"The time stamp was 3:37 a.m. two days ago," Shapiro said before tapping a key to start the video. The camera angle was directly above him. Directly over his shoulder and over his work station.

Russo stiffened. There was no surveillance camera directly above his work station. A chill ran through him as he realized Cotton had installed a hidden surveillance camera in the lab.

"Everything okay?" Shapiro asked.

Russo nodded slowly as he watched himself use a small knife to scrape a fleck of blood off the shirt. He then watched as he meticulously set the fleck in a miniature plastic vial.

Shapiro tapped a few keys and the video sped up. He stopped the video precisely on the frame he wanted as if he had watched the clip hundreds of times before. "You took a vial and then you spread its contents on another evidentiary item. Didn't you?"

Russo's eyes popped. He didn't know what to say. He pointed to the video. "That's misleading!"

Shapiro shook his head and squeezed his lips together. "Sorry brother, it's not. Not even close. We've got you dead to rights."

Russo looked stricken, unable to put words together.

"In full disclosure," Shapiro continued, waving the index card in front of Russo with the confident air of a cop who's built an open and shut case. "I should tell you for the past few days we've investigated you. We know that in at least 16 cases you overstated the strength of your results, misreported the frequency of genetic matches, reported inconclusive tests as conclusive, failed to report conflicting results and reported scientifically impossible results."

Russo's body sagged as if Shapiro's words drained him of all his strength.

"But I think you were just doing this to help others out," Shapiro added, sounding like an understanding friend.

Russo sat, blankly staring ahead as if he lost his sense of hearing.

"In my opinion, you were trying to be a team player. And there's nothing wrong with being a team player. In fact, most of the time being a team player is a damn positive thing."

Shapiro leaned closer to Russo and pulled a copy of the DNA analysis conducted on Irene Izak's clothes."Who were you trying to help by rigging these results?"

Russo's eyes retreated into his head.

Shapiro motioned to the troopers. "Grab him a bottle of water." One of the troopers left the room and returned with a plastic bottle of water. Shapiro unscrewed the cap and placed it down besides Russo. "Have some water and let's talk."

Russo sipped the water like a bird, a few drops at a time. His eyes were glassy, like he was watching his life slip away. The plastic water bottle crinkled loudly as he set it down on the table. "I am a team player" Russo said breathlessly.

Then he talked for over an hour and every word was captured on video.

CHAPTER THIRTY SIX

A dust cloud billowed below the belly of the Camry as it wound its way through the rows of aluminum storage units surrounded by rusting trailers and cracked fiberglass boats marooned on a gravel lot.

The Camry drove to the back of the deserted storage lot and parked. The driver's door creaked open and Francis Durkin stepped out. He surveyed the junk strewn about and questioned if he was at the right spot.

Durkin stood in silence until the sound of boots crunching dirt and gravel drew his attention. He turned and saw Colonel Robert Welsh in street clothes approaching him. The two men walked towards one another and stopped three feet apart, next to a rusted backhoe.

Welsh got right to the point. "I need to speak with Sam Rome, Angelo DeMartin and PJ McLevy."

Durkin sighed and wore an apologetic look. "I don't represent them anymore and I don't think an attorney worth her salt would agree to it."

Welsh kicked the tip of his boot into the gravel. "Yeah, I figured as much but I thought it was worth asking anyway." He then gently kicked a pile of loose gravel. "Then I need some information from you."

"I wasn't involved in anything that took place on the bridge."

Welsh bore his eyes into Durkin. He didn't have time for games. "A day ago you were about to be arrested for the murder of Irene Izak."

"And you now know that was all bullshit concocted by a corrupt trooper."

"Maybe. But I know if a prosecutor was ever indicted for murder his career would be over."

Durkin shrugged. "You're right. So?"

"So, wouldn't a prosecutor on the verge of being indicted do just about anything to avoid it?"

Durkin's nostrils flared. Welsh was right. His career, which was his entire life's purpose, would've been blown to bits by an indictment. He would've been put on leave and Roslyn Jones would've been pressured to terminate him. He wouldn't be able to teach at the law school. He would've been confined to his house for at least a year and when he was finally cleared

307

everyone would treat him as if he was radioactive. He'd be stained for life. And yes, Durkin would've done just about anything to avoid that.

"And off the record," Welsh added, "while you might not have been on the bridge, we both know you know what went down there."

Durkin's eyes and face would neither confirm or deny. "I wasn't there."

Welsh seemed to take interest in a rusted ATV propped up on cement blocks. He then turned back abruptly to Durkin. "I thought I've seen everything. But I was wrong." He paused for effect like a skilled storyteller. "Last night, the surveillance cameras on the bridge, below the bridge and at the entrance to the Welcome Center were all down. Terrible luck for us, right?"

Durkin nodded. Sometimes cops are shit-out-of-luck.

"But we had one stroke of luck. A camera on top of the Welcome Center was working. Seems it was set up temporarily and wasn't yet hooked into the Bridge Authority's security system. The odd thing is that when we enhance the video we see a moving bag of pipes or something. "

"A bag of pipes?"

"Yeah, green pipes. The same color as the bridge."

Durkin shook his head, trying to remain expressionless.

"We also found an underwater sea-scooter stashed below the bridge. We traced the sale back to a diving shop in Clayton. Thankfully that shop's surveillance camera was working." Welsh pinched his nose. "The customer was decked out like ZZ Top. Sunglasses. Long beard. Paid in cash and didn't touch anything so we can't even pull finger prints."

Again, Durkin shrugged. I don't know what to tell you. You're right. It sounds odd to his ear too.

Welsh studied Durkin's reaction. His face revealed nothing.

"Everything has the hallmarks of professionals. I'd think this was a CIA operation if I didn't know better." Welsh paused for a long beat. "But I know better. I know there is a man capable of staging a professional operation like that. That man was once a Marine sniper and spent a career as a Bridgeport cop."

A slight flicker of emotion surfaced on Durkin's face before he regained command of his emotions. "What are you getting at?"

"I don't have time to play coy so I'm going to get right to the point. Sam Rome and PJ McLevy were seen speaking to Father O'Brien two days before the priest had his head blown off."

Welsh grimaced as he pulled up a mental vision of the crime photos. Thick bits of Fr. Patrick O'Brien's brain clung to the confessional wall against a backdrop of splattered blood.

"Then we learned that Rome had been speaking to Clifford Putnam, whose bullet-ridden body was found off I-81. There's a connection here, no?"

"McLevy and Rome were trying to find the woman's killer."

"Yeah, but why would they want to speak to the priest?" Welsh pressed his lips together and then answered his own question. "My hunch is that they knew about the taped confession."

"I can't help you with that."

"Can you help me with who would be skilled enough to shoot Hennigan in both of his hands?"

"Huh?"

"About five hours ago, we found Hennigan's body. It was wedged in the side of a freighter. No one noticed it until it got a hundred miles down river. Some kid on a boat saw a human leg dangling from the side of a crane."

Durkin shook his head as he pictured the gruesome vision of Hennigan's body spiked on a ship's crane.

"There are bullet wounds in both of Hennigan's hands." Welsh paused as if he was letting his words settle in before springing a surprise. "Our divers found Hennigan's gun on the bottom of the river."

Durkin tried to conceal his surprise but his eyes widened. "The divers found a gun a 125 feet below the river's surface?"

"The gun had been fired three times but Rome has only one bullet wound in his leg."

Welsh paced his delivery with small breaths. "Hennigan always tested as a top marksman. If he wanted, he could've shot Rome through his heart."

Durkin pressed his lips together and shrugged. I don't know what to tell you.

"Who shot Hennigan?"

"I can't help you with that."

"Can you help me with why Sam Rome was wearing a bullet proof vest?"

Durkin shook his head. Nope. "You need to ask him."

"Unfortunately, Rome is staying tight lipped."

"You can't blame him, can you?"

"I guess not, but the investigation won't ever be closed if we can't determine how those bullet holes got into Hennigan's hands." Welsh sniffled as if he detected an objectionable odor. "We tested Sergeant DeMartin and

Rome's hands for gunpowder residue. If either of them discharged a gun, there'd be a trace of gunpowder on them. Both were negative."

Silence. Durkin stared blankly back at Welsh. Unraveling that mystery was Welsh's problem. "Did you find gun powder residue on Hennigan's hands?"

"Of course."

"And we know that Hennigan shot Rome, right?"

Welsh nodded.

"We also know that Hennigan was a religious nut."

Welsh nodded again. So far, he was in full agreement with Durkin.

"Maybe as part of a last-right, sort of penance, he shot himself in both hands as if re-enacting the scene of Jesus on the cross. You know, when they drove spikes through Jesus's hands."

Welsh's eyes scrunched up with displeasure. "That's exactly what one of our detectives came up with too. He says there's a group of Filipino Catholics who prove their devotion to God by being nailed to a cross. His theory was that if someone would let a person drive a spike through his hands, surely someone would be crazy enough to shoot themselves in their hands."

Both men grimaced at the thought of having spikes driven through their palms.

"But once you shoot yourself in one hand, is it possible to use the injured hand to shoot yourself in the other hand?"

Durkin shrugged. "I'm no gun expert." He then positioned an imaginary gun against his chest and demonstrated how he could pull a trigger with a wounded hand.

Welsh snorted. "That's exactly what the detective did when I asked him the question."

"Great minds think alike."

Welsh drew a long breath. He didn't buy it.

"Why are you telling me all this?"

Welsh blew out a breath of frustration. "I need to sort things out and I don't have much time."

Welsh paused and wore an expression that something important suddenly occurred to him. "If Sam Rome and Angelo DeMartin were on the bridge, there'd be a pretty good chance PJ McLevy was there too, no?"

"McLevy's pretty old, no?" Durkin countered, sounding like a skilled courtroom attorney planting a seed of doubt in a jury.

"Yeah, he is. About 70 or something."

"That'd be my guess."

"Did you know that he was a decorated Marine sniper?"

"Doesn't ring a bell."

"Did you know Rasmutin got a judge to issue a warrant allowing him to tap your cell phone?"

Durkin felt a bolt of fear rip through him. He was sure Welsh could see his chest heave and sweat form on his forehead. He commanded his exterior to remain calm as his insides churned with intense emotion as he mentally recounted every call he made the last week. He called Kyle Johnston to pick him up at the Boldt Castle Yacht House. He spoke to Cassie and Roslyn Jones. It might prove embarrassing to hear his words played in court but he was sure nothing he said would be incriminating. He also spoke with Rome but Rome never said anything more than he wanted to meet with him. Then he stiffened. He spoke to Alex Phillips. If it came out that Phillips tipped him off about the Connecticut troopers trying to seize his garbage, Phillips career would take a mortal hit.

"There is one curious thing, though," Welsh pressed on. "A call was made from a burner phone from the river last night."

Durkin nodded lightly. Tell me more. Welsh obliged. "The call was made to Cassie Johnston's cell phone. You know anything about that?"

Stress pulsed through Durkin's veins, setting off a cascade of uncontrollable bodily reactions. His heart raced. His hands turned clammy. Dry mouth set in. Before Durkin had a chance to reply, Welsh continued, "Coincidentally, we traced the location of Ms. Johnston's phone." Welsh paused for full dramatic effect. "It was at your cottage in the Thousand Island Park."

Welsh breathed loudly and pressed on. "Ms. Johnston then immediately made a call to Kyle Johnston who then was seen fishing not too far from the Thousand Islands Bridge. Hmm."

A long pause, laced with crackling tension, passed between the men. "Knowing what I know about PJ McLevy, Sam Rome and Sergeant DeMartin," Welsh added, "I'm positive that no amount of smart policing could pry information from them."

Durkin looked at Welsh. Why was he so sure?

"They're too damn experienced and smart. They know what to say and when to ask for a lawyer. The same goes for you." Welsh's tone sounded as if he held begrudging admiration for the cagey cops and wiley prosecutor.

"But do you know who I'm sure would crack under the stress of a professional interrogation?" Welsh paused as if trying to tease Durkin. "Kyle Johnston. Johnston was in the middle of that bird massacre on Little Galloo

Island. Those locals cracked like thin-shelled eggs once the feds said boo. And Cassie Johnston? I'm not sure how she's mixed up in this but she's a college professor and has no experience in the world of crime. She also might be inclined to speak with us."

Durkin's head swirled as if he just stepped off a merry-go-round. There was no way he could expose the woman he was falling in love with to intense interrogation. Even if he retained a defense lawyer for her, it was against her grain to refuse to talk to cops. No, their budding romance would shatter under the pressure of a police interrogation.

Welsh read Durkin's face. He recognized the tell-tale signs of anguish bubbling inside of a man with secrets he needed to remain secret. It was exactly how he wanted Durkin to feel.

"I know who murdered the girl. I know who murdered the priest. I also know who killed the tollbooth collector. What I don't know is who taped Hennigan's confession."

"Does it really matter?"

Welsh sucked in a mouthful of air. "Maybe in the scheme of things it doesn't. But it sure would help the investigation."

Welsh paused and nodded as if he was in conversation with himself. "I also don't think it's too far fetched to think that Kyle Johnston whisked PJ McLevy away from the river."

"Why are you telling me this?"

"Because you were seen on multiple occasions with Cassie Johnston. That's your business but there's a good chance she was with you when someone called her last night."

"Again, why are you telling me all this?"

"Because I want you to know I have you by your balls."

"Then why don't you just squeeze them?"

Welsh's eyes darted over the disintegrating boats and rotting golf carts littering the lot. He then slowly turned his attention back to Durkin. "Do you know why FBI agents from Connecticut are snooping around?"

Durkin instantly detected vulnerability. It was the same vulnerability he detected when a defense attorney approached him, seeking a plea bargain. Now, Welsh feared the consequences of having the FBI perform an investigative colonoscopy on the state police. And, most importantly, Welsh thought that Durkin could pull the FBI's stings.

"I'm not surprised that the FBI is interested in state police who cover up for murderers."

"Yeah but do you think it's just a coincidence that they're from Connecticut?" Welsh's lips scrunched leaving no doubt he didn't believe in coincidences. "They're a little far from home, no?"

"What's their names?"

"Special Agent in Charge Katherine Sharp and Agent Seth Brooks dropped by the Alexandria Bay barracks a couple of hours ago."

"Sharp and Brooks, eh?" Durkin said with a heavy dose of feigned familiarity.

"You know them?"

"Sure," Durkin replied. He dropped his eyes to the ground as if trying to mask his thoughts. He knew the Connecticut FBI Agents weren't in Alexandria Bay to look into the troopers' cover-up. He knew Sharp and Brooks were sniffing around to see if there was anything they could hang on Angelo DeMartin.

Durkin wore his best poker face. "I might be able to convince them to stay in Connecticut."

There was a long silence before Welsh nodded. "My only concern is that justice is served."

"Mine too."

Welsh carefully composed his next words. "As I said, we know Hennigan murdered Irene Izak. We are going to take a nasty hit once it becomes public that a trooper brutally murdered a young, defenseless woman while he was on patrol."

Welsh nodded somberly. "We also know Hennigan killed the priest and he killed the tollbooth collector. Justice won't be served but at least there will be closure."

Durkin mimicked Welsh's slight nod. "It's important to have closure."

"And don't get me wrong, I want to know what went down on the bridge but, as I said, in the scheme of things, it doesn't really matter."

Durkin's eyes widened. Welsh caught the eye movement; a glint of hope. It was the look of a man who suddenly believed there may be a resolution without a judge, without a courtroom, without the searing glare of the press. There was a chance his career wouldn't be racked by scandal.

"If the killer is dead, there's nothing more anyone can do," Welsh said.

Both of the men breathed heavily as if on the verge of an agreement. An agreement that could benefit both of them and allow the troopers to seal the case.

"What about Rasmutin?" Durkin asked.

"You speak to the FBI," Welsh said, before pointing to Durkin's bandaged face, "and if you let bygones be bygones, I'll handle Rasmutin."

Durkin patted his bandaids. "That works for me."

Welsh nodded confidently knowing that only hours ago Dante Russo had signed a confession that Rasmutin encouraged him to fabricate the DNA evidence against Francis Durkin.

"Let me just say that Commander Rasmutin may not be part of the law enforcement community for much longer. I can't say anything more at this time." Welsh inhaled and looked as if he was celebrating putting the final nail in Rasmutin's coffin.

Durkin relaxed. With Hennigan's death, there was nothing for the FBI to investigate; especially since Angelo DeMartin would be returning to Bridgeport, Connecticut soon. He'd heal up and forego suing the troopers and no one would investigate Kyle Johnston or Cassie. It had the ring of something that was too good to be true.

"So, this it?" Durkin asked. "We can all go home and get back on with our lives?"

"Pretty much."

"What about the lab report that put me at the scene of the murder?"

Welsh grinned. "There seems to have been some technical errors in the crime lab and the tests were rerun. My understanding is that your DNA was not found on the victim on the re-tests. You are officially not a suspect."

Durkin sagged with relief. He dodged a bullet.

"But there is one last thing," Welsh said.

"There always is."

"Forty thousand dollars."

"Huh?"

"The blackmail money. Hennigan's sister told us that Hennigan brought 40 thousand dollars to the bridge."

Welsh searched Durkin's eyes for a reaction. Durkin's eyes widened. He didn't detect deception.

"I know very little about this." That much was true. He only learned about the money a few hours ago. "You've got to believe me on this. Maybe he brought the money to the church before he blew the priest's brains out."

Welsh was unfazed. "Forty thousand dollars wasn't left in the church's collection box."

Durkin's face twitched as he worried about their agreement unraveling. "Could he have tossed the money over the bridge?"

Welsh shook his head. We all knew that didn't happen. "I want your word that no one will profit from this money."

Durkin quieted as he contemplated the solemnity of giving his word. He was old-school. If he gave his word he would have to make sure he honored it.

"If 40 thousand dollars are kicking around out there, no one will profit from it. You have my word."

Welsh relaxed. He knew Durkin's word was his bond. "Good. We're done." He extended his hand and the two men shook hands, made one last eye contact and headed towards their cars. Durkin took two steps and spun around with the sound of boots pivoting in dirt and gravel. "Hey, one last thing."

Welsh stopped and turned, standing 10 feet from Durkin. What is it?

"Why did Rasmutin do everything in his power to try to frame me?"

Welsh ran his tongue over his front teeth and then slid his tongue over his molars. His expression was hard for Durkin to read.

"You have to admit," Welsh said, "at the beginning you looked like a suspect."

A smile formed and then disappeared on Durkin's face as he envisioned himself pedaling a 50 year old bicycle down a deserted road at four in the morning. "I get that but when the dust settled, even a kid could see that Hennigan murdered the young woman."

"Yeah, I agree with that."

"Then why did Rasmutin keep pressing the case against me?"

Welsh blinked a few times and itched his nose as if Durkin's question triggered a nervous reaction. He had given the question a lot of thought.

"Well, for starters, he hated you. I don't know why but I know he did." Both men's thoughts raced to the scene of Rasmutin pummeling Durkin in the troopers' interrogation room.

"Yeah, I guess he did," Durkin said with a slight grin. "But he also knew Hennigan did it."

Welsh paused and itched his nose. "Rasmutin also knew if Hennigan was brought to justice it would be an indelible stain on his own record. The murder trial would be sensational and Rasmutin would never have a chance to sit behind the Superintendent's desk. And that is Rasmutin's life's ambition."

Durkin shook his head, thinking how close Rasmutin's blind ambition came to ending his career as a state's attorney.

"Oh, one more thing," Welsh added. "You'll soon be reading in the papers that the Jefferson County Coroner got it wrong. The bloody rocks found next to her body weren't used to murder her. A second medical examiner

315

discovered three identical lines pounded into her skull. The lines came from a man-made implement that was harder than bone, metal or ceramic." Welsh paused. "A trooper's flashlight has three metal ridges on the edge. The bastard killed the woman with his trooper's flashlight," Welsh said, shaking his head in disbelief.

"Let me guess," Durkin said, "no one can locate Hennigan's flashlight."

Welsh grinned. No comment. He then smiled like he was smiling at an old friend. "Take care of yourself."

Welsh and Durkin shared the pained look of men tasked with sweeping life's messy details under the rug. They exchanged waves and Francis Durkin walked to his car like a man who had the weight of the world lifted from his shoulders. He drove slowly to the road. Fifteen minutes later, Welsh pulled out of the storage depot, wearing the look of a cop who hadn't slept in weeks.

CHAPTER THIRTY SEVEN

Francis Durkin pulled into the cottage's dirt driveway, killed the engine and sat perfectly still, decompressing. His powerful legal mind dissected everything Welsh said. Did he misconstrue something or was his nightmare finally coming to an end?

In the quiet of his car, Durkin took a deep breath and thought of the legal charges he may have dodged. He could have been charged as an accessory for every crime committed on the bridge, too many to count.

As he stepped out of his car, Durkin's thoughts turned to Cassie. He hadn't seen her for a day and already missed her badly. He heard the crunch of the gravel under his shoes and then groans from the cottage windows.

Groans of pleasure.

He stopped and cocked his ear. The groans came from the second floor of his cottage. He opened the screen door and entered the kitchen as the sounds grew louder and more animated. Durkin heard Madeleine Marks's high-pitch groan rise and fall like a musical note just as Angelo DeMartin's powerful baritone followed. Her high pitched cry of ecstasy hung in the air as the brass bed's legs scraped along the wooden floor. The rocking reached a crescendo, followed by the grande finale; an explosion of springs, brass, wood, mattress and sheets moving all at the same time. The sexual music then ended with whimpers of euphoria.

Durkin tiptoed through the kitchen, sure that DeMartin and Marks thought they were alone in the cottage. He pictured them lying on their backs, spent and smiling wrapped in each other's arms. For an instant, Durkin's mind wandered, imagining Madeleine Marks naked. He pictured her perfectly proportioned body and silky skin; a sort of beautiful naked Barbie doll. He felt himself getting excited as his mind continued wandering.

The sounds of footsteps upstairs brought Durkin's fantasy to an abrupt end. He scampered around the kitchen and acted as if he was readying himself a cup of coffee. A few seconds later DeMartin hobbled into the kitchen dressed only in shorts and lumbering in his moon boot. He wore a distressed look. What was Durkin doing in the cottage?

Durkin tried to ignore DeMartin's sculptured physique. The guy was chiseled from granite, Durkin thought.

"How long have you been here?" DeMartin asked with a tone that suggested that Durkin was trespassing.

"Just a second."

"A second?"

"Maybe a minute."

A contagious grin sprung up on DeMartin's face. Durkin burst into a full smile. "Okay, maybe a couple of minutes."

DeMartin continued smiling and shrugged. "I hope we didn't embarrass you."

Durkin shrugged right back. "Embarrass me? Hell, you made me jealous," he joked.

The men quieted as the staircase creaked with Mark's light footsteps. The sound of slippers sliding across a wooden floor proceeded Marks entrance. Her face was aglow and she was draped in one of DeMartin's dress shirts. Her bare legs left the impression that was all she was wearing.

"Hi," Marks said without a trace of embarrassment.

"Hi," Durkin replied as he felt his face warming. "Uh," Durkin began as his mind searched for something to say as his cell phone's ring rescued him. He held up a finger and began his retreat out to the porch before he even pulled his phone out of his pocket. He was going to answer the call no matter who was calling.

On the porch, Durkin sighed at the sight of Roslyn Jones's name on his phone. Roslyn Jones complicated everything and he was sure her call was bringing more complications.

"Hello, Roslyn," Durkin answered lightly.

"We need to meet." Roslyn's voice was no-nonsense and clinical.

"Roslyn, I'm up in the Thousand Islands."

"I know where you are. I'm 30 minutes from Alexandria Bay."

Durkin's face contorted with confusion. What was so important that the chief state's attorney was driving 6 hours to meet face-to-face?

"There's an all-night diner on Route 12 called Pam's. I'll see you there in 30 minutes."

Jones disconnected the call without another word.

*****

318

Durkin spotted Roslyn Jones's navy blue BMW coupe as he turned into Pam's Diner's parking lot. Jones was sitting in the car, glued to her cell phone and seemed unhappy about whatever she was reading. The movement of Durkin's car caught her attention and she tossed her cell phone in her purse and pushed herself out of her car as if she was in a rush.

The chief state's attorney was dressed casually; at least for Roslyn Jones. She wore a cashmere sweater with pearls and jeans. With a beep of her keys, she locked her car and she instinctively hit the lock button again and watched her brake lights flash to confirm her car was locked. She moved in a matter of fact, business-like fashion as if she wanted to complete a tiresome chore as fast as possible.

Her body language triggered a flood of worry in Durkin. He was being fired. He was sure Jones drove up to tell him that he had lost his last threads of political support and now his enemies were going to cut off his balls.

"I drove 6 hours. This place better be good," she said, half-jokingly as she walked to the diner's entrance.

This place. Pam's Diner sat in a dusty parking lot on Rte. 12, twenty yards from a trailer park. A hand stenciled sign announced it operated from the last week in April to the week after Labor Day. It was closed Monday's except for holidays. No one drove 6 hours to eat at Pam's Diner.

"People come from all over the country just for their pancakes," Durkin joked back.

Durkin and Jones waited at the entrance in awkward silence as an elderly man and woman navigated their way out of the diner on wobbly knees and hips.

"Good morning," a late 60-ish waitress greeted them. "Take any table that's free."

Durkin and Jones scanned the restaurant. It was decorated in a duck hunter's motif. Duck wallpaper, duck drapes, plastic duck decoys and duck paintings. Sweatshirts, t-shirts and baseball caps embroidered with the diner's Mallard Duck logo were nailed to the wall.

Jones strode towards a booth in the corner, out of earshot from the other customers.

Another waitress with tired lines etched deep in her face, followed them to their table with a coffee pot. "Coffee?" she asked breathlessly as if was nearing the end of a long shift.

"Thanks," Jones said flatly as she eyed the mocha-colored coffee, quickly concluding Pam's coffee would be barely drinkable. Durkin pushed his coffee mug over to the woman. "Yes, thanks."

The waitress filled the mugs. "Do you know what you want?"

Before Jones had a chance to reply, Durkin said, "Give us a second. We may just have coffee."

The waitress scribbled something on her pad. "Sure thing," she said before disappearing into the kitchen.

Durkin ripped open a plastic creamer and poured it into his mug. "You really shouldn't have come all this way just for the coffee."

Roslyn Jones barely cracked a smile. "Francis, you may be brilliant but you're a pain in my ass. A royal pain in my ass." Her tone was light but had a serious edge. As she gripped her coffee mug, her mood turned even more serious. "As you probably guessed, I didn't drive all the way up here to have coffee."

"Yeah, the thought crossed my mind."

Durkin's other thought as he sipped his coffee was that Jones's face was going to explode with displeasure as her tastebuds came in contact with the watery brown liquid. She was a coffee snob. She ground her own beans and used a fancy French coffee press at her office. He smiled to himself in anticipation of her reaction.

Jones began haltingly. "What I have to say is difficult because it could be misconstrued." Her eyes danced away from his as if she was having difficulty in believing her own words. "You remember the sabbatical agreement I drafted for you?"

Durkin's eyes narrowed as he tried to figure out where she was headed.

"Well, my intention was for the agreement to say that you could do anything you wanted during the sabbatical. That's it."

Durkin palms turned up. And?

"I inadvertently specified that you could engage in legal services."

Durkin's brain instantly pulled up the two page document.

Employee may render either for-profit or pro bono legal services as long as such services do not bring the office into disrepute.

"My inadvertent addition may cause problems. Political problems," Jones explained.

"Who knows about our written agreement?"

Jones took a deep breath. "I'm not sure."

"Who's giving you heat about the agreement?"

Jones brushed his question aside. "Maybe it's my subconscious working overtime but I have my concerns."

"And you'd take a hit if the agreement leaked?"

"I'd lose my job," Jones said sharply.

Durkin rolled his eyes as if Jones was being overly dramatic.

"No, I would," she added. "It shows utter lack of judgment. I'd get roasted by McGonagle," she said, referring to the Chief Judge of Connecticut's Supreme Court who held sway over the Criminal Justice Commission which, in turn, held sway over the Chief State's Attorney.

"Roslyn, I don't——"

"Listen, I know what I'm talking about," Jones interrupted.

Durkin pushed himself back in the booth. She obviously wasn't telling him everything.

"Okay, what can I do?"

"I was wondering," she replied timidly, "if you'd consider signing an agreement that represents what I intended."

Before Durkin had a chance to reply, Jones pulled out a folded piece of paper from her purse and slid it across the table.

Employee may engage in any activities he so chooses as long as such activities do not bring the office into disrepute.

"Do you really think this is going to make any difference?"

"I do," she answered. "Besides there's a good chance this will never become an issue."

"But you think there's enough of a chance that you drove 6 hours up here to make sure your inadvertent mistake doesn't bite your career in your ass."

"That's a bit harsh, Francis."

"It is. And I'm sorry," Durkin said, pushing himself closer to the table. "You're a good friend and I know you've taken a lot of hits because of me." Durkin picked up the pen and signed the agreement.

"Who knows that I represented Angelo DeMartin?" he asked as he set the pen down.

"Rasmutin told the Connecticut State Troopers. It's kicking around the rumor mill but it may just dry up and blow away."

"I can live with it. Nothing I did that was unethical." Durkin sipped the coffee and grimaced. It was really awful.

"It may not have been orthodox but it wasn't unethical," Jones replied. Jones' voice drifted off and she blew a stream of air over her coffee before raising the mug to her lips. Her nose twitched as if she detected an offensive odor. "Ugh," she said pushing her coffee mug away from her without tasting it. "That's possibly the worst smelling coffee...." She let her sour expression finish her sentence.

Durkin grinned. The coffee snob wasn't even going to take a sip. He sipped his coffee and fought not to reveal his feelings. It was possibly the worst coffee he had ever tasted.

Jones shook her head as if a thought suddenly struck her. "You really poked the bear when you used the Benjamin Cardozo Lecture Series to advocate rolling back the Exclusionary Rule."

Durkin smiled. It was the exact reaction he had hoped for. "They didn't like that?" Durkin asked with a chuckle.

Jones shook her head. "They—I won't name names. You know who they are. They went bat shit." A laugh escaped from her mouth. "Absolutely bat shit."

Durkin waited until she stopped laughing. "Is there anything else you wanted to discuss?"

Jones pushed her coffee cup away from her. "There's rumors that the Criminal Justice Commission wants to hold hearings on your involvement in the murder investigation up here. It's all designed to sully your reputation."

"I can handle that," Durkin said breezily. "In fact, I welcome it."

"I know. That's the problem," Jones laughed wearily. She pushed herself to her feet and stuck the signed agreement in her pocket book.

"Okay, I'll stop practicing defense law," he said with a light chuckle. "But I need a day to wrap things up."

Jones gripped the side of the formica table top and pushed herself to her feet. "Okay. You've got 24 hours. Not one more."

The Chief State's Attorney shook her head as a light smile warmed her face. "I've got one last question."

Durkin pushed against the back of the booth as dread sprouted on his face.

"Who was the woman you brought to the Lecture Series?"

Durkin's face reddened like a teenager asked about his new girlfriend. The brilliant legal orator was momentarily tongue-tied. Finally, he said, "She's a friend."

Jones smiled widely. "I didn't think you had it in you."

Durkin laughed as Jones walked past him. "The coffee is on me," Durkin yelled with a dry smile. He dropped cash on the table and followed Roslyn Jones to the parking lot. As Jones got into her car, she paused and looked back at Durkin. "Until you're back in Connecticut, don't ride a bike."

Durkin grinned as he held his laughter until Jones pulled out of the parking lot. Then he let out a long, loud, barreling laugh.

CHAPTER THIRTY EIGHT

Francis Durkin sat on a park bench overlooking the Clayton town dock. A flock of grandparents and grandkids buzzed about on the river's edge as power boats crisscrossed the river. Dogs barked and a teenager drew a crowd with a kite dancing in the wind.

Durkin saw none of it. His thoughts were a million miles away as he dissected every thing that transpired over the past 10 days. He was forced take a sabbatical. He stumbled upon a gruesome murder scene. He clashed with the New York State Police, the Customs and Border Protection and was almost charged with murder. His friends almost died trying to exonerate him. And now he was falling in love.

"Hey, stranger," a friendly voice interrupted his trance. Durkin shook like a startled man as he broke free from the hold on his thoughts. He leveraged the back of the bench to push himself to his feet and held on to it until he steadied himself. Then he hugged Cassie tightly and whispered, "I missed you."

Cassie kissed him. "Me too."

As their lips parted, Durkin noticed PJ McLevy besides her, supporting himself on a cane. He released Cassie and embraced PJ.

"You guys snuck up on me," Durkin said with an embarrassed grin as he stepped back from PJ.

Cassie smiled back. "It wasn't too hard. You looked like your thoughts were a million miles away."

"Yeah, I," Durkin began explaining but then remembered his time as PJ's attorney was quickly running out. He turned to Cassie. "Would you mind if I have word with PJ and then we can grab something to eat?"

"Of course not. I'll grab us a table at HOPs," she said, pointing to the restaurant down the block as she began to make her way there.

Durkin's eyes followed Cassie as she headed down the road.

"She's a good woman," PJ said, sounding like an uncle talking to his favorite nephew. "You better hold on to her."

Durkin smiled, half with appreciation and half with embarrassment for receiving dating advice at his age. "Yeah, she's a special one."

"She's grounded. There's not a lot of people, men or women, who are as solidly grounded as Cassie. Besides," he paused and blew a mouthful of air, "She saved my life. She'll always have a special place in my heart."

Durkin considered PJ's words. "Yes. She very special."

Durkin motioned for PJ to take a seat on the bench. PJ slid down on the bench like a man who had lost most of the muscles that held his bones together.

"How are you?"

"I'll be fine," PJ said, sounding like a hard-headed ex-cop, deflecting unwanted attention. He held the cane up and made a motion like he wanted to toss it in the river. He then massaged the tip of his fingers and took a deep breath as he assessed whether he'd have permanent nerve damage in his finger tips.

Durkin studied PJ, who seemed to have aged a decade in the past 48 hours. "Are you really okay?"

PJ hesitated and wondered if he'd ever admit how close he came to dying from exposure in the river. "In a couple of days, I'll be back in fighting form."

Amoeba blobs floated across PJ's eyes like dizzying specs of dust. He blinked furiously, hoping his eyelids would wipe away the distracting particles. When he stopped, gelatin worms floated over his eyeballs like strands of wavy hair.

"You ever get floaters on your eyes?" PJ asked in a hollow, depressed voice.

Durkin shook his head, no. He had heard about the common eye disorder that came with age. He heard it was like having translucent worms slithering across your eyeballs.

"For the last couple of days, all I see are worms floating over my eyes as yellow and blue disco-lights flash in the corners. I called my eye doctor. He says it's nothing to worry about," PJ said with the tone of a man thinking of switching ophthalmologists.

Durkin took a deep breath through his nose as if signaling he needed to change the subject. "My sabbatical ends today," Durkin said matter-of-factly.

"Is that good or bad?"

Durkin shrugged as a tired smile spread across his face. "I'm not sure. I fought the sabbatical when Jones imposed it on me and now I wished it would last a couple more months."

"So this is our last discussion that's covered by the attorney-client privilege?"

Durkin's smile morphed to an amused look. The ex-cop with eye floaters was still sharp.

"Yep. Once I stop representing you, nothing we say is privileged. But everything you told me while you were my client remains privileged."

The men cast their eyes over the town dock. Kids throwing balls, chasing dogs, fishing off the dock. It was probably the last place in the world anyone would hold a serious legal discussion.

"While we're still covered by the attorney-client privilege, I want to ask you a few things."

PJ detected an ominous ring in Durkin's words.

"How the hell did you escape the police dragnet on the Thousand Islands Bridge?" Durkin asked.

PJ grinned as a long rush of air blew through his nostrils. That was not what he expected the state's attorney to ask him. He also wasn't sure how to respond. Where should he start?

"When I was a Marine sniper I got interested in camouflage. I guess you could say my interest then grew into an obsession. When I became a cop I spent most of my free time studying how to use light, color and spatial illusions to deceive the human eye. There are infinite things you can do to stretch and distort visual images to deceive the human eye."

Durkin nodded. "So you mastered the art of visual deception to catch bad guys?"

"I'm not a master," PJ replied humbly. "I've shamelessly stolen from all the great optical deceivers."

Vulnerability crept into PJ's face as if he was embarrassed to have shared an intensely private part of him.

"So how'd you make yourself invisible when an army of troopers descended upon the bridge?"

PJ shrugged. It wasn't that difficult. "It was nighttime. The shadows and bridge railings made visual deception easy. The color of the Thousand Islands Bridge was chosen to blend in with the trees and river. It was easy to create a canvas of beams to blend into the bridge." PJ paused and let out a loud breath and tapped his cane. "But I'm getting too old for this."

Durkin dropped his eyes and contemplated his own mortality. He raised his head and smiled. "I think everything is going to be resolved without any arrests."

"No one is going to get charged? Not even Sam or Dem?" PJ sounded relieved.

"It looks that way." Durkin paused and scanned the river. "But things could always unravel. If things unravel, there are a number of loose ends that could cause problems."

PJ turned serious and listened.

"The troopers found the sea-scooter and traced the sale back to a diving shop in Clayton."

PJ shrugged. He wasn't concerned. He decked himself out in a long beard and padded at least a 100 pounds onto him. He looked like a fat, bearded, mountain-man. He paid in cash. There'd be no way to trace the sea-scooter back to him.

"No. That's not going to be a problem."

"But what if a cop figures out that only a master of deception could've escaped from the bridge? There aren't too many masters of visual deception on Wellesley Island beside you."

"They'd never be able to prove it was me."

"You're probably right. But the FBI was up here. Sharp and Brooks."

McLevy expelled a heavy stream of air from his mouth. "They'll always be gunning for Dem." PJ shrugged. "But he'll be okay."

"They also found Hennigan's gun on the bottom of the river."

PJ shook his head in wonder. He didn't see that coming.

"The guy who's taken over the investigation is named Colonel Welsh. He tells me Hennigan fired three shots. Rome was hit by one in his leg and Hennigan has two bullet holes in his hands."

PJ quieted and looked around to confirm that no one could hear him. "I shot Hennigan. I hit him in his right hand. He dropped his gun and when he rushed Sam, I took out his left hand with another shot. He used his forearms to push himself over the side the railings."

Durkin eyed a large American flag on top of a high flag pole, whipping in the wind. "Do you think Hennigan thought the priest taped the confession?"

PJ nodded pensively. "That'd be my guess."

The men sat in silence thinking of how Rome was going to blame himself for Fr. O'Brien's death.

"And the toll collector?"

PJ explained how Putnam introduced Rome to Hennigan at the Graveyard bar. "He probably thought Putnam was working with Sam.'

"The poor bastard," Durkin muttered.

"Yep. I'm sure Rome will be pretty shook up about him too. He says Putnam was a solid guy."

Durkin cast his eye on a large freighter headed towards Lake Ontario. "Hey," he said, turning back to PJ. "Do you know how Sam released the tape?"

"We had a contingency plan in case everything went to shit. Sam gave the tape to Kyle. He told him that in the event he didn't hear from him by 7 a.m. to deliver it to that reporter who came by your cottage."

"He gave Kyle the tape?"

"Yep. Kyle came through for me in spades. I owe him." Both men shook their heads in agreement. Kyle Johnson saved PJ McLevy's life.

Durkin stood, signaling the end of their discussion. He learned what he needed and wanted to rejoin Cassie as fast as possible. PJ struggled to his feet and shook hands.

"It's been nice representing you," Durkin said with a sly grin. "Now let's go get something to eat."

*****

Cassie eyed the menu at an outside table surrounded by waiters whizzing around tables filled with tourists in t-shirts, shorts and sandals. As Durkin reached the table he motioned back to PJ, "Thanks for taking care of my buddy."

Cassie and PJ fixed eyes one another as if they shared a secret. "My pleasure," Cassie said with a smile. "He was the perfect patient." She turned back and eyed Durkin with the glint of teenager with a crush.

"Hey, would you mind if I grab a few things," PJ said, pointing to the general store across the street. Everyone knew it was a polite ploy to give Cassie and Durkin a moment alone. Before they could reply, PJ stabbed the ground with his cane and wobbled off like an old man with a bum knee.

Durkin reached over and grasped Cassie's hands. "What will your academic friends say when they see us holding hands?"

Cassie laughed loudly. "Probably the same things as your prosecutor buddies."

They smiled as they considered how opposites attract. Durkin motioned to PJ who pushed off his cane as he crossed the street. "He says he's fine but how is he really?"

Cassie shook her head in amazement. "He's an old war horse. Sadie was amazed his heart could take the shock of hypothermia."

"Sadie?"

Cassie understood Durkin's concern. It was another person who knew their secrets. "Sadie's one of us. She won't say anything."

Durkin's cheeks puffed up with doubt.

"She's a mid-wife who lives on Grindstone." Cassie thought of all the times she saw Sadie in action. Delivering babies. Setting casts on broken bones. Sticking thermometers in mouths. She was on call 24/7, attending to all the islanders' health needs.

"Sadie jet-skied over to Jolly Island and snatched PJ back from death's grip. She knows how to treat a person with serious hypothermia. She nursed him all-night. I told her PJ fell off his fishing boat and was rescued by Kyle. I don't think she believed me with all the news about the shooting on the bridge but she didn't ask any questions. Besides, I had no choice. I had to call her. She's an expert on treating hypothermia."

"So you think he's going to be okay?"

"He's got frostbite on several of his fingertips. If he's not lucky, his fingertips may have to be amputated."

Durkin blew a stream of air through his lips. Holy crap.

"What about you?" Cassie asked. "Do you think you'll still be charged?"

"No. The truth about Hennigan will come out shortly. I'll be cleared."

Durkin paused and assessed his criminal liabilities. As he mentally listed them, PJ neared, stabbing his cane into the ground with each step. When he reached the table he was electrified. "I thought you'd want to see this," he said, handing a copy of the *Watertown Daily Register* to Durkin.

TROOPER KILLS THREE. JUMPS FROM BRIDGE

By James Alexander Breen

A veteran New York State Trooper, who police believe is responsible for the recent Wellesley Island murder of 23-year-old Irene Izak, as well as a Sacred Heart Church priest and a Thousand Islands Bridge toll collector, jumped to his death early yesterday morning, according to an official not authorized to speak publicly about the investigation.

Trooper David Hennigan, who was a New York State Trooper for 22 years, reportedly killed Father Patrick O'Brien and Clifford Putnam, before shooting himself in both hands and jumping from the bridge.

Police would not confirm details about the shooting on the Thousand Islands Bridge, nor how Hennigan came to be their prime suspect, but sources allow that police initially considered Connecticut State's Attorney Francis X.

329

Durkin, a person of interest. Durkin was exonerated, sources report, when evidence emerged confirming Hennigan was the killer.

Another source, who is also unauthorized to discuss the on-going murder investigations, said police have a tape on which Hennigan confesses to the murder.

A spokesperson for the Watertown...

Durkin eyes jumped over several paragraphs.

Camelia Hennigan, David Hennigan's sister, stated that her brother was a righteous man in an evil world.
"He died doing God's work." She dismissed reports that her brother killed Irene Izak.
"Whatever he did, he did for the Lord."

The newspaper dipped in Durkin's hands, stunned his agreement with Welsh was falling in place. He passed the paper to Cassie who devoured the article.

"It sounds like the troopers are tying up the loose ends," she said slowly and deliberatively.

Durkin wore the look of a man who couldn't believe his good fortune. "Sounds like it."

"This gives us cause to celebrate," Cassie said.

Durkin squeezed her hand as if to communicate that he hoped to celebrate with her for many years to come.

"I wish Sam could join us," Durkin said.

"Well, you'll get your wish," PJ interjected. "He discharged himself this morning."

Durkin's eyes sought an explanation.

"He wore the doctors down. They finally threw a pair of crutches at him and told him to get out." PJ snorted with laughter. "Kyle picked him up on his boat."

Durkin grinned. "When the hell was he going to tell me?"

"All in due time."

Cassie punched a number on her phone. "Hi. We're at the Clayton dock. Want to pick us up? Great. See you in fifteen." She turned to PJ and Durkin. "Kyle is going to pick us up and take us to Jolly Island."

A young, bouncy waitress appeared with menus. "Can I take your drink orders?"

Durkin pulled out his wallet and dropped a $20 bill on the table. "Change of plans. Thanks, though."

The surprised waitress beamed at her tip. "Thanks."

Thirty minutes later, PJ McLevy and Angelo DeMartin sat on folding chairs next to Sam Rome, who sat perched on a tree stump with his crutches slung over his leg. The men gazed off into the St. Lawrence River with the smiles of soldiers who just learned the war was over and still shocked they'd be going home in one piece.

The cool breeze seemed to blow away their troubles and, for the moment, life was back on course.

Francis Durkin emerged from Cassie's cottage with a fistful of beers. As he handed them out, he thought of what each did for him. Sam Rome took a bullet. PJ McLevy almost died from hypothermia. DeMartin sat in a barracks for 8 hours and was almost arrested.

Rome, DeMartin and McLevy nodded with appreciation and cracked the beers.

"Cheers. Here's to George Putnam and Father Patrick," Rome said somberly.

The men raised their beers and tipped the cans into their mouths without another word, knowing Francis Durkin's sabbatical was officially over. He was a state's attorney and when Rome and PJ ever spoke about what happened on the Thousand Islands Bridge, they'd speak alone, far from Durkin.

As they sipped their beers, no one took notice of the two fishermen in ripped baseball caps perched on the trolling boat, steered by foot pedals. The boat floated inconspicuously less than a 100 yards from Jolly Island. The fisherman's foot constantly adjusted the boat's position as the wind and current buffeted his boat. To everyone it looked like the fishermen were steering the boat in search of fish. Not one of the cagey cops considered that the fishermen were undercover agents listening to their conversation through a long-range audio detector. Not one of the cops ever noticed the fisherman never caught a fish.

THE END

POST SCRIPT

-Two days after their celebration on Jolly Island, two fisherman drifted under the Thousand Islands Bridge a short distance where Robert Johnston and his men sunk the Sir Robert Peel in 1838. One fisherman stabbed the water with a long aluminum hook. On his second try, he pulled up a water-logged gym bag and quickly slid it under a canvas cover. The men then slowly glided up river.

Three days later, $5000 was left at the Alexandria Bay Community Care Center. This was repeated every Tuesday for 7 straight weeks.

-The *Times Union Daily* reported that New York State Police Forensic Scientist Dante Russo was found hanging by an electric cord in his garage. The NYSP ruled the death a suicide.

-Stephanie Cotton was appointed Director of the Albany Crime Laboratory. There was a single line noting that Director Darlene Chilletti accepted a teaching position at Albany State.

-Commander Igor Rasmutin retired three weeks after Trooper Hennigan plunged into the St. Lawrence River. A two-line notice in the NYSP newsletter noted his 26 years of service and plans to take up golf.

-Two weeks after Durkin's sabbatical ended, he drove 7 hours to visit Professor Cassie Johnston at St. Lawrence University in Canton, New York.

-James Alexander Breen won the IRE Award for best investigative reporting for his story about the first reported murder on Wellesley Island. He is currently living with Danielle Keegan half way between Watertown and Albany.

Reilly v. New York State Police

In late 2022, approximately 55 years after Izak's murder, I sought records from the New York State Police regarding the investigation of Izak's murder pursuant to the New York's Freedom of Information Law, known as FOIL in legal parlance.

The NYSP informed me in 2023 that its investigation of Ms. Izak's 1968 murder was still both "active " and "on-going" and disclosure of the records would interfere with the troopers' investigation.

I appealed the decision, noting that with the passage of a half century, it was beyond the pale of reasonableness for the NYSP to claim that it was still conducting an active and on-going investigation of Ms. Izak's murder. To ensure that my FOIL request was not mired in the NYSP's bureaucracy, I brought the matter to the Superintendent's attention, the NYSP's highest officer. I noted that my request concerned "records of historical interest and admittedly runs the risk of unearthing details that most agencies would rather remain forever buried. Simply, many reporters and law enforcement officials believe that a NYS trooper murdered Irene Izak in June 1968 and question why troopers never aggressively pressed the investigation at the time."

A few weeks later, a high ranking trooper upheld the NYSP's denial of my FOIL request, claiming that there was, in fact, an "active" and "on-going" investigation underway in 2024 for a murder that took place in 1968.

When you stretch the truth to the breaking point it becomes a lie. There's no plainer way of putting it. The NYSP were lying. And the lie was sanctioned at the highest levels of the state police. There was no "active" and "on-going" investigation 55 years after Ms. Izak was murdered.

My only option was to got to court to compel the NYSP to comply with the law. I filed my court papers on June 7, 2023, with a lengthy memorandum citing the legal precedents supporting my claims. (Copies of the legal papers and FOIL requests can be found at www.tomreillybooks.com)

The Assistant Attorney General representing the NYSP initially defended the NYSP's preposterous position. Then, a week before my trial date before Judge Elizabeth Walsh, the Assistant Attorney General informed me that the NYSP would turn over all the records I sought.

Why the sudden, 180 degree change?

There's no doubt in my mind the Assistant Attorney General and the New York State Police knew Judge Walsh would have held the NYSP to account for its blatant lies. The NYSP played chicken all the way to the steps of the

New York State Supreme Court and then, and only then, complied with the law

The documents I had to pry away from the NYSP revealed that in 1968 considerable evidence pointed at Trooper David Hennigan, and, in fact, that after the investigation was reopened in 1998, Hennigan became the trooper's main target.

Among other things, the FOIL documents revealed that:

• Trooper Hennigan stopped Izak on Interstate 81 less than an hour before she was murdered. In his sworn statement, Hennigan stated that he stopped Izak for speeding but when confronted with the evidence that her car could go no faster than 62 miles per hour, Hennigan changed his sworn statement and claimed he stopped Izak randomly because he was on the lookout for burglars.

• Trooper Hennigan crossed the Thousand Islands Bridge on to sleepy Wellesley Island only a minute before Izak. He did this despite the fact that he was on highway patrol, enforcing the speed limits on Interstate 81. Other troopers noted that Hennigan had no legitimate reason to be on Wellesley Island at 2 in the morning.

• Less than 26 minutes after Irene Izak crossed the Thousand Islands Bridge, Hennigan radioed in his gruesome "discovery" of Ms. Izak's body.

While the documents noted above were telling, one document drew my intense interest. In June 1968, Hennigan swore that he found Irene Izak lying face-down in the mud. According to his official statements, Izak was dead when he saw her near the entrance to the Dewolf Point State Park.

However, several eye witnesses reported seeing people speaking outside of Izak's VW Bug and a car with a search light before Hennigan reported finding the body. "I did observe a spotlight shining from the left front of the second car onto the Volkswagen...and I saw two people standing to the left front of the car..."

As the tollbooth collector reported, Trooper Hennigan was the only law enforcement official on Wellesley Island that morning and he was driving an unmarked police car—with a spotlight.

The only evidence that the troopers followed up on the eye witness accounts-which placed Izak alive, with another person with a search light

335

mounted on his dashboard—is a single follow-up from the troopers to the Chicago Police Department seeking background information on the witness.

The FOIL documents also revealed that:

- Trooper Hennigan claimed that Ms. Izak's blood was on his uniform because he picked her up and cradled her head to see if she was alive when he "found" her body. He changed his account about how he picked her up several times.
- A trooper reported seeing blood on Hennigan's patrol car and that Hennigan washed the bumper before he went home.
- In 2009, when Hennigan was still alive, the NYSP exhumed Ms. Izak's body. The autopsy indicated that her skull contained indentations— three small lines—in several places. Investigators believed the indentations were consistent with the design of the large flashlights used by troopers.

Despite the strong evidence implicating Hennigan in the murder, the New York State Police did not zero in on him for the first three decades after the murder. All evidence indicates that, in fact, some troopers likely did just the opposite: they turned a blind eye to the truth.

Jefferson County District Attorney

Ms. Izak was murdered on Wellesley Island, New York which is in Jefferson County. In 1968, the then-District Attorney William McClusky, issued strong declarations of support for Trooper Hennigan, as he came under suspicion. D.A. McClusky said "the investigation has proven that [Trooper Hennigan] definitely had nothing to do with [Irene Izak's murder] and…if it had not been for the tremendous police job conducted by [Hennigan] the investigation would not have been progressed as favorably as it was."

Why was McClusky making such an effort to tamp down rumors that Hennigan was the murderer despite the overwhelming evidence against Hennigan? The FOIL records contained information that McClusky, drove alone with Hennigan to "reconstruct" Hennigan's trip after he crossed the Thousand Islands Bridge shortly before he reported finding Ms. Izak's bludgeoned body. McClusky then traveled to Colorado in late 1968 to "investigate" a lead.

Intrigued by McClusky's role in the murder investigation, I sought the D.A.'s records regarding the 55 year old murder.

My request, like my initial request to the troopers, was denied on the basis there was an "open" investigation in the 1968 murder. My appeal was granted but my FOIL request was "deemed moot in light of the lack of possession of any responsive records." I was informed that, pursuant to a court order, District Attorney Kristyna Mills destroyed all the records regarding Irene Izak's murder in 2018. I was provided with a "copy of the order and proof of destruction of the records." However, upon inspection, the "proof of destruction" did not identify the files related to Ms. Izak's murder investigation. I requested clarification. More than five months later, I have not received any clarification on whether the District Attorney destroyed the documents or possesses any records regarding Ms. Izak's infamous murder investigation.

Ms. Izak's murder investigation is still shrouded in mystery and the historical stink of injustice still hangs over it. It was a horrific crime that screamed for justice. A young woman, in the prime of her life, was murdered in cold blood.

Justice was never served.

State of Connecticut v. Terrance Police

The discussion about Terrance Police in *State v. Police* between Cassie and Durkin is a real case. After I gathered the facts I sent the following letter to Connecticut's then-Chief State's Attorney and copied the two state judges who I believe got it right. Unfortunately, Connecticut's State's Attorney chose not to appeal the case.

From:Thomas K. Reilly
March 10, 2023

Honorable Patrick J. Griffin
Chief State's Attorney
State of Connecticut
Division of Criminal Justice
300 Corporate Place
Rocky Hill, CT 06067

State of Connecticut v. Terrance Police ("Police")

Dear Chief State's Attorney Griffin,

I recognize you may be perplexed why, out of the blue, I've sent this letter regarding *Police*. I have no logical explanation other than to say that upon learning about the case I was perplexed by the lack of commentary on it and feel it should have been appealed.

Connecticut's Supreme Court framed the central question in *Police* as whether or not the John Doe arrest warrant complied with the U.S. Constitution's Fourth Amendment's particularity requirement. While technically correct, the Court should have drilled deeper to avoid being mired in tangential issues which led to its faulty conclusion. The more precise issue in *Police* was whether or not the genetic placeholder utilized in the John Doe arrest warrant sufficiently identified Terrance Police as required by the Fourth Amendment.

The U.S. Supreme Court has long held that the Fourth Amendment requires an arrest warrant to identify a person with "sufficient certainty." Courts have repeatedly held that the "sufficient certainty" standard is met by a genetic marker because of DNA's "unparalleled ability" to exonerate the innocent and identify the guilty. In turn, because of the confidence placed in DNA, the statute of limitations are stayed when a John Doe arrest warrant has been issued with genetic markers until the police discover a "match." When this occurs, the police utilize a corroborating genetic analysis to seek an arrest warrant which "swaps" the name of the suspect for the genetic placeholder. This is what occurred in *Police*.

It bears noting that judges are required to take a leap of faith in allowing a genetic marker to be deployed in lieu of a name in a John Doe arrest warrant. By and large, judges cannot make heads or tails of a loci table; nor should they attempt to. The genetic markers employed as placeholders in John Doe arrest warrants are beguiling codes that can only be deciphered by a separate DNA analysis and statistical guidance. Courts simply rely on experts to opine (with the assistance of complex computer programs) on the likelihood that the

338

DNA found at crime scenes "matches" a suspect's DNA. It is completely different from a judge ruling on whether an arrest warrant naming "James West" sufficiently identifies "Vandy West." In the same vein, if the alleles and loci noted in the John Doe arrest warrant and affidavit were transcribed incorrectly, say an "11" was listed as a "13" the John Doe arrest warrant would likely be voided.

In *Police,* Judge White was presented with a six page warrant and affidavit utilizing boilerplate forms. In paragraph 20 of the affidavit, the Norwalk PD listed the genetic codes to use as the placeholder for the John Doe's identity.[1] Specifically, the affidavit cited genetic markers from fifteen different locations in the DNA strands extracted from:
   1) saliva found inside the cuff and neckline of a hoodie;
   2) DNA found on the victim's cell phone cover; and
   3) DNA from the left pocket of the hoodie.

The key legal issue was whether or not the genetic markers, which came from several individuals (as opposed to a sole source) identified Terrance Police with "sufficient certainty." There is no magic required to answer this question. The answer is arrived at in precisely the same manner regardless of whether the genetic markers emanate from a single source or from multiple sources: the court must turn to the laboratory analyses which compare the suspect's DNA to the DNA found at the crime scene. In *Police,* the corroborating DNA analysis found that the DNA extracted from the cuff and neckline of the hoodie was "at least 100 billion times more likely to occur if it originated from Terrance Police and three unknown individuals than if it originated from four unknown individuals."[2] Based on this forensic analysis the trial court correctly concluded that the DNA identified Terrance Police with "nearly irrefutable precision."

As for Terrance Police's appeal, that should have been game, set and match. Unfortunately, the Connecticut Supreme Court arrived at a very different conclusion. It appears the court took the wrong turn by reasoning that the multi-source DNA was not unique to Terrance Police and a judge could not make an informed ruling analyzing a loci table without statistical guidance.[3] As noted above, the genetic markers, even multi-source markers, are essentially codes. If they work with great reliability, then the code should

---

[1] It is puzzling why the NPD did not include the tests of more swabs, especially the swabs from the gun used in the crime.

[2] Conclusion # 4. DESPP, April 13, 2018, Supplemental DNA Report II, Lab case ID-12-001734.

[3] "We agree with the many courts that have held that "a warrant identifying the person to be arrested for [an]…offense by description of the person's unique DNA profile…." 343 Conn. 274, 299 (2022).

be recognized as valid. Further, the particularity requirement in no way mandates that a placeholder in a John Doe arrest warrant utilize a unique identifier. "John Smith" is legally sufficient in an arrest warrant if, in fact, the individual's name is "John Smith." There is nothing unique about the name John Smith. As the trial court noted, courts have rightly held that a genetic placeholder cannot conceivably eliminate all possibilities of error and the Fourth Amendment does not require it to do so.

The Supreme Court also gave short shrift to the plethora of physical evidence that connected Terrance Police to the items that were tested for DNA. Even a cursory reading of the May 1, 2017 warrant leaves little doubt (surveillance cameras, eye witness accounts and the fact that NPD found the hoodie where the perpetrator was seen fleeing) that the lone perpetrator wore the hoodie in question, used the gun found by the NPD used to shoot Ms. Williams and handled the victim's Kate Spade cell phone case. It is a travesty that the judicial 'gatekeepers' have shut the door on the use of multi-source DNA to mete out justice when the link to the perpetrator and the DNA samples was so strong.

The Connecticut Supreme Court's numerous references to its "independent research" implies that a little reading on the human chromosome bestowed the court with a mastery of the subject. This should give everyone pause. The Supreme Court notes the FBI's requirement that a minimum of twenty loci be included in a genetic marker uploaded to the nation's CODIS system. It notes the relation of homozygote and heterozygote in DNA markings. The opinion explains alleles and loci at a basic level. The court would have been well advised to recognize its limits like another court which noted that "judges are, far and away, not the people best qualified to explain science."[4]

The Supreme Court's failure to recognize its limitations has led to major errors. One such glaring error is the court's characterization of the DNA extracted from the crime scene and behind Best Buy as "trace" DNA. First, no where in any laboratory analysis is the term "trace DNA" found. The Court's own independent research presumably led it to this conclusion. However, as the trial court noted, the laboratory found saliva on the dark hoodie.[5] Studies show that up to seventy-four percent of the DNA in saliva originates from white blood cells which are a source of high quality genomic DNA.[6] Simply, the DNA found on the hoodie which Terrance Police wore the day he

---

[4] *People v. Collins*, 15 N.Y.S.3d 564 (N.Y. Sup. Ct. 2015).

[5] See paragraph 19 of May 1, 2017 arrest warrant.

[6] Thiede, C. et al. Buccal swabs but not mouthwash samples can be used to obtain pre-transplant DNA fingerprints from recipients of allogeneic bone marrow transplant. (2000). Bone Marrow Transplantation. 25(5): 575-577.

committed the crime bore not "trace" DNA but high quality "wearer" DNA. This fundamental error allowed the court to paint the DNA samples in question as scientifically wobbly and suspect.

The Connecticut Supreme Court admonished the trial court for not limiting its analysis to the four corners of the May 1, 2017 John Doe arrest warrant. The key question in the case was whether the genetic placeholder in the May 1, 2017 warrant identified Terrance Police with sufficient certainty. So, yes, the first step in the analysis should be solely focused on the four corners of the John Doe arrest warrant. However, the court seems oblivious to the fact that a judge tasked with signing off on an arrest warrant which "swaps" a name for a genetic marker previously used in a John Doe arrest warrant, must verify whether another DNA analysis (or a CODIS 'hit') "matched" the suspect. It is a two-step process. That is, perfecting a John Doe arrest warrant requires a judge to go beyond the four corners of the original John Doe arrest warrant.

The Court further states that the judge signing the arrest warrant must be given statistical guidance because, presumably without such guidance, the judge cannot make an informed decision. Again, a little knowledge is a dangerous thing. The court's independent research should have uncovered the risk that the complexity of matching mixed "trace" DNA to an unknown suspect may prevent a crime lab to opine on such probabilities with a high degree of confidence at that time. Again, the genetic markers are a "code" that requires deciphering later. If the "deciphering" does not confirm a "match" then the John Doe arrest warrant cannot be perfected. Thus, the judiciary's"gatekeeping" function would not be compromised by utilizing multi-source 'trace' DNA in a John Doe arrest warrant.

The Connecticut Supreme Court noted that *Police* presented a significant issue of first impression for both our state and country. In such times, the Court needed to step up and provide judicial leadership and insight. Instead, unfortunately, the court dropped the ball. Should anyone care? I think so. Despite the court's claim that it recognizes DNA's probative value, the *Police* ruling could restrict its admittance in future criminal trials. While that prospect is distressing, I am perhaps most concerned about the total lack of commentary on the *Police* decision. It landed like a tree falling deep in the forest.

Ms. Williams and Connecticut residents deserve that no stone should be left unturned until *Police* is overturned.

Sincerely,
Thomas K. Reilly

cc: Honorable John F. Blawie & Honorable Gary J. White

Made in the USA
Middletown, DE
28 June 2024